HINDI-ENGLISH
DICTIONARY

स्टैण्डर्ड हिन्दी-अंग्रेज़ी डिक्शनरी

HINDI-ENGLISH DICTIONARY

DR. R.C. TIWARI
DR. R.S. SHARMA
& KRISHNA VIKAL

HIPPOCRENE BOOKS
New York

For information, please address:
Hippocrene Books
171 Madison Ave.
New York, NY 10016

ISBN 0-87052-824-6

ABBREVIATIONS
USED IN THE DICTIONARY

a — adjective
adv— adverb
conj — conjugation
ind — indeclinable
int — interjection
nf — noun, feminine
nm — noun, masculine
phr — phrase
pref — prefix
pron — pronoun
v — verb

स्टैण्डर्ड हिन्दी-अंग्रेजी कोश

HINDI-ENGLISH DICTIONARY

अ

अ the first vowel and the first letter of Devnagri alphabet; a prefix denoting negation as अतुल, अतृप्त, अन्याय

अंक (*nm*) a number; marks; a mark; embrace; an act of a drama; — गणित Arithmetic

अंकन (*nm*) marking; writing

अंकित (*a*) marked; written

अंकुर (*nm*) a sprout

अंकुश (*nm*) a hook; an iron hook with which elephants are driven; control

अंग (*nm*) body; limb; part; portion; — रक्षक a body-guard; — हीन limbless

अंगार, अंगारा (*nm*) a burning charcoal

अंगिया (*nf*) a bodice

अंगी (*nm*) creature in the corporal form

अंगीकार (*nm*) an agreement; acceptance

अंगीठी (*nf*) a portable oven

अंगूठा (*nm*) the thumb

अंगूठी (*nf*) a finger-ring

अंगूर (*nm*) grape

अंगोछा, अंगौछा (*nm*) a towel

अंचल (*nm*) the border of a cloak or that portion of a sari which covers the shoulder; a region

अंजन (*nm*) collyrium

अंजर-पंजर (*nm*) the joints of the body; skeleton

अंजाम (*nm*) result; end; — देना to complete

अंट-शंट (*a*) irrelevant; meaningless, nonsense

अंड-बंड (*a*) see अंट-शंट

अंडा (*nm*) an egg

अंत:करण (*nm*) the inner self, conscience.

अंतः प्रेरणा (nf) inspiration; intuition

अंत (nm) the end; — हीन endless

अंततः (adv) at last, finally; eventually

अंतरंग (a) intimate; internal

अंतर (nm) difference; distance; the inner self

अंतरात्मा (nf) the soul, spirit, inner self

अंतराल (nm) gap; inner space

अंतरिक्ष (nm) sky, space; — यात्री an astronaut

अंतरिम (a) interim

अंतरीप (nm) cape (a land surrounded by water from three sides)

अंतर्गत (a) included; hidden

अंतर्जातीय (a) inter-caste

अंतर्दृष्टि (nf) insight

अंतर्देशीय (a) inland; inter-state

अंतर्द्वंद्व (nm) inner conflict

अंतर्धान (nm) disappearance; (a) invisible, vanished; — होना to disappear

अंतर्निहित (a) understood; included, implied

अंतर्राष्ट्रीय (a) international

अंतिम (a) final, last, conclusive, ultimate; — चेतावनी ultimatum

अंदाज़ (nm) a guess, an estimate; style; gesture; — न roughly

अंदाज़ा (nm) see अंदाज़

अंधकार (nm) darkness; cloudiness; gloom

अंधविश्वास (nm) superstition

अंधा (a) blind; unthinking; careless; thoughtless

अंधाधुंध (adv) blindly; at random; ignorantly

अंधापन (nm) blindness; folly; carelessness

अंधिया/रा (a) dark black; — री (a faminine) dark; black

अंधेर (nm) wrong; injustice; outrage; — खाता/गर्दी mismanagement, complete lawlessness

अंधेरा (nm) darkness; dimness; — घुप्प black out, pitch dark. -री (nf) dust storm (आंधी)

अंबार (nm) bulk, heap, pile

अंश (nm) portion, part; share, division; degree

अंशतः (adv) partly, partially

अकड़ (nf) stiffness; haughtiness; — बाज़ haughty

अकड़ना (v) to be stiff; to be haughty

अकर्मक (a) intransitive (verb)

अकर्मण्य (a) idle

अकस्मात् (adv) all of a sudden, suddenly

अकारथ (a) useless; (adv.) in vain

अकाल (nm) famine; scarcity; (a) untimely; — मृत्यु untimely death

अकिंचन (a) poor; destitute

अकुलाना (v) to feel uneasy

अकेला (a) single; solitary;

—पन loneliness, solitude

अक्खड़ (a) rude and rough; haughty; —पन rudeness, fearlessness

अक्ल (nf) wisdom; sense; intellect; —का दुश्मन (nm) a foolish person; —दौड़ाना to reason; —पर पर्दा पड़ना to be stupid

अक्ल/मंद (a) intelligent; sensible; —मंदी intelligence; sensibility

अक्षम्य (a) unpardonable

अक्षय (a) imperishable, durable

अक्षर (nm) the letter of an alphabet; (a) undecaying, permanent

अक्षरश: (adv) literally, word by word, in toto

अक्षुण्ण (a) unbroken; entire, whole

अक्सर (adv) often; usually

अखंड, अखंडित (a) the whole; undivided

अखबार (nm) a newspaper.

अखरना (v) to feel unpleasant

अखरोट (nm) a walnut

अखिल (a) all, entire, whole

अगर (ind) in case, if; —बत्ती incense-stick

अगला (a) next, following; yet to come; —भाग front portion

अगवानी (nf) welcome

अगाध (a) bottomless; very deep, profound

अगुआ (nm) a leader; chief, pioneer; —ई leadership

अग्नि (nf) fire; the god of fire; appetite; —बोट a steam boat

अग्र (a) first, chief; —भाग fore part

अग्रणी (a) leading, outstanding

अग्रसर (nm) going ahead

अग्रिम (a) first, chief; (adv) prior, before

अघाना (v) to be satisfied

अचंभा (nm) astonishment, surprise, wonder

अचरज (nm) a miracle, surprise, wonder —भरा wonderful

अचल (a) stationary, immovable; fixed; firm

अचानक (adv) suddenly, all of a sudden

अचार (nm) pickles

अचूक (a) unfailing; sure

अचेत (a) senseless; unconscious; —न unconscious

अच्छा (a) good; fine; healthy; lucky; useful; (adv) well; (int) well done ! all right; —ई goodness; merit; —बुराई virtue and vice

अछूत (a) untouchable

अछूता (a) not used; fresh —untouched

अजनबी (a) stranger, unknown; (nm) a stranger

अजब (a) peculiar; strange

अजायबघर (nm) a museum

अजीब (a) (see अजब)

अज्ञात (a) unknown

अज्ञा/न (nm) ignorance; —नी

ignorant

अटपटा (a) absurd; odd

अटूट (a) unbroken; unbreak-able

अटटहास (nm) a horse-laugh, loud laughter

अड़ंगा (nm) an obstruction, an obstacle

अड़चन (nf) hitch; difficulty; hindrance

अड़ना (v) to insist; to halt; to stick

अडिग (a) steady; unflinching

अड़ियल (a) stubborn; inflexi-ble; obstinate

अड़ोस-पड़ोस (nm) neighbour-hood

अड्डा (nm) meeting place; a stand

अणु (nm) atom; (a) atomic

अत: (ind) therefore; hence; thus

अतएव (ind) so; hence

अतल (a) bottomless; fathom-less

अति (pref) a prefix denoting extremity etc.; very much, too much

अतिक्रम (nm) violation; devia-tion

अति/चार (nm) violation; trans-gression; —चारी violator

अतिथि (nm) a guest, stranger

अति प्राकृतिक (a) supernatural

अति/मानव (nm) a superman; —मानवीय superhuman

अति/रंजना (nf) exaggeration;

—रंजित exaggerated

अतिरिक्त (a) besides; additio-nal; extra

अतिवृष्टि (nf) excessive rains; heavy downpour of rain

अतिशय (a) excessive

अतिशयोक्ति (nm) exaggeration; —पूर्ण exaggerated

अतीत (a & nm) past; (adv) beyond

अतुल (a) immense, unpara-lleled

अतृप्त (a) unfulfilled, unsatis-fied

अत्यंत (adv & a) very much, extremely; exceedingly

अत्याचा/र (nm) tyranny; atro-city; —री atrocious, (nm) a tyrant

अथ (nm) the beginning, com-mencement

अथक (a) untiring, not fatigued

अथवा (ind) or, or even

अथाह (a) very deep; bottomless

अदद (nm) a number, figure; a piece

अदना (a) ordinary; low, in-ferior

अदब (nm) manners; respect; politeness; literature; —क़ायदा good manner

अदम्य (a) indomitable; irrepr-essible. unyielding

अदरक (nf) ginger

अदला-बदली (nf) exchange, alt-eration

अदा (nf) discharge; performance; —करना to discharge, to pay off

अदायगी (nf) payment; fulfilment

अदा/लत (nf) a court of law; —लती judicial

अदावत (nf) enmity; opposition; hostility

अदृश्य (a) out of sight, invisible

अदृष्ट (nm) fate; (a) unseen; unforeseen

अद्भुत (a) fantastic, wonderful

अद्वितीय (a) matchless; unparalleled

अघ:पतन (nm) ruin, downfall

अघकचरा (a) half-baked, imperfect, immature

अघम (a) low, mean, base, worthless

अघमरा (a) half-dead, near dead

अघर (nm) lip; underlip

अघ/र्म (nm) sin; vice; —र्मी sinful, wicked, immoral

अघार्मिक (a) irreligious; impious

अधिक (a) surplus; more. —तम maximum. —तर mostly

अधिकांश (a) most; majority

अधिकाधिक (a) more and more

अधिकार (nm) authority; right

अधिकारी (nm) an owner; an officer. (a) worthy

अधिनायक (nm) a dictator

अधिमास (nm) a leap month

अधिवेशन (nm) a session; meeting

अधीक्षक (nm) a superintendent

अधीन (a) subordinate; dependent —ता subordination

अधीर (a) impatient; nervous; restive; —ता impatience

अधुना (ind) at present; now; —तन modern

अधूरा (a) unfinished, incomplete

अघेड़ (a) middle-aged

अघोगति (nf) downfall; misfortune

अध्यक्ष (nm) head; president; owner

अध्ययन (nm) study; —कक्ष study-room

अध्यवसाय (nm) diligence; enterprise

अध्यात्म (nm) spiritual contemplation, spiritual knowledge

अध्यादेश (nm) an ordinance

अध्या/पक (nm) master, a teacher; —पन teaching

अध्याय (nm) a canto; a chapter, a lesson

अध्येता (nm) a scholar; student

अनंत (a) eternal; endless; (nm) Vishnu

अनंतर (ind) afterwards; soon after

अन (pref) in sense of without, (as-बन, —मोल)

अनगढ़ (a) unformed, crude; in the natural form

अनगिनत (a) countless, numberless

अनजान (a) ignorant; unknown

अनदेखा (a) unseen

अनधिकार (a) unauthorised

अनन्नास (nm) pineapple tree or its fruit

अनन्य (a) intimate (as मित्र)

अनपचा (a) undigested

अनपढ़ (a) illiterate, uneducated

अनबन (nf) enmity; discord

अनभिज्ञ (a) ignorant; less informed

अनमना (a) mentally disturbed

अनमिल (a) irrelevant; discordant

अनमेल (a) inharmonious, heterogeneous

अनमोल (a) very costly, priceless

अनर्गल (a) useless; absurd; unbarred

अनर्थ (nm) contrary meaning; grievous wrong; a great loss

अनल (nm) fire

अनवरत (a) always, incessant, continuous

अनशन (nm) fast

अनश्वर (a) eternal, immortal

अनसुना (a) unnoticed, unheard

अनहोनी (nf) the impossible; (a) unusual; impossible

अनागत (a) the future

अनाचार (nm) wrong doing; misconduct

अनाज (nm) corn, grain

अनाड़ी (a) stupid; unskilled

अनाथ (nm) an orphan; (a) helpless

अनाथालय, अनाथाश्रम (nm) an orphanage

अनादर (nm) disrespect; insult

अनादि (a) eternal, having no beginning; an epithet of God

अनाप-शनाप (a & nm) nonsense; meaningless (talk)

अनामिका (nf) the finger between the middle and the little finger; the ring finger

अनायास (adv) suddenly; without effort

अनार (nm) a pomegranate; —दाना dried seeds of pomegranate

अनार्य (nm) a non-Aryan; (a) not respectable; not noble

अनावरण (nm) exposure

अनावर्ती (a) non-recurring

अनावश्यक (a) unimportant

अनावृत (a) open

अनिंद्य (a) faultless, irreproachable

अनिच्छा (nf) unwillingness; reluctance

अनिमेष (a) without a wink

अनियंत्रित (a) uncontrolled

अनियत (a) not fixed, indefinite

अनियमित (a) irregular

अनिर्वचनीय (a) ineffable; indescribable

अनिवार्य (a) compulsory; unavoidable

अनिश्चय (nm) uncertainty; suspense

अनिश्चित (a) undecided,

uncertain

अनिष्ट (*nm*) undesired, harm,
— कारी harmful

अनीति (*nf*) impropriety;
injustice

अनु (*pref*) meaning after,
along with, etc. (as अनुगमन,
अनुचर)

अनुकंपा (*nf*) kindness.

अनु/करण (*nm*) imitation;
— करणीय imitable

अनुकूल (*a*) suitable; agreeable;
— ता suitability

अनुक्रम (*nm*) sequence, succession

अनुक्रमणिका(*nf*)an index, a table
of contents

अनुगत (*a*) succeeding, following, obedient; (*nm*) a
follower

अनुगृहीत (*a*) grateful, obliged

अनुग्रह (*nm*) kindness, help

अनुचर (*nm*) servant; follower

अनुचित (*a*) unsuitable, wrong

अनु/ज (*nm*) a younger brother;
— जा a younger sister

अनुज्ञा (*nf*) permission

अनुताप (*nm*) dissatisfaction;
remorse

अनुदान (*nm*) a grant

अनुदार (*a*) miserly; not liberal

अनुदेश (*nm*) instruction

अनुनय (*nm*) prayer, request

अनुनासिक (*a*) nasalised (*nm*)
a nasalised vowel

अनुपम (*a*) matchless, unequalled; excellent

अनुपयुक्त (*a*) undeserving,
unsuitable

अनुपयो/गी (*a*) useless, unavai-
ling; — गिता uselessness

अनुपस्थित (*a*) absent

अनुपस्थिति (*nf*) absence

अनु/पात (*nm*) ratio, proportion;
— पाती proportional

अनुपूरक (*a*) supplementary

अनुपूर्ति (*nf*) supplementation;
subsidy

अनुप्राणित (*a*) imbued; inspired

अनुप्रास (*nm*) alliteration

अनुबंध (*nm*) contract

अनुभव (*nm*) experience

अनुभवी (*a*) experienced

अनुभूत (*a*) experienced; tried

अनुभूति (*nf*) emotional experience

अनुमति (*nf*) order, assent,
approval

अनुमान (*nm*) supposition,
guess; — त: about

अनुमो/दन (*nm*) approval, — दित
approved

अनुयायी (*nm*) a follower

अनु/रक्त (*a*) attached, fond;
— रक्ति attachment, fond-
ness

अनु/राग (*nm*) affection, love,
— रागी loving, fond

अनुरूप (*a*) fit; like; resembling;
congruent

अनुरोध (*nm*) entreaty; solicitation

अनुवाद (*nm*) translation;
interpretation

अनु/शासन (*nm*) discipline;
—शासक a disciplinarian

अनुशासित (*a*) disciplined

अनुशीलन (*nm*) constant study;
contemplation

अनु/श्रुत (*a*) traditional —श्रुति
tradition

अनुष्ठान (*nm*) ceremony,
ritual; undertaking

अनुसं/धान (*nm*) research;
—धाता a researcher

अनुसार (*a & adv*) according to;
in confirmity with

अनुस्वार (*nm*) the mark of nasal
sound used in writing
Devnagri

अनूठा (*a*) uncommon, unparalleled

अनूदित (*a*) translated

अनूप (*a*) unequalled; best

अनेक (*a*) several, many; more
than one

अनैतिक (*a*) immoral; —ता
immorality

अनोखा (*a*) rare; peculiar; —पन
novelty, peculiarity

अनौचित्य (*nm*) indecency;
impropriety

अनौपचारिक (*a*) informal,
unofficial

अन् a Sanskrit prefix showing
negation to words begin-
ning with vowels (e.g)
अनर्थ, अनादि (see अ)

अन्न (*nm*) food, corn

अन्न-जल (*nm*) bread and butter

अन्नदाता (*nm*) a supporter, a
patron

अन्य (*a*) other, diffrent; —पुरुष
the third person

अन्यत्र (*ind*) in some other
place

अन्यथा (*adv*) otherwise; (*a*)
against

अन्यमनस्क (*a*) unmindful,
absent-minded; —ता
absent-mindedness

अन्याय (*nm*) injustice, wrong;
—पूर्ण unjust, wrong

अन्यायी (*a*) lawless, unjust;
(*nm*) an unjust person

अन्योक्ति (*nf*) an allegory

अन्योन्य (*a*) each other, reciprocal

अन्वय (*nm*) the prose order

अन्वीक्षण (*nm*) investigation

अन्वेष/ण (*nm*) exploration;
discovery; —क an explorer

अपंग (*a*) cripple; maimed

अप (*pref*) a Sanskit prefix
denoting down & action of
inferiority etc. (as अपमान
अपबाद)

अपकर्ष (*nm*) downfall

अपकार (*nm*) damage; harm;
disservice

अपकारी (*a*) harmful

अपच (*nm*) stomach derange-
ment; indigeition

अपढ़ (*a*) unlettered, illiterate

अपथ्य (*a*) undigestible

अपदस्थ (*a*) dismissed, depos-
ed

अपना (*a*) personal; one's own; mine; —पन cordiality

अपनाना (*v*) to adopt; to own

अपभ्रंश (*nm*) one of the middle Indo-Aryan languages

अपमान (*nm*) disgrace, insult

अपयश (*nm*) disrepute, infamy

अपरंच (*ind*) besides, more-over

अपर (*a*) another, moreover, too

अपराध (*nm*) fault, crime; —विज्ञान criminology

अपराधी (*a*) guilty, criminal; offender

अपराह्न (*nm*) afternoon

अपरिचित (*a*) unknown; un-acquainted; (*nm*) a stranger

अपरिमित (*a*) limitless; infinite

अपरिमेय (*a*) immeasurable

अपरिष्कृत (*a*) crude; unrefined

अपरिहार्य (*a*) indispensible; unavoidable

अपरूप (*a*) odd, ugly, ill-shaped

अपर्याप्त (*a*) insufficient, short

अपलक (*a & adv*) unblinking

अपवाद (*nm*) censure; excepti-on; defamation

अपविचार (*nm*) a bad idea; mistrial

अपवित्र (*a*) unholy

अप/व्यय (*nm*) expenditure, waste; —व्ययी a wasteful

अपशकुन (*nm*) bad omen

अपशब्द (*nm*) a vulgar word, abusive language

अपहरण (*nm*) kidnapping; usurpation

अपादान (*nm*) the ablative case

अपार (*a*) immense; boundless

अपारदर्शी (*a*) opaque.

अपार्थिव (*a*) spiritual; un-earthly

अपाहिज (*nm & a*) disabled; crippled

अपितु (*ind*) on the other hand, but

अपील (*nf*) an appeal

अपूर्ण (*a*) deficient; in-complete

अपूर्व (*a*) wonderful; novel; unique

अपेक्षा (*nf*) expectation, neces-sity; की— in comparison with

अपेक्षित (*a*) expected

अप्रकाशित (*a*) unexposed; unpublished; kept secret

अप्रचलित (*a*) out of date, out of currency

अप्रत्यक्ष (*a*) indirect

अप्रत्याशित (*a*) sudden; unexpected

अप्रधान (*a*) minor, secondary

अप्रयुक्त (*a*) obsolete; unused

अप्रसन्न (*a*) displeased; un-happy

अप्रस्तुत (*a*) indirect

अप्राकृ/त —तिक (*a*) unnatural; uncommon

अप्राप्य (*a*) rare; unobtainable

अप्रामाणिक (*a*) inauthentic;

unauthoritative

अप्रासंगिक (*a*) out of context, irrelevant

अप्रिय (*a*) unloving, unpleasant

अप्सरा (*nf*) fairy; nymph

अफरा (*nm*) swelling of stomach due to over-eating

अफरा-तफरी (*nf*) hurry-skurry, confusion

अफलातून (*nm*) a person of overweening pride; the Greek philosopher 'Plato'

अफवाह (*nf*) a rumour

अफसर (*nm*) an officer

अफसाना (*nm*) a tale, story

अफसोस (*nm*) regret, sorrow

अफीम (*nf*) opium

अफीमची (*nm*) an opium-addict

अब (*adv.*) now; —की/के this time; —जाकर at long last; —से in future

अबरक (*nm*) mica

अबरी (*nf*) marble paper

अबला (*nf*) a woman

अबाध (*a*) free; without restraint

अबूझ (*a*) stupid; unintelligible

अबे (*ind*) to use words of disrespect

अबोध (*a*) innocent

अभागा (*a*) unfortunate; unlucky

अभा/व (*nm*) shortage, lack; —वात्मक negative

अप्रसन्न (*a*) displeased; unhappy

अभि (*pref*) a Sanskrit prefix denoting towards, over,

above, excessive etc. (as अभिनंदन, अभिमुख)

अभिजात (*a*) well born; aristocratic; (*nm*) aristocrat

अभिज्ञ (*a*) knowing all, well-conversant

अभिधा (*nf*) denotation, the literal sense of a word

अभिधान (*nm*) a name

अभिधेय (*nm*) predicable, literal meaning

अभिनंदन (*nm*) a ceremonious welcome; greeting

अभिनय (*nm*) acting

अभिनव (*a*) new; recent

अभि/नेता (*nm*) an actor; —नेत्री (*nf*) an actress

अभिन्न (*a*) clase; sameness, not different

अभिप्राय (*nm*) purpose; intention

अभिभावक (*nm*) a guardian

अभिभाषण (*nm*) a public speech

अभिभूत (*a*) overpowered; astonished

अभि/मान (*nm*) vanity; pride; —मानी arrogant; proud

अभिमुख (*ind*) facing, directed towards

अभियान (*nm*) an expedition; a campaign

अभियुक्त (*nm* & *a*) an accused

अभियोग (*nm*) charge, accusation

अभिराम (*a*) lovely, beautiful

अभिरुचि (*nf*) taste

अभिलषित (*a*) longed for,

desired

अभिलाषा (nf) desire

अभिवादन (nm) greeting

अभिवृद्धि (nf) development

अभिव्यंजना (nf) expression; —वाद expressionism

अभिव्यक्ति (nf) manifestation; expression

अभिशाप (nm) a curse

अभिसार (nm) appointment of lovers; meeting

अभिसारिका (nf) a woman who goes to meet her lover

अभी (adv) this moment, just now

अभीष्ट (a) cherished, desired

अभूतपूर्व (a) never existed before; unprecedented

अभेद (nm) absence of difference, identity

अभेद्य (a) indivisible

अभ्यर्थना (nf) request; welcome

अभ्यागत (nm) visitor, a guest

अभ्यास (nm) exercise; practice; habit

अभ्युत्थान (nm) elevation; rise

अभ्युदय (nm) rising

अमचूर (nm) dried mango parings

अमन (nm) tranquillity, peace

अमर (a) undying, immortal; (nm) a god

अमरता (nf) immortality

अमरूद (nm) guava

अमर्त्य (a) eternal, deathless

अमल (a) pure

अमल (nm) conduct, authority, application, —पानी (nm) intoxication

अमलदारी (nf) government, rule

अमला (nm) officers, agents, staff

अमली (a) habitual, (nm) an addict

अमानत (nf) charge, something given in trust

अमानुषिक (a) devellish; inhuman

अमावस (nf) the last day of the dark fortnight

अमिट (a) fixed, indelible

अमित (a) endless, immeasurable; enormous

अमीर (a) wealthy, rich; (nm) a noble man

अमीरी (nf) richness

अमुक (a) a certain person, so and so

अमूर्त (a) abstract

अमूल्य (a) costly, valuable; priceless

अमृत (nm) nectar

अमोघ (a) effectual, unfailing

अम्माँ (nf) mamma, mother

अम्ल (nm) acid; (a) sour; —ता acidity, sourness

अयोग्य (a) unworthy; unqualified, unfit, improper

अरक्षित (a) unguarded, undefended; insecured

अरब (a) a thousand million; (nm) the Arab country; an

Arab

अरमान (*nm*) wish, desire, ambition

अरसा (*nm*) a space of time, period; delay

अराजकता (*nf*) the state of being without a king, anarchy

अरारोट (*nm*) arrow-root

अरि (*nm*) an enemy

अरुचि (*nf*) sickness of stomach; dislike; —कर disgusting

अरुणोदय (*nm*) the first appearance of the Sun; day-break

अरे (*int*) O! a form of address

अर्क (*nm*) the Sun; essence

अर्ग/ल—ला (*nm & nf*) a log for fastening a door

अर्घ्य (*nm*) precious, valuable; fit for presentation to a deity, etc

अर्च/न—ना (*nm & nf*) worship, adoration

अर्ज़ (*nm*) prayer, request, solicitation

अर्जित (*a*) gathered, gained, earned

अर्ज़ी (*nf*) petition; an application

अर्ज़ीदावा (*nm*) a plaint submitted in a law-court

अर्थ (*nm*) sense; meaning; money; —गर्भित significant —वत्ता significance

अर्थ-व्यवस्था (*nf*) economy

अर्थ/शास्त्र (*nm*) Economics; the science of wealth; —शास्त्री an economist

अर्थहीन (*a*) moneyless; meaningless

अर्थात् (*ind*) that is to say, namely

अर्थी (*nf*) a bier; (*a*) desirous; (*nm*) a petitioner

अर्दली (*nm*) attendant, an orderly

अर्ध (*a*) half; semi; demi

अर्धचंद्र (*nm*) half moon, the symbol of nasalisation to a vowel

अर्धवृत्त (*nm*) semi-circle

अर्धव्यास (*nm*) radius

अर्धांगिनी (*nf*) wife, better half

अर्पण (*nm*) an offering, —करना to deliver

अर्राना (*v*) to fall down with a violent noise; to rush to

अर्वाचीन (*a*) new, recent; modern, up-to-date

अर्ह (*a*) competent; qualified; —ता (*nf*) competence; qualification

अलंकार (*nm*) ornament; figure of speech

अलक (*nf*) a ringlet of hair

अलकतरा (*nm*) pitch, coal-tar

अलग (*a & adv*) aside, separate, apart

अल्ल/गरज़ (*a*) careless; —गरज़ी (*nf*) carelessness

अलगाव (*nm*) separation;

breach, severance

अलबत्ता (*ind*) certainly, nevertheless

अलबेला (*nm*) hubble -bubble, a dandy; (*a*) dandy

अलभ्य (*a*) unattainable; rare

अलमबरदार (*nm*) a standard-bearer

अलमस्त (*a*) gay; free from anxiety

अलमारी (*nf*) a cupboard; a bookcase

अलसाना (*v*) to be drowsy; to feel lazy

अलसी (*nf*) linseed; —का तेल (*nm*) linseed oil

अलह/वा (*a*) different, separate, aloof — वगी aloofness

अलापना (*v*) to converse, to tune the voice

अलावा (*ind*) moreover, besides, except

अलोना (*a*) without salt

अलौकिक (*a*) heavenly, unearthly

अल्प (*a*) small, few; —ता (*nf*) smallness

अल्लाह (*nm*) God, the Almighty

अल्हड़ (*a*) carefree; —पन inexperience

अव (*pref*) a Sanskrit prefix denoting — downwards, smallness, decay etc. (as —अवगुण, अवतरण, अवमान)

अवकाश (*nm*) leave; recess; leisure

अवगुण (*nm*) fault, defect

अवचेतन (*nm* & *a*) subconscious

अवज्ञा (*nf*) disregard; contempt

अवतरण (*nm*) descent; crossing over; birth; copy —चिह्न quotation marks (" ")

अवतरित (*a*) descended

अवतार (*nm*) exhibition into human form, an incarnation

अवतीर्ण (*a*) manifested, descended

अवधि (*nf*) time; period; limit; duration

अवयव (*nm*) body; limb; a part, portion

अवर (*a*) under; junior; low

अवरुद्ध (*a*) stopped, shut up; hindered; restrained

अवरोध (*nm*) hindrance; restraint

अवर्णनीय, अवर्ण्य (*a*) unspeakable, indescribable

अवलंब (*nm*) a prop and stay; support

अवलोकन (*nm*) beholding, viewing, seeing

अवशिष्ट (*a*) remainder, left; (*nm*) remains, remnant

अवशेष (*nm*) remains, remnant

अवश्य (*adv*) surely, certainly; —मेव undoubtedly

अवसर (*nm*) chance, opportunity, occasion; —वादी

opportunist

अवस्था (nf) situation, condition; age

अबहेलना (nf) disrespect, neglect, carelessness

अवांछनीय (a) undesirable

अवांछित (a) undesired

अवाक् (a) stunned, wonderstruck; speechless

अविकारी (a) permanant condition; immutable

अविचल (a) unmoved, steady, motionless

अविनाशी (a) everlasting, immortal

अविभाज्य (a) indivisible

अविलंब (adv) immediately, at once

अविवाहित (a & nm) unwedded, bachelor

अविवे/क (nm) imprudence; —की stupid

अविश्वसनीय (a) incredible; untrustworthy

अविश्वास (nm) discredit, distrust; doubt

अविश्वासी (a) unfaithful, suspicious; (nm) an unbeliever

अवैज्ञानिक (a) unscientific

अवैतनिक (a) honorary

अवैध (a) unlawful, illegal, —ता illegality

अव्यय (nm) an indeclinable

अव्यवस्था (nf) hotch-potch, disorder, lawlessness

अव्यावहारिक (a) impractical

अव्वल (a) first

अशक्त (a) feeble, weak

अशांत (a) unquiet, restless

अशांति (nf) disturbance, restlessness

अशिक्षित (a) savage, uneducated

अशिष्ट (a) indecent; ill mannered; rude; —ता (nf) rudeness

अशुद्ध (a) impure; incorrect, wrong

अशुभ (a) bad, evil, inauspicious

अशोभन (a) ugly, unbecoming

अश्रु (nm) a tear, —पात shedding of tears

अश्लील (a) indecent, vulgar; obscene; —ता obscenity

असंख्य (a) countless, untold, numberless

असंग/त (a) absurd; irrelevant; —ति absurdity; irrelevance.

असंतुलित (a) unbalanced

असंतुष्ट (a) discontented, aggrieved, dissatisfied

असंतो/ष (nm) discontentment, dissatisfaction; —षी insatiable

असंबद्ध (a) disconnected

असंभव (a) impracticable, impossible

असंस्कृत (a) unrefined; uncultured

असत्य (nm) untruth, a lie

असफल (a) unsuccessful; —ता failure

असबाब (nm) baggage, luggage

असभ्य (a) impolite, vulgar, rude; —ता uncivility

असमंजस (nm) suspense, a dilemma

असमय (adv & a) out of season; untimely

असमर्थ (a) unable; —ता inability, incompetence

असमान (a) dissimilar; unequal

असर (nm) impression; effect

अस/ल—ली (a) real; pure

असलियत (nf) truth, reality

असहमति (nf) disagreement

असहयोग (nm) non-co-operation

असहाय (a) helpless; single-handed; lonesome

असहिष्णु (a) unenduring, peevish —ता intolerance, peevishness

असह्य (a) unendurable, intolerable

असाधारण (a) unusual, extra-ordinary —ता unusualness

असाध्य (a) incurable; impracticable

असामयिक (a) untimely, ill-timed, immature

असावधानी (nf) negligence, carelessness

असीम (a) boundless, limitless

असीमित (a) unlimited, unbounded

असुविधा (nf) inconvenience

असैनिक (a) non-military; civil; (nm) a civilian

अस्त (a) set; hidden, sunk —प्राय almost set

अस्त-व्यस्त (a) scattered; confused

अस्तित्व (nm) entity, existence

अस्तु (ind) well, however

अस्त्र (nm) a weapon, missile

अस्त्र-शस्त्र (nm) armament, weapons

अस्त्रागार (nm) armoury

अस्थायी (a) provisional, temporary

अस्थि (nf) a bone

अस्थिर (a) unstable, unsteady

अस्पताल (nm) a hospital

अस्पष्ट (a) vague; dim, obscure

अस्पृश्य (a) untouchable; —ता untouchability

अस्वस्थ (a) unhealthy

अस्वाभाविक (a) artificial, un-natural

अस्वीकृत (a) refused; unaccepted; rejected

अहं (nm) ego; —वाद egoism

अहंका/र (nm) egotism; vanity —री egotist

अहम (a) significant, important

अहमियत (nf) significance, importance

अहिंसक (a) non-violent

अहिंसा (nf) benevolence, non-violence

अहित (nm) enmity; harm, evil; —कर harmful

आ

आ the second vowel and the second letter of Devnagri alphabet; the long form of अ a Sanskrit prefix denoting the sense upto, through-out etc. (as आजन्म, आजीवन)

आंकड़े (*nm plural*) figures; data; numerals

आंकना (*v*) to assess; to mark

आँख (*nf*) an eye; sight; vision, the eye of a needle; — मिचौली — मिचौनी the game of hide and seek; — डबडबाना to have the eyes filled with tears; — देखा self-witnessed

आँगन (*nm*) a courtyard

आँच (*nf*) fire, the heat of flame

आँचल (*nm*) the end of cloth, sari and shawl etc

आँत (*nf*) intestines

आंतरिक (*a*) innate; internal

आंदोलन (*nm*) an agitation, a movement, campaign; tumult

आँधी (*nf*) a dust-storm, storm; tempest

आंशिक (*a*) fractional; partial

आँसू (*nm*) tear

आईंदा (*adv*) in future

आइना (*nm*) mirror, a looking-glass

आकर (*nm*) source; a mine; treasury

आकर्षक (*a*) attractive, charming, magnetic

आकर्षण (*nm*) charm, attraction, affinity; — शक्ति the power of attraction

आकर्षित (*a*) drawn, attracted

आकस्मिक (*a*) accidental, unexpected, sudden

आकांक्षा (*nf*) wish, aspiration

आकांक्षी (*a & nm*) expectant, aspirant

आकार (*nm*) appearance, form; structure; size; — प्रकार shape and size

आकाश (*nm*) the sky, heavens; — गंगा the milky way; — मंडल the celestial sphere; cosmos

आकाशवाणी (*nf*) an oracle; a proper name given to All India Radio

आकुल (*a*) confounded; uneasy; distressed

आकुलता (*nf*) agitation; mental distress, uneasiness; restlessness

आकृति (*nf*) form; structure; features

आक्रमण (*nm*) invasion, attack, thrust

आक्रामक (*nm*) aggressor; attacker

आक्रोश (*nm*) a curse, an abuse; fury

आक्षेप (*nm*) allegation; charge

आखिर (*nm*) end; (*adv*) at last; —कार finally

आगंतुक (*nm*) a new-comer, visitor

आग (*nf*) fire

आगज़नी (*nf*) arson

आगमन (*nm*) precedence; arrival; approach

आगा (*nm*) the fore part of any thing; before; in future

आगामी (*a*) future; about to come; next

आगे (*adv*) before; in future; a head

आग्रह (*nm*) obstinacy, insistence

आघात (*nm*) stroke, blow, shock

आचरण (*nm*) behaviour; conduct; practice

आचार (*nm*) custom; conduct; —विचार morals and manners

आचार्य (*nm*) a professor; the teacher

आज (*adv*) today, now, this day

आजकल (*adv*) now-a-days; —का modern; —में in a couple of days

आज़माइ/श (*nf*) experiment, trial; test —शी experimental

आज़माना (*v*) to test, to try

आज़ाद (*a*) free, independent

आज़ादी (*nf*) liberty, freedom

आजीवन (*adv*) throughout the life

आजीविका (*nf*) profession, livelihood

आज्ञा (*nf*) command, order; —पत्र a written order; a passport

आज्ञाका/री (*a*) obedient; —रिता (*nm*) obedience

आटा (*nm*) flour

आडंबर (*nm*) pomp, ostentation, affectation

आड़ (*nf*) curtain, a cover, shield; block

आड़ा (*a*) transverse; oblique

आतंक (*nm*) fear; terror, panic

आततायी (*nm & a*) an assailant; tyrant; oppressive

आतिथ्य (*nm*) hospitability

आतुर (*a*) restless, distressed; anxious; hasty

आतुरता (*nf*) restlessness, distress; anxiety; hastiness

आत्म (*nm*) one's own, personal; —कथा autobiography; —केंद्रित self-centered; —गौरव self-respect; —घात suicide; —चरित an autobiography; —ज्ञान self-knowledge; —त्याग self-sacrifice; —निंदा self-condemnation; —निरीक्षण introspection —हत्या suicide

आत्मा (*nf & nm*) spirit, soul

आत्माभिमान (*nm*) self-respect

आत्मिक (*a*) spiritual

आदत (*nf*) a habit

आदम (*nm*) Adam (the first man created on earth

according to Islamic, Christian and Jewish mythology)

आदमी (*nm*) human being, man

आदर (*nm*) honour, respect, deference; —णीय respectable

आदर्श (*nm*) a model, an ideal, norm; pattern; (*a*) model

आदान (*nm*) taking, receiving; —प्रदान exchange, giving and taking

आदाब (*nm*) salutation; manners

आदि (*nm*) a beginning, origin; (*a*) first; —कालीन primitive

आदिक (*ind*) etcetera, and so forth

आदिम (*a*) early, primitive; first

आदिवासी (*nm*) an aboriginal

आदी (*a*) accustomed, habituated

आदेश (*nm*) instruction; command; injunction

आद्यंत (*adv*) from the beginning to the end

आद्य (*a*) first, initial

आद्योपांत (*adv*) from the beginning to the end

आधा (*a*) half; middle; a part

आधार (*nm*) a supporter, basis; —भूत fundamental; —रेखा base; —शिला foundation-stone

आधारित (*a*) based (on)

आधिकारिक (*a*) authoritative, official; —कथानक (*nm*) the main plot or story of a novel, drama or an epic

आधिक्य (*nm*) excess, surplus; abundance.

आधिपत्य (*nm*) lordship, supremacy; power

आधिभौतिक (*a*) caused by animals, material

आधुनि/क (*a*) modern; —कीकरण modernisation

आधृत (*a*) based (on)

आध्यात्मिक (*a*) pertaining to soul, spiritual

आनंद (*nm*) pleasure, delight, joy

आन (*nf*) dignity, honour, prestige

आनन-फ़ानन (में) (*adv*) at once

आना (*v*) to come;

आना-कानी (*nf*) neglect, procrastination

आनुवंशिक (*a*) hereditary; —ता heredity

आप (*pron*) one's self; self; you (second person, formal or honorific)

आपत्काल (*nm*) emergency

आपत्ति (*nf*) objection, calamity, trouble

आपदा (*nf*) trouble, distress, adversity

आपस (*pron*) one another, each other

आपसदारी (*nf*) mutual relationship

आपसी (*a*) reciprocal; mutual

आपा (*nm*) one's own existance; ego, vanity

आपात (*nm*) an emergency

आपा-धापी (*nf*) hasty selfserving, a mad race for self-interest

आपेक्षिक (*a*) relative, comparative

आप्लावन (*nm*) a dip, a plunge

आफत (*nf*) trouble, disaster

आब (*nf*) brilliance, lustre; water — दार brilliant

आबकारी (*nf*) excise

आबपाशी (*nf*) irrigation

आबरू (*nf*) respect, honour

आबहवा (*nf*) weather; climate of a place.

आबाद (*a*) populated; inhabited

आबादी (*nf*) population; habitation

आभा (*nf*) splendour; beauty; —मंडल a halo

आभार (*nm*) burden; obligation

आभारी (*a*) grateful; obliged

आभास (*nm*) reflection, shadow; false knowledge

आभासी (*a*) unreal; pseudo

आभूषण (*nm*) ornaments, jewels; decoration.

आभूषित (*a*) decorated

आभ्यंतर (*nm & a*) interior; internal

आमंत्रण (*nm*) solicitation, invitation

आमंत्रित (*a*) invited

आम (*a*) common —आदमी common man

आम (*nm*) the mango

आमद (*nm*) coming, approach; income; revenue

आमदनी (*nf*) revenue, income

आमना-सामना (*nm*) opposition, coming face to face

आमने-सामने (*adv*) opposite to one another, face to face

आमरण (*ind*) till death, throughout one's life

आमादा (*a*) ready, bent upon

आमाशय (*nm*) the stomach

आमुख (*nm*) the prelude of a drama; introduction

आमोद (*nm*) pleasure, delight, joy; —प्रमोद marriment; orgy

आमोदित (*a*) happy, delighted

आय (*nf*) income, receipt

आयत (*nf*) a rectangle; (*a*) wide; stretched

आयतन (*nm*) a resting place; volume

आयताकार (*a*) rectangular

आया (*nf*) a female attendant for children, a nurse; (*ind*) whether, or

आयात (*nm*) import

आयाम (*nm*) length; dimension

आयु (*nf*) age

आयुर्विज्ञान (*nm*) Medical Science

आयुर्वेद (*nm*) the Indian medicinal system

आयुष्मान् (*a*) blessed with a long life (used for youngers)

आयोग (*nm*) a commission

आयोजन (*nm*) arrangement

आरंभ (*nm*) origin; beginning, start

आरजू (*nf*) desire; request

आरती (*nf*) the ceremony performed in the worship of gods by moving a lighted lamp

आर-पार (*adv*) over, across; (*nm*) the two banks of a river

आरा (*nm*) a saw

आराधक (*nm*) a worshipper

आराधना (*nf*) worship; adoration

आराम (*nm*) comfort; rest; relief; —कुर्सी an easy chair

आरामतलब (*a*) lazy, indolent; ease-loving

आरोग्य (*nm*) freedom from disease; health

आरोप (*nm*) charge, allegation; imputation

आरोहण (*nm*) climb; ascension

आर्त (*a*) aggrieved; distressed; afflicted

आर्थिक (*a*) economic, monetary

आर्द्र (*a*) wet; moist; damp; tender

आर्य (*nm*) an Aryan; (*a*) noble

आर्यावर्त (*nm*) the land of Aryans (the country lying between the Himalayas and the Vindhya mountains)

आलंकारिक (*a*) ornamental; rhetorical

आलस (*nm*) idleness, laziness

आलसी (*a*) lazy

आलस्य (*nm*) laziness, lethargy, idleness

आला (*nm*) an instrument; (*a*) excellent; superior

आलिंगन (*nm*) embracing; clasping

आली (*nf*) (a woman's) female friend; range; a row; (*a*) grand; excellent

आलीशान (*a*) magnificent, grand

आलू (*nm*) potato

आलो/क (*nm*) brightness; enlightenment; light; —कित lit, lighted

आलोचक (*nm*) a critic

आलोचना (*nf*) criticism

आलोच्य (*a*) worth criticising

आवभगत (*nf*) hospitality

आवरण (*nm*) covering; envelope

आवर्ती (*a*) recurring

आवश्यक (*a*) important; necessary; essential

आवश्यकता (*nf*) need, requirement, necessity

आवागमन (*nm*) coming and going; transmigration

आवाज (*nf*) voice, sound; echo

आवारा (*nm*) wicked, loafer; (*a*) wandering, vagrant

आवारागर्दी (*nf*) loitering, vagrancy; loafing

आवा/स (*nm*) place of residence, house —सी resident

आवाहन (*nm*) a calling; summoning

आविर्भाव (*nm*) manifestation; advent; emergence

आविर्भूत (*a*) manifested; become visible

आविष्कर्ता (*nm*) an inventor

आविष्कार (*nm*) an invention

आवृत (*a*) covered

आवृत्त (*a*) repeated; turned round

आवृत्ति (*nf*) repetition; frequency; edition

आवेग (*nm*) passion; emotion; impulse; wave

आवेदन (*nm*) petition, an application; —पत्र an application

आवेश (*nm*) intense emotion; wrath

आशंका (*nf*) doubt; fear; alarm

आशय (*nm*) meaning; intention

आशा (*nf*) hope; expectation; —जनक hopeful

आशातीत (*a*) unexpected, beyond hope

आशा/वाद (*nm*) optimism; —वादी optimistic; an optimist

आशिक़ (*nm*) a lover, a suitor; —माशूक़ the lover and beloved

आशिष (*nf*) blessings

आशीर्वाद (*nm*) blessings

आशु (*a*) speedy, swift, prompt, quick, spontaneous

आश्चर्य (*nm*) astonishment, wonder, surprise

आश्रम (*nm*) hermitage, asylum

आश्रय (*nm*) support; shelter, refuge

आश्रित (*a*) enjoying the support of; (*nm*) refugee; a dependent

आश्वस्त (*a*) assured; consoled; encouraged

आश्वासन (*nm*) assurance; guarantee; repose; solace

आस (*nf*) desire; hope

आसक्त (*a*) fond; attached

आसक्ति (*nf*) attachment, addiction

आसन (*nm*) act of sitting, a posture; stage; seat

आस-पास (*adv*) all around, near about

आसमान (*nm*) the sky; heaven

आसमानी (*a*) the colour of sky, light blue; pertaining to the sky

आसरा (*nm*) shelter; reliance; support

आसा/न (*a*) simple; easy; convenient; —नी easiness

आस्तिक (*nm*) a theist

आस्था (*nf*) belief, faith

आह (*int*) ah! (*nf*) a sigh indicating pain, sorrow etc

आहट (*nf*) sound; noise; sound of footsteps

आहत (*a*) wounded, injured

आहार (*nm*) meal, food, diet

आहिस्ता (*adv*) softly, slowly,

gently

आह्लाद (*nm*) delight, gladness,

joy

आह्वान (*nm*) a call, a summon

इ

इ the third vowel and the third letter of Devnagri alphabet

इंगित (*nm*) sign, hint; gesture

इंतज़ाम (*nm*) arrangement; management

इंतज़ार (*nm*) expectation; wait

इंतहा (*nf*) extremity; limit

इंद्रजाल (*nm*) trickery; magic

इंद्रधनुष (*nm*) a rainbow

इंद्रिय (*nf*) sense, an organ of sense; —निग्रह self-control; —सुख sensual pleasure

इंसाफ़ (*nm*) equity; justice

इकट्ठा (*a*) gathered, collected; (*adv*) in one lot, together

इकहरा (*a*) single-folded, single

इकाई (*nf*) a unit

इक्का (*nm*) a small one horse carriage; an ace

इच्छा (*nf*) intention; desire; wish; —शक्ति will-power

इच्छित (*a*) willed, desired

इच्छुक (*a*) willing; desirous

इजाज़त (*nf*) consent; permission; sanction

इज़्ज़त (*nf*) prestige; dignity; respect; honour

इठलाना (*v*) to express tenderness by gesture, to act

affectionately

इतना (*a*) so much; this much

इतमीनान (*nm*) assurance; conviction; confidence

इतराना (*v*) to behave in a self-conceited manner

इति (*nf*) conclusion, end; (*ind*) a word denoting conclusion

इतिहास (*nm*) history; —कार a historian

इत्तफ़ाक़ (*nm*) coincidence; friendship, unity; chance; understanding

इत्तला (*nf*) intimation; information; notice

इत्यादि (*ind*) etcetera

इत्र (*nm*) scent; perfume; essence

इघर (*adv*) here; this side, this way

इनकलाब (*nm*) revolution

इनकार (*nm*) denial; refusal; disapproval

इनसान (*nm*) a human being, mankind; man

इनसानियत (*nf*) humanity; human nature; nobility

इनाम (*nm*) reward, prize;

award

इने-गिने (*a*) selected, very few

इमारत (*nf*) structure, building

इम्तहान (*nm*) test; examination; trial

इरादा (*nm*) idea, intention; desire

इर्द-गिर्द (*adv*) about; nearby, around

इलज़ाम (*nm*) allegation, blame, accusation, charge

इलाक़ा (*nm*) area; locality; zone, region

इलाज (*nm*) medical treatment; remedy, cure

इल्म (*nm*) learning, knowledge

इशारा (*nm*) signal; hint; indication

इश्क़ (*nm*) passion, love; amour

इश्तहार (*nm*) poster; advertisement

इस (*pron*) this, it

इस्पात (*nm*) steel

इस्लाम (*nm*) the religion of Mohammedans

इस्तरी (*nf*) a smoothing iron; —करना to smooth garment with a heated iron

इस्तीफ़ा (*nm*) resignation

इस्तेमाल (*nm*) use; application

ई

ई the fourth vowel and the fourth letter of Devnagri alphabet

ईंट (*nf*) brick

ईंधन (*nm*) firewood, fuel

ईख (*nf*) sugar-cane

ईजाद (*nf*) an invention

ईमान (*nm*) belief, faith, truth

ईमानदार (*a*) faithful; honest

ईमानदारी (*nf*) faithfulness, honesty

ईर्ष्या (*nf*) jealousy; —लु jealous

ईश्वर (*nm*) God; —वादी a theist

ईश्वरीय (*a*) Godly

ईसवी (*a*) pertaining to Christ; —सन the christian era A.D

ईसा (*nm*) Jesus Christ

ईसाई (*nm*) a Christian

उ

उ the fifth vowel and the fifth letter of Devnagri alphabet

उंगली (*nf*) a finger

उंडेलना (*v*) to pour out; to pour into

उऋण (*a*) free from debt

उकता/ना (*v*) to be tired of, to fret; —हट weariness, boredom

उकसाना (*v*) to excite, to instigate; to raise

उक्त (*a*) spoken, told, mentioned

उक्ति (*nf*) speech, voice, statement

उखड़ना (*v*) to be rooted up, to be raised

उखाड़-पछाड़ (*nf*) ado; manoeuvring

उगना (*v*) to grow, to rise; to spring up

उगलना (*v*) to vomit, to spit out; to eject

उग्र (*a*) sharp; violent; radical; —वादी radicalist, terrorist

उघाड़ना (*v*) to open, to uncover, to bare

उचकना (*v*) to leap, to stand on tip-toe

उचक्का (*a*) a swindler

उचाट (*a*) mentally wearied, indifferent

उचित (*a*) reasonable, proper, suitable

उच्च (*a*) lofty, tall, high; —ता excellence, distinction

उच्चारण (*nm*) utterance; pronunciation

उच्छिष्ट (*a*) leavings, waste

उच्छृंखल (*a*) rude, undisciplined

उच्छ्वास (*nm*) breath, inspiration; chapter of a book

उछल-कूद (*nf*) a hopple, jumping

उछलना (*v*) to jump, to leap, to spring

उजड्ड (*a & nm*) rash, uncivil

उजबक (*a*) foolish, stupid, idiot

उजला (*a*) white; bright; clean; clear

उजागर (*a*) bright, shining; famous; clear

उजाड़ (*a*) deserted, ruined; barren

उजाड़ना (*v*) to lay waste, to root up; to destroy

उजाला (*nm*) splendour, light, brightness; (*a*) clear, bright, shining

उज्ज्वल (*a*) clear, bright, clean; without blemish

उठना (*v*) to stand up; to rise; to get up (*adv*)

उठाईगीर (*nm*) a petty thief

उड़द (*nf*) black-gram.

उड़ना (*v*) to fly, to wing; to vanish, to disappear

उड्डाऊ (a) squanderer; extravagant

उड्डाकू (a) capable of flying; an aviator

उड्डान (nf) act of flying, flight

उड़ाना (v) to cause to fly, to blow up

उतना (a) that much, so much

उतरना (v) to come down from a height; to descend

उतार (nm) fall, descent

उतार-चढ़ाव (nm) rise and fall

उतारू (a) determined, bent on

उतावला (a) hasty, rash

उतावली (nf) haste, rashness

उत् a Sanskrit prefix denoting over, above etc (as उक्षेप, उत्थान, उन्नति)

उत्कं/ठा (nf) longing; curiosity; craving; —ठित curious

उत्कट (a) keen, excessive, intense

उत्कर्ष (nm) climax; excellence; prosperity

उत्कृष्ट (a) good, superior, excellent

उत्तम (a) the best, the greatest; —पुरुष first person (in grammer)

उत्तर (nm) an answer, north, response —प्रत्युत्तर reply and counter-reply

उत्तरदायित्व (nm) burden, responsibility

उत्तरदायी (a) responsive, answerable

उत्तराधिका/र (nm) succession, inheritance; —री an heir, inheritor, successor

उत्तरार्ष (a) the latter half

उत्तरी (a) northern

उत्तरोत्तर (a & adv.) continuous; more and more; continuously

उत्तीर्ण (a) successful, passed (in test or examination)

उत्तेजक (a) exciting; stimulating

उत्तेजना (nf) excitement, thrill; stimulation

उत्थान (nm) act of rising; progress

उत्पत्ति (nf) birth; origin; creation; production

उत्पन्न (a) born; produced; originate, —करना to bear, to produce

उत्पात (nf) mischief, nuisance, disturbance

उत्पादक (nm) an originator; a creator; (a) originating; creating

उत्पादन (nm) giving birth to; production; —करना to produce

उत्पीड़क (nm) an oppressor

उत्पीड़न (nm) vexation, oppression

उत्पीड़ित (a) oppressed

उत्फुल्ल (a) expanded, blossomed

उत्सर्ग (nm) abandonment; sacrifice

उत्सव (nm) great occasion,

festival, gala

उत्साह (nm) enthusiasm, joy, zeal

उत्साही (a) zealous; an enthusiast

उत्सुक (a) eager, keen

उथल-पुथल (nf) state of being capsized or confused

उथला (a) shallow

उदय (nm) dawn, rise; accent

उदर (nm) stomach, abdomen

उदात्त (a) generous, sublime

उदार (a) bountiful, generous; liberal —ता generosity, liberality

उदास (a) dejected, sad, dull, doleful

उदासी (nf) sadness

उदासीन (a) neutral; indifferent; —ता indifference

उदाहरण (nm) example, instance

उदीयमान (a) ascending, rising

उद्गम (nm) appearance, rising; commencement

उद्गार (nm) feelings (of mind)

उद्घाटन (nm) opening, inauguration

उद्घोष (nm) proclamation

उद्दंड (a) arrogant, rude; insolent

उद्दाम (a) free from restraint, unchecked, self-willed

उद्दीपन (nm) the act of exciting, stimulation

उद्देश्य (nm) aim; object; import; purpose

उद्धत (a) arrogant, rude, impudent

उद्धरण (nm) extract, quotation

उद्धार (nm) salvation; restoration; uplift

उद्धृत (a) quoted, extracted

उद्बोधन (nm) knowledge, awakening

उद्भव (nm) origin; birth

उद्यत (a) prepared, ready; —होना to be bent on

उद्यम (nm) business, enterprise; exertion

उद्यमी (nm) active, hard-working, an entrepreneur

उद्योग (nm) effort; industry; —धंधा industry; —पति an industrialist

उद्योगीकरण (nm) industrialisation

उद्विग्न (a) distressed, sulky, troubled

उद्वेग (nm) anxiety, restlessness

उघड़ना (v) to be unsewn, to be unfold

उधर (adv.) thither, on the other side

उधार (nm) loan; debt; credit; —खाता credit account; —देना to lend; —लेना to borrow

उघेड़ना (v) to unsew, to unfold

उन (pron) third person plural, oblique form, those

उनींदा (a) sleepy, dozy

उन्नत (a) tall, high; improved; progressed

उन्नति (nf) increase;

promotion; progress; improvement; development

उन्नयन (*nm*) development; progress

उन्मत्त (*a*) crazed; intoxicated

उन्माद (*nm*) rabidity; insanity; hysteria

उन्मुक्त (*a*) free; unrestrained

उन्मुख (*a*) looking upwards, intent, ready

उन्मूलन (*nm*) ruin; uprooting, destroying; abolition

उन्मेष (*nm*) twinkling of the eyes; blooming

उप a Sanskrit prefix used in the sense of down, under, near etc (as उपहास, उपमंत्री)

उपकरण (*nm*) materials; appliance; equipment

उपकार (*nm*) favour, help, kindness

उपकारी (*a*) helping, beneficent

उपक्रम (*nm*) beginning, preparation

उपचार (*nm*) remedy, medical treatment

उपज (*nf*) product; crop; fruitfulness; origin

उपजाऊ (*a*) productive, fertile.

उपदेश (*nm*) counsel; lesson, advice; preaching

उपद्रव (*nm*) riot, disturbance, turmoil; —करना to mob

उपनगर (*nm*) a suburb

उपनाम (*nm*) a family name, surname, nickname; pen name

उपनिवे/श (*nm*) a colony; —शीय colonial

उपन्या/स (*nm*) fiction, novel; —सकार novelist

उपभोक्ता (*nm*) a consumer; one who enjoys

उपभोग (*nm*) consuming; enjoyment

उपमा (*nf*) comparison; a simile

उपयुक्त (*a*) fit, suitable, proper; used; —ता suitability, propriety

उपयोग (*nm*) utility, use.

उपयोगिता (*nf*) service, usefulness

उपयोगी (*a*) proper; useful; helpful

उपरांत (*adv*) afterwards, in future

उपरिलिखित (*a*) above-mentioned

उपर्युक्त (*a*) above-mentioned; aforesaid

उपलक्ष्य (*nm*) में on account of

उपलब्ध (*a*) acquired, received; available

उपलब्धि (*nf*) acquisition, achievement; availability

उपवास (*nm*) a fast; starvation

उपसंहार (*nm*) end, conclusion

उपसर्ग (*nm*) a prefix

उपस्थित (*a*) ready; present

उपस्थिति (*nf*) attendance; presence

उपहार (*nm*) gift, present

उपहास (nm) mockery; sarcasm

उपहासास्पद (a) ridiculous,

उपाख्यान (nm) a story, narrative

उपादेय (a) acceptable, useful

उपाधि (nf) attribute, title; qualification

उपाध्यक्ष (nm) Vice-President; Vice-Chairman; Deputy Speaker

उपाय (nm) measure; remedy; step

उपार्जन (nm) acquiring, gain; earning

उपालंभ (nm) reviling, complaint

उपासक (nm) a worshipper, a devotee

उपासना (nf) prayer, worship

उपास्य (a) worthy of worship, adorable

उपेक्षा (nf) slight, neglect, disregard

उपेक्षित (a) slighted, neglected, disregarded

उफनना (v) to boil over

उफान (nm) a boiling

उबकाई (nf) nausea, vomit

उबटन (nm) an unguent, a paste for smearing the body with

उबरना (v) to be free, to remain over

उबलना (v) to boil

उबारना (v) to release, to set free

उबाल (nm) boiling, seething

उबालना (v) to boil

उबासी (nf) a yawn

उभय (a) both of them, the two

उभरना (v) to emerge

उभार (nm) swelling, projection

उमंग (nf) ambition, aspiration; zeal

उमदा (a) fine, excellent, nice

उमस (nf) heat, sultry weather

उम्मीद (nf) expectation, hope

उम्मीदवा/र (nm) a candidate; —री candidature

उम्र (nf) time of life, age

उर्फ़ (ind) alias

उर्वर (a) fertile, fruitful

उलझन (nf) tangle, complication

उलझना (v) to dispute, to be entangled

उलटना (v) to be turned over, to reverse, to overturn

उलट-फेर (nm) a change, upsetting

उलटा (a) contrary, opposite; reversed

उलटी (nf) vomiting, vomit; nausea

उलाहना (nm) reproach; complaint

उल्का (nf) a flame, fire brand, a falling star

उल्था (nm) rendering, translation

उल्लंघन (nm) transgression, violation

उल्लास (nm) splendour, joy, delight

उल्लू (nm) an owl; a fool

उल्लेख (nm) description, mention, quotation; —करना to mention, to refer

उल्लेखनीय (a) worth mention-ing, remarkable, fit for being written

उस(pron) the inflexional form of वह

उसाँस (nf) long breath, a sigh

उसूल (nm) cause, principle

उस्तरा (nm) a razor

उस्ताद (nm) a tutor, teacher; (a) clever, tricky, expert

ऊ

ऊ the sixth vowel and the sixth letter of Devnagri alphabet

ऊँघना (v) to slumber, to doze

ऊँच-नीच (nf) ups and downs; good and evil

ऊँचा (a) tall, high; —सुनना to be hard of hearing

ऊँचाई (nf) height, loftiness

ऊँट (nm) a camel

ऊँ हूँ (ind) denoting refusal, no, never !

ऊटपटाँग (a) disorderly; absurd, meaningless

ऊत (a) foolish

ऊदा (a) violet

ऊष/म (nm) uproar; distur-bance; —मी naughty

ऊन (nf) wool; (a) less, worthless

ऊनी (a) wollen

ऊपर (adv) upward; upon

ऊपरी (a) superficial, showy; upper

ऊब (nf) feeling of aversion arising from continuous work

ऊबना (v) to feel irked, to be bored

ऊर्जस्वी (a) powerful, glorious

ऊर्जा (nf) vigour; energy

ऊल-जलूल (a) irrelevant, disconnected; rude, foolish

ऊसर (a & nm) sandy fallow land

ऊहापोह (nf) reasoning, arguing

ऋ

ऋ the seventh vowel and the seventh letter of Devnagri alphabet

ऋचा (*nf*) a Vedic hymn

ऋजु (*a*) not crooked; straight; easy

ऋण (*nm*) debt; minus; loans

ऋणात्मक (*a*) concerning a debt; negative

ऋणी (*a*) beholden, indebted; (*nm*) a debtor

ऋतु (*nf*) season; menses, menstrual discharge

ऋद्धि (*nf*) wealth, name of medicinal plant; —सिद्धि wealth and prosperity

ऋषि (*nm*) a seer; sage

ए

ए the eighth vowel and the eighth letter of Devnagri alphabet

एक (*a*) an, alone, single, one

एकक (*nm*) a unit

एकटक (*adv*) without a wink

एकड़ (*nm*) an acre

एकतंत्र (*nm*) autocracy

एकतरफ़ा (*a*) one-sided; one way

एकता (*nf*) oneness, unity

एकत्र (*a*) collected, in the same place, together

एकत्रित (*a*) gathered, collected; assembled —करना to collect, to assemble

एकदम (*ind*) in one breath; suddenly; completely

एकबारगी (*adv*) suddenly; completely; all of a sudden

एकमत (*a*) agreeing, unanimous

एकमात्र (*a*) the only one, solitary

एकमुश्त (*a & adv*) lump; in a lot

एकरंगा (*a*) not diverse; monochromatic

एकवचन (*a*) singular

एकसार (*a*) uniform, even

एकांकी (*a & nm*) one-act (play); —कार a one-act play-wright

एकांगी (*a*) one-sided, partial

एकांत (*a*) alone, solitary; (*nm*) solitude; privacy

एकांतर (*a*) alternate (angle)

एका (*nm*) unity

एकाएक (*adv*) at once, suddenly

एकाकी (*a*) alone; solitary

एकाग्र (*a*) undisturbed, concentrated on the same point

एकाग्रता (*nf*) intentness, concentration

एकादशी (*nf*) the eleventh day in the fortnight of a lunar month

एकाधिकार (*nm*) exclusive right, monopoly

एकीकरण (*nm*) unification, integration

एकबार (*nm*) faith; confidence

एतबार (*nm*) faith; confidence

एतराज़ (*nm*) objection, opposition

एलान (*nm*) an announcement

एवज़ (*nm*) recompense, substitution

एवज़ी (*nm*) one officiating for another, substitute

एहतियात (*nm*) caution; warning

एहसान (*nm*) obligation, gratefulness

एहसानमंद (*a*) obliged, grateful

एहसास (*nm*) feeling

ऐ

ऐ the ninth vowel and the ninth letter of Devnagri alphabet

ऐंठ (*nf*) twist, cramp

ऐंठना (*v*) to twine, to twist

ऐंद्रिय (*a*) pertaining to senses

ऐक्य (*nm*) oneness; unity

ऐच्छिक (*a*) intentional, voluntary, unrestrained

ऐतिहासिक (*a*) traditional; historical

ऐन (*a*) just, exact

ऐनक (*nf*) an eyeglass; spectacles for weak eyes

ऐब (*nm*) defect; blemish; vice

ऐबी (*a*) wicked, defective

ऐयारी (*nf*) deception, wiliness, fraud

ऐयाश (*a & nm*) luxurious, licentious person

ऐयाशी (*nf*) luxurious living

ऐरा-गैरा (*a*) stranger, unknown

ऐश्वर्य (*nm*) wealth, fortune; glory

ऐसा (*a*) so, such, like; —वैसा trifling

ऐहिक (*a*) pertaining to this world; temporal; worldly

ओ

ओ the tenth vowel and the tenth letter of Devnagri alphabet

ओंकार (*nm*) the mysterious syllable called प्रणव

ओछा (*a*) shallow; narrow-minded

ओज (*nm*) strength; vigour; —स्वी vigorous; powerful —स्विता vigorousness

ओझल (*a*) impediment, out of sight

ओट (*nm*) protection, shelter

ओठ (*nm*) a lip

ओढ़ना (*v*) to cover the body with something

ओढ़नी (*nf*) a woman's mantle

ओत-प्रोत (*a*) full of, well mixed

ओफ़ (*int*) expressing pain and wonder; Ah me !

ओम् (*nm*) the sacred syllable called प्रणव

ओर (*nm*) direction, side

ओर-छोर (*nm*) the beginning and the end; the two ends

ओला (*nm*) hail; hailstone

ओषधि (*nf*) a medicine herb

ओस (*nf*) dew

ओह (*int*) an exclamation of sorrow and wonder, oh !

ओहदा (*nm*) rank, position

ओहो (*int*) expressing regret, Alas ! Heigh-ho !

औ

औ the eleventh vowel and the eleventh letter of the Devnagri alphabet

औंधा (*a*) overturned, with the face downwards

औंस (*nm*) an ounce

औकात (*nf*) capability; status

औचित्य (*nm*) propriety; righteousness

औज़ार (*nm*) tool, an instrument

औटना (*v*) to thicken by evaporation

औद्योगिक (*a*) industrial

औपचारिक (*a*) pertaining to service, formal

औपन्यासिक (*a*) pertaining to a novel

और (*conj*) and, also (*adv*) else; other; more

औरत (*nf*) a woman; one's wife

औरस (*a*) legitimate child

औलाद (*nf*) descendent, progeny, child

औषध (*nm*) a medicine, drug

औषधालय (*nm*) a dispensary, pharmacy

औसत (*a*) average; mean

क

क the first member of the first pentad of consonants in Devnagri alphabet

कंकड़ (*nm*) a small piece of stone; pebble

कंकण (*nm*) a bangle, a bracelet

कंकरीट (*nm*) a mixture of gravel, lime, cement and sand; concrete

कंकाल (*nm*) a skeleton

कंगन (*nm*) a bracelet

कंगाल (*nm*) poor, miserable

कंगाली (*nf*) misery, poverty

कँगूरा (*nm*) tower; parapet wall; ornament on crowns

कंघा (*nm*) a comb

कंचन (*nm*) wealth; gold

कंचुक (*nm*) a bodice, brassieres; skin of a snake

कंजू/स (*a*) parsimonious, miserly —सी niggardliness and miserliness

कँटीला (*a*) prickly, thorny

कंठ (*nm*) neck, the throat; —हार a necklace

कंठस्थ (*a*) learnt by heart

कंठाग्र (*a*) learnt by heart

कंद (*nm*) an esculent tuber root; sugar candy

कंदरा (*nf*) a cave

कंधा (*nm*) a shoulder

कंपन (*nm*) shiver, thrill

कंपायमान (*a*) oscillating, quivering

कंबल (*nm*) a rug, a blanket

ककड़ी (*nf*) cucumber

कक्ष (*nm*) chamber, a room

कक्षा (*nf*) a class room; an orbit

कचरा (*nm*) sweepings, rubbish

कचहरी (*nf*) a court of justice; assembly

कचूमर (*nm*) anything well-crushed

कचोट (*nf*) a lingering agony

कच्चा (*a*) unripe, immature

कछुआ (*nm*) a tortoise, a turtle

कटकटाना (*v*) to grind teeth

कटना (*v*) to be cut; to pass away time; to be ashamed; to complete; to die in battle; to be disconnected

कटाई (*nf*) act of cutting, harvesting

कटाक्ष (*nm*) ogling, a side-look; taunt

कटार (*nf*) a large knife, a dagger

कटु (*a*) sharp; unpleasant; bitter

कटोरेदान (*nm*) a brass pot with a lid for keeping articles of food

कटोरा (*nm*) a big bowl, cup

कटौती (*nf*) deduction; reduction

कट्टर (*a*) strict, fanatic; dogmatic

कठघरा (*nm*) a dock; bar

कठपुतली (*nf*) a wooden toy, a puppet

कठमुल्ला (*nm*) a dogmatic Mullah, bigot

कठि/न (*a*) hard, difficult; —नता a difficulty

कठोर (*a*) rough, hard; unkind

कड़वा (*a*) unpleasant; bitter

कड़ा (*a*) stiff; hard; stony; (*nm*) a ring of metal

कड़ाह (*nm*) a big boiling pan

कढ़ाई (*nf*) the art of embroidery

कण (*nm*) jot, particle; a small fragment of rice or wheat

कतई (*adv & a*) altogether, wholly, completely, whole, complete

कतरना (*v*) to cut; to clip, to chip

कतरा (*nm*) portion cutt off, a drop, fragment

कतराना (*v*) to cause to be cut out; to avoid an encounter or coming face to face

कताई (*nf*) spinning

कतार (*nf*) row, a line

कत्ल (*nm*) slaughter; murder

कथन (*nm*) mention, statement; saying

कथनी (*nf*) speech, narration

कथा (*nf*) a tale, fable; a religious discourse

कथानक (*nm*) a small story, the plot

कथोपकथन (*nm*) conversation; the dialogue

कथ्य (*nm*) subject matter

कद (*nm*) height; size

कदम (*nm*) footstep; step, pace

कदाचित् (*adv*) may be, possibly, by chance

कदापि (*adv*) seldom, ever; —नहीं never

कदावर (*adj*) of tall stature, giant like

कद्दू (*nm*) gourd, pumpkin

क़द्र (*nf*) merit; appreciation; respect —दान patron; just appreciator

कनखी (*nf*) a glance of the eye, ogle, leer

कनस्तर (*nm*) a canister

कनात (*nf*) a screen of canvas, walls of a tent

कनी (*nf*) a small particle; uncooked grain of rice

कन्नी (*nf*) edge; border; ends of kite; a tool of a mason

कन्या (*nf*) a girl; virgin; daughter

कप/ट (*nm*) guile; fraud; hypocrisy; —टी cunning,

trickish

कपड़ा (*nm*) cloth, fabric; —लत्ता wearing fabrics or clothes

कपाट (*nm*) a screen, a door leaf

कपाल (*nm*) the head, skull; a begging bowl; —क्रिया the ceremony of breaking the head of a burning corpse

कपास (*nf*) cotton

कपूत (*nm*) a son of bad character, an undutiful son

कपूर (*nm*) camphor

कप्तान (*nm*) a captain

कफ (*nm*) phlegm, mucus

कफ (*nm*) a cuff

कफन (*nm*) coffin, pall, shroud

कब (*adv*) at what time, when

कबड्डी (*nf*) an Indian outdoor game of boys

कबाड़ (*nm*) worthless articles; rubbish

कबाड़ी (*nm*) one who sells old and broken articles

कबीला (*nm*) a tribe

कबूतर (*nm*) a pigeon; —ख़ाना a pigeon house

कबूल (*nm*) agreement, con-sent; confession; —करना to confess, to admit

कब्ज़ (*nm*) constipation

कब्ज़ा (*nm*) grip, possession; a hinge

कब्र (*nf*) a tomb, a grave

कब्रिस्तान (*nm*) cemetery, a graveyard

कभी (*ind*) seldom, sometimes; —कभी occasionally

कमजो/र (*a*) feeble, weak —री feebleness, weakness

कमबख़्त (*a*) unlucky, illfated, cursed

कमनीय (*a*) desirable, beautiful

कमर (*nf*) the waist

कमरा (*nm*) a chamber, room

कमल (*nm*) a lotus flower

कमाई (*nf*) earnings; wages

कमाऊ (*a*) laborious, earning a livelihood

कमान (*nm*) a bow; an arch; command

कमाना (*v*) to earn; to process

कमानी (*nf*) a spring of steel

कमाल (*nm*) perfection, excellence

कमी (*nf*) decline, deficiency, shortage

कमीज़ (*nf*) a shirt

कमीन (*a*) low-born; mean

कमीना (*a*) mean, wicked —पन vulgarity, meanness

कयामत (*nf*) the day of resurrection, the last day of judgement

कर (*nm*) tusk of an elephant; hand; ray of the Sun or Moon; tax; custom

करतब (*nm*) work, performance, skill, jugglery

करतार (*nm*) master, husband, the creator

करतूत (*nf*) misdeed, evil doing

करना (*v*) to act; to perform; to

use; to do

करनी (*nf*) action, deed

करवट (*nf*) a sleeping on the side, a turning from one side to the other side

करामात (*nf*) a wonderful feat, a miracle

करार (*nm*) a contract, an agreement; —नामा a written agreement

करारा (*a*) hard; rigid; crisp; befitting (reply)

कराहना (*v*) to cry in pain, to moan

करिश्मा (*nm*) a magic, miracle

क़रीना (*nm*) manner, mode, orderliness

क़रीब (*adv*) close by, near, almost

करुण (*a*) merciful, touching

करुणा (*nf*) mercy, pity, tenderness of feeling

करोड़ (*a*) ten million; —पती a very rich person, a millionaire

कर्कश (*a*) husky, cruel

क़र्ज़ (*nm*) debt; loan; —दार a debtor

कर्ण (*nm*) the ear, hypotenuse, helm of a ship

कर्तव्य (*nm*) duty; (*a*) necessary

कर्ता (*nm*) the creator; doer; —धर्ता all in all

कर्म (*nm*) act, work, occupation, fate, grammatical object —चारी a worker

—फल the outcome of one's deeds; —शील industrious —हीन unlucky; idle

कर्मठ (*a*) active, energetic; —ता hard work

कर्मण्य (*a*) hard working, laborious

कलंक (*nm*) aspersion, blemish

कलंकित (*a*) blemished, defamed

कल (*a*) melodious; (*nm*) yesterday; tomorrow; (*nf*) comfort; a machine or its part

कलई (*nf*) tin; white wash; external grandeur

कलपना (*v*) to grieve, to lament

कलफ़ (*nm*) starch; a pimple or spot on the face

कलम (*nf*) pen

कलसा (*nm*) a waterpot, a jar

कलह (*nm*) scramble, quarrel

कला (*nf*) a division, moon's phase; art; —कार an artist

कलाई (*nm*) the fore-arm, the wrist

कली (*nf*) bud, a gusset

कलुष (*nm*) impurity, sin; (*a*) dirty, sinful

कलूटा (*a*) of black complextion; sun-burnt

कलेजा (*nm*) heart; the liver

कल्पना (*nf*) supposition; imagination; —शक्ति ingenuity

कल्पनातीत (*a*) beyond imagination, unimaginable

कल्याण (nm) welfare, good fortune

कल्लोल (nm) frolic, play

कवच (nm) armour, helmet

कवयित्री (nf) a poetess

कवायद (nm) military exercise, drill

कवि (nm) a poet

कविता (nf) a poem; poetry

कवित्व (nm) poetic genius

कश (nm) lash, whip, pulling, flogging

कशमकश (nf) tension

कशीदा (nm) embroidery

कष्ट (nm) distress; pain; trouble; —साध्यburdensome

कसक (nf) griping pain, strain

कसकना (v) to cause a pain (or strain)

कसना (v) to tighten, to fix firmly

कसबा (nm) a town

कसम (nf) an oath

कसर (nf) deficiency; draw back

कसर/त (nf) physical exercise; —ती athletic

कसाई (nm) a butcher

कसाव (nm) astringency, tightness

कसूर (nm) error, fault; —वार a guilty person. (see कुसूर)

कसैला (a) pungent, astringent

कसौटी (nf) an assay, touch stone

कहकहा (nm) a boisterous laugh

कहना (v) to relate, to say, to utter; (nm) saying, order, command

कहा (nm) order, precept, saying; —सुनी altercation

कहानी (nf) a tale, story

कहावत (nf) a saying, proverb

काँच (nm) glass

काँटा (nm) a thorn; fishing hook

काँटेदार (a) prickly; thorny

कांड (nm) sectional division; chapter; incident

कांत (nm) the lover; husband; (a) pleasing; lovely

कांति (nf) beauty, loveliness; lustre

काँपना (v) to shiver, to shudder

काँसा (nm) bronze

काइयाँ (a) shrewd, cunning

काई (nf) lichen, moss

काक (nm) a crow; cunning fellow

कागज़ (nm) paper; written document

कागज़ी (a) made of paper; delicate

काजल (nm) lampblack for use on eyes, soot

काजू (nm) the cashew-nut

काट (nm) act of cutting, a cut; bite, wound

काटना (v) to cut; to bite; to reap; to trim

काठ (nm) timber; wood

काठी (nf) structure; frame; a saddle

कादना (v) to embroider

कातना (v) to spin

कातिक (nm) the eighth month of the Hindu calender

कातिल (nm) a murderer

कान (nm) an ear

काना (a) one eyed; partly rotten (fruit); —फूसी an inkling, a whisper

कान/न (nm) law; —नन lawfully; —नी legal

कापी (nf) an exercise book

काफ़िर (nm) a disbeliever in Mohammedanism; cruel; pitiless

काफ़िला (nm) a caravan

काफ़ी (a) sufficient, enough; (nf) coffee

काबिल (a) qualified; able

काबू (nm) possession, control

काम (nm) task; employment; job; desire; —कला the art of love; —देव Cupid, god of love; —बाण the fire of passion, the flowery arrow of Cupid

कामकाजी (a) busy; active, laborious

कामगार (nm) labourer, worker

कामचलाऊ (a) ad hoc

कामचोर (a) inactive, lazy; shirker

काम/धंधा (nm) occupation; work; —धाम work

कामना (nf) wish, desire

कामया/ब (a) successful; —बी success

कामिनी (nf) a beautiful lady, a lustful woman

कामी (a) loving, lustful

कामुक (a) sensual, amorous; —ता lewdness

कायदा (nm) regulation practice; —क़ानून rules and regulations

कायम (a) settled; established

कायर (a) timid, coward —ता timidity

कायल (a) convinced by argument; —होना to be convinced

काया (nf) the body, person

कारखाना (nm) mill; factory; workshop

कारगर (a) effective

कारण (nm) cause, purpose, reason

कारतूस (nm) a cartridge

कारनामा (nm) deed, doing

कारबार (nm) business; profession; occupation

कारवाँ (nm) a caravan

कारागृह (nm) a jail; prison

कारावास (nm) imprisonment, captivity

कारिंदा (nm) one who works for another, an agent

कारिस्तानी (nf) trickery, cunningness

कारीग/र (nm) a mechanic, a craftsman, an artisan; —री workmanship

कारोबार (nm) occupation; business

कार्य (*nm*) work; vocation; job

कार्यकर्ता (*nm*) an employee; a worker

कार्यकुशल (*a*) efficient; —ता efficiency

कार्यक्रम (*nm*) programme

कार्यवाहक (*a*) officiating; acting

कार्यवाही (*nf*) proceedings

कार्यसूची (*nf*) agenda

कार्यान्वित (*a*) executed

कार्यालय (*nm*) an office

कालकोठरी (*nf*) solitary cell

काला (*a*) dark, black; —कलूटा pitch black; —कानून black law —पानी imprisonment for life

कालिख (*nf*) lampblack, stain, soot; blackness

कालिमा (*nf*) blemish; blackness

कालीन (*nm*) a carpet

काल्पनिक (*a*) unreal, imaginary

काव्य (*nm*) poetry; —कार a poet

काश (*int*) Had God willed thus ! May it happen !

काश्त (*nf*) tenancy, cultivation; —कार a tenant; a cultivator, a farmer

काहि/ल (*a*) indolent; lazy; —ली indolence, laziness

किंचित (*a*) somewhat, a little

किंतु (*ind*) but

किंवदंती (*nf*) false report, rumour

किचकिच (*nf*) useless prattling, quarrel

कितना (*a*) how much

कितने (*a*) how many

किधर (*a*) where, whither

किनारा (*nm*) side, edge; bank; border

किफायत (*nf*) thrift, economy

किरण (*nf*) ray of light, a beam

किरायेदार (*nm*) a hirer, the tenant

किराना (*nm*) grocery

किराया (*nm*) hire, rent, fare

किलकना (*v*) to shout in joy

किलकारी (*nf*) sound of joy

किला (*nm*) a castle; fort, tower

किवाड़ (*nf*) a door-leaf

किशमिश (*nf*) small stoneless raisins, currants

किशोर (*a*) youthful; adolescent

किश्ती (*nf*) a boat

किसान (*nm*) a peasant, farmer, cultivator

किस्त (*nf*) a portion of debt, instalment

किस्म (*nf*) kind; sort; type

किस्सा (*nm*) tale, a story; dispute; —कहानी fiction

कीचड़ (*nm*) clay, mud

कीटाणु (*nm*) a germ

कीड़ा (*nm*) a worm, an insect

कीम/त (*nf*) cost, price; worth; /ती valuable, costly

कीर्ति (*nf*) fame, reputation

कील (*nf*) a pin, peg, nail

कुँआरा (*a*) unmarried, bachelor

कुंकुम (*nf*) saffron

कुंजड़ा (*nm*) a vegetable vendor

कुंजी (*nf*) a key

कुंठा (*nf*) frustration

कुंडल (nm) a large ring worn on the ears

कुंद (nm) a lotus flower

कुआँ (nm) a well

कुकरे (nm) trachoma

कुक/र्म (nm) sin, misdeed; —र्मी sinner

कुख्यात (a) defamed, of bad repute

कुचलना (v) to tread, to crush

कुछ (pron & a) some, a little, anything

कुटनी (nf) procuress, a bawd

कुटिल (a) cruel, crooked; —ता crookedness

कुटी (nf) a hut, cottage

कुटीर (nm) cottage

कुटुंब (nm) family

कुढ़ना (v) to grudge, to fret

कुतरना (v) to nibble; to gnaw

कुतूहल (nm) eagerness, curiosity

कुत्ता (nm) a dog

कुत्सित (a) vile; shabby, contemptible

कुदरत (nf) the nature, power, God

कुनबा (nm) household, family

कुपित (a) angry, offended, irate

कुबड़ा (a) crook-backed; bent

कुमक (nf) reinforcement; aid; assistance

कुमार (nm) a boy; a son; (a) unmarried (man)

कुमुद (nm) lily, red lotus

कुम्हलाना (v) to wither, to shrivel, to fade

कुम्हार (nm) a potter

कुरबानी (nf) a sacrifice

कुरेदना (v) to scratch, to scrape

कुर्सी (nf) a chair

कुल (a) all, entire, complete; (nm) lineage; dynasty —पति Vice-Chancellor; —मर्यादा the dignity of a family; —वधू the virtuous woman of a noble family

कुलटा (nf) an unchaste woman

कुलबुलाना (v) to rumble, to creep; to be restless

कुली (nm) a labourer, a coolie

कुलीन (a) well born, of noble descent, of gentle blood

कुल्ला (nm) rinsing and washing of mouth, gargle

कुल्हा/ड़ा (nm) an axe, hatchet; —ड़ी a small hatchet

कुशल (a) expert, skilful; (nm) safety, prosperity; —क्षेम good-health; —मंगल welfare

कुशलता (nf) trick, skill; well-being

कुशाग्र (a) sharp; penetrating —बुद्धि of keen intelligence

कुशासन (nm) maladministration

कुश्ती (nf) duel, wrestling

कुष्ठ (nm) leprosy

कुसुम (nm) a flower

कुसूर (nm) omission, fault; —वार defaulter

कुहकना (v) to twiter; to coo

कुहरा (nm) damp, fog, mist

कुहराम (nm) uproar, outcry

tumult

कुहासा (*nm*) fog, mist

कूकना (*v*) to cackle, to warble

कूच (*nm*) departure; march

कूचा (*nm*) a narrow path, a lane

कूट (*a*) false; counterfeit; —नीति diplomacy

कूटना (*v*) to macerate; to crush; to beat

कूड़ा (*nm*) sweepings; rubbish; waste; —करकट waste materials

कूद (*a*) dull-headed, stupid; —मग्ज़ a dullard

कूदना (*v*) to leap; to jump

कूबड़ (*nm*) a hunch, hump

कूल्हा (*nm*) the bones of the hip; hip

कृतकृत्य (*a*) successful, fulfilled

कृतघ्न (*a*) thankless, ungrateful

कृतज्ञ (*a*) indebted, grateful

कृतार्थ (*a*) satisfied, gratified; obliged

कृति (*nf*) a work; —कार the author

कृती (*a*) creative, (*nm*) creator

कृत्य (*nm*) duty, performance, work which ought to be done

कृत्रिम (*a*) bogus, artificial, fictitious; laboured

कृदंत (*nm*) participle

कृपण (*a*) stingy, miser; —ता illiberality

कृपया (*ind*) favourably, kindly, please

कृपा (*nf*) grace, kindness; pity; —कांक्षी seeking favour

कृपालु (*a*) compassionate, kind; —ता kindness

कृश (*a*) thin, lean

कृषक (*nm*) a peasant, a farmer

कृषि (*nf*) agriculture, farming

कृष्ण (*a*) dark, black; (*nm*) Sri Krishna, —पक्ष the fortnight of the waning moon

केंचुआ (*nm*) an earthworm

केंचुली (*nf*) the slough of a snake

केंद्र (*nm*) the centre

केंद्र/क (*nm*) a nucleus; —कीय nuclear

केंद्रित (*a*) concentrated; centralised

केंद्रीकरण (*nm*) centralisation

केंद्रीय (*a*) central

केतली (*nm*) a kettle

केला (*nm*) a banana

केलि (*nf*) frolic, pastime, sport

केवट (*nm*) a boat man

केवड़ा (*nm*) the fragrant flower pandanus

केवल (*a & ind*) alone, only, mere; simply

केसर (*nf*) the tendrils of a flower, saffron

केसरी (*nm*) a lion

कैंची (*nf*) scissors, shears

कैंसर (*nm*) cancer

कै (*nf*) vomiting, nausea

कै/द (*nf*) imprisonment; —दी a prisoner

कैफियत (*nf*) statement; description; remarks

कैसा (*a*) of what sort; (*adv*) how

कोंपल (*nf*) a new sprout, a new and tender leaf

कोई (*pron*) anybody; a few; someone; —कोई some one

कोख (*nf*) womb

कोट (*nm*) a fort, citadel; a coat

कोटा (*nm*) quota

कोटि (*nf*) rank; category; ten million

कोठरी (*nf*) a small room, cabin

कोठा (*nm*) a big room; a ware house

कोठी (*nm*) a mansion, bungalow

कोड़ा (*nm*) a lash, a whip

कोढ़ (*nm*) leprosy

कोण (*nm*) a corner; an angle

कोतवाली (*nf*) the chief police station in a city

कोताही (*nf*) want, deficiency

कोप (*nm*) anger, wrath

कोफ्त (*nf*) tedium

कोमल (*a*) tender, mild; soft

कोयल (*nf*) a cuckoo

कोयला (*nm*) coal

कौल (*nm*) agreement; contract; promise

कौशल (*nm*) art, welfare, skill

क्या (*pron*) what

क्यों (*ind*) why; —कर how; —कि because

क्रम (*nm*) system; chain; series; —बद्ध consecutive; —हीन out of order

क्रमश: (*adv*) by degrees, respectively

क्रमांक (*nm*) roll number

क्रमिक (*a*) serial, successive

क्रांति (*nf*) a revolution; —कारी revolutionary

क्रिया (*nf*) activity, action, work

क्रियात्मक (*a*) active; functional

क्रियान्विति (*nf*) implementation

क्रियाविधि (*nf*) procedure

क्रियाशील (*a*) active

क्रिस्तान (*nm*) a christian

क्रीड़ा (*nf*) amusement, sport

क्रुद्ध (*a*) infuriated, angry, wrathful

क्रूर (*a*) unkind, ruthless, cruel; —ता savagery, ruthlessness; cruelty

क्रोध (*nm*) fret, anger; —वश out of anger

क्रोधित (*a*) resentful, lofty, angry

क्रोधी (*a*) wrathful, high-tempered

क्लांति (*nf*) fatigue, weariness

क्लिष्ट (*a*) difficult

क्लेश (*nm*) trouble, suffering, pain

क्वार (*nm*) the seventh month of the Hindu calendar

क्षण (*nm*) an instant, a moment

क्षणिक (*a*) momentary

क्षत (*a*) hurt, wounded —विक्षत wounded all over

क्षति (*nf*) harm; injury; wastage

क्षतिपूर्ति (*nf*) reparation; compensation

क्षमता (*nf*) fitness, ability; competence

क्षमा (*nf*) forgiveness; mercy

क्षम्य (*a*) forgivable

क्षय (*nm*) decrease, loss; erosion, — रोग tuberculosis

क्षार (*nm*) alkali, (*a*) alkaline, salty

क्षितिज (*nm*) the horizon

क्षीण (*a*) weak, feeble

क्षुद्र (*a*) contemptible; small

क्षुब्ध (*a*) impatient, angry

क्षेत्र (*nm*) ground, field

क्षेत्रफल (*nm*) area

क्षेम (*nf*) protection, welfare

क्षोभ (*nm*) excitement; agitation, fret

ख

ख the second member of the first pentad of consonants in Devnagri alphabet

खँखारना (*v*) to hawk; to make effort before spitting

खंजर (*nm*) a poniard, dagger

खंड (*nm*) part, section

खंडन (*nm*) denial, repudiation; —मंडन repudiation and vindication

खंडहर (*nm*) debris, the ruins of a house

खंडित (*a*) destroyed; broken

खंदक (*nm*) a moat round a fort, a deep ditch

खंभा (*nm*) a post, pillar

खचाखच (*a & adv*) overcrowded

खच्चर (*nm*) a mule

खज़ांची (*nm*) a treasurer

खज़ाना (*nm*) treasury; treasure

खटकना (*v*) to throb; to feel disgusted

खटका (*nm*) fear; doubt; knocking

खटखटाना (*v*) to knock, to tap

खटना (*v*) to spend money, to labour hard

खटपट (*nf*) strife, wrangling, quarrel

खटमल (*nm*) a bed bug

खटाई (*nf*) sourness; tartness

खटाखट (*nf*) sound of beating constant clicking; (*adv*) quickly

खटास (*nf*) tartness, sourness

खट्टा (*a*) tart, sour

खड़ा (*a*) erect, standing; upright

खड्ड (*nm*) a deep pit

खत (*nm*) a letter; handwriting

खतरनाक (*a*) risky, dangerous

खतरा (*nm*) risk, danger

खता (*nf*) error, mistake; —वार

a guilty person

खत्म (*a*) end, complete, finished

खदेड़ना (*v*) to drive away

खद्दर (*nm*) hand-spun cloth.

खनकना (*v*) to clink, to jingle

खनिक (*nm*) a miner

खनिज (*a & nm*) a mineral substance

खपत (*nf*) consumption; sale

खपना (*v*) to be expended, to be
consumed

खफ़ा (*a*) angry, enraged,
displeased

ख़बर (*nf*) intelligence; news

खंबरदार (*a*) careful, cautious

ख/ब्त (*nm*) madness, mania;
— ब्ती mad, crazy

ख़मियाज़ा (*nm*) retribution; loss

ख़रगोश (*nm*) hare, rabbit

खरबूज़ा (*nm*) a musk melon

खरा (*a*) pure, sincere, candid

खरा/ब (*a*) spoiled; bad;
wicked; defected; —बी
defect; badness

ख़रीद (*nf*) purchase, buying

ख़रीदना (*v*) to purchase, to
buy

ख़रीदा/र (*nm*) a purchaser,
— री purchasing

ख़रीफ़ (*nf*) the crop which
is reaped in autumn

खरोंचना (*v*) to scrape, to
scratch

ख़र्च (*nm*) expenditure,
expense

ख़र्चा (*nm*) see ख़र्च

ख़र्चीला (*a*) extravagant, lavish;
costly, expensive

खर्रा (*nm*) a long sheet

खर्राटा (*nm*) snoring

खलबली (*nf*) alarm, agitation,
commotion

खलल (*nm*) confusion,
interruption

खलिहान (*nm*) a grainary, barn

खसखस (*nm*) mawseed, poppy
seed

खसम (*nm*) husband, master

ख़सरा (*nm*) measles

खसोटना (*v*) to pull out, to
scratch

खस्ता (*a*) very brittle; crisp

खाँड (*nf*) unrefined sugar

खाँसना (*v*) to cough

खाँसी (*nf*) cough

खाई (*nf*) a dike, ditch; trench

ख़ाक (*nf*) dirt; ashes; anything
trivial; nothing

ख़ाका (*nm*) a map; diagram,
sketch

ख़ाकी (*a*) dusky, brown

खाट (*nf*) a bedstead; cot

खाड़ी (*nf*) a bay; a gulf

खाता (*nm*) ledger; account

ख़ातिर (*nf*) hospitality; (*ind*)
for, for the sake of

ख़ातिरी (*nf*) hospitality

खाद (*nf*) manure; fertilizer

खाद्य (*nm*) food; (*a*) eatable

खान (*nf*) mine

खान/दान (*nm*) family, —दानीof
high family

खाना (*v*) to live on; to eat

खाना (nm) a house; compartment; shelf

खानाबदोश (nm) a rover, an idle scamp

खामी (nf) a defect

खामो/श (a) taciturn, silent; —शी silence

खारा (a) salty, brackish; —पन salinity

खारिज (a) expelled, dismissed, discharged

खारिश (nf) itch, scab

खाल (nf) skin; hide

खालिस (a) unmixed; pure

खाली (a) void, empty, vacant

खास (a) peculiar; special; proper

खासा (a) good, noble

खासियत (nf) quality; characteristic

खिंचना (v) to be drawn; to be pulled

खिंचाव (nm) tightness; attraction

खिचड़ी (nf) a dish prepared from rice and pulse boiled together; a mixture; hotchpotch

खिड़की (nf) a window

खिताब (nm) a title

खिदमत (nf) duty, service

खिन्न (a) wearied, sad, glum, gloomy

खिलखिला/ना (v) to laugh loudly; —हट laughter

खिलना (v) to blow; to blossom

खिलवाड़ (nf) pastime, frolic

खिलाड़ी (nm) a player, sportsman

खिलाफ़ (a) contrary, opposite, against

खिलौना (nm) a plaything, toy

खिल्ली (nf) jest, joke

खिसकना (v) to slip away, to move slowly

खिसिया/ना (v) to grin, to giggle; —हट giggle

खींचना (v) to wrest; to pull; to haul

खीज/खीझ (nf) anger, vexation

खीरा (nm) a cucumber

खुजली (nf) itch, eczema

खुजाना (v) to scratch

खुद (pron) self; (adv) of one's own accord

खुदगरज़ (a) selfseeking, selfish

खुदरा (a) small coins; retail

खुदा (nm) God, the Almighty; —ई creation

खुदाई (nf) providence, digging

खुफ़िया (a) secret; (nm) a spy

खुरचना (v) to scrape something

खुरदरा (a) coarse, rough.

खुराक (nf) diet; dose

खुर्दबीन (nf) a microscope

खुलना (v) to be unravelled; to be opened; to be untied

खुलासा (nm) brief, summary, gist; (a) brief

खुल्लम-खुल्ला (a) without

reservation, publicly

खुश (*a*) pleased, merry, happy

खुशकिस्मत (*a*) fortunate

खुशख़बरी (*nf*) glad findings, happy news

खुशनसी/ब (*a*) fortunate; — बी good luck

खुशबू (*nf*) odour, fragrance

खुशमिज़ाज (*a*) cheerful, good-tempered

खुशहाल (*a*) prosperous, in good circumstances

खुशामद (*nf*) false praise, flattery

खुशी (*nf*) delight, cheerful-ness, happiness

खुश्क (*a*) withered; dry

खुश्की (*nf*) drought; dryness

खूँख्वार (*a*) ferocious, cruel

खूँटी (*nf*) a peg

खून (*nm*) murder; blood

खूनी (*nm*) a murderer, an assassin

खूबसूर/त (*a*) handsome; beautiful; — ती handsome-ness; beauty

खूबी (*nf*) goodness; speciality; merit

खेत (*nm*) a field, farm

खेतिहर (*nm*) a peasant, a farmer

खेती (*nf*) agriculture; farming

खेद (*nm*) sorrow, gloominess; regret

खेमा (*nm*) a tent, pavilion

खेल (*nm*) fun, game, sport; -कूद sports

खेलना (*v*) to sport, to play; to stage

खैर (*nf*) welfare, happiness; (*ind*) all right, well

खैरा/त (*nf*) alms, charity; — ती charitable

खैरियत (*nf*) safety; welfare

खोखला (*a*) empty, hollow

खोज (*nf*) search, investiga-tion; discovery

खोजना (*v*) to seek, to search, to investigate, to discover

खोटा (*a*) faulty, defective

खोदना (*v*) to scratch, to dig

खोना (*v*) to lose, to squander, to destroy

खोपड़ी (*nf*) the pate, skull

खोलना (*v*) to unfold; to open; to unbind

ख़ौफ़ (*nm*) dread, fear; —नाक fearful

खौलना (*v*) to bubble; to boil

ख्याति (*nf*) renown, fame, repute

ख्याल (*nm*) attention; thought, idea, opinion

ख्वाब (*nm*) a dream

ख्वाहमख्वाह (*ind*) without any purpose, uselessly

ख्वाहिश (*nf*) desire; wish

ग

ग the third member of the first pentad of consonants in Devnagri alphabet

गंज (nf) treasure, pile; (nm) baldness

गंजा (a) scald-headed, bald

गँठबंधन (nm) a custom in marriage ceremony in which the skirts of bridegroom's and bride's mantles are tied together

गंदगी (nf) impurity, dirtiness

गंदा (a) filthy, dirty, nasty

गंदला (a) dirty, muddy

गंध (nf) odour, smell, scent

गंभीर (a) sober; grave, reserved —ता gravity; sobriety; reservedness

गँवाना (v) to waste; to lose

गँवार (a) vulgar, ill-bred; —पन vulgarity

गँवारू (a) rude, rustic

गऊ (nm) a cow; (a) gentle

गज (nm) an elephant, a yard; a yardstick

गज़ब (nf) a calamity

गटकना (v) to eat, to swallow, to gulp

गट्ठर (nm) a big bundle; package

गठन (nf) construction

गठरी (nf) a parcel, bundle

गठिया (nf) a sack; pains in the joints, rheumatism

गठीला (a) full of knots, robust

गड़गड़ा/ना (v) to rumble, to gurgle; —हट a rumble

गड़पना (v) to glut, to swallow

गड़बड़ (nf) confusion; shuffling; —झाला bustle, disorder

गड़डी (nf) a pack, bundle

गड़ढा (nm) ditch; hollow

गढ़ (nm) a castle; a battery

गढ़ना (v) to form, to mould

गण (nm) multitude, union

गणतंत्र (nm) a Republic

गणना (nf) reckoning, calculation, counting

गणराज्य (nm) a government by the people

गणिका (nf) harlot, a prostitute

गणित (nm) Mathematics; —ज्ञ a mathematician

गति (nf) movement; speed; condition

गतिमान (a) on the move, moving

गदर (nm) a rebellion

गवगद (a) overwhelmed, very happy, greatly delighted

गद्दा (nm) a bed cushion

गद्दार (nm & a) traitor

गद्दी (nf) a stuffed pad or cushion

गद्य (nm) prose

गधा (nm) a donkey; a stupid fellow

गन्ना (*nm*) a sugarcane

गप (*nf*) a gossip, chat; —शप tittle -tattle

गपोड़ (*nm*) a gossiper; —बाज़ी gossiping

गफ़ (*a*) thick, dense, compact

गफ़लत (*nf*) mistake, careless - ness

गबन (*nm*) misappropriation of money; embezzlement

गम (*nm*) woe, sorrow; —गीन gloomy

गंमला (*nm*) a flower -pot

गमी (*nf*) the period of observing mourning; death

गरज (*nf*) thunder; roar

गरज़ (*nf*) concern; need

गरजना (*v*) to bluster, to roar

गरदन (*nf*) the neck

गरम (*a*) burning, warm, hot; woollen (cloth)

गरमागरम (*a*) heated; hot; fresh

गरमागरमी (*nf*) exchange of hot words

गरमाना (*v*) to be hot; to be in excitement

गरमी (*nf*) heat; anger; summer

गरिमा (*nf*) grace, dignity

गरिष्ठ (*a*) indigestible, heavy

गरीब (*a*) mild, meek; poor; —खाना humble dwelling; —परवर supporter of the poor people

गरूर (*nm*) pride, vanity

गर्त (*nm*) a pit, crack in a wall

गर्द (*nf*) dust, dirt

गर्दन (*nf*) the neck

गर्दिश (*nf*) circulation; distress

गर्भ (*nm*) pregnancy; the womb; —धारण conception; —पात abortion; —स्राव miscarriage

गर्भाधान (*nm*) conception, impregnation

गर्भाशय (*nm*) uterus; the womb

गर्भिणी (*a*) pregnant

गर्व (*nm*) conceit, pride; elation

गर्हित (*a*) vile, wicked, ignoble

ग़लत (*a*) incorrect, wrong, untrue

ग़लतफ़हमी (*nf*) misunderstand - ing

ग़लती (*nf*) error, mistake

गलना (*v*) to be dissolved; to decay; to be boiled; to rot

गला (*nm*) throat, neck

गली (*nf*) a lane, street

गलीचा (*nm*) a carpet

गल्प (*nf*) a small tale

गल्ला (*nm*) produce; daily income of a shop kept in a chest

गँवाना (*v*) to waste; to suffer

गवाह (*nm*) a deponent, witness

गवाही (*nf*) testimony, evidence

गवैया (*nm*) a singer

गश्त (*nf*) beat, patrol

गहन (*a*) deep; profound

गहना (*nm*) an ornament; jewellery; (*v*) to handle

गहरा (*a*) profound; deep; bold; sound; intimate

गहराई (nf) depth, profoundity

गहराना (v) to be deep; to excavate

गाँठ (nf) a knob, knot, tie

गांभीर्य (nm) gravity; depth; importance

गाँव (nm) a village

गाज (nf) roar; thunderbolt; lighting

गाजर (nf) carrot

गाड़ना (v) to lay; to bury; to pitch

गाड़ी (nf) a car, a cart, a carriage; —वान a cartman, coachman

गाढ़ा (a) dense; thick; close; (nm) hand woven cloth

गाना (v) to chant, to sing; (nm) a song

गाफ़िल (a) careless, stupid, negligent

गाय (nf) a cow; (a) meek and humble

गायक (nm) a singer

गायन (nm) chant, singing

ग़ायब (a) lost; vanished

गाल (nm) a cheek

गाली (nf) rebuke, abuse

गावदी (a) dull-headed, stupid

गाहक (nm) a client, a purchaser, a customer

गिचपिच (a) not clearly written; illegible

गिड़गिड़ाना (v) to implore, to beseech in an humble manner

गिद्ध (nm) a vulture

गिनती (nf) calculation; reckoning

गिनना (v) to figure, to count; regard

गिरगिट (nm) chameleon; opportunist

गिरजाघर (nm) a church

गिरना (v) to come down, to fall, to drop

गिरफ़्ता/र (a) seized, arrested; —री an arrest

गिरबी (a) pledged, mortgaged

गिरावट (nf) lapse, spill

गिरोह (nm) a gang

गिला (nm) accusation, complaint

गिलाफ़ (nm) a pillow-cover

गीत (nm) a song

गीदड़ (nm) a jackal; (a) coward

गीला (a) wet

गुंजन (nm) humming sound

गुंजाइश (nf) capacity; accommodation

गुंजार (nm) buzzing

गुंडा (nm) a rogue; (a) wicked; —गर्दी foppishness, hooliganism

गुंबद (nm) vault, dome

गुच्छ (nm) a bunch; tuft

गुज़र (nf) passing of time; —बसर livelihood; —करना to maintain

गुज़रना (v) to cross over; to pass away

गुज़रना (v) to pass time

गुज़ारा (nm) livlihood; subsistence

गुट (nm) group; a block

गुड़ (nm) raw sugar; jaggery

गुड़िया (nf) a doll

गुड्डी (nf) a kite

गुण (nm) quality; attainment

गुनन (nm) calculation, multi-plication

गुणा (nm) multiplication; —करना to multiply

गुत्थमगुत्था (nm) entanglement, a scuffle

गुत्थी (nf) entanglement, a knot

गुदगुदा (a) fleshy, soft

गुदगुदाना (v) to titillate, to tickle

गुनगुना (a) slightly warm

गुनगुनाना (v) to buzz, to hum

गुनहगार (a) guilty, sinful, (nm) a criminal

गुना a suffix denoting times or fold

गुनाह (nm) guilt; sin, fault

गुप्त (a) hidden, concealed, confidential

गुप्त/चर (nm) a spy; —चर्या espionage

गुफा (nf) a cave

गुबार (nm) dust; vexation

गुब्बारा (nm) a balloon

गुम (a) hidden; missing; lost; —नाम nameless; —राह depraved; —शुदा missing

गुमान (nm) imagination, fancy; doubt; pride

गुमाश्ता (nm) manager, an agent

गुर (nm) a simplified method;

a formula

गुरदा (nm) kidney

गुरु (nm) a teacher; a spiritual guide

गुरुता (nf) weight, heaviness; greatness, gravity

गुरुत्वाकर्षण (nm) gravitation

गुरुघंटाल (a) very crafty, a great knave

गुर्गा (nm) a servant, a spy; low fellow

गुर्राना (v) to snarl, to roar, to gnarl

गुलछर्रे (nm pl) revelry, merry-making; —उड़ाना to enjoy freely

गुलाब (nm) rose; —जल rose-water

गुलाबी (a) ruddy, rosy, of light red colour

गुला/म (nm) a slave; —मी slavery

गुसलखाना (nm) a bathroom

गुस्ता/ख (a) rude, arrogant; —खी (nf) arrogance, rudeness

गुस्सा (nm) rage; anger

गुस्सैल (a) choleric, furious

गूँगा (a) dumb

गूँज (nf) buzzing, echo

गूँजना (v) to buzz, to resound; to echo

गूँधना (v) to knead

गूढ़ (a) obscure, secret

गूदड़ (nm) a bundle of old tattered clothes, rags

गूदा (nm) pulp; essential

portion of a thing

गृह (*nm*) a house; residence

गृहस्थ (*nm*) a householder

गृहस्थी (*nf*) household; family

गृहिणी (*nf*) wife.

गेरुआ (*a*) red brown

गेहुआँ (*a*) of the colour of wheat

गेहूँ (*nm*) wheat

ग़ैर (*a*) alien, other; —क़ानूनी unlawful; —ज़िम्मेदार irresponsible

ग़ैरत (*nf*) modesty, emulation; —मंद having a sense of honour

गोंद (*nm*) gum, wood-gum

गो (*nf*) a cow; —दानthe gifting away of a cow; —धनcattle-wealth; —मांस beef; —रक्षा cow protection

गो (*ind*) though

गोचर (*a*) visible

गोता (*nm*) immersion, dive; —मार diver

गोद (*nf*) the lap; —लेना to adopt

गोदना (*v*) to puncture

गोदाम (*nm*) a storehouse, a warehouse

गोदी (*nf*) the lap; a dock

गोपी (*nf*) a cowherd's wife

गोबर (*nm*) cow-dung

गोया (*ind*) as if

गोरा (*a*) fair-skinned, white

गोलंदाज़ (*nm*) a marksman, gunner

गोल (*a*) globular; round; —मटोल vague

गोला (*nm*) a ball; a cannon ball; —ई roundness; —बारी bombardment

गोलार्ध (*nm*) hemisphere

गोली (*nm*) pill; a bullet; tablet

गोशाला (*nf*) cow-shed, enclosure of cattle

गोश्त (*nm*) flesh; —ख़ोर a meat-eater

गोष्ठी (*nf*) assembly, discourse

गौ (*nf*) a cow

गौण (*a*) secondary, inferior

गौर (*a*) white, fair

ग़ौर (*nm*) considration; pondering (*v*) (करना) to ponder; to take note of

गौरव (*nm*) heaviness, pride, glory

ग्रंथ (*nm*) a book, volume; —कार an author

ग्रीष्म (*nm*) the summer

ग्लानि (*nf*) lassitude; repentance

ग्वाला (*nm*) a cowkeeper, a milkman

घ

घ the forth member of the first pentad of consonants in Devnagri alphabet

घंटा (*nm*) a gong, a bell; an hour; —घर a clock-tower

घंटी (*nf*) a small bell

घटक (*nm*) an intermediary, a factor

घटना (*nf*) happening, incident; (*v*) to decrease, to decline; —स्थल scene

घटा (*nf*) a gathering of clouds

घटिया (*a*) low in price, cheap, of bad quality

घड़ा (*nm*) an earthen pot, jug

घड़ी (*nf*) time; a space of 24 minutes; a watch

घन (*nm*) cloud; sledge-hammer, assembly; —घोर roaring of clouds

घना (*a*) thick; close

घनिष्ठ (*a*) most intimate; close.

घपला (*nm*) bungling

घबरा/ना (*v*) to be confused, to be nervous; —हट nervousness

घमं/ड (*nm*) pride; conceit; —डी arrogant; vain

घमासान (*a*) a fierce

घर (*nm*) house; home

घराना (*nm*) a family

घरेलू (*a*) domestic; private

घसीटना (*v*) to trail; to drag

घहराना (*v*) to thunder

घाघ (*a*) a shrewd, cunning

घाटा (*nm*) deficit; loss

घात (*nf*) killing; ambush; opportunity; power (like a^x)

घातक (*a*) fatal, savage; (*nm*) a murderer

घायल (*a*) hurt; wounded

घाव (*nm*) injury; wound

घास (*nf*) grass

घासलेट (*nm*) vegetable oil; inferior stuff

घिनौना (*a*) hateful, odious

घिसना (*v*) to be worn out; to rub

घुंघराले (*a pl*) curly

घुग्घू (*nm*) an owl; a fool

घुटना (*v*) to be suffocated, (*nm*) the knee

घुट्टी (*nf*) a medicine which is given to newborn infants to clear out the bowels

घुड़ an allomorph of घोड़ा used as the first member in compound words; —घुड़-सवार a horse rider; —साल a stable for horses

घुड़की (*nf*) a reprimand, a threat, rebuking

घुन (*nm*) wood-worm

घुन्ना (*a*) one who conceals his emotions, reticent, taciturn

घुप्प-अंधेरा (*a*) pitch dark,

obscure

घुमक्कड़ (a) a rover, fond of wandering about; (nm) wanderer

घुमड़ना (v) the gathering up of clouds in the sky

घुमाव (nm) curvature; a turning; twist; —दार circu-itous, winding

घुलना (v) to be lean and thin; to be dissolved in a liquid; to be melted

घुसना (v) to pierce; to enter; to thrust into

घुसपैठ (nf) access; entrance; infiltration; —घुसपैठिया an infiltrator

घुसाना (v) to pile; to poke; to penetrate

घुसेड़ना (v) to pierce; to thrust in; to stuff in

घूँसा (nm) buffet; a blow with the fist; boxing

घूँघट (nm) a veil which conceal the face

घूँघर (nm) a curl of hair; —वाले curly

घूँट (nm) a sip, draught

घूमना (v) to wander; to roam, turn; to stroll

घूरना (v) to ogle; to stare; to frown

घूरा (nm) rubbish, sweepings

घूस (nf) emolument; bribe; —खोरbribee; —खोरीbribery

घृणा (nf) hatred, dislike

घृणित (a) despicable, abominable, abhorred

घृत (nm) clarified butter; ghee

घेरना (v) to encircle, to encompass, to enclose

घेरनी (nf) the handle of a spinning wheel

घेरा (nm) circumference; enclosure; fence

घेवर (nm) a kind of sweetmeat

घोंघा (nm) conch, slug, snail, (a) foolish; worthless

घोंसला (nm) a nest

घोटना (v) to rub for smoo-thening; to cream up; to commit to memory

घोटाला (nm) turmoil; bungling; confusion

घोड़ा (nm) a horse; hammer of a gun

घोड़ी (nf) a mare; a song sung at the time of marriage

घोर (a) horrible, terrible; awful

घोल (nm) a solution

घोलना (v) to mix; to dissolve

घोषणा (nf) announcement; a declaration

ड़.

ड़. the fifth member of the first pentad of consonants in

Devnagri alphabet

च

च the first member of the second pentad of consonants in Devnagri alphabet

चंगा (a) healthy, sound, healed

चंगुल (nm) grasp, claw

चंचरीक (nm) the buzzing bee

चंचल (a) restless; unsteady; flickering

चंचलता (nf) unsteadiness; inconsistancy

चंट (a) willy, cunning; (nm) a cheat, a cunning fellow

चंड (a) violent, fierce; powerful

चंडाल (nm) a low born; an outcaste; cruel

चंडालिका (nf) an epithet of Durga

चंदन (nm) sandalwood

चंदराना (v) to deceive, to beguile

चंदला (a) bald-headed

चंदा (nm) the moon; contribution, subscription

चंद्र (nm) the moon; —ग्रहण lunar eclipse; —बिंदु the nasal sign represented by a crescent with a dot over it (ँ); —बिंब the lunar disc; —मंडल the halo of the moon; — मुखी woman blessed with a moon-like face; —वार Monday; —हार a kind of broad necklace; —लोक the sphere or heaven of the moon

चंद्रमा (nm) the moon

चंद्रिका (nf) moonlight, moonbeams

चंपत (a) disappearing, vanishing; —होना to abscond, to disappear

चंपा (nm) the tree *Michelia Champacca* which bears fragrant yellow flowers

चंपू (nm) a literary work which is composed in alternations of prose and verse

चँवर (nm) a whisk, a flapper made of the tail of a yak

चक (nm) a plot of land

चकई (nf) a whirling toy like a pulley; the female of a ruddy goose

चकती (nf) patch of leather; a round plate of metal

चकता (nm) a blotch on the skin

चकनाचूर (a) broken into fragments; much weary

चकबंदी (nf) marking the boundaries of plots of land

चकमक (nm) a kind of hard stone, flint

चकमा (nm) deception; trick; —खाना to be tricked; —देना to play a trick

चकराना (v) to revolve; to feel dizzy; to be confused

चकल्लस (nf) jocularity, fun; —बाज़ी drollery, fun

चकाचौंध (nf) the dazzling effects of light on the eyes

चकित (a) surprised, astonished, amazed

चक्कर (nm) multitude, circle, whirl; a wheel; vertigo; —काटना to revolve

चक्की (nf) mill, grinding mill

चक्र (nm) a wheel; cycle; disc; — वर्ती (राजा) an universal (monarch); an emperor; —वात a whirlwind; —वृद्धि ब्याज compound interest

चक्राकार (a) circular

चक्षु (nm) an eye; —गोचर visible

चखना (v) to taste

चखाना (v) to cause to taste

चचा (nm) paternal uncle

चची (nf) paternal aunt

चचेरा (a) descended from the paternal uncle

चचोड़ना (v) to sip by pressing under the teeth

चट (a) quickly, instantly; —पट immediately

चटक (nf) splendour, brilliance; (a) sharp, bright; —दार of bright colour

चटकना (v) to snap, to make a sound of breaking up

चटकनी (nf) a click, the bolt of a door. (see also चटखनी)

चटक-मटक (nf) gaudiness; wantonness; ornamentation

चटकीला (a) of rich colour; shining, brilliant; glittering

चटचट (nf) a crackig sound

चटखनी (nf) tower bolt, a bolt

चटनी (nf) sauce, मीठी —, jelly

चटपटा (a) delicious, saucy, pungent

चटाई (nf) the act of licking; a mat

चटाक (nf) a crackling sound

चटुल (a) agile; fickle; clever

चटोरा (a) fond of spicy food-stuff. greedy

चट्टान (nf) cliff, rock, ledge shelf

चट्टा-बट्टा (nm) a play thing for children

चढ़ना (v) to ascend; to rise; to go up; to attack

चढ़ाई (nf) invasion; ascent;

assault; attack

चढ़ावा (*nm*) an offering to a god; exaltation

चणक (*nm*) gram

चतुरंग (*nm*) chess; an army consisting of pedestrians, chariots, horses and elephants

चतुरंगिणी (*a*) having four divisions of an ancient Indian army (see चतुरंग)

चतुर (*a*) dexterous, ingenious, expert, clever; —ता cleverness

चतुर्दिक (*nm*) the four quarters; (*adv*) on all sides

चतुर्भुज (*a*) quadrilateral; four sided figure

चतुर्भुजी (*nf*) the four armed one; a Vaishnava cult

चतुर्मास (*nm*) the four months of the rainy season

चतुर्मुख (*a*) four faced; (*nm*) the god Brahma

चतुर्विध (*a*) of four types, fourfold

चतुराई (*nf*) ingenuity, cleverness

चना (*nm*) gram

चपटा (*a*) flat

चपड़ा (*nm*) shellac, a kind of red insect

चपत (*nm*) a slap; a push; loss

चपरकनाती (*nm & a*) foolish, stupid

चपरासी (*nm*) a peon

चपल (*a*) a variable; unsteady; wanton

चपलता (*nf*) variability, nimbleness, unsteadiness

चपला (*nf*) the goddess Lakshmi; lighting (*a*) faminine form of चपल

चपाती (*nf*) a thin cake or bread (of the Indian style)

चपेट (*nf*) a blow, a slap; a sudden misfortune

चप्पल (*a*) a sandal, a slipper

चप्पा (*nm*) a fourth part; a small portion; a hand's breadth

चप्पू (*nm*) an oar, a paddle

चबाना (*v*) to masticate; to chew; to munch

चबारा (*nm*) a room in the upper most storey of a house

चबूतरा (*nm*) stand; platform; stage; dais

चमक (*nm*) brilliancy, sheen, flash; —दमक brilliancy, glitter; —दार sheeny, shining

चमकना (*v*) to flash; to sparkle, to glitter

चमकनी (*nf*) an irritable woman

चमकाना (*v*) to burnish, to varnish; to sparkle

चमकीला (*a*) sunny, glossy, clear, splendid

चमगादड़ (*nm*) a bat; a vampire

चमचम (*nf*) a kind of Bengali sweetmeat; (*a*) glittering, bright

चमचमाना (v) to glitter, to shine, to brighten

चमचमाहट (nm) brightness, glow, glitter

चमचा (nm) a large spoon; flatterer

चमड़ा (nm) skin; leather; hide

चमत्का/र (nm) wonder; marvel; surprise; —रिक marvellous; — री marvellous, amazing

चमन (nm) bed of a garden, a small garden

चमर (nm) the tail of a yak used as a flapper to whisk off flies

चमाचम (adv) brightly, shining

चमार (nm) a shoemaker; a skinner; a cobbler

चमेली (nf) the jasmine plant, its fragrant flower

चम्मच (nm) spoon

चयन (nm) work of collecting or picking; selection

चयनिका (nf) a collection

चर (nm) a secret messenger, a spy; sound made when tearing cloth

चरई (nf) manger, trough which is used for feeding cattle

चरक (nm) a spy, a secret messenger; a traveller; a treatise on Indian system of medicine

चरकटा (nm) a chaff-cutter; a non entity

चरका (nm) a slight wound; loss; trick, fraud

चरख़ (nm) a revolving wheel, a lathe

चरख़ा (nm) a revolving wheel, a spinning wheel.

चरखी (nf) a winch; a reel

चरचराना (v) to crackle, to sputter

चरण (nm) the foot; the line of poetry; root; —चिह्न foot-mark —तल sole of the foot

चरणामृत (nm) ambrosia of the feet

चरपरा (a) hot, pungent, acrid

चरबी (nf) grease; fat; tallow

चरम (a) final, last, ultimate

चरमराना (v) to produce a creaking sound

चरवाई (nf) the work or wages paid for grazing cattle

चरवाना (v) to cause to graze

चरवाहा (nm) a shepherd, a herdsman

चरस (nm) a large bucket of leather used in irrigation; an intoxicating drug prepared from the flowers of hemp

चरसी (nm) one who smokes

चरागाह (nm) a pasturage; meadow

चराचर (a) sentient and lifeless, movable and immovable

चराना (v) to graze; to make a fool of

चरित (nm) conduct; character; biography

चरितार्थ (a) gratified, successful

चरित्र (nm) conduct; custom; character; —चित्रण characterisation, —हीन characterless

चरित्रांकन (nm) characterisation

चर्चा (nf) discussion; mention; rumour

चर्चरी (nf) a song sung in the spring season; çlapping of hands

चर्पटी (nf) a kind of thin cake

चर्म (nm) skin; leather; —कार shoemaker; a cobbler

चलन (nm) motion; use; method; custom

चलना (v) to go, to walk, to proceed

चलनी (nf) a sieve

चलाऊ (a) lasting, durable

चलायमान (a) movable, wavering, unsteady

चवर्ग (nm) the palatals च, छ, ज, झ, ञ

चश्मा (nm) spectacles, eyeglasses; a fountain; a spring

चसका (nm) an ardent desire, relish; habit

चस्पाँ (a) stuck, fixed, affixed

चहकना (v) to warble, to be talkative, to chirp

चहचहाना (v) to warble, to chirp

चहलकदमी (nf) walking of a person at a slow pace

चहलपहल (nf) mirth, merriment, hustle -bustle

चहारदीवारी (nf) the four surrounding walls of a palace or house

चहेता (a) dear, beloved

चहेती (nf) beloved

चाँटा (nm) a slap, a blow

चांडाल (nm) the untouchable, a sinful person

चाँद (nm) the moon

चाँदतारा (nm) a kind of kite, a kind of fine muslin on which stars of coloured silk are woven

चाँदनी (nf) moonlight, bedsheet

चाँदी (nf) silver; argent

चाँप (nf) pressure; a thrust; the lock of a gun

चांसलर (nm) the highest officer of a University, Chancellor

चाक (nm) a wheel; a potter's wheel; a circular mark

चाकर (nm) servant, menial; waiter

चाकरनी (nf) a house maid, a female servant

चाकरी (nf) service, attendance

चाकू (nm) a knife

चा/चा (nm) paternal uncle; ची paternal uncle's wife, aunt

चाट (nf) a spicy preparation of cut fruits, vegetables etc.

चाटना (v) to lap, to lick

चाटु (nm) favourable conversation; —कार a flatterer; —कारिता false praise, flatteʁy

चाणक्य (*nm*) the famous statesman of ancient India

चातक (*nm*) a kind of cuckoo which is supposed to drink only drops of rain

चातुरी (*nf*) cleverness, art

चातुर्य (*nm*) skill, cleverness

चादर (*nf*) a sheet; plate; bedsheet

चान्द्रायण (*nm*) a fast which is observed for one month

चाप (*nm*) a bow; semi-circle; pressure (*nf*) sound of stepping

चापना (*v*) to press

चापलूस (*a*) servile; flattering; obsequious

चापलूसी (*nf*) adulation, flattery

चापी (*nm*) an archer; the god Shiva

चाबना (*v*) to masticate, to chew (see also चबाना)

चाबी (*nf*) a key;— देना to wind a clock or watch

चाबुक (*nm*) a whip, lash

चाम (*nm*) skin; hide; leather

चामुंडा (*nf*) an apithet of Durga

चाय (*nf*) tea;— घर a tea-house; — दानी a tea pot; —पानी breakfast

चारखाना (*nm*) chequered cloth

चारण (*nm*) a bard, a panogyrist, a wandering minstrel

चारदीवारी (*nf*) an enclosure

चारपाई (*nf*) bedstead, cot, bed

चारपाया (*nm*) a quadruped

चारा (*nm*) food for cattle, fodder, pasture

चारु (*a*) attractive, elegant, beautiful

चारुता (*nf*) beauty

चारों ओर (*adv*) about, around, on all sides

चाल (*nf*) walk; gait, movement; step; —चलन conduct, behaviour; —ढाल gait, air, fashion; —बाज़ deceitful, crafty; —बाज़ी fraud, deception

चालक (*a*) a driver

चाला/क (*a*) sharp, clever, cunning; —की cleverness, craftiness

चालान (*nm*) invoice; a challan

चालू (*a*) tenable; current; prevalent; cunning

चाव (*nm*) ardent desire; eagerness

चावल (*nm*) rice

चाशनी (*nf*) syrup; taste

चाह (*nm*) desire, will; love, liking; want, need

चाहत (*nf*) longing, fondness; affection

चाहना (*v*) to desire; to love; to need, to want

चाहे (*ind*) either or; —कोई whichever; —जो हो come what may

चिउँटा (*nm*) the black ant of bigger species

चिउँटी (*nf*) an ant

चिंघाड़ (nf) a shrillery

चिंघाड़ना (v) to scream, to trumpet like an elephant

चिंतक (a) musing, thinker

चिंतन (nm) study; thinking, reflection

चिंता (nf) anxiety; worry; care

चिंत्य (a) refletive; thinkable

चिकन (nf) embroidered fine muslin

चिकना (a) smooth; glossy; clean, slippery, —चुपड़ा looking smart; full of flattery

चिकनाई (nf) gloss; smoothness; oiliness; fattiness

चिकनापन (nm) greasiness; smoothness

चिकित्सक (nm) a doctor; a physician

चिकित्सा (nf) treatment; medication;—शास्त्र medical science

चिकित्सालय (nm) dispensary, hospital

चिकोटी (nf) pinch; twitch

चिट्ठा (nm) detailed list; account book

चिट्ठी (nf) a letter; —पत्री correspondence

चिड़चिड़ा (a) peevish, irritable; —पन testiness, surliness, peevishness

चिड़िया (nf) a bird

चिढ़ (nf) vexation, irritation; hatred

चिढ़ना (v) to be irritated

चिढ़ाना (v) to tease, to huff

चित (a) supine; (nm) attention; mind; —चोर heart-stealing; beloved

चितकबरा (a) spotted

चितवन (nf) glance, look

चिता (nf) funeral pyre

चितेरा (nm) a painter

चित्त (nm) mind; (a) supine; —चुराना to bewitch, to charm; —देना to attend to

चिती (nf) a scar, a spot; —दार spotted

चित्र (nm) painting; picture; —कला the art of painting; —कार an artist; a painter; —शाला a picture gallery

चित्रण (nm) drawing; portrayal

चिथड़ा (nm) a rag, shred

चिथाड़ना (v) to tear to pieces

चिनगारी (nf) a spark, an ember

चिनाई (nf) bilge and cantline, brick-laying

चिपकना (v) to stick, to cling

चिपचिपा (a) waxy, limy, gummy

चिपचिपाना (v) to feel sticky

चिपटना (v) to stick, to adhere to

चिपटा (a) stuck, flat; चिपटी नाक वाला pug-nosed

चिबुक (nm) the chin

चिमटना (v) to embrace, to cling, to hold fast

चिमटा (nm) tongs, pincers

चिमनी (nf) a chimney, a funnel

चिरंजीव (a) blessed with longevity; — (nm) son

चिरंतन (a) ever lasting, perpetual

चिर (a) lasting for a long time; (ind) ever; —काल since a long time; —जीवी immortal; —निद्रा death; — परिचित long known; —प्रतीक्षित long-awaited; —स्थायी enduring; permanent; —स्मरणीय ador-able

चिरना (v) to be sawed

चिराग़ (nm) a light; lamp;-गुल करना to put out the lamp

चिरौंजी (nf) the tree Chironji, its edible nut

चिलगोजा (nm) fruit of the pine tree of tubular form

चिलचिलाना (v) shine scorch-ingly; चिलचिलाती धूप (nf) scorching sun

चिलम (nf) the part of a hubble-bubble which contains the fire

चिलमची (nf) a metal basin to wash the hands in

चिल्ल-पों (nf) a scream, a cry, a noise

चिल्लाना (v) to cry out, to shout

चिल्लाहट (nf) clamour, scream, call

चिह्न (nm) sign; mark

चिह्नित (a) marked, stained, spotted

चीं (nf) chirp, —चपड़ speaking something againt; — बोलना to confess helplessness; to own defeat

चींटी (nf) an ant

चीख़ (nf) screech, scream; —पुकार shriek and scream

चीख़ना (a) to shriek, to scream

चीज़ (nf) a commodity; a thing; — बस्त belongings

चीता (nm) a panther; a leopard

चीत्कार (nf) shouting; uproar

चीथड़ा (nm) rag

चीनी (nf) chinese (language); sugar; (a) a chinese; —मिट्टी clay

चीर (nm) cloth; bark of tree; rag

चीरना (v) to rip, to cleave, to tear

चीरा (nm) a surgical operation, incision

चील (nf) a kite, a snap

चुंगल (nm) claw, talon, a handful

चुंगी (nf) cess, octroi; —घर custom-house

चुंधियाना (v) to see dimly; to be dazzled

चुंबक (nm) a loadstone; a magnet

चुंबन (nm) kissing, a kiss

चुंबित (a) kissed, loved

चुकंदर (nm) a tuberous vege-table, beet root, beet, sugar beet

चुकाना (v) to settle; to pay off

चुगना (v) to pick up food with beak

चुग़ल-ख़ोर (nm) a tell tale, a back biter; —ख़ोरी back-biting

चुग़ली (*nf*) whispering, back-biting

चुगाई (*nf*) act of picking

चुगाना (*v*) to cause to peck

चुटकी (*nf*) a pinch

चुटकुला (*nm*) a joke; an anecdote

चुड़ैल (*nf*) a hag, a witch

चुनना (*v*) to extract, to pick, to gather

चुनरी (*nf*) a piece of coloured cloth worn by women

चुनाँचे (*ind*) thus, therefore

चुनाव (*nm*) pick; choice; election; selection; —क्षेत्र constituency;—मंडल electorate

चुनिंदा (*a*) selected

चुनौती (*nf*) a challenge

चुप (*a*) quiet, silent

चुपचाप (*adv*) quietly, silently

चुपड़ना (*v*) to besmear, to flatter

चुप्पा (*a*) secretive

चुप्पी (*nf*) silence

चुभना (*v*) to be pierced; to be fixed in the mind; to feel pain

चुमकारना (*v*) to coax, to fondle, to produce a kissing sound

चुराना (*v*) to steal, to pinch

चुलबुला (*a*) restless, gay, fidgeting; —पन fickleness

चुल्ली (*nf*) a fire place; a chimney of stove

चुल्लू (*nm*) hollowed palm, handful of liquid

चुस्की (*nf*) a suck, a sip

चुसना (*v*) to be sucked

चुसनी (*nf*) a child's coral, feeding bottle for babies

चुसाना (*v*) to cause to be sucked

चुस्त (*a*) tight, narrow, active, smart; —चालाक sharp and smart

चुस्ती (*nf*) agility, smartness

चुहटना (*v*) to crush with feet, to trample

चुहल (*nf*) merriment, jollity; —बाज a jester; a buffoon

चुहिया (*nf*) a small mouse

चैं (*nm*) chirping of a small bird

चूँकि (*ind*) for this, because

चूकना (*v*) to slip, to err, to miss

चूज़ा (*nm*) a chicken

चूड़ा (*nf*) the top, crest, a bracelet

चूड़ी (*nf*) ring; a bangle

चून (*nm*) wheat-meal, flour

चूना (*v*) to drap; to leak; (*nm*) mortar, lime

चूमना (*v*) to kiss

चूरन (*nm*) a powder, digestive powder

चूरमा (*nm*) a sweetmeat made of crushed bread

चूरा (*nm*) sawdust, a broken part

चूर्ण (*nm*) digestive powder, powder

चूल्हा (*nm*) a stove, a fireplace, hearth

चूसना (v) to sip, to suck, to drink

चूहा (nm) mouse; a rat;

चूहेदानी (nf) a rat trap

चेचक (nf) small-pox

चेट (nm) a servant

चेटी (nf) a female servant

चेतना (nf) feeling, conscious-ness; (v) to understand; to think

चेताना (v) to acquaint; to awaken; to tease

चेतावनी (nf) a warning; alarm

चेरी (nf) a female slave

चे/ला (nm) a disciple; a pupil; —ली a female disciple

चेष्टा (nf) bodily action, spirit; effort

चेहरा (nm) face; countenance; front part of a thing

चैत (nm) the first month of the Hindu calender

चैतन्य (a) perceiving, sensitive, conscious; (nm) intelligence

चैन (nm) rest; tranquillity; relief

चोंगा (nm) a funnel, a tele-phone's receiver

चोंच (nf) neb, bill, beak

चोखा (a) pure; clear; keen; fine

चोगा (nm) a long coat, a gown

चोचला (nf) coquettishness, playfulness

चोट (nf) a hurt; stroke; blow; attack; —करना to strike a

blow

चोटी (nf) braided hair of a woman; an apex; crown; braid

चोर (nm) burglar; a thief

चोरी (nf) burglary, theft

चोली (nf) corset, bodice, brassieres

चौंकना (v) to start up in sleep, to be alarmed

चौंकाना (v) to alarm, to startle

चौंगा (nm) wheedling, bait

चौंधियाना (v) to flash, to daze

चौ an allomorph of चतु: (चार); — कन्ना cautious, alert; —कोर quadrangular; —खटा door-frame; —खाना cheq-uered cloth; —गिर्द all round, on all sides; —गुना fourfold; —तरफा all round; —पाया a quadruped; cattle; neat; —पाल an assembly hall; —मासा the four months of the rainy season beginning from Asharha; —मुखा having four mouths or burners of lamp; —रस flat, plane, square; —राहा cross road

चौक (nm) a square plot of ground, a courtyard

चौकी (nf) a stool; a bench for sitting; a police station; an outpost

चौकीदार (nm) a sentry, a guard, a watchman

चौकीदारी (nf) the business of a

watchman

चौगान (*nm*) the game of polo

चौड़ा (*a*) wide, broad; —ई width, breadth

चौथा (*a*) the fourth; (*nm*) the fourth lunar day; the fourth day of somebody's death

चौथाई (*a*) the fourth part

चौथापन (*nm*) the fourth stage of life, old age

चौदस (*nf*) the fourteenth day of a lunar month according to Hindu calendar

चौधरी (*nm*) the headman of a village, a foreman

चौपड़ (*nm*) a game like backgammon which is played with three long dices

चौपाई (*nf*) a metre or verse consisting of four lines

चौबाइन (*nf*) the wife of a choube

चौबारा (*nm*) an open room built on the roof of a house

चौबे (*nm*) a subcaste among Brahmans

चौमंज़िला (*a*) built of four storeys

चौसर (*nm*) a game played with oblong dice

चौहान (*nm*) a caste among Rajputs

च्यवन (*nm*) dripping, oozing, a leak; the name of a sage

च्यवनप्राश (*nm*) an Ayurvedic medicine

च्युत (*a*) dropped, fallen, degraded

च्युति (*nf*) falling, perishing

छ

छ the second member of the second pentad of consonants in Devnagri alphabet

छँटना (*v*) to be separated on being cut, to be removed, to be lean and thin

छँटा हुआ (*a*) selected; cunning

छँटाई (*nf*) the work or wages for cleaning or pruning

छँटनी (*nf*) retrenchment

छंद (*nm*) metre, stazna; — शास्त्र prosody

छंदोबद्ध (*a*) in the form of a verse

छकड़ा (*nm*) a wooden car; cart

छकना (*v*) to be satisfied; to be intoxicated

छकाना (*v*) to satiate, to intoxicate, to cheat

छक्का (*nm*) a group of six, the sixth at cards; a six in cricket

छगन (*nm*) a baby, a darling

छछूंदर (*nf*) mole, musk-rat

छछूंदरी (*nf*) a vole

छज्जा (*nm*) terrace; a balcony; drip stone

छटंकी (*nf*) a weight of one chhatank

छटकना (*v*) to slip off, to keep aloof

छटपटाना (*v*) to toss; to struggle; to be restless

छटपटी (*nf*) restlessness, struggling

छटाँक (*nf*) one sixteenth of a seer

छटा (*nf*) brilliance, glory, lustre

छटाव (*nm*) separation

छठ (*nf*) the sixth day of a fortnight in a lunar month

छठी (*nf*) the ceremony performed on the sixth day after child birth

छड़ी (*nf*) a rod, a cane, a stick

छत (*nf*) roof; the ceiling

छतरी (*nf*) an umbrella

छत्ता (*nm*) a covered footpath, carrior, bee-hive

छत्र (*nm*) an umbrella, a parasol; —छाया protection, a mushroom

छत्रक (*nm*) a temple, a pavilion

छत्रधारी (*a*) carrying an umbrella; (*nm*) a prince

छद्म (*nm*) pretext, trick, fraud

छद्मी (*a*) crafty, impersonating

छनकना (*v*) to emit a hissing sound

छनना (*nm*) a filter

छनाई (*nf*) percolation

छपाई (*nf*) work of stamping or printing

छपाका (*nm*) the sound produced by striking against water

छपाना (*v*) to cause to be printed

छप्पर (*nm*) a booth, a thatched roof

छबड़ा (*nm*) a shallow basket

छबि (*nf*) aspect, beauty

छबीला (*a*) handsome, graceful

छरहरा (*a*) light, swift, slim and smart

छर्रा (*nm*) a small shot

छल (*nm*) deception, —कपट duplicity, trick

छलकना (*v*) to spill out, to over flow

छलनी (*nf*) strainer; a sieve

छलाँग (*nf*) a spring, a vault, a leap, jumping

छलावा (*nm*) the shadow of a ghost, magic, will-o'-the-wisp

छलिया (*a & nm*) artful, crafty, cunning

छल्ला (*nm*) a ring worn on the fingers; a bangle; eye Curl

छवि (*nf*) features; beauty; brilliance

छाँटना (*v*) to sort out, to select; to cut

छांदोग्य (*nm*) an Upanishad of the Samaveda

छाँव (*nf*) shadow; shade

छांह (*nf*) reflection, shadow;

shade; —वार shadowy —से
बचना to keep away from
shadow

छठ (nf) butter-milk, whey

छज (nm) a winnowing basket,
a thatch

छजन (nm) covering, cloth

छता (nm) an umbrella

छती (nf) chest, breast; bosom;
heart

छत्र (nm) a pupil, a scholar, a
student; —वृत्ति scholarship

छत्रावास (nm) a boarding house,
hostel

छन (nf) frame work for that-
ching with straw

छनना (v) to strain, to filter, to
investigate

छन-बीन (nf) search, investigation, critical research

छना (v) to thatch, to cover; to
spread; to stay

छप (nf) stamp; print; impression; brand

छपना (v) to stamp; to imprint;
to impress

छपा (nm) impression; stamp;
seal, —मार a raider; guerilla

छपाखाना (nm) a printing press

छाया (nf) shade; shadow; करना
to shade; —वार sunless,
shadowy; —पन shadiness;
—पूर्ण umbrageous; —मात्र
phantom; —तरु a large tree
which gives ample shade;
—ग्राहिणी a demon who had
pulled Hanuman by his

reflection while he was
crossing the ocean; —दान
the giving as a gift of oil in
which a person has seen his
reflected image; —पथ the
Milky way; —पुरुष a
reflected image of a person;
—छूना to pursue the unreal

छार (nm) ashes; salt; dirt

छल (nf) rind, bark, skin

छला (nm) a blister; a pimple

छलिया (nf) betel nut

छावनी (nf) thatch, encampment, cantonment

छावा (nm) a boy, son

छि: (ind) a word used to
express contempt, tush

छिंकाना (v) to cause someone to
sneeze

छिछला (a) thin, shallow; —पन
shallowness

छिछली (nf) the play of ducks
and drakes

छिछोरा (v) trivial, petty; —पन
meanness

छिटकना (v) to be scattered, to
be dispersed

छिटकाना (v) to spread all round,
to scatter

छिटकी (nf) a speck

छिड़कना (v) to spill, to sprinkle,
to patter

छिड़काव (nm) the act of
sprinkling

छिड़ना (v) to begin, to
commence

छितरना (v) to be scattered

छिद्र (nm) hole, gap, slot; defect

छिनना (v) to be snatched away; to be taken by force

छिनाल (a & nf) adulterous, sluttish

छिन्न (a) cut; divided; rent; —भिन्न broken up; destroyed

छिपकली (nf) a lizard

छिपना (v) to be concealed, to be hidden

छिपाना (v) to cover; to hide, to conceal

छिपाव (nm) hiding, secrecy

छिलका (nm) rind, crust, peel, skin

छिलना (v) to be rubbed away, to be excoriated

छींक (nf) a sneeze

छींकना (v) to sneeze

छींट (nf) fine drops especially of water

छींटना (v) to scatter, to diffuse

छींटा (nm) a slap, a casual glance, spot made by a drop of water; —कशी ironical utterance

छींका (nm) network of strings for hanging anything in

छीछड़ा (a) tough flesh of an animal

छीछालेदर (nf) embarrassment

छीज (nf) diminution, waste

छीनना (v) to take possession of, to extort, to snatch

छीना-झपटी (nf) extortion, forcible seizing

छींबर (nf) thick calico

छीलना (v) to peel; to pare; to scrap

छुआछूत (nf) untouchability

छुईमुई (nf) the sensitive plant, the mimosa plant

छुगनू (nm) small bells attached to an ornament

छुटकारा (nm) escape; exemption; riddance

छुटपन (nm) infancy, childhood

छुट्टा (a) free, alone, not bound

छुट्टी (nf) leave, vacation; holiday

छुड़वाना (v) to cause to be dismissed from service; to cause someone freed

छुड़ाव (nm) discharge

छुपना (v) to hide oneself

छुरा (nm) a razor; dagger

छुरी (nf) a knife; a small dagger

छुहारा (nm) the date palm

छू (nm) the act of blowing or uttering, an incantation; —मंतर होना to disappear from sight, to fly away, to vanish

छूट (nf) remission, discount; rebate

छूटना (a) to lag; to be dismissed; to get rid of

छूत (nf) touch, infection, contagion

छूना (v) to touch, to feel, to excel

छेक (nm) a hole, a division

छेड़खानी (nf) act of provoking, teasing

छेड़छाड़ (nf) teasing; provocation

छेड़ना (v) to irritate, to excite, to tease

छेद (nm) aperture, breach, hole

छेदक (a) boring or cutting, a divisor

छेदना (v) to perforate, to drill, to bore

छैला (nm) a fap, spark, dandy; (a) dandical

छोकरा (nm) a boy, lad

छोकरी (nf) a girl

छोटा (a) little; narrow; junior; —मोटा minor, ordinary

छोटी इलायची (nf) cardamom

छोड़ना (v) to relinquish, to remit, to let go; to leave

छोर (nm) border; end; the edge

छोरा (nm) a boy, lad

छोला (nm) gram

छौंकना (nm) to fry

छौना (nm) a young one

ज

ज the third member of the second pentad of the consonants in Devnagri alphabet

जंग (nf) battle, fight

जंग (nm) rust

जंगम (a) movable; moving; living

जंगल (nm) a forest; wood; wilderness

जंगली (a) wild; savage; boorish

जंगी (a) military, warlike, martial; large

जंघा (nf) thigh

जंजाल (nm) perplexity, embarrassment; entanglement

जंजीर (nf) a shackle; a chain

जंतु (nm) an animal, a creature

जंभाई (nf) yawning

जकड़ना (v) to tighten, to grasp

जखीरा (nm) a treaxiry; collection; a store-house

जख्म (nm) injury, a wound

जख्मी (a) injured, wounded, hurt

जग (nm) the universe, the world

जगत (nm) the universe, the world; —सेठ a very rich man

जगदंबा (nf) the goddess Durga

जगदीश (nm) the Lord of the universe

जगना (v) to be awakened; to be careful

जगमगा/ना (v) to glint, to shine

to twinkle; —हट glimmer, splendour

जगह (nf) place, locality; space; —जगह everywhere

जगाना (v) to raise; to awake

जघन्य (a) abominable; detested; low

ज़च्चा (nf) a woman in child-bed; —ख़ाना maternity home

जज़्ब (a) assimilated; absorbed

जज़्बा (nm) feeling, emotion; —ती emotional

जटिल (a) very difficult, intricate

जठ/र (nm) the womb, the stomach; —शग्नि the fire of the stomach which helps to digest food

जड़ (nf) root; (a) senseless, material, inert; —बुद्धि stupid

जड़ता (nf) stupor, immovable-ness, stiffness

जड़ना (v) to fit, to join; to set with jewels

जड़ाऊ (a) studded or set with jewels

जड़ाना (v) to cause to be set

जड़ी (nf) a medicinal root; —बूटी medicinal herbs

जताना (v) to inform, to make known, to remind

जत्था (nm) gang; a band

जन (nm) mankind, a person, people; —गणना census; —जीवन public life; —तंत्र democracy; —प्रिय popular; —मत public opinion; —श्रुति rumour; —संख्या population; —समूह crowd; —साधारण the commonman; —हित public welfare

जनक (nm) father; originator; the father of Sita —नंदिनी Sita

जनजाति (nm) a tribe

जनता (nm) the public, masses

जननी (nf) mother

जनाना (a) female; (nm) female apartment

जनाब (a & nm) your honour, your highness; mister

जनार्दन (nm) an epithet of Lord Vishnu

जनेऊ (nm) the sacred thread of a Brahman

जनोक्ति (nf) a proverb

जन्म (nm) birth; production; origin

जन्मोत्सव (nm) birthday celebration

जप (nm) the silent repetition of a Mantra

जपना (v) to repeat silently the name of any deity, to mutter prayers

जपमाला (nf) a rosary for counting prayers

जब (adv) when, at whatever time; —कि when; —तब sometime

जबड़ा (nm) a jaw

जबरद/स्त (a) strong, powerful,

violent;—स्त्री injustice, high-handedness

जबरन (adv) forcibly, with force

ज़बह (nm) slaughter

ज़बहा (nm) spirit, courage

ज़बान (nf) the tongue, language

ज़बानी (a) by word of mouth, vocal; (adv) orally, verbally

जबाब (nm) answer

जवाबदेह (a) accountable, liable; subject

जवाबदेही (nf) liability, responsibility

जबून (a) bad, wicked

ज़ब्त (a) confiscated, forfeited; —करना to impound

ज़ब्ती (nf) forfeiture, forfeit

जब्र (nm) oppression, force, violence

जमघट (nm) throng, crowd, assembly

जमदग्नि (nm) the name of a sage

जमना (v) to be coagulated, to be frozen, to be fixed

जमवट (nf) the wooden foundation of a well

जमहाई (nf) a gaping, yawning

जमा (a) accumulated, collected, stored; —खर्च debit and credit;—पूँजी total accumulation

जमाई (nm) a son-in-law

जमात (nm) assembly; a class

जमादार (nm) head of soldiers, a

person on guard

ज़मानत (nf) bond; surety; bail

ज़मानती (nm) a surety, guarantor

ज़माना (nm) time; world, (a) age, period

जमाव (nm) crowd, accumulation, collection

ज़मींकन्द (nm) the yam

ज़मीं/दार (nm) a cultivator; a landlord; — दारी an estate, a landed property.

ज़मीन (nf) land, the earth; soil; ground

ज़मीनी (a) earthly, pertaining to the earth

जम्बुक (nm) a jackal

जम्बूद्वीप (nm) one of the seven divisions of the world as described in the Puranas

जम्बूरा (nm) a swivel, small pliers

जम्हाई (nf) yawning; —लेना to yawn

जयंत (a) victorious, triumphant; (nm) the name of Indra's son

जयंती (nf) jubilee; Durga

जय (nf) victory, conquest

जयकार (nf) cheers, rejoicings

जयघोषणा (nf) noise of victory

जयद्रथ (nm) brother-in-law of king Duryodhana

जयध्वज (nm) the name of an ancient king of Avanti; banner of victory

जयपत्र (nm) a bond of victory

जयमंगल (*nm*) the elephant on which a king mounts

जयश्री (*nf*) the goddess of victory

जयस्तंभ (*nm*) the monument erected to commemorate a victory

जया (*nf*) an epithet of Durga; green grass

ज़र (*nm*) riches, wealth; —ख़रीद purchased

ज़रा (*nf*) senility, an old age

ज़रा (*a*) little, less; (*adv*) a little, somewhat; —सा a small amount

जराग्रस्त (*a*) aged, old

जरामीरू (*nm*) cupid

जरासंघ (*nm*) the name of an ancient king of Magadha

ज़रिया (*nm*) connection, means, agency

ज़री (*nf*) a cloth woven with gold thread

जरीब (*nf*) chain used in measuring land

ज़रूर (*adv*) of course, certainly, necessarily

ज़रूरत (*nf*) need, want, necessity

ज़रूरी (*a*) necessary, needful; important

ज़र्क-बर्क (*a*) shining, brilliant

जर्जर (*a*) old, decrepit, worn out

जर्जरित (*a*) tattered, crushed

ज़र्दी (*nf*) yellowness, paleness

ज़र्रा (*nm*) a particle, an atom

जराह (*nm*) a surgeon, an anatomist

जराही करना (*v*) to operate

जलंधर (*nm*) the name of a demon, dropsy

जल (*nm*) water, aqua; hydro; —मार्ग channel waterways; —यात्रा a voyage; —यान a ship, vessel; boat

जलज़ला (*nm*) an earthquake

जलन (*nf*) inflammation, a burning sensation; jealousy

जलना (*v*) to flame, to burn

जलनिधि (*nm*) sea, ocean

जलपक्षी (*nm*) an aquatic bird

जलपात्र (*nm*) ewer, urn, flagon

जलपान (*nm*) breakfast; light refreshment

जलप्रणाली (*nf*) sluice of water

जलप्रपात (*nm*) a waterfall

जलप्रवाह (*nm*) a torrent; the act of throwing something into water

जलप्रलय (*nm*) the destruction of the world by water

जलप्लावन (*nm*) a flood

जलबेंत (*nm*) a water-cane

जलभँवर (*nm*) a whirl pool

जलभँवरा (*nm*) a water bee

जलमय (*a*) watery

जलमानुष (*nm*) a merman

जलयन्त्र (*nm*) an appliance to raise water, water wheel

जलवायु (*nf*) climate

जलशास्त्र (*nm*) hydromechanics

जलसा (*nm*) a meeting; a function; social gathering

जलसेना (*nf*) navy

जलस्तंभ (*nm*) a lighthouse; a water-sprout

जलाना (*v*) to light, to kindle; to burn; to scold

ज़लालत (*nf*) meanness

जला-भुना (*a*) hot-tempered

जलाई (*a*) moist, wet

जलाल (*nm*) splendour, glory; power

जलावतन (*nm*) exile; (*a*) exiled

जलाशय (*nm*) a tank; lake

ज़लील (*a*) wretched, base, mean

जलूस (*nm*) a procession

जलेबी (*nf*) a kind of sweetmeat

जल्दी (*nf*). quickness, hurry; (*adv*) hastily, quickly

जल्प (*nm*) babbling

जल्पना (*v*) to brag, to boast

जल्लाद (*nm*) an executioner, a cruel person

जवनिका (*nf*) a theatrical screen

जवाँमर्द (*a*) brave, heroic

जवाँमर्दी (*nf*) gallantry, bravery, heroism

जवान (*a*) young, youthful; brave, (*nm*) a youth; a soldier or sepoy

जवानी (*nf*) youth,

जवाब (*nm*) answer; reply; retaliation; —देह answerable; responsible; —देही liability

जवाबी (*a*) requiring a reply; pertaining to answer

जवाहर (*nm*) a jewel, a gem

जश्न (*nm*) merriment, festivity, festival

जस्ता (*nm*) zinc

जहन्नुम (*nm*) hell

ज़हमत (*nf*) affliction, trouble; injury

ज़हर (*nm*) venom, poison; —बाद a carbuncle; septic

ज़हरमोहरा (*nm*) the bezoar, a kind of green stone supposed to be an antidote to poison

ज़हरीला (*a*) poisonous, venomous

जहाँ (*adv*) wherever; —तक as far as;—तहाँ everywhere, here and there

जहाँगीरी (*nf*) a kind of bracelet

जहाँपनाह (*nm*) the protector of the world, His Imperial Majesty

जहाज़ (*nm*) a ship; a vessel, a sail; —रानी shipping, navigation

जहाज़ी (*a*) marine, nautical; (*nm*) a sailor

जहान (*nm*) the world

जहानी (*a*) worldly, terrestrial

जहालत (*nf*) ignorance, barbarity, stupidity

जहीं (*adv*) wherever, at whatsoever place

ज़हीन (*a*) intelligent, sagacious, wise

जहेज़ (*nm*) dowry, gift in marriage; (see also दहेज़)

जह्नु (nm) the name of the sage who adopted the river Ganga as his daughter

जाँघ (nf) thigh

जाँघिया (nm) a lower under-wear, short drawers

जाँच (nm) trial, assay, investigation; — पड़ताल enquiry

जाँचना (v) to ascertain; to examine; to try; to investigate

जागना (v) to get up from bed, to awake; to be careful

जागता हुआ (adv) vigilant, unwinking

जागरण (nm) watch, vigil, wakefulness

जागरित (a) wide-awake, watchful, alert

जागरूक (a) wakeful, vigilant

जागीर (nf) a rent-free grant given by the Government as a reward for some services, grant

जागृति (nf) wakefulness, an awakening

जाज्वल्यमान (a) shining, lustrous

जाट (nm) a tribe among Rajputs

जाड़ा (nm) winter; cold

जाड्य (nm) lack of sensation,

जातक (nm) a child, a newborn babe

जात-पाँत (nf) caste and community

जाता (nf) a girl, daughter

जाति (nf) race; sex; caste; community

जाती (a) personal, individual

जातीय (a) pertaining to tribe or caste

जातीयता (nf) communal feeling

जादू (nm) juggling, magic, spell; charm; — टोना socre-ry; voodooism

जादूगर (nm) juggler, magician; conjurer

जादूगरनी (nf) a witch

जादूगरी (nf) magic, sorcery, a charm

जान (nf) understanding; life; spirit; — बीमा life insurance; — व माल life and property

जानका/र (a) conversant; knowing; experienced; — री acquaintance; knowledge

जानकी (nf) Sita; — नाथ Shri Rama

जानवार (a) animate, having life

जानना (v) to know; to under-stand

जान-पहचान (nf) acquaintance

जानवर (nm) an animal, a beast

जाना (v) to go; to depart; to lose

जानु (nm) the knee

जानी (a) dear, beloved, animate; — दुश्मन a mortal enemy; — दोस्त a fast friend

जाप (nm) a rosary for counting mantras

जापक (nm) one who repeats

the names of a deity on a rosary

जाफ़रान (*nm*) saffron

जाबालि (*nm*) the preceptor of king Dasharatha

ज़ाब्ता (*nm*) regulation, rule; —दीवानी Civil Procedure Code; —फौजदारी Penal Code

जाम (*a*) jammed; (*nm*) jam; a peg; a period of three hours

जामन (*nm*) rennet used in coagulating milk;

जामा (*nm*) a garment, a raiment, a robe

जामाता (*nm*) a son-in-law

जामुन (*nm*) a black plum, jambo

जाम्बवती (*nf*) one of the wives of Lord Krishna

जाम्बवंत (*nm*) a minister of King Sugreeva

जाय/का (*nm*) relish, taste; केदार tasteful, relishing

जायदाद (*nf*) property

जाया (*a*) waste, ruined

जार (*nm*) a lover, an adulterer

जारण (*nm*) burning, reducing to ashes

जारी (*a*) proceeding, running, in force

जालंधर (*nm*) dropsy

जाल (*nm*) mesh, net, network; plot; —साज़ a deceiver, a cunning person; —साज़ी forgery, deception

जाला (*nm*) a net, cobweb

ज़ालिम (*a*) tyrannical, cruel, oppressive; (*nm*) a tyrant

जाली (*nf*) network, guaze, grating

जासू/स (*nm*) an emissary, a spy; —सी the work of a spy or secret agent

ज़ाहिर (*a*) obvious, clear, plain, manifest

जाहिल (*a*) foolish; ignorant; illiterate; rude

जाह्नवी (*nf*) an epithet of river Ganga

ज़िंदगी (*nf*) duration of life, age

ज़िंदा (*a*) living, alive; —दिल jolly, jovial, merry; —दिली liveliness

ज़िक्र (*nm*) recital, mention

जिगर (*nm*) the liver; the heart

जिगरा (*nm*) courage, bravery

जिगरी (*a*) intimate, friendly; — दोस्त very intimate friend

जिगीषा (*nf*) desire for victory, superiority

जिज्ञासा (*nf*) curiosity

जिज्ञासित (*a*) questioned, enquired

जिज्ञासु (*a*) inquisitive, curious

जित/ना (*a*) as much as, however; ने as many

जितात्मा (*a*) self-controlled

जिताना (*v*) to cause to win

जितेंद्रिय (*a*) having the sense subdued; (*nm*) an ascetic, virtuous person

ज़िद (nf) persistence, obstinacy

ज़िद्दी (a) obstinate

जिधर (adv) whither, wherever

जिन (nm) the Jain Tirthankars; Vishnu; the Sun; the plural form of जिस

जिमाना (v) to feed at a table

ज़ि/म्मा (nm) trust, charge, duty; —म्मेदार responsible; —म्मेदारी responsibility

जिरह (nf) fault-finding, cross-examination

ज़िला (nm) a district

जिलाना (v) to give life, to bring back to life

ज़िलाधीश (nm) the district magistrate

जिल्द (nf) skin, leather, binding of a book; —बंदी book-binding work; —साज a bookbinder

जिस (pron) who, whom, which

जिस्म (nm) the body of an animate being or animal

जिहाद (nm) crusade

जिह्वा (nf) the tongue

जिह्वाग्र (nm) the tip of the tongue

जी (nm) soul, spirit, mind; a term of respect — sir, madam etc

जीजा (nm) husband of one's elder sister

जीजी (nf) an elder sister

जीत (nf) mastery; victory, success

जीतना (v) to conquer, to win; to overcome

जीता (a) living, alive; —जागता living

जीना (v) to live, to be alive

जीना (nm) a ladder, staircase

जीभ (nf) the tongue

जीरा (nm) cuminseed; pollen contained in a flower

जीरी (nf) a kind of fine rice

जीर्ण (a) old, ragged, decayed

जीर्णता (nf) triteness, old age

जीर्णोद्धार (nm) restoration, repair of broken objects

जीवंत (a) living, alive

जीव (nm) a creature; life; soul; —जंतु tiny creatures; —धारी having life, animate

जीवट (nm) adventure; courage

जीवन (nm) existence, breath; life; —चरित biography; —चर्या livings — दान sacrifice of life; —वृत्तांत bio-data; —संघर्ष struggle for existence

जीवनी (nf) biography

जीवाणु (nm) microbe; bacteria

जीवात्मा (nm) the vital principle, the spiritual essence in man

जीविका (nf) allowance, livelihood

जीवित (a) animate, alive, living

जुआ (nm) the yoke; gambling

जुआरी (nm) a gambler

जुकाम (nm) a cold, catarrh

जुगाली (nf) the chewing of the

cud

जुगुप्सा (*nf*) aversion, abuse, censure

जुटना (*v*) to unite, to be entangled

जुड़वाँ (*nm*) twins

जुदा (*a*) separate, different; — ई separation

जुर्म (*nm*) sin; crime; fault

जुर्माना (*nm*) penalty, fine

जुर्रत (*nf*) courage

जुर्राब (*nf*) socks, stocking

जुलाब (*nm*) a purgative

जुलाहा (*nm*) a weaver

जुलूस (*nm*) a procession

जुल्फ (*nf*) curling lock of hair, a ringlet

जुल्म (*nm*) tyranny, oppression, outrage

जुल्मी (*a*) oppressive, tyrannical

जुहार (*nf*) salutation

जुहारना (*v*) to ask for assistance, to be obliged

जुही (*nf*) a kind of jasmine

जूँ (*nf*) a louse

जूझना (*v*) to fight; to quarrel

जूट (*nm*) jute, matted hair

जूठन (*nf*) garbage, offal, leavings

जूठा (*a*) what is left off after eating

जूड़ा (*nm*) a plait, a tress, a tuft

जूता (*nm*) shoe; boot; slipper

जूताखोर (*a*) beaten with shoes; degraded, shameless

जूती (*nf*) shoes worn by ladies; slippers

जूस (*nm*) broth, soup

जूही (*nf*) a kind of jasmine, a kind of fireworks see also जुही

जुम्भक (*a*) one who yawns; a certain demon

जेठ (*nm*) the third month of the Hindu year; elder brother of one's husband

जेठा (*a*) first born, elder

जेठानी (*nf*) the wife of husband's elder brother

जेतव्य (*a*) conquerable

जेब (*nf*) a pocket; — कतरा pickpocket; — खर्च pocket money;-घड़ी a pocket watch

जेल (*nf*) jail, prison

जेलर (*nm*) a jailor

जेब/र (*nm*) ornament, jewel, — रात jewellery, ornaments

जेहन (*nf*) intellect

जैतून (*n*) olive tree, its fruit

जैमिनी (*nm*) the founder of the Purva Mimansa school of Hindu philosophy

जैसा (*a*) like, similar to; (*adv*) as, according to

जैसे (*adv*) in the manner, in which; — जैसे as far as; — तैसे some how

जोंक (*nf*) a leech

जोंकी (*nf*) a nail which is pointed at both ends

जो (*pron*) who, which, that; (*ind*) if; — कुछ whatever, whatsoever

जोखा (nm) (mostly used after लेखा-) account

जोखिम (nm) enterprise; danger, risk

जोगिया (a) ascetic, of reddish colour

जोगी (nm) a saint; an ascetic

जोड़ (nm) connection; joint; sum; match

जोड़ना (v) to rejoin; to supplement; to affix; to mix; to link; to collect

जोड़ा (nm) a pair; couple; twin; a pair of shoes; suit of clothes

जोड़ी (nf) couple; a pair

जोत (nf) the strap of leather or rope; flame

जोतना (v) to plough a field, to till; to yoke

जोताई (nf) the worker's wages tilling a land

जोबन (nm) bloom of youth, lustre, brilliance

ज़ोर (nm) force, strength, power; effort

ज़ोरदार (a) strong, powerful

जोरू (nf) wife, better half

जोश (nm) heat; zeal; passion

जोशाँदा (nm) a medicinal decoction

जोशीला (a) enthusiastic, zealous

जौहर (nm) a precious stone, a jewel; excellence; collec- tive sacrifice in fire by Rajput ladies when their husbands die in the battle

जौहरी (nm) a jeweller

ज्ञा/त (a) acquainted, known, understood; —ता one who knows

ज्ञातव्य (a) knowable, worth knowing

ज्ञान (nm) knowledge, percep- tion, understanding

ज्ञानी (a) experienced; one who has knowledge of self; intel- ligent

ज्ञानेंद्रिय (nf) the organs of perception and intellect

ज्ञापक (a) giving information, making known; memo

ज्ञापन (nm) memorandum

ज्ञेय (a) knowable, fit to be known

ज्या (nf) a bow string, the earth; sine - - - - (Maths)

ज्यादती (nf) abundance, excess, increase

ज्यादा (a) too much; more

ज्यामिति (nf) conic section, geometry

ज्येष्ठ (a) best; elder; (nm) the third month of the Hindu year

ज्यों (adv) as; if; —ज्यों in which order, as much; —त्यों somehow or other; —ही as soon as; —का त्यों precisely the same

ज्योति (nf) a flood of light; lustre, brilliance; flame

ज्योतिष (nf) astrology; astronomy

ज्योतिषी (*nm*) an astrologer; astronomer

ज्योत्स्ना (*nf*) moonlight

ज्वर (*nm*) fever

ज्वरांकुश (*nm*) a medicine which is used to remove fever; a kind of fragrant grass

ज्वरांश (*nm*) feverishness

ज्वरार्त (*a*) suffering from fever

ज्वलन (*nm*) a burning, inflammation

ज्वार (*nm*) flood tide; — भाटाthe flood tide and ebb-tide

ज्वाला (*nf*) blaze, flame, fire, heat

ज्वालादेवी (*nf*) a goddess whose place of worship is in the Kangra district in Himachal Pradesh

ज्वालामुखी (*nm*) a volcano

झ

झ the fourth member of the second pentad of consonants in Devnagri alphabet

झंकार (*nf*) jingling, tinkling; ringing

झंकारना (*v*) to produce a jingling

झंख (*nf*) wailing, lamenting; a fish

झंझट (*nm*) difficulty; botheration; trouble

झंझोडना (*v*) to shake a thing with a violent jerk

झंडा (*nm*) a flag, streamer, banner

झंडी (*nf*) a small flag, a bunting

झक (*nf*) whim, crank; craze; (*a*) clean

झकझक (*nf*) nonsensical talk, chattering

झकझोरना (*v*) to give a violent jerk

झकना (*v*) to prattle, to chatter, to speak inproperly in wrath

झकाझक (*a*) shining, glittering, polished

झक्कड़ (*nm*) a strong wind, hurricane, a gale; (*a*) crazy, cranky

झक्की (*a*) prattling, crazy, daft

झगड़ना (*v*) to quarrel; to altercate

झगड़ा (*nm*) dispute, variance, quarrel

झगड़ालू (*a*) contentious, disputatious, quarrelsome

झट (*adv*) quickly, instantly, immediately

झटकना (*v*) to give a jerk to a

thing, to toss violently

झटका (*nm*) a push, a jolt, a concussion.

झटकारना (*v*) to toss, to give a jerk to

झटपट (*adv*) very soon, quickly, hastily

झड़ना (*v*) to fall off in small fragments, to drop, to be shed off; erosion

झड़प (*nf*) skirmish, quarrel

झड़पना (*v*) to fight, to snatch away something forcibly

झड़पा-झड़पी (*nf*) skirmish, altercation

झड़वाना (*v*) to cause to be swept

झड़ी (*nf*) continued fall of rain

झनक (*nf*) a tinkling sound

झनकना (*v*) to jingle, to tinkle

झपक (*nf*) a wink; a moment, a very short time

झपकना (*v*) to nap, to wink; to twinkle

झपका (*nm*) a gust of wind

झपकी (*nf*) a nap, drowsiness, doze

झपट (*nf*) a rush; a snatch

झपटना (*v*) to pounce upon; to rush; to snap

झपट्टा (*nm*) an assault, a swoop, a snatch

झमेला (*nm*) disturbance, turmoil

झमेलिया (*nm*) one who creates disturbance

झरझर (*nf*) sound of rain or the flowing of water

झरना (*nm*) a spring, fall; a stream; (*v*) to fall off, to flow

झरोखा (*nm*) window; peep-hole; loophole

झलक (*nf*) glitter; glimpse; glance

झलकना (*v*) to sparkle, to glitter, to shine

झलमलाना (*v*) to twinkle; to glitter, to gleam

झल्लाना (*v*) to be displeased, to be fretful, to excite

झाँकना (*v*) to peer, to peep

झाँकी (*nf*) a glance, a look, a scene

झाँझर (*nf*) anklet, a sieve

झाँसना (*v*) to deceive, to pilfer

झाँसा (*nm*) deception, fraud, trickery

झाँसिया (*nm*) a deceiver, a cheat

झाग (*nm*) scum; foam; yeast, —दार yeasty, scumy

झाड़ (*nm*) a shrub, a bush, (*nf*) scolding; —फानूस chandelier, lights

झाड़खंड (*nm*) a junble, a wood

झाड़दार (*a*) thick, thorny

झाड़न (*nf*) sweepings; duster

झाड़ना (*v*) to brush, to sweep, to clean

झाड़ी (*nf*) covert, brake, thicket

झाड़ू (*nm*) a swab, a broom, a

comet

झापड़ (nm) a slap

झालर (nf) a frill, fringe, tatting

झिझक (nf) hitch, hesitation

झिझकना (v) to feel shy; to hasitate

झिड़कना (v) to scold, to speak snapishly

झिड़की (nf) rebuke, snubbing, snap

झिपना (a) to be shut

झिलमिलाना (v) to sparkle, to flash, to twinkle

झींकना (v) to grumble; to fret

झीना (a) very fine; thin; threadbare

झील (nf) a lake

झुंझला/ना (v) to be fretful, to be peevish; —हट acrimony, bitterness of language

झुंड (nm) cluster, flock, crowd

झुकना (v) to droop, to bow

झुकाव (nm) bent, leaning; tilt

झुटपुटा (nm) twilight

झुठलाना (v) to falsify, to prove to be false

झुनझुना (nm) a child's rattle

झुर्री (nf) furrow, wrinkle, blemish

झुलसना (v) to be singed; to be charred; to be scorched

झुलाना (v) to swing, to rock, to dandle

झूठ (a) untrue, false; (nm) lie, falsehood, fiction; —मूठ falsely, uselessly

झूठा (a) fictitious, dishonest, untrue

झूमना (v) to wave, to swing, to toss the head

झूमर (nm) an ornament worn on the head; a kind of song

झूलना (v) to swing; to linger in suspense; to wobble

झूला (nm) a swing, a swinging rope

झेंपना (v) to be ashamed

झेलना (v) to bear, to endure, to suffer

झोंकना (v) to cast something into fire; to push violently

झोंका (nm) a blast; puff, gust

झोंपड़ी (nf) a small cottage, a hut

झोलदार (a) soupy; loose

झोला (nm) a bag, knapsack

झोली (nf) a small bag; —फैलाना to beg

ञ

ञ the fifth member of the second pentad of conso- nants in the Devnagri alphabet

ट

ट the first member of the third pentad of consonants in Devnagri alphabet

टंकी (*nf*) a large tub for storing water or oil; tank

टैगना (*v*) to be hung; to be suspended; (*nm*) the rope on which clothes are hung up to be dried

टंटा (*nm*) quarrel, wrangling, altercation

टकटकी (*nf*) stare, gaze, fixed look; —बाँधना to gaze intently

टकराना (*v*) to be knocked or dashed together, to clash

टकसाल (*nm*) a mint; —में बने सिक्के mintage

टकसाली (*a*) pertaining to mint; genuine

टका (*nm*) a rupee; a brass coin worth half an anna

टक्कर (*nf*) pushing, knocking; a collision

टखना (*nm*) the ankle joint

टटोलना (*v*) to touch, to feel with the hand; to sound

टट्टी (*nf*) latrine; stool; fence; hedge

टट्टू (*nm*) a pony

टन (*nf*) a tinkling sound; (*nm*) ton, a weight of about twenty eight maunds

टपकना (*v*) to drop; to drip, to gutter

टपना (*v*) to jump over, to overleap

टपाटप (*a*) successively, continuously

टब (*nm*) a tub

टमटम (*nm*) a gig, a tandem

टमाटर (*nm*) a tomato

टर (*nm*) harsh sound, obstinacy, croaking of frogs

टरकना (*v*) to disappear, to abscond

टरकाना (*v*) to remove; to postpone; to evade

टरटर (*nm*) crackle, chattering, murmur

टर्राना (*v*) to chatter, to quack, to grumble

टलना (*v*) to vanish, to slip, to disappear

टसक (*nf*) throbbing or shooting pain in the body

टसर (*nm*) a kind of coarse silken cloth

टसुआ (*nm*) tear

टहनी (*nf*) a spray, sprig, twig

टहल (*nm*) service, attendance

टहलना (*v*) to roam, to walk, to stroll

टाँकना (*v*) to stitch; to cobble; to jot down

टाँका (*nm*) a solder; a stitch; a patch work

टाँग (*nf*) the leg

टाँगना (v) to hang

टाँगा (nm) a kind of two wheeled carriage

टाई (nf) neck-tie

टाट (nm) canvas, sack-cloth; floor mat

टाप (nm) sound of a horse's hoof

टापना (v) to be left helpless

टापू (nm) an island

टाल (nf) a heap, a fuel; postponement; —मटोल prevarication; avoidance

टालना (a) to put aside, to postpone

टिकिट (nm) a ticket; stamp; —घर booking-office

टिकड़ा (nm) a disk, a thick bread which is fried on fire

टिकना (v) to stop; to abide; to continue; to stay

टिकाऊ (a) lasting, durable

टिकाना (v) to lodge; to station

टिकिया (nf) a small cake; a tablet

टिक्की (nf) round circular piece; a tablet

टिड्डा (nm) a grasshopper

टिड्डी (nf) a locust; —दललocust swarm

टिपटिप (nf) sound made by the fall of water in drops

टिप्पणी (nf) annotation; a note; comment; critical remark

टिप्पस (nf) manipulation

टिमटिमाना (v) to give a faint light, to glimmer

टीका (nm) annotation; commentary, note; mark made on the forehead with sandal paste; an ornament for the head

टीकाकार (nm) a commentator

टीन (nm) tin, sheet of tinned iron

टीप (nf) pressure; raising of voice in singing; —टाप tip-topping

टीपना (v) to record; to point; to copy

टीम (nm) a team of players

टीमटाम (nf) empty show; ostentation; dressing

टीला (nm) a rising ground, mound, small hill

टीस (nf) a throbbing pain in a part of body

टीसना (v) to throb, to palpitate

टुकड़ा (nm) a piece, fragment, bit; a part, portion

टुकड़ी (nf) a small piece; part of an army

टुच्चा (a) trivial, insignificant

टुटपुँजिया (a) of meagre means

टूटना (v) to break, to fall; to rupture

टूटा (a) broken, decayed

टेंटुआ (nm) neck, throat

टेक (nf) prop, support; habit

टेकना (v) to support; to rest; to lean

टेढ़ा (a) bent, crooked, uneven; difficult; —पन obliquity, crookedness; —मेढ़ा crooked, zigzag

रेव (nf) habit, wont

रेवा (nm) horoscope, calculation of nativity

टोंटी (nf) a tap

टोकना (v) to interrogate, to question; to prevent

टोकरा (nm) a large wicker work basket

टोकरी (nf) a small basket

टोटका (nm) spell, charm; remedy for a disease

टोटा (nm) deficiency; loss; part (of a cigarette etc.)

टोना (nm) spell, magic, enchantment

टोप (nm) a hat; a helmet; cover

टोपी (nf) a cap

टोल (nm) a band, group

टोला (nm) part of a town or city

टोली (nf) band, group, crowd

टोह (nf) search, secret watching

टोहना (v) to seek, to be in search of

ठ

ठ the second member of the third pentad of consonants in Devnagri alphabet

ठंड (nf) coldness, chilliness; —क coolness

ठंडा (a) cold; cool; dull; lifeless; unfeeling

ठंडाई (nf) a cooling medicine; an indigeneous cold drink prepared from almond

ठक (nf) a tapping sound

ठकठक (nf) a knock; difficulty, uneasiness

ठकुराइन (nf) wife of Thakur; landlady

ठग (nm) a cut throat, cheat

ठगई (nf) cheating, robbing; theft

ठगना (v) to cheat, to swindle; to rob

ठगपन (nm) the work of cheating

ठट्ठा (nm) fun, jest, joke, gibe

ठठरी (nf) a skeleton; a bier

ठठेरा (nm) a brazier; a tinker

ठठोली (nf) joking, humour, fun

ठनठन-गोपाल (nm) a worthless object, a penniless-person

ठप (a) reduced; at a standstill

ठपना (v) to fix on the mind; to settle anything

ठप्पा (nm) a dice, stamp, matrix

ठर्रा (nm) a kind of cheap spirituous liquor

ठस (a) solid, thick, heavy; dull; miserly

ठसाठस (a) filled up to brim; crowded

ठहरना (v) to stop, to halt; to rest

ठहराव (nm) pause; settlement, agreement

ठहाका (nm) a peal of laughter, explosion

ठाकुर (nm) god; idol; lord; leader

ठाकुरी (nf) mastery

ठाठ (nm) splendour, pomp, magnificence; —बाट pomp, splendour

ठानना (nm) to intend, to determine, to resolve

ठिकाना (nm) place; station, destination

ठिगना (a) dwarfish, short

ठिठकना (v) to step short, to shrink, to hesitate

ठिठोलिया (nm) a jester, a buffoon, a joker

ठिठोली (nf) buffoonery, banter

ठीक (a) accurate; just; fit; right; (adv) accurately; all right

ठीक-ठाक (adv) regularly, properly

ठीकरा (nm) a broken piece of earthen ware

ठुकराना (v) to strike with the toes, to kick off; to reject contemptuously

ठुकवाना (v) to cause to be beaten

ठुड्डी (nf) chin

ठुनकना (nm) sobbing of a child; (v) to sob

ठुमकना (v) to strut, to walk with grace

ठुमका (a) dwarfish, of low stature; (nm) a strutting round in a dance

ठुसाना (v) to feed to the fill, to cause to be stuffed

ठूंठ (nm) stump, snag

ठूंठा (a) leafless; stubby

ठूंसना (v) to stuff, to be crammed

ठेंगा (nm) a thumb

ठेका (nm) support; a contract; —ठेकेबार a contractor

ठेठ (a) genuine; pure; un-mixed

ठेलना (v) to push forward, to shove

ठेलमठेल (nf) hustle and bustle; rush

ठेला (nm) push; stroke; trolley, wheel-barrow

ठेस (nf) shock;

ठोकना (v) to beat, to tap; to hammer

ठोकर (nf) blow, stroke, thump, kick

ठोढ़ी (nf) the chin

ठोस (a) dense, solid, hard; sound

ठौर (nf) place, —ठिकाना whereabouts

ड

ड the third member of the third pentad of consonants in Devnagri alphabet

डंक (nm) the sting of a wasp-bee

डंका (nm) a big drum, a kettle drum

डंगर (nm) a beast, cattle

डंठल (nm) stem, a small shoot or spring of a plant

डंड (nm) a kind of exercise; —पेलना to take exercise in the form of डंड

डंडा (nm) a bar, rod, stick

डंडी (nf) thin stick, beam of a scale

डैंसना (v) to bite; to sting

डकार (nf) belch, eructation

डकारना (v) to belch; to swallow up

डकै/त (nm) a robber, dacoit; —ती robbery, piracy

डग (nm) pace, step in walking

डगमगाना (v) to stagger, to totter, to falter

डगर (nm) path, road

डटना (v) to stop; to stay; to stand firmly

डपट (nm) rebuke, objurgation

डपटना (v) to rebuke, to shout at

डबडबाना (v) to be filled with tears

डब्बा (nm) a tin box; a railway wagon

डर (nm) terror, fear, awe, dread

डरना (v) to be frightened, to dread

डरपोक (a) timid; shy; cowardly

डरावना (a) awful, horrible, terrible

डरावा (nm) anything told to frighten

डाँट (nf) subjugation, intimidation

डाँटना (v) to rebuke, to chide, to browbeat

डाँडी (nf) handle, shaft, beam of a balance

डाइन (nf) a witch

डाक (nf) post, mail, dak; —खर्च postage; —खाना post-office

डाका (nm) robbery, plunder, dacoity

डाकिनी (nf) a hellcat

डाकिया (nm) a postman

डाकू (nm) a robber, bandit, dacoit

डाट (nf) a plug, a cork

डायरी (nf) a diary

डाल (nf) a branch, a bough

डालना (v) to put in, to throw

डाली (nf) a small branch

डावाँडोल (a) unsteady, wandering, fluctuating

डाह (nf) envy; jealousy; spite

डिगना (v) to deviate; to be shaken

डिबिया (nf) a small box or case

डींग (nf) boasting, bragging; —मारना to boast

डीलडौल (nm) figure, stature

डुगडुगी (nf) a small drum

डुबकी (nf) a plunge, a dip

डूबना (v) to dive, to set in the horizon, to sink

डेढ़ (a) one and a half

डेगची (nf) a kettle

डेरा (nm) dwelling, abode, a camp; tent

डैना (nm) a wing of a bird

डोम (nm) the sweeper or scavenger class among the Hindus

डोर (nf) thick cord or thread

डोरा (nm) thread, string

डोल (nm) a bucket, agitation

डोलना (v) to roam, to wander, to swing

डौल (nm) form, mode, shape, manner

ड्यौढ़ा (a) one and a half times

ड्यौढ़ी (nf) the main gate of a house

ठ

ठ the fourth member of the third pentad of consonants in Devnagri alphabet

ढंग (nm) method, mod; manner

ढकना (v) to conceal; to cover; (nm) a cover, a lid

ढकेलना (v) to push, to press against, to ram

ढकोस/ला (nm) affectedness, hypocrisy; —लेबाज़ a hypocrite, humbug

ढक्कन (nm) a cover, lid

ढब (nm) ways, manner

ढर्रा (nm) method; system; path

ढलना (v) to decline, to roll, to flow

ढलाई (nf) casting, moulding

ढलान (nm) a slope, descent

ढहना (v) to fall or tumble down; to be destroyed

ढाँचा (nm) frame; skeleton; sketch; outline

ढाँपना (v) to cover up, to conceal

ढाई (a) two and a half

ढाक (nm) the tree Butea frondosa; a war trumpet

ढाढस (nm) comfort, solace, consolation; —बँधाना to console

ढाना (v) to destroy, to pull to the ground, to demolish

ढाबा (nm) a small common hotel

ढाल (nf) buckler, shield; slope

ढलना (v) to pour out, to shape; to found

ढालू (a) descending, sloping

दिंढोरची (nm) a public crier, one who proclaims by beat of drum

दिंढोरा (nm) proclamation; —पीटना to proclaim aloud

ढिठाई (nf) impudence, pertness, impertinence

ढिबरी (nf) an earthen lamp

ढिलाई (nf) looseness, sluggishness, laziness

ढीठ (a) impudent, pert

ढीला (a) loose; sluggish; —ढाला loose; sluggish

ढुलमुल (a) unsteady; vacillating

ढुलकना (v) to roll down, to let fall

ढूंढना (v) to investigate, to search

ढेर (nm) pile; heap; hoard; lump; (a) abundant, plenty

ढेला (nm) a clod; a lump of earth

ढोंग (nm) trick; fraud, deceit

ढोंगी (nm) deceitful, fraudulent, impostor

ढोना (v) to carry; to bear on head or shoulders; to maintain

ढोर (nm) cattle

ढोल (nm) a drum, a kettledrum

ढोलक (nf) a small drum

ण

ण the fifth member of the third pentad of consonants in Devnagri alphabet

त

त the first member of the fourth pentad of consonants in Devnagri alphabet

तंग (a) narrow; tight; troubled; scarce

तंगदस्त (a) poor

तंगदस्ती (nf) poverty, miserliness

तंगी (nf) tightness; want; trouble; poverty

तंडुल (nm) rice

तंतु (nm) tendril; thread, yarn

तंतुवादक (*nm*) one who plays on a stringed musical instrument

तंतुवाय (*nm*) a weaver of cloth

तंत्र (*nm*) thread, filament; system; technique

तंत्रिका (*nf*) nerve

तंत्री (*nf*) strings or wires which are used in musical instruments

तंदुरुस्त (*a*) free from illness, healthy

तंदुरुस्ती (*nf*) good health, healthiness

तंदूर (*nm*) an oven

तंदूरी (*a*) fried in an oven

तंद्रा (*nf*) sleepiness, drowsiness; lassitude

तंद्रालु (*a*) drowsy, sluggish, sleepy

तंबाकू (*nm*) tobacco

तंबू (*nm*) a tent

तंबूर (*nm*) a kind of a small drum

तंबूरची (*nm*) one who plays on a Turkish guitar

तंबूरा (*nm*) a Turkish guitar

तंबोली (*nm*) the man who sells betel leaves

तअज्जुब (*nm*) wonder, astonishment

तअल्लुक़ (*nm*) relation; connection between things

तक (*ind*) till, until, upto, for, as long as

तकदीर (*nf*) fate, destiny, luck

तकना (*v*) to gaze at, to stare at, to look at

तकरार (*nf*) dispute, altercation; quarrel

तक़रीबन (*ind*) nearly, approximately

तक़रीर (*nf*) speech, lecture

तकला (*nm*) the spindle of a spinning wheel

तकली (*nf*) a bobbin of cotton

तकलीफ़ (*nf*) affliction; difficulty, distress

तकल्लुफ़ (*nm*) formality, conventionality

तक़सीम (*nf*) distribution; division

तक़ाज़ा (*nm*) demand; importunity

तकिया (*nm*) a pillow, cushion

तकिया-कलाम (*nm*) the favourite phrase which a man is habituated to use repeatedly in his speech

तकियादार (*nm*) the Mohammedan Fakir who dwells in a तकिया

तक्र (*nm*) butter milk

तक्षक (*nm*) one of the eight principal serpents

तक्षण (*nm*) wood or stone modelling pattern

तक्षणी (*nf*) a carpenter's jackplane, long plane

तक्षशिला (*nf*) an ancient city of India

तख़्त (*nm*) a royal seat, throne; a seat made of planks

तख़्ता (*nm*) a board; plank;

rack

तख्ती (*nf*) a small plank; a school boys' board to write on

तगड़ा (*a*) robust, strong, sturdy, powerful

तगड़ी (*nf*) a gold or silver chain worn round the waist

तगमा (*nm*) a medal

तजना (*v*) to leave, to quit, to give up

तजुरबा (*nm*) test, trial; experience; experiment

तजुरबेकार (*a*) experienced

तट (*nm*) bank; shore

तटस्थ (*a*) indifferent; neutral; —ता neutrality

तड़क-भड़क (*nm*) tawdriness, pompous exhibition

तड़का (*nm*) dawn, peep of day, early morning

तड़प (*nf*) throbbing, palpi-tation, fury

तड़पना (*v*) to flutter, to palpitate; to writhe in pain

ततैया (*nf*) a wasp

तत्काल (*adv*) instantly, immediately

तत्कालीन (*a*) contemporary

तत्क्षण (*adv*) at the same time, instantly

तत्त्व (*nm*) essence; element; principle; truth

तत्त्वज्ञ (*nm*) a philosopher, a metaphysician

तत्त्वज्ञान (*nm*) knowledge of the divine, philosophy

तत्त्वत: (*ind*) essentially, in essence

तत्त्वदृष्टि (*nf*) intuition, inner sight

तत्त्वप्रकाश (*nm*) superficial knowledge of the supreme soul

तत्त्वभाषी (*a*) one who describes the real facts

तत्त्वशास्त्र (*nm*) metaphysics

तत्त्वावधान (*nm*) investigation of true knowledge, under the auspices of

तत्पर (*a*) ready, engaged; clever; —ता readiness, alertness

तत्र (*adv*) there, at that place

तथा (*ind*) and, so, thus

तथाकथित (*a*) so-called

तथापि (*ind*) too, nevertheless, also

तथाविध (*adv*) in that manner

तथ्य (*nm*) truth, reality, fact

तदनंतर (*adv*) afterwards, here-after

तद्नुसार (*ind*) accordingly

तदबीर (*nf*) arrangement, method; effort

तदर्थ (*a*) ad hoc

तन (*nm*) body

तनख्वाह (*nf*) pay, salary

तनाव (*nm*) tension; strain

तनिक (*a*) slight, little, small

तप (*nm*) devotion, penance, religious austerity

तपन (*nf*) warmth, heat, burning

तपना (*v*) to glow; to be heated;

to burn with grief

तपस्या (*nf*) penance, austerity, devotion

तपाक (*nm*) warmth

तपिश (*nf*) mental anguish; heat

तपेदिक (*nf*) tuberculosis

तफ़्तीश (*nf*) an investigation, probe

तफ़रीह (*nf*) recreation, fun

तफ़सील (*nf*) details; particulars

तब (*adv*) then, at that time; afterwards

तबका (*nm*) a class; a group

तबदी/ल (*a*) altered; changed; —ली change

तबाह (*a*) destroyed, ruined

तबाही (*nf*) ruin, destruction

तबियत (*nf*) disposition; temperament; nature

तबेला (*nm*) a stable

तभी (*adv*) at the same moment, on this account

तमंचा (*nm*) a small musket; a pistol

तमग़ा (*nm*) a royal charter, a medal

तमतमाना (*v*) to grow red in the face owing to heat of Sun or wrath

तमतमाहट (*nf*) ardour, heat

तमन्ना (*nf*) an aspiration, longing

तमाचा (*nm*) a slap

तमाम (*a*) whole, entire, complete

तमाशबीन (*nm*) an onlooker, a spectator, a sightseer

तमाशबीनी (*nf*) luxury, libertinism

तमाशा (*nm*) spectacle, show; sport

तमीज़ (*nf*) sense; good manner's

तय (*a*) settled; completed; fixed

तरंग (*nf*) ripple, wave, billow

तरंगिणी (*nf*) a river

तरंगी (*a*) unsteady, whimsical, fantastic

तर (*a*) wet; damp

तरकश (*nm*) a quiver

तरकारी (*nf*) cooked or green vegetable

तरकीब (*nf*) way; tact

तरक्क़ी (*nf*) increase; promotion; progress

तरखान (*nm*) a carpenter

तरजीह (*nf*) priority, preference

तरणि (*nf*) a boat, a raft or float

तरफ़ (*nf*) direction, side, quarter; —दार a follower; —दारी partisanship, bias

तरबूज़ (*nm*) a water-melon

तरल (*a*) liquid, fluid; —ता fluidity

तरस (*nm*) pity, mercy; —खाना to feel pity for

तरसना (*v*) to long, to desire

तरसाना (*v*) to cause to long or desire

तरह (*nf*) kind, sort

तराई (*nf*) marshy ground, a

valley

तराजू (nf) a scale, a balance

तराना (nm) a kind of song

तरावट (nf) moisture, humidity, coolness

तराश (nf) trimming, cutting; paring

तराशना (v) to trim, to cut, to clip; to pare

तरीक़ा (nm) mode, manner; custom; method

तरु (nm) a tree

तरुण (a) young; adult

तरुणाई (nf) youth, puberty

तरुणी (nf) a young woman

तर्क (nm) reasoning; argument; —वितर्क argumentation

तर्जनी (nf) the fore-finger

तल (nm) surface; bottom; under part

तल/ख़ (a) pungent, bitter; acrid; —ख़ी acridity; bitterness

तलछट (nf) sediment; —संबंधी sedimentary or dregs

तलना (v) to fry

तलब (nf) wages, salary; demand

तलवा (nf) the sole of the foot

तलवार (nf) sabre; a sword

तलहटी (nf) a vale, a valley

तला (nm) bottom; sole of a shoe; support

तलाक़ (nm) a divorce; —शुदा divorced

तलाश (nf) search; investigation

तलाशी (nf) a search

तल्ला (nm) floor; a storey; sole of a shoe

तल्लीन (a) deeply involved; immersed; identified with

तवा (nm) the round plate of iron on which bread is baked, a griddle

तवाज़ा (nf) respect, hospitality, entertainment

तवायफ़ (nf) a harlot, a prostitute; a dancing girl

तशरीफ़ (nf) a term signifying respect; —रखना welcome (your) coming

तश्तरी (nf) a tray; a small plate

तसकीन (nf) satisfaction; consolation

तसदीक़ (nf) attestation; verification

तसल्ली (nf) comfort, solace; satisfaction

तसबीर (nm) portrait, a picture

तस्कर (nf) a thief, a smuggler

तस्करी (nf) the act of smuggling

तह (nf) fold; layer; bottom; —ख़ाना a cell

तहकीक़ात (nm) investigation, enquiry, inquest

तहज़ीब (nf) civilization

तहमद (nf) loin cloth

तहरीर (nf) style of writing, a testimonial

तहलका (nm) agitation, havoc

तहस-नसह (a) destroyed, ruined

तहसील (nf) the office or court

of a Tehsildar, a part of a district

ताँगा (*nm*) a tonga

तांडव (*nm*) a dance, dancing of Shiva

ताँता (*nm*) a row; series

तांबा (*nm*) copper

तांबूल (*nm*) betel leaf

ताई (*nf*) paternal (elder) uncle's wife, aunt

ताईद (*nf*) support, confirmation

ताऊ (*nm*) father's elder brother, uncle

ताकझाँक (*nf*) gazing at intervals

ताकत (*nf*) strength, force, might, power; —वर powerful

ताकना (*v*) to see; to stare at; to view

ताकि (*ind*) therefore, so that

ताकीद (*nf*) instruction

तागा (*nm*) thread

ताज (*nm*) crown; the Taj

ताज़गी (*nf*) greenness; freshness, health

ताज़ा (*a*) new; fresh; green

ताज़िया (*nm*) a model of the tomb of Imam Husain which is buried by Mohammedans under the earth in the Moharram festival

ताज्जुब (*nm*) astonishment, wonder

ताड़ (*nm*) the palmyra tree

ताड़ना (*nf*) whipping, admonition, rebuke; (*v*) to whip; to guess

ताड़ित (*a*) beaten, rebuked, chided

ताड़ी (*nf*) the juice of a toddy tree

तात (*nm*) father; a revered person; dear and younger

तात्कालिक (*a*) immediate, quick

तात्पर्य (*nm*) sense, meaning

तात्त्विक (*a*) essential, real; elementary

तादात्म्य (*nm*) similarity, identity

तावाद (*nf*) number

तानना (*v*) to expand, to stretch; to spread

ताना (*nm*) a taunt

ताना (*nm*) the warp; loom for weaving carpet; —बाना warp and woof

तानाशाह (*nm*) a dictator

तानाशाही (*nf*) dictatorship

ताप (*nm*) warmth, heat; fever; —मान temperature; —मापी a thermometer

तापना (*v*) to warm oneself, to heat

तापस (*nm*) one who performs religious austerities

ताबड़तोड़ (*adv*) incessantly, successively

ताबूत (*nm*) a coffin, a bier

तार (*nm*) thread; wire; chord

तारक (*nm*) a planet, a star; the pupil of the eye; the name of a demon

तारकोल (nm) coal-tar, tarmac

तारघर (nm) a telegraph office

तारतम्य (nm) proportion, comparative value; accordance

तारना (v) to free, to deliver from sin

तारा (nm) a star; pupil of the eye

तारापथ (nm) the sky

तारामंडल (nm) the starry sphere, firmament

तारिका (nf) cine-actress

तारीख़ (nf) a date; an appointed day; —वार datewise

तारीफ़ (nf) praise; introduction

तारुण्य (nm) youth

तार्किक (nm) a logician, a metaphysician

ताल (nm) musical measure, rhythm, tune; a pond

तालमेल (nm) concordance; co-ordination

ताला (nm) a lock; —बंदी a lock-out

तालाब (nm) a tank, pool

तालिका (nf) key; a list; table

ताली (nf) a key; clapping of hands together

तालीम (nf) education

तालु (nm) the palate

ताल्लुक (nm) relationship, connection

ताल्लुकेदार (nm) a landlord

ताव (nm) a sheet of paper; heat; anger

तावीज़ (nm) an amulet

ताश (nm) playing cards

तिकड़म (nf) manipulation; unfair means

तिकोन (nm) a triangle

तिकोना (a) triangular

तिक्त (a) pungent; acrid

तिगुना (a) triple, three-times

तिजारत (nf) trade, commerce

तिजोरी (nf) an iron safe

तितर-बितर (a) dispersed; diffused; scattered

तितली (nf) butterfly, lady-bird; glamour girl

तिथि (nf) a date

तिनका (nm) a bit of dry grass, straw

तिपाई (nf) a three-legged table, tripod, teapoy

तिबारा (adv) a third time

तिमंज़िला (a) three-storied building

तिमाही (a) quarterly

तिमिर (nm) darkness; a disease of the eye in which objects are not clearly seen

तिरंगा (a) tricolour; (nm) the tri-colour flag

तिरछ (a) transverse, bent, crooked, oblique

तिरना (v) to float on water

तिरपाल (nm) tarred canvas, tarpaulin

तिरस्कार (nm) disregard, disrespect; insult

तिरस्कारी (a) insulting, scorning; disregarding

तिरस्कृत (a) censured, reproached; hidden

तिराहा (nm) a junction of three roads or paths

तिल (nm) a mole; small particle; sesamum plant and its seeds

तिलकना (v) to slip

तिलचट्टा (nm) a cockroach

तिलपट्टी (nf) a kind of sweet-meat which is made of fried sesamum and treacle

तिलमिलाना (v) to dazzle; to be in the grip of impotent anger

तिलस्म (nm) miracle, wonder, spell

तिलहन (nm) oilseed

तिलांजलि (nf) oblations to the dead with sesamum seeds and water; abandonment

तिहाई (a) one-third

तीक्ष्ण (a) sharp; keen

तीक्ष्णता (nf) severity, sharpness

तीक्ष्णदृष्टि (a) hawk-eyed

तीखा (a) harsh; sharp; pungent

तीज (nf) the third day of the each half of a lunar month

तीतर (nm) a partridge

तीन (a) three

तीमारदा/र (nm) a person attending on a patient; an attendant; —री nursing the sick and invalid person

तीर (nm) bank; arrow

तीरंदाज़ (nm) an archer

तीर्थ (nm) a sacred place; a place of pilgrimage; —यात्रा pilgrimage; —यात्री a pilgrim

तीव्र (a) pungent; fast; high; sharp

तीसमारखाँ (nm) a very brave person (said ironically), a sham hero

तीसरा (a) a third

तुंग (a) lofty, high, tall; (nm) a mountain

तुक (nf) part of a song, rhyme, alliteration; —जोड़ना grotesque rhyming of verse; — बंदी poetry of an inferior or grotesque type

तुकांत (a) rhyming

तुक्का (nm) a kind of arrow which is blunt at one end; unsure means, vain bid; —लगाना to make conjecture

तुच्छ (a) trivial; contemptible; insignificant; —ता insignificance, meanness, lowness

तुड़वाना (v) to cause to be broken

तुड़ाई (nf) the work or wages for breaking a thing

तुतलाना (v) to speak indistinctly as a child, to lisp

तुमुल (a) noisy, excited, tumultuous

तुम्हारा (pron) your, yours

तुम्हीं (pron) you alone

तुम्हें (pron) to you, unto you

तुरंग (nm) a horse; mind

तुरंत (adv) rapidly, at once, quickly, soon

तुर्श (a) sour, acid; harsh

तुर्शी (nf) sourness, tartness

तुलना (nf) similarity, compari - son; (v) to be weighed; —त्मक comparative

तुला (nf) balance

तुल्य (a) like; equivalent, similar

तुल्यता (nf) parity, balance

तुषार (nm) cold, frost, thin rain

तुष्टि (nf) satisfaction, delight

तूफ़ान (nm) deluge; storm, tempest; false accusation

तूफ़ानी (a) strong, violent; quarrelsome

तूलिका (nf) a painter's brush

तृण (nm) grass, sedge

तृणकुटी (nf) thatched hamlet

तृतीय (a) the third

तृ/प्त (a) satisfied, contented, pleased; —प्ति satisfaction, gratification

तृ/षा (nf) thirst, desire, wish; —षित thirsty, desirous

तृष्णा (nf) thirst; ambition, desire

तेंदुआ (nm) a leopard

तेज (nm) glory, ardour, magni - ficence; brilliance

तेज़ (a) sharp, keen, pointed; swift; hot; smart

तेजहीन (a) spiritless; muzzy, lack-lustre

तेजपुंज (nm) stream of light

तेजपत्ता (nm) cassia, bay tree and its leaf

तेजवान् (a) glorious, energetic, strong

तेजस्विता (nf) radiance, nobility, lordliness, lustre

तेजस्वी (a) lustrous, glorious, brilliant

तेज़ाब (nm) an acid

तेज़ी (nf) pungency, sharpness, smartness; intelligence

तेरा (pron) thy, thine

तेल (nm) oil; petrol

तेली (nm) an oilman

तेवर (nm) an angry look, the eyebrow

तैनात (a) appointed, engaged

तैया/र (a) ready, prepared; ready-made; —री pre - paration, readiness

तैरना (v) to swim (for ani - mate); to float. (for inanimate)

तैराई (nf) the act of swimming

तैरा/क (a) an expert swimmer; —की swimming

तैराना (v) to cause some -one to swim

तैश (nm) anger, wrath, passion; — में आना to be provoked

तैसा (a) similar

तैसे (adv) in the same manner, accordingly

तोंद (nf) pot belly, abdomen, paunch

तो (ind) therefore; then; moreover; however

तोड़ (nm) break; rent —फोड़ (nm) breakage; sabotage

तोड़ना (v) to break; to burst, to violate; to pluck

तोतला (a) stammering, lisping

तोतलाना (v) to stutter, to lisp

तोता (nm) a parrot

तोप (nf) a cannon, a gun —खाना the place where cannon and artillery are kept; —ची a gunner

तोय (nm) water

तोल (nf) weight

तोलना (v) to balance; to weigh

तोला (nm) a weight of rupee or twelve Mashas

तोहफ़ा (nm) a gift, a present

तोहमत (nf) false accusation, calumny

तौबा (nf) solemn assertion for not doing a forbidden act in future; —करना to vow never to repeat

तौर (nm) manner, mode, way; —तरीका conduct, manners

तौलिया (nf) a towel

तौहीन (nf) disrespect; insult

त्यक्त (a) abandoned; rejected

त्यजनीय (a) liable to be abandoned

त्याग (nm) avoidance; a abandonment, forsaking

त्यागना (v) to lose, to desert

त्यागी (a) a hermit

त्यों (adv) in like manner, so like

त्योरी (nf) glance; angry look, wrinkles of the forehead

त्योहार (nm) a festival; fete

त्रसित (a) frightened, terrified; trembling

त्राण (nm) protection, shelter; security

त्राता (nm) a protector; a deliverer

त्रास (nm) fear, fright, dread; awe

त्रासदायी (a) terrifying, dreadful

त्रासदी (nf) a tragedy

त्राहि (int) save me, protector;

त्रि (a) three

त्रिकालदर्शी (nm) the omniscient one

त्रिकोण (a) triangular, (nm) a triangle

त्रिगुण (nm) an aggregate of the three principal qualities of human nature

त्रिपथगामिनी (nf) an epithet of the river Ganga

त्रिफला (nf) a mixture of three kinds of myrobalan

त्रिभुज (nm) a triangle

त्रिशूल (nm) a trident

त्रिया (nf) a female; —चरित्र the wiles of a female

त्रुटि (nf) diminution, imperfection; mistake

त्रेता (nm) the second Yuga

त्रैकालिक (a) eternal, permanent

त्रैमासिक (a) quarterly, three-monthly

त्वक् (nm) the bark of a tree; skin

त्वचा (nf) the skin

त्वरा (nf) haste, quickness,

speed   quickly

त्वरित (*a*) swift; (*adv*) hastily,

थ

थ the second member of the fourth pentad of consonants in Devnagri alphabet

थंबा, थंभ (*nm*) a pillar; support or prop

थकना (*v*) to be wearied, to be tired; to be stagnant

थकान (*nf*) weariness, tiredness, fatigue

थका-माँदा (*a*) weary, tired

थकावट (*nf*) fatigue, exhaustion, weariness

थक्का (*nm*) lump; clot

थन (*nm*) udder, nipple

थपकना (*v*) to tap, to pat, to strike gently with the palm

थपकी (*nf*) a pat, a tap

थपथपाना (*v*) to tap, to dab

थपेड़ा (*nm*) a slap; a box; blow, stroke

थप्पड़ (*nm*) a slap, clap

थमना (*v*) to stay; to stop; to have patience

थरथर (*a*) shuddering, trembling

थरथराना (*v*) to quiver, to tremble, to shake

थरथराहट (*nf*) shivering, trembling

थर्मामीटर (*nm*) a thermometer

थर्राना (*v*) to shake, to shudder, to tremble

थल (*nm*) a dry land

थलथल (*a*) undulating owing to flabbiness of flesh

थाती (*nf*) a thing given in charge, a trust; capital

थान (*nm*) a long piece of cloth of fixed length

थाना (*nm*) a police-station

थानेदार (*nm*) the officer in-charge of a police-station

थामना (*v*) to assist; to grasp; to hold; to prop

थाल (*nm*) a large flat dish; basin

थाली (*nf*) a dish, tray, a plate

थाह (*nm*) depth of water; bottom, limit

थिगली (*nf*) a patch which is used for mending holes in cloths

थिरकना (*v*) to dance with expressive action and gestures

थू (*nf*) the sound made in spitting; (*ind*) word of contempt

थूक (*nm*) spittle; saliva

थूकना (v) to spittle, to spit; to curse

थूथन (nm) the snout of an animal

थैला (nm) a bag, a wallet; a purse

थैली (nf) a small bag; a purse

द

द the third member of the fourth pentad of consonants in Devnagri alphabet

दंग (a) astonished, wonder-struck

दंगल (nm) a wrestling

दंगा (nm) mutiny, confusion; disturbance; riot; —दंगेबाज़ quarrelsome

दंड (nm) punishment; a staff; a stick; —विधि the law of crimes

दंत (nm) a tooth; —कथा a legend

दंपती (nm) a (married) couple, husband and wife

दं/भ (nm) boast, pious fraud, deceit; —भी vain-glorious, conceited

दंश (nm) a sting, biting

दकियान/स (a) conservative person; —सी conservative idea or thinking

दक्खिन/न (nm) the South; —नी southern

दक्ष (a) able; expert; astute, clever; —ता readiness, expertness

दक्षिण (nm) the South; right; —पंथी rightist

दक्षिणा (nf) reward, present given to Brahman

दख़ल (nm) interference; authority, possession

दगा (nm) deception; treachery; —बाज़ deceitful, fraudulent

दगाबाज़ी (nf) treachery, cheating

दढ़ियल (a) having a long beard

दत्तक (पुत्र) (nm) an adopted son

दत्तचित (a) concentrating one's mind in performing a work, fully attentive to do a work

दादिहाल (nm) paternal grand father's family

दधि (nm) curd

दनादन (adv) non-stop

दफ़नाना (v) to entomb; to bury

दफ़ा (nf) one time, one turn — होना (v) to go to hell

दफ़ादार (*nm*) an official in the Indian Army

दफ़्तर (*nm*) an office

दफ़्तरी (*nm*) one who is employed in an office for ruling registers; a book-binder

दबंग (*a*) influential; fearless, overbearing

दबकाना (*v*) to check, to threaten

दबदबा (*nm*) state; dignity, sway

दबना (*v*) to be pressed down, to go down, to yield

दब जाना (*v*) to with-draw, to retire

दबाव (*nm*) pressure, compulsion; repression

दबोचना (*v*) to subdue, to seize suddenly

दब्बू (*a*) tame

दम (*nm*) life; breath

दमक (*nf*) brilliance; glimmer

दमकना (*v*) to shine, to glisten, to glow

दमकल (*nf*) a water pump, the fire brigade, fire engine

दमदमा (*nm*) a mound of sand used in warfare, grandeur

दमदार (*a*) strong, enduring; sharp

दमन (*nm*) subdual, sup-pression, subjugation

दमनशील (*a*) fit to be subdued, restrianable

दमा (*nm*) asthma

दमित (*a*) repressed, suppressed

दयनीय (*a*) inspiring pity, pitiable

दया (*nf*) tenderness, affection, kindness

दयाकर (*a*) generous, benevo-lent, pitiful

दयादृष्टि (*nf*) favour, kindness

दयावान् (*nm*) kind-hearted, merciful

दयानत (*nf*) genuineness; honesty; —वार genuine; honest; —दारी honesty

दयानिधान (*nm*) one who is very generous; an epithet of God

दयार्द्र (*a*) tender-hearted; charitable

दयालु (*a*) tender, kind-hearted, a kind

दर (*nf*) price, rate; (*nm*) door; —असल in reality, in fact; —दर door to door, place to place

दरकार (*a*) necessary, needed; (*nf*) necessity

दरख्वास्त (*nf*) application, petition; request

दरख़्त (*nm*) a tree

दरगाह (*nf*) a doorsill, a shrine; holyplace; tomb

दरबान (*nm*) a porter, a door-keeper, watchman

दरबार (*nm*) hall of audience, a royal court

दरबारदारी (*nf*) paying visit to a person very often and flattering to please him

दरबारी (*nm*) a courtier

दरमियान (*nm*) a middle; (*adv*) among, during, between

दरमियानी (*nm*) a middle man, an umpire

दरवाज़ा (*nm*) door; doorleaves

दरवेश (*nm*) a beggar, dervish

दराज़ (*nf*) the compartment of a box, a drawer; (*a*) long

दरार (*nf*) leak; gap

दरिंदा (*nm*) a carnivorous, meat-eating beast

दरिद्र (*a*) poor, needy; indigent, poverty-stricken; of low qualities

दरिद्रता (*nf*) poverty, wretched-ness

दरिद्रनारायण (*a*) the have-not; the poor

दरिया (*nm*) a river; — दिल liberal, large-hearted

दरियाफ़्त (*a*) known; (*nm*) an enquiry

दरी (*nf*) a cotton carpet

दर्ज (*a*) entered, recorded

दर्जन (*nm*) a dozen

दर्जा (*nm*) degree; a class; rank; gradation

दर्जी (*nm*) a tailor

दर्द (*nm*) pain, ache; —नाक painful, tragic

दर्प (*nm*) pride, arrogance, boastfulness

दर्रा (*nm*) a valley, a cleft between hills

दर्शक (*nm*) spectator, a looker

on; visitor

दर्शन (*nm*) seeing, prospect, looking, sight; philosophy

दर्शनीय (*a*) worth seeing, agreeable, handsome, beautiful

दर्शित (*a*) exposed to view

दल (*nm*) leaf; a party

दलबल (*nm*) an army of followers and supporters

दलदल (*nm*) fen, swamp, marsh, mire

दला/ल (*nm*) tout, a broker; an agent; — ली brokerage

दलित (*a*) rent, broken, torn, depressed

दलिया (*nf*) coarse meal, hominy

दलील (*nf*) an argument, proof, plea

दवा (*nf*) medicine, drug; remedy; —ख़ाना a clinic, dispensary; —दारू medical treatment; medicine

दवात (*nf*) an inkpot

दशक (*nm*) a decade

दशमलव (*nm*) a decimal fraction

दशा (*nm*) state, condition; degree

दस (*a*) ten; (*nf*) the number ten

दस्त (*nm*) the hand; loose faeces

दस्तक (*nf*) a tapping noise made with hands, a knock at the door

दस्तकार (nm) craftsman, an artisan

दस्तकारी (nf) handicraft

दस्तख़त (nm) signature

दस्ता (nm) handle of an instrument, bunch of flowers, a small band of soldiers

दस्ताना (nm) glove, gauntlet

दस्तावर (a) purgative

दस्तावेज़ (nm) a note of hand; a document; deed

दस्तूर (nm) custom, fashion; regulation

दहकना (v) to burn with a red hot flame, to blaze

दहन (nm) burning, combustion; — शील combustible

दहलना (v) to tremble, to shake, to be terrorised

दहलीज़ (nf) a corridor, gallery, threshold

दहशत (nf) fear, dread; terror; panic

दहाड़ना (v) to roar; to weep loudly, to shout aloud

दही (nm) curd

दहेज (nm) dowry

दाँत (nm) a tooth

दांपत्य (a) pertaining to husband and wife; (nm) conjugal relations

दाँव (nm) a stake, a bet, a wager

दाई (a) pertaining to the right

दाई (nf) a nurse; a midwife

दाख़िल (a) entered; admitted; produced

दाख़िला (nm) entry; admission

दाग़ (nm) scar; speck; stigma

दाग़ (nm) act of burning

दाग़ना (v) to burn, to brand; to fire a gun

दाढ़ (nf) jaw-tooth, grinder

दाढ़ी (nf) chin; beard

दाता (nm) a donor, benefactor, a generous man

दातुन (nm) a native tooth-brush (made of a spray of a tree)

दाद (nf) shingles, ring worm; praise

दान (nm) the act of giving alms; charity, donation

दान-धर्म (nm) almsgiving; charity

दान-पात्र (nm) a fit person for the bestowal of alms

दानशील (a) charitable, liberal bountiful

दान/व (nm) giant; demon; — वीय giant-like; demonic

दाना (nm) grain; food; seed; corn; — पानी food; seed;

दानी (a & ' nm) charitable, generous, liberal

दाब (nf) pressure; force; control

दाबना (v) to suppress, to press down

दाम (nm) price; value; cost

दामन (nm) the skirt of a garment

दामाद (nm) a son-in-law

दामिनी (nf) the lightning; an ornament for the head

दाय (nm) nuptial present, inheritance, heritage

दायरा (nm) a ring; a circle; range

दायाँ (a) right

दायाधिकार (nm) heritage

दायित्व (nm) responsibility; liability

दारा (nf) wife

दारुण (a) horrible; dreadful; difficult

दारू (nf) medicine, drug; liquor

दारोग़ा (nm) a sub-inspector of police

दार्शनिक (nm) a metaphysician, a philosopher

दाल (nf) pulse

दालान (nm) a lobby; verandah

दाव (nm) chance; stake; a trick; —पेंच strategical moves

दावत (nf) banquet; feast; invitation for a feast

दावा (nm) suit; claim

दावात (nf) an inkpot

दावानल (nm) forest conflagration

दावेदार (nm) a claimant

दास (nm) servant; slave, helot, —ता vassalage, enslavement; —प्रथा slavery

दास्तान (nf) account, narration, story, tale

दाह (nm) inflammation; burning, heat

दाहकर्म (nm) cremation, burning of the dead

दाहिना (a) right

दिक् (nf) quarter, direction

दिक्कत (nf) trouble; difficulty, perplexity

दिक्सूचक (nm) a compass

दिखना (v) to be seen

दिखाऊ (a) presentable, worth seeing, showy

दिखावट (nf) exhibition; show, display

दिखावा (nm) pomp, ostentation, show

दिग्an allomorph of दिक् —विजय the world conquest; —विजयी conqueror of whole of the world

दिग्दर्श/क (nm) a director; —न survey; something exhibited as a sample

दिन (nm) day, time; -ब-दिनday by day

दिनचर्या (nf) daily routine

दिन-भर (adv) all day long

दिनमान (nm) the length of a day

दिनांक (nm) date

दिमाग़ (nm) mind, brain; pride, arrogance

दिमाग़ी (a) proud, haughty; pertaining to mind, mental

दिया (nm) a lamp; (a) given

दियासलाई (nf) a match box; a match stick

दिल (nm) mind; heart;

courage; spirit; —कश attractive; —दार beloved; corageous

दिलगीर (a) sorry, afflicted

दिलचस्प (a) attractive, beautiful, interesting

दिलचस्पी (nf) attractiveness, interest

दिलचोर (a) lazy, slow in doing a work; a lover

दिलजला (a) greatly afflicted

दिलदरिया (a) bountiful, liberal

दिलाना (v) to cause to be given

दिलावर (a) brave, courageous, intrepid

दिलासा (nm) comfort, consolation, encouragement, solace

दिली (a) pertaining to the heart, hearty; sincere

दिलेर (a) proud, courageous

दिलेरी (nf) daring; boldness; bravery

दिल्लगी (nf) jest, joke, fun; —बाज़ a jester, a jocular

दिवंगत (a) deceased, late

दिवस (nm) a day

दिवाकर (nm) the Sun

दिवाचर (nm) a bird

दिवानिश (nf) day and night

दिवावसान (nm) evening, close or decline of day

दिवाला (nm) insolvency, bankruptcy

दिवालिया (a) a bankrupt, insolvent

दिव्य (a) heavenly, divine, supernatural

दिव्यता (nf) brilliancy, godliness; beauty

दिव्य/दृष्टि (nf) supernatural power

दिशा (nf) direction, way; region, quarter

दीक्षा (nf) investiture of sacred thread; initiation

दीक्षित (a) initiated, consecrated

दीखना (v) to look, to appear

दीदार (nm) sight, interview, meeting or conference

दीन (a) badly off, poor, miserable; (nm) religion

दीनता (nf) distress, want, poverty

दीन-दुनिया (nf) this world and the next world

दीनबंधु (nm) friend of the poor; (nm) an epithet of God

दीनार (nm) a gold coin used in Arabic countries, denarius

दीपक (nm) a lamp, a light

दीपगृह (nm) a lighthouse

दीप्त (a) luminous, radiant, bright

दीप्ति (nf) light, flash, lustre; splendour

दीप्तिमान (a) shining, glittering

दीमक (nf) white ant, termite

दीर्घ (a) large; long; wide; huge; —सूत्री a slow coach; dilatory

दीर्घायु (a) long lived, of long

दीवट (nf) a lamp-stand

दीवान (nm) a royal court, a court-minister

दीवाना (a) mad, insane; —पन insanity, madness

दीवानी (nf) the post of minister; (a) civil (court)

दीवार (nf) a wall

दीवारगीर (nm) a bracket fixed in a wall for keeping articles on it

दीवाल (nf) a wall

दुंदुभि, दुंदुभी (nm) a kettle-drum

दु:ख (nm) suffering, distress; sorrow, unhappiness

दु:खदायक (a) troublesome, painful, vexatious

दु:खमय (a) full of trouble or pain

दु:खांत (a) ending in sorrow

दु:खात्मक (a) lugubrious; tragic

दु:खित (a) unhappy, sorrowful

दु:खी (a) sad, sorrowful, unhappy

दु:शील (a) wicked, of bad character

दु:सह (a) intolerable, un-bearable

दु:साध्य (a) arduous, difficult, difficult to do

दु:साहस (nm) a futile enter-prise, rashness

दु:साहसी (a) bold; rash, arrogant

दु:स्वप्न (nm) a bad dream, a nightmare

दु:स्वभाव (nm) evil nature, wickedness

दु an allomorph of दो used as the first member in compound words — गुना double; —तरफ़ा two-sided; —नाली double-barrelled; —पहर noon, mid-day; —बारा a second time; — भाषिया an interpreter; —मंज़िला double-storeyed; —मुँह double mouthed; —रंगा two-coloured

दुआ (nf) blessings

दुकान (nf) a shop; —दार a shop-keeper, a seller; —दारी the business of shopkeeping

दुखड़ा (nm) description of one's sufferings, trouble

दुखाना (v) to trouble, to inflict pain; to torement

दुखिया (a) afflicted with pain, troubled; —रा ill, unwell

दुतकार (nf) reproof; reprimand; —ना (v) to reprove, to show contempt

दुधमुँहा (nm & a) still feeding on mother's milk; an infant

दुधारू (nf) yielding much milk

दुनिया (nf) people; the world; —दार worldlywise; —दारी worldliness

दुनियावी (a) wordly

दुबला (a) weak, lean, gaunt, thin; —पतला lean and thin

दुम (nf) tail; end

दुरभिसंधि (nf) a secret plot, stratagem

दुराग्रह (nm) prejudice, wilful-
ness, prejudgement

दुराग्रही (a) grumpy, mulish,
prejudicial

दुरा/चरण (nm) villainy,
misbehaviour, bad conduct;
—चार crime, misconduct;
—चारी (a) wicked

दुरात्मा (a) (a) vile, wicked

दुराव (nm) trick, concealment;
reservation

दुराशय (nm) evil intention;
(a) wicked, vicious

दुरुपयोग (nm) perversion,
abuse, misapplication

दुरुस्त (a) fit, proper, just,
correct

दुरुस्ती (nf) exactitude,
propriety, fitness

दुरूह (a) difficult to underst-
and, hidden, obscure

दुर्गंध (nf) bad or offensive
smell; stink

दुर्ग (nm) castle, fort; citadel

दुर्गति (nf) poverty, misfortune,
meanness

दुर्गम (a) inaccessible, out of
the way, deep, difficult

दुर्गुण (nm) flaw; defect,
blemish, fault

दुर्घटना (nf) tragedy, accident;
misadventure

दुर्जन (nm) a rascal, wicked
person, mischief-maker

दुर्जेय (a) difficult to be subdued, indomitable, in-
conquerable

दुर्जित (a) wicked, miserable

दुर्द/म (a) irrepressible;
unyielding; difficult to
subdue; —मनीय impregn-
able; —म्य difficult to be
subdued

दुर्दशा (nf) adversity, plight,
misfortune, calamity

दुर्दिन (nm) bad weather,
cloudy or rainy day; a bad
time

दुर्दैव (nm) ill-luck, misfortune,
a mishap

दुर्घर्ष (a) difficult to subdue,
invincible

दुर्नि/वार (a) unrestrainable;
—वार्य irrepressible;
inevitable

दुर्नीति (nf) bad policy, injustice, evil behaviour

दुर्ब/ल (a) infirm, faint, slight,
weak; —लता thinness,
feebleness

दुर्बुद्धि (a) foolish, senseless,
evil-minded

दुर्बोध (a) difficult to be understood, hard to conceive

दुर्भाग्य (nm) ill-luck, mis-
chance, tragedy

दुर्भाव (nm) malice, ill-temper,
bad conduct

दुर्भिक्ष (nm) scarcity, dearth,
famine

दुर्भेद्य (a) unable to be
penetrated, impregnable

दुर्लभ (a) scarce, rare, difficult
to be attained

दुर्वचन (*nm*) abuse, reproach

दुर्व्यवस्था (*nf*) mismanagement

दुर्व्यवहार (*nm*) bad treatment, misconduct; misuse

दुर्व्यसन (*nm*) dissipation, evil habit

दुविधा (*nf*) fix, dilemma

दुश्चरित्र (*nm*) an evil purpose, misconduct; (*a*) bad conduct, deprave

दुश्म/न (*nm*) foe, enemy; —नी animus, hostility, enmity

दुष्कर (*a*) difficult to be performed, impossible, arduous

दुष्कर्म (*nm*) sin, wrong, vice

दुष्ट (*a*) bad, mean, wicked sly, faulty; (*nm*) a rascal, scamp, villain

दुष्टता (*nf*) knavery, guilt, improperiety, wickedness

दुष्टात्मा (*a*) malicious; (*nm*) a very wicked person

दुष्प्राप्य (*a*) difficult to be attained, rare

दुस्तर (*a*) difficult to cross, insuperable, impassable

दुहना (*v*) to milk; to squeeze, to extract the essence of

दुहरा (*a*) double-folded; dual, two-fold

दुहराना (*v*) to do over again; to repeat; to revise

दुहिता (*nf*) a daughter

दूत (*nm*) legate, messenger, envoy

दूतावास (*nm*) residence of a foreign embassy

दूध (*nm*) milk; juice of certain plants

दूधिया (*a*) milky; white as milk; (*nm*) an opal

दूभर (*a*) arduous; difficult

दूरदर्श (*a*) prudent, far-sighted

दूर (*adv & a*) away, aloof, fro, distant; —गामी gone afar or away; —दर्शक यंत्र a field-glass, a telescope; —दर्शिता prudence, far-sightedness; —बीन a telescope; —संचार telecommunication

दूरी (*nf*) distance; separation

दूल्हा (*nm*) a bridegroom; a husband

दूषण (*nm*) defect, flaw, calumny

दूषित (*a*) corrupted, defield, sullied

दूसरा (*a*) other, second, another; next

दृढ़ (*a*) hard, firm, iron-bound, powerful

दृश्य (*nm*) a sight, view, scene; (*a*) visible

दृश्यमान (*a*) seen, visible

दृष्टांत (*nm*) illustration, citation, instance

दृष्टि (*nf*) seeing; sight; vision; view; —कोण point of view; —गोचर visible, perceptible; —पात glance, look; —हीन blind

देखना (*v*) to look, to see, to behold; to observe; to view

देखभाल (*nf*) maintenance; care; supervision

देख-रेख (*nf*) supervision; care, guidance

देन (*nf*) giving; gift; a prize; —दार a debtor; —दारी indebtedness; due

देना (*v*) to grant; to give, to afford; to confer

दे/र (*nf*) delay; —री suspension, delay

देव (*nm*) a deity, a respectable person, god; a demon; —दूत an angel, a divine messenger; —स्थान a temple

देव/ता (*nm*) deity, god; —त्व godliness

देवर (*nm*) husband's younger brother, brother-in-law

देवरानी (*nf*) wife of the younger brother of a woman's husband

देवांगना (*nf*) a celestial damsel

देवालय (*nm*) paradise, the temple of a god

देश (*nm*) land; country; —ज local; native; —भक्त a patriot; —भक्ति nationalism, patriotism

देश/द्रोह (*nm*) disloyalty to one's country; —द्रोही a traitor

देशनिकाला (*nm*) banishment, exile

देशांतर (*nm*) foreign country, longitude

देशाटन (*nm*) a wandering through a country

देशी (*a*) pertaining to a country; local; native

देसावर (*nm*) marketing centre; a foreign country

देसी (*a*) native, not foreign

देह (*nf*) figure, body; person; —धारी possessing a body, corporal, —त्यागना to die; —धरना to be born

देहरी (*nf*) doorsill, the threshold

देहांत (*nm*) demise, death

देहा/त (*nm*) village; country; —ती rural, rustic

देही (*nm*) the body

दैत्य (*nm*) giant, a demon, evil spirit

दैनंदिन (*a & adv*) pertaining to each day; daily

दैनिक (*a*) daily, quatidian

दैन्य (*nm*) poverty; humbleness

दैव (*nm*) destiny, fate, fortune; —गति a supernatural occurrence, misfortune; —ज्ञ an astrologer; —योग chance; —वश luckily, haply; —वाणी the Sanskrit language

दैहिक (*a*) bodily, physical; material

दो (*a*) two; (*nm*) the number two; —गला a bastard; —टूक decisive, crystal clear; —पहर noon; midday

दोज़ख़ (*nm*) hell

दोष (*nm*) harm, blemish,

defect, guilt

दोषी (*a & nm*) a criminal, a culprit

दोषारोपण (*nm*) impeachment, charge, imputation

दोस्त (*nm*) a friend

दोस्ताना (*a*) friendly

दोस्ती (*nf*) friendship

दोहनी (*nf*) a milk pail, the act of milking a cow

दोहरा (*a*) twofold, duplicate, double

दोहराना (*v*) to double, to renew, to repeat, to fold

दोहा (*nm*) a couplet (in Hindi)

दोहित्र (*nm*) a daughter's son

दौड़ (*nf*) running; a race, gallop; —धूप hard-labour, tumult

दौड़ना (*v*) to gallop, to run, to go fast

दौना (*nm*) a plant with fragrant leaves; rosemary; a bowl made of leaves

दौर (*nm*) roaming, revaluation, round

दौरा (*nm*) circuit, tour; attack of disease

दौलत (*nf*) wealth, riches, property; —खाना a place of residence; —मंद rich, wealthy; —मंदी wealthiness

दौवारिक (*nm*) a porter, a door keeper

द्यु (*nm*) day; sky; heaven

द्युति (*nf*) glow, radiance

द्यूत (*nm*) playing at dice, gambling

द्योतक (*a*) making manifest, showing, explaining

द्रव (*nm*) fluid, a liquid

द्रवित (*a*) moved by emotion; melted

द्रव्य (*nm*) matter, substance; wealth, property

द्रष्टव्य (*a*) worthy to be seen, attractive

द्रष्टा (*nm*) one who sees, a looker on, spectator

द्रुत (*a*) swift, quick

द्रुति (*nf*) motion

द्रो/ह (*nm*) malice, hostility, rancour —ही (*a*) rancorous, malicious

द्वंद्व (*nm*) a pair; a quarrel; uproar

द्वार (*nm*) gate; door; a doorway; —पाल watchman, a door-keeper

द्वारा (*ind*) by means of, by, through

द्विज (*nm*) a twice born; a bird; a Brahman

द्वितीय (*a*) second

द्विधा (*ind*) in two ways, in two parts

द्वीप (*nm*) an island, isle

द्वे/ष (*nm*) hatred, malice, spite; —षी inimical, hostile

ध

ध the fourth member of the fourth pentad of consonants in Devnagri Alphabet

धंधलाना (v) to play a false trick, to make ostentation

धंधा (nm) occupation; business, employment; work

धँस (nm) a dip into water

धँसना (v) to be penetrated; to enter a place; to sink

धक (nf) agitation, excitement, palpitation

धकधकाहट (nf) palpitation

धकधकी (nf) palpitation

धकपकाना (v) to be frightened, to be in fear

धकापेल (nf) jostling; (adv) vigorously, non-stop

धकियाना (v) to jostle, to jerk, to elbow

धकेलना (v) to push, to thrust

धकैत (a) pushing, thrusting

धक्कम-धक्का (nm) pushing, jostling

धक्का (nm) a shove; a push, concussion, dash; shock; —देना to hustle, to jostle; to shock; —मारना to buffet; —देनेवाला jerky, knocky; —मुक्की pushing and jostling

धड़ (nm) trunk of body or tree, a torso

धड़कन (nf) pulsation, palpita-tion, throbbing

धड़कना (v) to pulsate, to throb

धड़धड़ (nf) the noise produced by a thing falling from a height, a knocking sound

धड़धड़ाना (v) to palpitate, to walk heavily and briskly

धड़ाका (nm) crash, thump, explosion

धड़ाधड़ (adv) continuously, incessantly, quickly

धड़ाम (nm) the sound which is produced by a heavy object falling on the ground

धड़ी (nf) a weight of five seers

धत् (ind) be off! a word of contempt

धतकारना (v) to drive away with contempt, to reprove

धतूर (nm) a kind of trumpet

धधक (nf) flame, heat of fire

धधकना (v) to flare, to blaze, to burn with a flame

धन (nm) treasure, wealth, riches, property; —दौलत wealth and affluence; —धान्य all round prosperity; मूल — capital; —वान wealthy; —हीन moneyless, poor

धनिक (a) rich, wealthy; (nm) a wealthy person

धनिया (nm) coriander seed

धनी (a) wealthy, rich, substantial; (nm) owner;

—मानी eminent

धनुर्धर (nm) a bowman, an archer

धनुर्विद्या (nf) archery

धनुष (nm) an arch, a bow

धन्य (a & nm) prosperous, lucky, blessed; (ind) well done! how fortunate!

धन्यवाद (nm) expression of gratitude, thanks-giving; (ind) thanks!

धब्बा (nm) spot, speck, blemish, stain, taint

धमकाना (v) to reprimand, to threaten, to intimidate

धमकी (nf) intimidation, threat, bluster; —में आना to be frightened or terrified

धमधमाहट (nm) a stumping over head, a thump

धमनी (nf) an artery; —संबंधी arterial, pertaining to artery

धमाका (nm) a bump, thud, crash; the report of a gun

धमाचौकड़ी (nf) bustle, turmoil, noise

धमाधम (a) with incessant thumping; (nf) sound of stamping on something

धर/षि —षी (nf) the earth, ground

धरती (nf) the earth, ground; the world

धरना (v) to place; to hold, to keep, to apply; (nm) picketing

धरा (nf) earth, soil, the world

धरातल (nm) the earth, area; surface of earth

धराशायी (a) razed to the ground, fallen

धरोहर (nf) trustmoney, deposit

धर्म (nm) religion; faith; duty; —ग्रंथ Holy Scriptures; —च्युत fallen from religion; —ध्वज the name of an ancient king of Mithila; —ध्वजी a hypocrite; —निरपेक्ष secular; —परायण religious, religious-minded; —युद्ध crusade; —रक्षक a protector of religion; —रत dutiful; —शास्त्र theology; —संकट a dilemma; —सुधार reformation

धर्मार्थ (a) for the sake of religion or justice, chartable

धर्मांध (a) fanatic; —ता fanaticism

धर्मात्मा (a) religious, devout

धर्मिष्ठ (a) pious, virtuous

धर्षण (nm) disrespect, attack, assault

धवल (a) clear; white; bright; beautiful

धवलता (nf) whiteness

धसक (nf) a dry cough

धसकना (v) to sink, to fear

धाँचल (nf) turmoil, disturbance, fraud

धाँचली (nf) chaos, outrage

धाँस (nf) the smell of a dry

tobacco leaf which causes constant sneezing

धाँसना (v) to cough as a horse

धाक (nf) pomp, renown, commanding

धागा (nm) thread, cord

धाता (nm) the creator, an epithet of Brahma

धातु (nf) a semen ; a mineral, a metal; root

धात्री (nf) mother; a wet nurse

धान (nm) the rice plant, paddy

धान्य (nm) a measure equal to four sesamum seeds, corn, crop

धाम (nm) a house; dwelling; seat of a diety

धार (nf) sharp edge; an edge; current; flow

धारण (nm) maintaining; holding; wearing

धारणा (nf) resolution, impression; concept, idea

धारा (nf) a current of water; stream, river; section; —प्रवाह non-stop, fluent

धार्मिक (a) virtuous, religious, holy

धार्मिकता (nf) piety, virtuousness, sanctity

धावक (nm) a harbinger

धावा (nm) quick running, incursion, assault, attack; — बोलना to launch an attack

धावित (a) cleansed, purified

धिक (int) a word denoting blame, censure, fie !

shame !

धिक्कार (nm) contempt, repulse, curse, repudiation

धिक्कारना (v) to disdain, to curse, to upbraid

धीमा (a) tardy, slow, mild, gentle; —चलने वाला tardigrade; —पन slowness, tardiness; —स्वर undertone

धीर (a) grave, solemn, patient, firm

धीरज (nm) a consollation, patience, gravity

धीरता (nf) patience, satisfaction, solace

धीरे (adv) slowly, lazily; — धीरे little by little; gradually; slowly

धीवर (nm) a fisherman; a sailor

धुंकार (nf) a loud noise, a roar

धुंध (nf, nm) haziness, mist, fog

धुंधकार (nm) darkness, mistiness, thunder

धुंधलका (nm) darkishness, twilight

धुंधला (a) dim, misty; faded; foggy

धुआँ (nm) smoke, fume, reek; — धार violent; fiery; eloquent

धुकधुकी (nf) the middle portion of the heart; fear, throbbing

धुन (nf) propensity, assiduity

धुनकना (v) to card cotton

धुनना (v) to comb, to wool, to

card cotton

धुरंधर (a) one who carries a weight, leading

धुरा (nm) axis, hub, shaft

धुरी (nf) pivat, axis

धुर्रा (nm) a fragment; —उड़ाना to break a thing into small pieces, to destroy

धुलना (v) to be washed or cleaned with water

धुलाई (nf) the work or wages which is paid for washing

धुलाना (v) to cause to be washed

धूर्त (a) wicked cunning; rascal

धू-धू (nm) noise which is made by a flaming fire

धूनी (nf) incense, fire lighted by a Hindu mendicant who sits near it and inhales the smoke; —रमाना to practise austerity

धूप (nf) incense, burnt perfume, the light and heat of the sun; —घड़ी a sun-dial; —छाँह sun and shade; —बत्ती incense-stick

धूम (nm) smoke, vapour; (nf) funfare, tumult; boom; —धाम hustle and bustle; pomp

धूमकेतु (nm) fire, a comet, an epithet of Shiva

धूम-धड़क्का (nm) noise, tumult, pomp

धूमिल (a) smoky, hoary, vague

धूल (nf) dirt, dust

धूलि (nf) dust, dirt

धूसर (a) grey, dusk-coloured

धूसरित (a) full of dirt

धृत (a) held, possessed; sustained, kept up

धृष्ट (a) insolent, impudent; saucy, impertinent

धृष्टता (nf) insolence, impudence; sauce; impertinence

धृष्या (nf) a woman of loose character; (a) shameless

धेनु (nf) a cow

धैर्य (nm) patience, firmness; constancy, endurance

धोखा (nm) deceit, deception; guile; —देना to outwit, to deceive, —खाना to be deceived; —धड़ी cheating; beguilement

धोखेबाज़ (nm) a cheat; a deceitful, fraudulent

धोती (nf) loin cloth worn by Indians

धोना (v) to wash; to launder; to cleanse

धोबिन (nf) a washer-woman

धोबी (nm) a washer-man, a laundry-man

धोवन (nm) work of washing; water in which anything has been washed

धौंकना (v) to blow with bellows

धौंकनी (nf) bellows

धौंस (nf) bluster, threat, awe

धौंसना (v) to frighten, to chide,

to threaten

ध्याता (*nm*) one who thinks on a subject, a contemplator

ध्यान (*nm*) consideration, reflection; attention; meditation —देना to pay attention to; —न देना to ignore; —धरना to contemplate; —लगाना to meditate; to concentrate —से उतरना to forget

ध्यानी (*a*) contemplative, meditative; (*nm*) one who

applies himself to religious meditation

ध्येय (*nm*) end, aim

ध्रुव (*nm*) the pole; the polestar; (*a*) fixed, a permanent, firm; —तारा the polestar

ध्वंस (*nm*) destruction; loss

ध्वज (*nm*) a flag, symbol, banner

ध्वजा (*nf*) a flag, banner, ensign

ध्वनि (*nf*) sound; suggested meaning, purport

न

न the fifth member of the fourth pentad of consonants in Devnagri alphabet; (*ind*) no, not

नंग-धड़ंग (*a*) completely naked

नंगा (*a*) undraped, naked, nude; shameless; wicked; —पन nakedness; shamelessness; wickedness

नंदोई (*nm*) the husband of husband's sister

नंबर (*nm*) number; counting, marks

नंबरदार (*nm*) the Zamindar cf a village who helps the co-sharers in realising rent

नंबरबार (*adv*) one by one

नंबरी (*a*) numbered, bearing a number; notorious

नई (*a*) new

नकटा (*a, nm*) noseless; a nose-clipped person; shameless

नकद (*a*) hard cash; (*nm*) cash, ready money; (*adv*) in lieu of cash, in cash

नकल (*nf*) imitation; copy, duplicate, transcription; —करना to copy, to duplicate; —करनेवाला (*nm*) a copyist

नकली (*a*) false, counterfeit; artificial, not genuine

नकशा (*nm*) a plan, map; —बनाना to sketch, to plan; —बनाने वाला (*nm*) a draftsman; — नापने का यंत्र (*nm*) pantograph

नकसीर (*nf*) bleeding from the nose

नकाब (nf) a veil; a mask; visor;
—पोश masked, visored

नकार (nm) refusal; denial;
negation

नकारना (v) to deny; to refuse,
to decline

नकारा/नाकारा (a) useless,
worthless

नकाशी (nf) see नक्काशी

नकुल (nm) a mongoose

नकेल (nf) the string fixed in a
camel's, ox's or bear's nose
to serve as a rein

नक्कारा (nm) a huge kettle-
drum

नक्काशी (nf) carving, engraving;
designing; —दार carved;
carving designs

नक्श (nm) features

नक्षत्र (nm) a star

नख (nm) nail; claw

नखरा (nm) prudery, coquetry

नखरीला (am) coquetish, prude

नख-शिख (nm) from top to toe

नग (nm) a jewel, precious
stone; piece; mountain

नगण्य (a) insignificant,
ordinary; worthless

नगदी (nf) hard cash

नगमा (nm) a song; melody

नगर (nm) town; city

नगाड़ा (nm) a tymbal, kettle-
drum, tomtom

नगीना (nf) a precious stone,
gem

नग्न (a) naked, nude; —ता
nakedness

नज़दीक (adv) near, close;
almost, about

नज़र (nf) eyesight; glance,
look; vision; attention

नज़राना (nm) a gift, present

नज़ला (nm) cold, catarrh

नज़ाकत (nf) tenderness,
delicacy

नज़ारा (nm) sight, view, scene

नज़्म (nf) poem; verse

नट (nm) dancer; an acrobat,
tumbler, an actor

नटखट (a) naughty, mischive-
ous

नटखटी (nf) trickery, naughtiness

नटनी (nf) an actress, a female
of the rope-dancer's class

नत (a) twisted, bent, curved;
—मस्तक respectful

नतीजा (nm) consequence;
result

नत्थी (a) annexed; attached;
tagged

नथ (nf) a ring-shaped
ornament for the nose

नदारद (a) absent, disap-
pearing from view

नदी (nf) a river

ननद (nf) sister-in-law,
husband's sister

ननसाल (nf) mother's paternal
home

नंदिनी (nf) daughter; the river
Ganga

नन्हा (a) small; tiny; wee

नपुंसक (nm) a eunuch; a

coward; an impotent person; (a) cowardly

नफ़रत (nf) contempt; hatred, disgust

नफ़ा (nm) gain; profit; advantage

नफ़ासत (nf) delicacy, refinement, nicety

नफ़ीस (a) excellent, fine, good, clean

नब्ज़ (nf) the pulse; —देखना to feel the pulse; —छूटना stopping of the pulse, death

नभ (nm) the sky; firmament

नम/क (nm) table salt; salt; —कहराम ungrateful; —कीन (a) salty

नमस्/कार (nm) adieu; salutation; —ते salutation to you

नमाज़ (nf) a formal prayer by the muslims

नमी (nf) dampness; humidity

नमूना (nm) specimen, model; a sample; pattern

नम्र (a) humble; polite; submissive

नय/न (nm) an eye; —नाभिराम (a) charming, beautiful

नया (a) fresh; new; modern; young; inexperienced

नर (nm) a male; a man; (a) male; —बलि human sacrifice; —भक्षी a man-eater

नरक (nm) inferno, hell, the infernal regions, a very dirty place

नरकगामी (a) one who goes to hell after death

नरगिस (nf) narcissus flower

नरम (a) delicate; soft; pliant; timid

नरमी (nf) delicacy; softness; kindness

नरमेध (nm) the sacrifice of a human-being

नराधम (nm) a mean person

नराधिप (nm) a king

नरेंद्र (nm) a king

नरेश (nm) a king

नर्त/क (nm) a dancer; —की a dancing girl

नर्स (nf) a nurse

नल (nm) a long pipe; tap; —कूप a tube-well

नलिनी (nf) a lotus; a lily

नली (nf) pipe; tube; barrel of a gun

नव (a) fresh; new; young; recent; —युवक a young man; —युवती a young lady

नवधा (a) of nine kinds; —भक्ति the nine ways of devotion

नवनीत (nm) butter

नवरंग (a) beautiful, of new design

नवरत्न (nm) the nine precious stones; the nine gems of the court of Vikramaditya (also in the court of Akabar)

नवल (a) fresh; recent; new, modern; young

नवासा (nm) a daughter's son; —सी a daughter's daughter

नवी/न (a) novel, new; fresh; youthful; young; —नीकरण renewal; —नता freshness; novelty; modernity

नव्य (a) recent; new; modern

नशा (nm) intoxication; pride; —पानी some intoxication; —बंदी prohibition

नशी/ला (a) inebrient; intoxicating; hence —ली (fam. form of नशीला)

नशे/बाज़ (nm & a) a drunkard, addict; hence —बाज़ी the habit of drinking

नश्तर (nm) surgical knife; a lancet

नश्वर (a) destructible, transient

नश्वरता (nf) destructibility

नष्ट (a) destroyed, annihilated

नष्टचित्त (a) insane, mad

नष्टचेष्ट (a) having lost the power of moving limbs

नष्टचेतना (nf) torpor, trance

नष्टबुद्धि (a) stupid, dull

नष्ट-भ्रष्ट (a) broken asunder, destroyed; —होना to be smashed to wear

नष्टात्मा (nm) a mean fellow, a rogue

नस (nf) vein, sinew; nerve, —चढ़ना to have sprain in a part of the body; नसवार snuff; —बंदी vasectomy

नसल (nf) genealogy, pedigree

नसीब (nm) fortune, fate luck; destiny

नसीहत (nf) advice, instruction, counsel; —देना to counsel

नहर (nf) a channel, canal; waterway

नहरनी (nf) an instrument for cutting the nails

नहलाना (v) to cause to be bathed or washed

नहाना (v) to bathe; to perform ablution

नहीं (ind) not, no; —तो or, else, otherwise, if not

नौद (nf) an earthen trough; manger

ना (ind) no, not; —इंसाफ़ी injustice; —उम्मीद hopeless; —क़ाबिल undeserving; —कारा good for nothing; idle; —खुश displeased; —गवार unbearable; —चीज़ worthless; trifling; —जायज़ undue; improper; —दान ignorant; —बालिग under age; —मंजूर rejected; —मर्द impotent; coward; —मुमकिन impossible; —मुराद ill-fated; —वाक़िफ़ a stranger; ignorant

नाई (ind) like

नाई (nm) a barber

नाक (nf) the nose; honour; pre-eminent person; a symbol of prestige; (nm) the heaven

नाक-नक़्शा (nm) features

नाकाबंदी (nf) posting guards to stop the entry in a place

नाखून (nm) nail, claw

नाग (*nm*) snake; serpent; a cobra; an elephant; (*a*) treacherous

नागर (*a*) pertaining to the city, civil; urban; (*nm*) a civilian

नागरिक (*a*) civilian; urbane; (*nm*) a citizen; civilian; —सभा municipality; —अधिकार की प्राप्ति enfranchisement; —संस्था body politic; —ता citizenship

नागलोक (*nm*) the Hades

नागा (*nf*) absence from work

नागिन (*nf*) a female serpent

नाच (*nm*) dance, a ball, a dramatic entertainment; —गाना dance and music, ballet; —घर a dancing hall

नाचना (*v*) to dance; to frisk, to gambol

नाचरंग (*nm*) dancing entertainment, nautch party

नाज़ (*nm*) pride; airs; —उठाना to show coquettishness

नाज़नीन (*nm*) delicate beauty

नाजायज़ (*a*) unlawful, illegal; improper, unjust

नाज़िर (*nm*) a supervisor, a superintendent

नाज़ुक (*a*) soft, delicate, fine, tender; —बदन of a delicate frame; —मिज़ाज one who is unable to bear even a little hardship

नाटक (*nm*) a play; a drama; a dramatic performance;

—कार a dramatist, playwright

नाटकशाला (*nf*) stage, theatre

नाटकीय (*a*) pertaining to a stage or drama, dramatic; —ता dramatic character

नाटना (*v*) to break a promise; to deny; to negate

नाटा (*a*) short, dwarfish; stunted; —मोटा stocky; —मनुष्य a pigmy

नाटिका (*nf*) a short drama consisting of four acts

नाट्य (*nm*) the act of dancing, a mimic play

नाट्यकला (*nf*) stage craft

नाट्यकार (*nm*) a dramatist; an actor; the performer of a drama

नाट्यशास्त्र (*nm*) dramaturgy

नाड़ा (*nm*) untwisted thread, a tape

नाड़ी (*nf*) nerve, vein, pulse

नाता (*nm*) relationship, relation

नाती (*nm*) a son's son; a daughter's son

नाते (*adv*) in relation with, for the sake of some one

नातेवा/र (*adv*) relation; (*nm*) a relative; —री kinship, relationship

नाथ (*nm*) lord, master; husband

नाथना (*v*) to pierce the nose of a cattle and pass a rope through it to have a complete control over it

नाद (*nm*) a sound; noise; music

नादिरशाही (*nf*) great tyranny and injustice; (*a*) very harsh and terrible

नान (*nf*) bread

नानखताई (*nf*) a kind of sweet-meat

नाना (*nm*) maternal grand-father, grandsire; (*a*) different, varied, miscel-laneous

नानारूप (*nm*) different shapes

नानी (*nf*) mother's mother, maternal grand mother

नाप (*nm*) measurement; survey; dimension; —जोख/तोल work of measuring something

नापना (*v*) to measure; to survey

नापाक (*a*) polluted, defiled, impure

नाभि (*nf*) the navel; hub

नाम (*nm*) title; name; fame; —करण the ceremony of naming a child; —कीर्तन constant repetition of god's name; —ज़द nominated; -धाम name and address; —पट्ट a name-plate; —मात्र को nominal

नामक (*a*) named, bearing the name

नामांकन (*nm*) nomination

नामी (*a*) bearing the name of; famous, reputed

नायक (*nm*) a guide, leader, chief, hero; a military official of a low rank

नायकत्व (*nm*) lead, captainship

नायब (*a*) deputy; (*nm*) an agent, an assistant

नायिका (*nf*) the heroine of drama etc.

नारंगी (*nf*) an orange; (*a*) of orange colour; —का बगीचा orangery

ना/रा (*nm*) a slogan; —रेबाज़ a slogan-monger

नाराज़ (*a*) displeased, dissatis-fied

नाराज़गी (*nf*) displeasure

नारियल (*nm*) the coconut

नारी (*nf*) a woman, lady

नाल (*nf*) hollow tubular stalk, a tube; barrel of gun

नाला (*nm*) a canal; a rivulet; a gutter

नालायक़ (*a*) unfit; improper; wretched, worthless

नालिश (*nf*) plaint, law suit

नाली (*nf*) sewer, drain; tube

नाव (*nm*) a boat, a sailing vessel

नाविक (*nm*) a boatman, sailor

नाश (*nm*) damage; ruination; waste

नाशक (*a*) destroying; killing

नाशपाती (*nf*) a pear

नाशवान् (*a*) perishable, destructible, liable to decay

नाश्ता (*nm*) breakfast

नासमझ (a) ignorant; stupid; dull

नासमझी (nf) ignorance; stupidity; folly

नासिका (nf) the nose

नासूर (nm) cancer, ulcer, sinus

नास्तिक (nm) an atheist, an unbeliever; —ता atheism, disbelief

नाहक (adv) improperly, unjustly, in a useless manner

निंदक (nm) a calumniator; (a) abusive

निंदना (v) to defame, to calumniate, to abuse

निंदनीय (a) blamable, reprehensible, censurable

निंदा (nf) scorn, blame, slander

निंदिया (nf) sleep

नि:स्पृह (a) free from wish or desire, contented

नि:स्वार्थ (a) unselfish, disinterested, impartial; hence —ता (nf) selfless-ness

निकट (adv & a) close, near, proximate; —वर्ती standing or residing near, ready; (n) a neighbour

निकम्मा (a) worthless, useless, idle, indolent

निकलना (v) to issue; to get out; to rise; to be extracted

निकष (nm) touchstone, emerystone

निकाह (nm) marriage ceremony performed according to Mohammedan rites and customs

निकृष्ट (a) wretched; vile, low, base; —ता wretchedness; baseness

निखट्टू (a, nm) earning nothing; unemployed; lazy, idle

निगरानी (nf) supervision, watch

निगलना (v) to swallow, to gulp

निगाह (nf) look, glance; observation; attention

निगूढ़ (a) secret, hidden, obscure

निगोड़ा (a) supportless, unfortunate, wicked; (nm) an idler

निग्रह (nm) obstruction, restraint

निचला (a) lower; low-lying

निचोड़ (nm) summary, gist, essence; —ना to wring, to press, to squeeze

निजी (a) own, personal; private; unofficial

निठल्ला (a) without employ-ment; idle; (nm) an idler; —पन idleness

निडर (a) fearless, dauntless; daring, intrepid

निढाल (a) languid, wearied; slow

नित (adv) daily, everyday, each day

नितांत (a) complete, excessive,

entire, whole

नित्य (a) perpetual, constant, eternal, permanent; (adv) constantly, for ever; —प्रति every day, daily

नियार (nm) distilled water, decantation

नियारना (v) to decant, to purify, to distil

निवर्शन (nm) illustration; example; evidence

निदान (nm) cause of disease; diagnosis

निदेश (nm) order, command; instruction

निदेशालय (nm) a directorate

निद्रा (nf) sleep, slumber

निघड़क (adv) without reflection, boldly, fearlessly

निघन (nm) death

निघान (nm) receptacle, support, abode

निधि (nf) fund; treasure, hoard

निनाद (nm) a sound

निपट (adv) exceedingly, very, sheer

निपटना (v) to be settled, to be decided

निपटारा (nm) settlement; termination

निपात (nm) fall, ruin; death

निपुण (a) clever, eminent, perfect

निपुणता (nf) adoritness; talent; efficiency

निबंघ (nm) an essay, a treatise

निबटना (v) to be settled, to be decided, to be finished

निबल (a) feeble, weak

निबाह (nm) maintenance, accomplishment, arrangement

निबाहना (v) to perform; to achieve; to conduct; to maintain

नि/भना (v) to be accomplished; —भाना to accomplish, to fulfil

निमंत्रण (nm) invitation for feast; —पत्र invitation card

निमग्न (a) drowned; engaged

निमज्जन (nm) dipping bath

निमित्त (nm) motive; cause; account

निमेष (nm) twinkling of an eye, blink

निम्न (a) sunken, depressed, low; — लिखित the following

नियंता (nm) ruler, governor, master

नियंत्रक (nm) a controller

नियंत्रण (nm) fixing up a rule and following it

नियंत्रित (a) restrained, controlled

नियत (a) fixed, prescribed

नियति (nf) fate, destiny, luck

नियम (nm) regulation; principle

नियमावली (nf) rules and regulations

नियमित (a) regulated, regular; —ता regularity

नियुक्त (a) appointed; engaged;

posted

निर्युक्ति (*nf*) appointment; posting

नियोजक (*nm*) one who appoints men in different occupations

निरंकुश (*a*) unrestrained, uncontrolled; self-willed

निरंतर (*a*) incessant, ceaseless, continuous

निरपराध (*a*) guiltless, innocent

निरपेक्ष (*a*) without expectation, unconcerned

निरभिमान (*a*) prideless, humble

निरर्थक (*a*) useless, purpose-less, insignificant

निरस्त्र (*a*) unarmed, not equipped

निरस्त्रीकरण (*nm*) disarmament

निरा (*a*) mere, single; (*adv*) entirely

निराकरण (*nm*) removing, abrogation

निराकार (*a*) formless, shape-less; (*nm*) God

निरादर (*nm*) disrespect, dis-honour, disregard

निराधार (*a*) without support; baseless; groundless

निरापद (*a*) protected, pro-sperous

निरामिष (*a*) vegetarian

निराला (*a*) strange, excellent, peculiar

निराश (*a*) disappointed; desperate

निराशा (*nf*) hopelessness, dis-appointment, despondency

निराश्रय (*a*) having no refuge, helpless, shelterless

निराहार (*a & adv*) fasting, without food

निरीक्षक (*nm*) a foreman; an inspector; a superintendent

निरीक्षण (*nm*) observation; supervision

निरीह (*a*) not desiring anything, disinterested

निरुत्तर (*a*) without an answer, unable to answer, wordless

निरुत्साह (*a*) without enthusi-asm, cowardly, supine

निरुद्देश्य (*a & adv*) without purpose, aimless

निरोध (*nm*) control; obstruc-tion, restriction, hold

निर्गंध (*a*) devoid of fragrance, without smell

निर्गत (*a*) coming out, departed

निर्गम (*nm*) exit, a going out, departure

निर्गुण (*a*) without qualities; bad

निर्जन (*a*) uninhabited; lonely, solitary

निर्जल (*a*) without water; dry; (*nm*) a desert

निर्जीव (*a*) dead, lifeless, inanimate

निर्णय (*nm*) judgement, conclusion, decision

निर्णायक (*nm*) a judge, umpire; (*a*) critical

निर्दय (*a*) cruel, hard-hearted;

ruthless; —ता cruelty, oppression

निर्दलीय (a) independent

निर्दिष्ट (a) described, pointed out, mentioned

निर्देश (nm) description, order, command; —क director; —न direction

निर्दोष (a) guiltless; correct; harmless; innocent

निर्द्वंद्व (a) carefree

निर्धन (a) moneyless, penniless, indigent, poor; —ता poverty

निर्धारण (nm) settlement; fixation

निर्बल (a) powerless, weak, —ता weakness

निर्बोध (a) ignorent; foolish, stupid

निर्भय (a) fearless, brave, daring

निर्भर (a) dependent, relying on

निर्भीक (a) audacious, fearless; —ता fearlessness, intrepidity

निर्मम (a) ruthless, cruel, heartless; —ता cruelty

निर्मल (a) pure; clear; clean, holy; —ता clearness, cleanness

निर्माण (nm) creation, structure, construction

निर्माता (nm) a builder; creator; constituent; a producer

निर्मित (a) made, constructed, formed

निर्मुक्त (a) free; —करना to unbay, to acquit

निर्मूल (a) rootless, unfounded, baseless; —न ruin, destruction

निर्मोही (a) without affection, cruel, unkind

नियांत (nm) export

निर्लज्ज (a) immodest, shameless, bare-faced

निर्लज्जता (nf) effrontery; immodesty; shamelessness

निर्लिप्त (a) unconnected, unengrossed, unengaged

निर्लेप (a) sinless, pure

निर्लोभ (nm) absence of greed, unselfishness

निर्वंश (a) **without a family,** childless

निर्वा/चन (nm) work of selector, election; —चक an elector;

निर्वाचन-क्षेत्र (nm) constituency

निर्वाचित (a) elected

निर्वाण (a) extinguished, liberated from existence

निर्वात (a) without air, unmoving

निर्वासित (a) exiled; expelled, banished

निर्वाह (nm) maintenance; accomplishment

निर्विकल्प (a) fixed; settled

निर्विकार (a) unaltered, passionless, immutable

निर्विघ्न (a) unchecked, unimpeded, uninterrupted; (adv) freely; —ता

immunity, exemption

निर्विरोध (*a & adv*) uncontested, unanimous, unanimously

निर्विवाद (*a*) incontestable, indisputable

निवारक (*a*) hindering; prohibitive; deterrent

निवारण (*nm*) prohibition, hinderance

निवास (*nm*) dwelling, abode, residence; house

निवासी (*a*) inmate, inhabitant, resident

निवेदक (*nm*) applicant; informant

निवेदन (*nm*) a petition; tender

नि:शंक (*a*) dauntless, fearless

निशा (*nf*) night; —कर the moon; —चर a demon

निशान (*nm*) mark, spot, sign; flag; signal

निशा/ना (*nm*) aim; target; —नेबाज़ a marksman; —नेबाज़ी marksmanship

निशानी (*nf*) sign; token; memorial

निश्चय (*nm*) certainty, determination; trust; (*adv*) undoubtedly, really

निश्चिंत (*a*) free, careless; —ता carelessness

निश्चित (*a*) assured, carefree

निश्चेष्ट (*a*) devoid of motion; in a trance; powerless

निश्छल (*a*) without wiles; simple

निश्शंक (*a*) dauntless, intrepid,

fearless

निषिद्ध (*a*) prohibited; forbidden; banned

निषेध (*nm*) prohibition; prevention; negation; denial

निष्कर्ष (*nm*) conclusion, substance; essence

निष्काम (*a*) free from any wish; disinterested

निष्का/सन (*nm*) expulsion; —सित expelled

निष्क्रिय (*a*) doing no work, idle —ता idleness

निष्ठा (*nf*) faith, belief; devotion

निष्ठावान् (*nm*) one who fulfils his religious duties, loyal, sincere

निष्ठुर (*a*) harsh, brutal, merciless, cruel; —ता brutality, severity

निष्णात (*a*) very learned; competent; adept

निष्पक्ष (*a*) unbiased, unprejudiced, neutral; —ता neutrality

निष्पाप (*a*) innocent; sinless

निष्प्रभ (*a*) deprived of light; obscure

निष्फल (*a*) unproductive; of no avail, vain

निसर्ग (*nm*) nature, creation of universe

निसार (*a*) sacrificed

निस्तब्ध (*a*) immovable, quiet; —ता silence

निस्तार (*nm*) a passing out,

quittance

निस्तेज (a) spiritless; powerless, cold

निस्यंद (a) motionless, still object

निस्पृह (a) free from desire, contented

निस्संकोच (a) without hesitation

निस्संदेह (adv) certainly, undoubtedly, of course

निस्सहाय (a) helpless; —ता helplessness

निस्सार (a) worthless, having no essence, of no value

निस्स्वार्थ (a) unselfish, selfless; —ता selflessness

निहंग (a) naked, shameless

निहत्था (a) unarmed; —करना to disarm

निहारना (v) to look, to see, to behold

निहित (a) inherent, under-stood, implied

नींद (nf) sleep, slumber

नींव (nf) base; foundation; ground

नीच (a) vulgar, mean, vile; —ता lowness, meanness

नीचा (a) low, down,

नीचे (adv) below, under, down, beneath

नीति (nf) morality; policy; —ज्ञ a statesman, a politi-cian; —मान a moral person; —शास्त्र the science of ethics

नीबू (nm) lime, lemon, citron; —का शर्बत lemonade

नीम (nm) the margosa tree; (a) half, semi; —हकीम (a) quack

नीयत (nf) intention, motive

नीर (nm) water; —ज lotus

नीरव (a) without sound, silent; —ता silence

नीरस (a) devoid of juice or sap, dry, dry flat; uninteresting; hence —ता

नीरोग (a) hale, healthy; free from disease

नील (a) blue; (nm) indigo, woad; mark made on the body by bruise

नीलम (nm) a sapphire

नीला (a) blue, azure

नीलाथोथा (nm) sulphate of copper, blue vitriol

नीलाम (nm) public sale, auction

नीहार (nm) mist, fog

नुकसान (nm) loss; harm; dis-advantage

नुकीला (a) sharp, pointed

नुक्कड़ (nm) a point, a pointed end, protruding corner

नुक्स (nm) flaw, defect; fault

नुमाइंदा (nm) a representative

नुमाइ/श (nf) show, display, exhibition; —शी gaudy, showy, boastful

नुसखा (nm) recipe; prescrip-tion

नूतन (a) new; fresh; recent; modern

नूपुर (nm) an ornament for the

ankles, an anklet

नूर (nm) splendour, light

नृत्य (nm) dancing; a dance, —शाला a ball room

नृशंस (a) cruel, tyrannical, harmful; —ता cruelty

नेक (a) gentle, good; —दिल gentle; virtuous; —नीयत of good intentions, honest

नेकी (nf) virtue, goodness

नेता (nm) a pioneer; a leader; —गीरी leadership

नेतृत्व (nm) leadership

नेम (nm) religious practice; routine

नेस्ती (a) lazy; ominous; —पन ominousness

नैतिक (a) pertaining to duty, moral; —ता morality

नैसर्गिक (a) spontaneous; natural

नैहर (nm) a woman's paternal home

नोक (nf) tip; point; end; forepart; —झोंक taunt, mutual repartee

नोचना (v) to pluck; to pinch; to scratch

नोट (nm) paper money; bank note; draft

नोटिस (nm) a notice; a bill

नौ (a) nine; new; (nm) the number nine; (nf) a boat; —जवान a young man; —निहालthe growing genera- tion; —सिखिया a learner, a novice, not well-trained; —सेना navy

नौकर (nm) servant; an employee; —शाही bure- aucratic

नौकरी (nf) service, labour for another

नौबत (nf) turn, condition; kettle-drum

न्याय (nm) justice; fairness; logic

न्यायाधीश (nm) justice; judge

न्यायालय (nm) a court of justice, judicature

न्यायोचित (a) equitable, just, fair

न्यारा (a) separate, different; uncommon; unique, pecu- liar

न्यास (nm) deposit; a trust; —धारी a trustee

न्यून (a) deficient, lacking; less; low

न्यूनता (nf) want, shortage; weakness

न्योता (nm) invitation

न्यौछावर (nm) sacrifice

प

प the first member of the fifth pentad of consonants in Devnagri alphabet

पंक (*nm*) mire, mud, bog, sin

पंकज (*nm*) a lotus

पंक्ति (*nf*) row, line; series; rank

पंख (*nm*) feather; wing; fin

पंखड़ी (*nf*) blade, petal

पंखा (*nm*) fan

पंगु (*a*) lame, crippled

पंच (*a*) five; (*nm*) the number five; council, arbiter, assembly, a juror

पंचकोण (*nm*) a pentagon

पंचफैसला (*nm*) arbitration

पंचायत (*nf*) village assembly; arbitration

पंछी (*nm*) a bird

पंजर (*nm*) a skeleton, the ribs, the bones of human body

पंजा (*nm*) an aggregate of five; claw; paw; palm of hand

पंडित (*nm*) learned, literate, wise, skilful

पंथ (*nm*) a path, a sect; a custom, a religious order

पंथी (*nm*) a traveller; a sectarian, the follower of a sect

पंसारी (*nm*) a grocer

पकड़ (*nf*) hold; seizure; catch; grasp; —धकड़ holding and seizing

पकड़ना (*v*) to seize; to take hold of; to grasp, to catch

पकना (*v*) to be cooked; to ripen

पकवान (*nm*) dressed food, pudding, victuals which are fried in clarified butter

पकाना (*v*) to cook; to fry; to bake; to ripen

पक्का (*a*) strong; prepared, boiled or cooked; expert, clever

पक्ष (*nm*) side; alternative party; a fortnight; wing

पक्ष/पात (*nm*) bias, partiality, partisanship; —पाती a partisan, partial

पक्षाघात (*nm*) palsy, hemiplegia

पक्षीशाला (*nf*) an aviary

पक्षी (*nf*) a bird; aves

पक्ष्म (*nf*) the eye-lashes

पखवाड़ा (*nm*) a period of fifteen days, one half of a lunar month, a fortnight

पखारना (*v*) to wash, to cleanse

पखेरू (*nm*) a bird

पग (*nm*) pace; foot; step; —पग पर at every step

पगडंडी (*nf*) a path, track, footpath

पगड़ी (*nf*) a turban

पगला (*a*) mad

पगार (*nf*) salary, wages

पचड़ा (*nm*) wrangling, quarrel, disturbance, trouble

पचना (*v*) to be digested; to be

consumed

पचनीय (a) digestible

पछताना (v) to rue, to repent, to regret, to grieve

पछतावा (nm) penitence; repentance, remorse

पछाड़ (nf) falling down in a trance; —खाना to fall senseless on the ground

पछाड़ना (v) to throw down, to defeat in wrestling

पट (nm) a piece of cloth, a garment; a screen, covering

पटकना (v) to knock, to let fall with a jerk, to overthrow

पटकाना (v) to dash or beat against a thing

पटना (v) to be covered; to be levelled; roof to be made over a well

पटरा (nm) a plank, the board of a washerman

पटरानी (nf) the queen who is installed with the king, the head queen

पटरी (nf) rail; pavement

पटल (nm) screen; board; layer

पटवाना (v) to have the work of roofing done by some one

पटवारी (nm) a person who keeps a record of village accounts

पटसन (nm) jute

पटाक (nm) a crash, a thump, an explosion

पटाक्षेप (nm) curtain fall, ringing down of the curtain; closing of an affair

पटाखा (nm) a cracker; explosion

पटाना (v) to level a floor, to repay in full

पटिया (nf) a slab of stone, slate; a board

पटु (a) clever, smart, skilful

पटुत्व (nf) cleverness, dexterity

पटिटका (nf) a small board; ribbon

पट्टी (nf) a slip, strip, banage; wooden plate; —पढ़ाना to misguide; to persuade for selfish motives

पट्ठा (nm) full grown youth, a wrestler; flesh, muscle

पठनीय (a) able to read, readable

पठान (nm) people inhabiting the hilly country in Afghanistan

पठाना (v) to send, to dispatch

पठित (a) read, recited, studied

पड़ताल (nf) survey; investigation; search

पड़तालना (v) to survey; to investigate; to examine

पड़ना (v) to drop, to fall down; to lie on bed

पड़ाव (nm) a halting place, a camp

पड़ो/स (nm) vicinity, environment, neighbourhood; —सी a neighbour

पढ़ना (v) to study; to read; to recite

पढ़वाना (v) to cause to be read

पढ़ाई (nf) teaching; education; study

पढ़ा (a) well-read, learned; —लिखा literate, educated

पतंग (nm) a bird; a grasshopper; a kite

पतंगा (nm) a moth

पतझर (nm) the fall of leaves, autumn, defoliation

पतन (nm) fall; down fall, decline; ruin, deterioration

पतला (a) thin; slim; lean; weak; —पन thinness; weakness, slimness

पतलून (nf) pantaloon; trousers

पतवार (nf) helm, rudder

पता (nm) address; information

पताका (nf) flag; banner

पति (nm) husband; lord; owner; —त्व ownership, —व्रता faithful, virtuous wife, chaste

पतित (a) degraded; fallen, corrupt, wicked

पतीली (nf) a pan, a kettle, a vessel for boiling

पतोहू (nf) daughter-in-law, son's wife

पत्तल (nf) a plate made of leaves (food served on such a plate)

पत्ता (nm) leaf, blade of grass

पत्ती (nf) a leaf, foliage; share; —दार co-sharer

पत्थर (nm) stone; heartless; hard-hearted

पत्नी (nf) wife, better-half; —व्रत attachment for one's wife only

पत्र (nm) a leaf; a piece of paper; letter; newspaper; —कार the editor of a newspaper; journalist; —वाहक the bearer or carrier of a letter, postman —व्यवहार correspondence

पथ (nm) way, path, road

पथरी (nf) a whetstone; stone in the kidney or bladder

पथ्य (nm) regimen, diet

पद (nm) a word, a foot, a step; rank, status

पदक (nm) a badge, a medal

पदवी (nf) rank, dignity; surname, degree

पदार्थ (nm) stuff, material, a thing

पदोन्नति (nf) promotion

पद्धति (nf) a way, method, system

पद्म (nm) a lotus, a kind of tree like the almond

पधारना (v) to proceed, to arrive at a place; to take leave

पनघट (nm) a quay from which people draw water

पनचक्की (nf) a water-mill

पनडुब्बी (nf) a submarine ship

पनपना (v) to prosper, to flourish, to revive

पनवाड़ी (nm) a seller of betel leaves

पनाला (nm) a drain, a gutter

पनाह (*nf*) protection, shelter, refuge

पनीर (*nm*) cheese

पनीला (*a*) mixed with water

पन्ना (*nm*) leaf of a book; page; emerald

पपड़ी (*nf*) the upper hard surface of a thing

पपीहा (*nm*) the sparrow hawk

पपीता (*nm*) the papaya fruit

पपोटा (*nm*) the eyelid

पयोद (*nm*) a cloud

पयोधर (*nm*) cloud; udder, female breasts

परंतु (*ind*) however; but

परंपरा (*nm*) order, succession; tradition; —गत traditional; —वादी traditionalist; traditional

पर (*ind*) yet; but; even so; after; (*a*) distant; other, separate; (*nm*) feather; —पुरुष a man other than a woman's husband

परकार (*nf*) a compass

परकोटा (*nm*) a rampart constructed around a fort

परख (*nf*) examination, test, inspection

परखना (*v*) to examine, to assay

परचून (*nm*) flour, rice etc., grocery; (*a*) retail

परचूनी (*nm*) a grocer

परछत्ती (*nf*) a thatch made over mud-walls

परछाईं (*nf*) shade; shadow; reflection

परजीवी (*nm*) a parasite; (*a*) parasitic

परतंत्र (*a*) subdued, dependent; —ता reliance; dependence; heteronomy

परत (*nf*) fold; layer; scale

परती (*nf*) uncultivated waste land, fallow land

परदा (*nm*) a screen; a curtain; veil; obstruction

परदादा (*nm*) great grandfather (paternal)

पर/देश (*nm*) a country other than one's native land, foreign country; —देशी an alien; stranger, foreigner

परदु:ख (*nm*) trouble of others

परधाम (*nm*) Heaven, Paradise

परनाना (*nm*) great grand father (maternal)

परनाला (*nm*) a drain, a gutter, a kennel

परपीड़क (*nm*) one who afflicts pain on others

परम (*a*) best; supreme; uttermost

परमल (*nm*) a kind of fried cereal used as food

परमाणु (*nm*) an atom, —बम an atom bomb; —युद्ध atomic warfare

परमात्मा (*nm*) the Supereme Spirit, the oversoul; God

परमानंद (*nm*) the highest pleasure; the blissful soul, God

परमार्थ (*nm*) the best end, the

subtle truth

परमार्थी (a) one in search of the highest truth; a philosopher

परमेश्वर (nm) God, the Almighty

परराष्ट्र (nm) foreign land, another country

परला (a) of the other side; —सिरा the other end

परलोक (nm) the next world; the other world;—गमन death

परवरदिगार (nm) the Almighty

परवरिश (nf) fostering; protection; patronising

परवर्ती (a) subsequent, later

परवश (a) subservient; dependent; —ता dependence, submission

परवाह (nf) care; concern, anxiety

परशु (nm) an axe, a battle axe

परसना (v) to touch

परसर्ग (nm) a postposition

परसों (ind) the day before yesterday; the day after tomorrow

परस्पर (ind) reciprocal; mutual; (a) each other, one another; —भिन्न diametrically opposed; —मिलन to intermingle; —विरुद्ध inconsistent, irreconcilable; —व्यवहार reciprocity

परहित (nm) beneficence, benevolence

परहेज़ (nm) abstinence;

temperance, sobriety

परौंठा (nm) a kind of fried cake made in several layers

पराकाष्ठा (nf) the end; the highest degree, climax, peak

पराक्रम (nm) strength, might, power

पराक्रमी (a) valiant, strong, brave, bold

पराग (nm) the pollen of a flower; a fragrant powder used before bathing

पराङ्मुख (a) disinclined; backward, averse

पराजय (nf) repulse, defeat

पराजित (a) defeated

पराधीन (a) dependent; subjugated, subjugative —ता dependence

पराभव (nm) disregard, defeat

पराभूत (a) vanquished; defeated; ruined

परामर्श (nm) consultation; discussion, inference; advice; —दाता an advisor

परायण (a) wholly occupied, intent, devoted

पराया (a) pertaining to another; foreign, strange

परार्थ (nm) other's work or business

पराश्रित (a) dependent

परास्त (a) vanquished; defeated; ruined

पराह्न (nm) the afternoon

परिंदा (nm) a bird

परिक्रमा (*nf*) circumambulation; a going round an idol as a mark of reverence

परिचय (*nm*) acquaintance; introduction; —पत्र a letter of introduction; identity-card

परिचर्या (*nf*) service, attendance, tending a sick person

परिचायक (*a*) introductory; (*nm*) one who makes an introduction to a person

परिचा/रक (*nm*) a servant, an attendant, a retainer; —रिका (*nf*) a nurse

परिचित (*a*) known, acquainted with, familiar

परिणति (*nf*) ripeness, end; development

परिणय (*nm*) marriage ।

परिणाम (*nm*) result; effect, issue; —स्वरूप as a result of

परितप्त (*a*) hot, ardent

परिताप (*nm*) heat; affliction; pain

परितापी (*a*) causing pain or sorrow, teasing

परि/तुष्ट (*a*) much pleased, very satisfied, hence —तुष्टि much satisfaction, much pleasure

परितोष (*nm*) gratification, satisfaction; pleasure

परित्यक्त (*a*) abandoned, left off

परित्याग (*nm*) repudiation, abandonment, desertion

परित्रस्त (*a*) terrified

परित्राण (*nm*) a shelter, a protection; deliverance, salvation

परित्राता (*nm*) a saviour, a protector, deliverer

परिधान (*nm*) a dress, a garment, a clothing

परिधि (*nf*) compass, circumference, boundary

परिपक्व (*a*) perfectly ripe; developed, matured

परिपाक (*nm*) digestion; perfection, maturity

परिपाटी (*nf*) a convention; tradition

परिभव (*nm*) disrespect, disregard

परिभाषा (*nf*) definition

परिभाषित (*a*) explained, defined

परिभ्रमण (*nm*) travel, tour, stroll; circulation

परिभ्रष्ट (*a*) degraded, corrupted, sinful

परिमंडल (*nm*) circumference, circle, orbit

परिमल (*nm*) fragrance, sweet scent

परिमाण (*nm*) quantity; measure, size, volume

परिमार्जक (*nm*) one who washes or cleanses

परिमा/र्जन (*nm*) the work of cleansing or washing a thing; —र्जित cleansed,

washed
परिमित (a) finite, limited
परिमिति (nf) measure, quantity
परिमेय (a) able to be measured or weighed, limited
परिरक्षण (nm) thorough protection from injury or harm
परिलिखित (a) surrounded by lines
परि/वर्तन (nm) alteration, chang; revolution; —वर्तित changed, altered
परिवर्धन (nm) increase in quantity or number of a thing
परिवहन (nm) transportation
परि/वाद (nm) reproach, abuse; censure, slander; —वादी (a) calumnious, abusive; —वादक one who plays on a guitar
परिवार (nm) family
परिवृत (a) covered, concealed; surrounded
परिवेश (nm) boundary; environment
परिशीलन (nm) a touch, reading a book with attention and thought
परिश्रम (nm) pain; work, labour
परिश्रमी (a) laborious, painstaking
परिषद (nf) an assembly, a meeting, congregation
परि/ष्कार (nm) purification, cleanness, initiation; —ष्कृत cleansed, purified, adorned

परिस्थिति (nf) surroundings, circumstances
परिहार (nm) remedy; avoidance
परिहास (nm) jest, joke, fun, humour; —प्रिय humorous
परी (nf) a fairy, elf, nymph; a very beautiful lady
परीक्षक (nm) an examiner; an experimenter; a judge
परीक्षण (nm) examining; trial
परीक्षा (nf) an examination, test
परीक्षार्थी (nm) an examinee
परुष (a) hard-hearted, cruel, harsh; pitiless
परे (ind) on the other side, apart, above
परेशान (a) troubled, distressed, harassed
परेशानी (nf) distress, perplexity, trouble
परोक्ष (nm) absence; invisibility, (a) invisible, out of sight
परोपकार (nm) charity; beneficence, benevolence
परोपकारी (a) hospitable, benevolent; kind
परोसना (v) to serve food
पर्जन्य (nm) cloud, Indra
पर्चा (nm) a question paper
पर्ची (nf) a slip of paper
पर्यंक (nm) a bed, bedstead
पर्यंत (ind) upto, till, until
पर्यटन (nm) wandering from place to place; roaming; trip
पर्याप्त (a) ample, adequate;

sufficient

पर्याय (nm) a synonym

पर्यायवाची (nm) synonymous

पर्यालोचना (nf) a thorough investigation, survey

पर्व (nm) festival; division of a book

पर्वत (nm) a hill, mountain

पर्वतारोही (nm) a mountaineer

पर्वतीय (a) mountainous, hilly

पलंग (nm) a bed; —पोश a sheet which is spread on a bedstead; a bed-sheet

पल (nm) a measurement of time which is equal to twenty four seconds

पलक (nf) the eyelid; a movement

पलटन (nf) a brigade, corps, battalion, regiment

पलटना (v) to turn back, to revert; to alter; to convert

पलड़ा (nm) one of the pans of a balance

पलना (nm) a cradle; (v) to be nourished, to be reared, to brought up

पलायन (nm) a running away, flight; escape, retreat

पलाश (nm) the tree butea, frondosa, a leaf

पलीत (nm) a ghost

पलीद (a) impure, unclean, wicked; —करना to pollute

पल्लव (nm) a new tender leaf; —ग्राही a smatterer; superficial

पल्ला (nm) border of a garment; —पकड़ना to seek the support of

पवन (nm) wind; air; breeze

पवित्र (a) pure, holy, spiritual; —ता sanctity, purification, holiness

पशु (nm) brute, beast, animal, cattle; —ता (nf) condition or nature of a beast; —त्व foolishness, brutality

पश्चात (ind) afterwards, behind, after a time

पश्चाताप (nm) remorse, repentance

पश्चिम (nm) West

पश्चिमी (a) western

पसंद (nf) liking, choice

पसली (nf) a rib

पसारना (v) to expand; to spread; to stretch

पसीजना (v) to ooze, to perspirate; to be compassionate

पसीना (nm) perspiration, sweat

पहचान (nf) recognition; acquaintance, familiarity

पहचानना (v) to recognise; to discriminate, to distinguish

पहनना (v) to put on, to wear

पहनवाना (v) to cause to wear

पहनावा (nm) clothing; dress; vestment

पहर (nm) duration of three hours' time

पहरा (nm) a watch; patrol

पहरे/दार (nm) warder, guard;
— दारी watchmanship

पहल (nf) initiative

पहलवान (nm) a stout person, a wrestler

पहलवानी (nf) the work or profession of wrestling

पहला (a) first; primary; maiden

पहले (ind) firstly; in olden times; in the beginning; before; — पहल first of all

पहाड़ (nm) a hill, mountain; a large heep of any thing

पहाड़ा (nm) a multiplication table in Arithmetic

पहाड़ी (a) hilly, mountainous, (nf) hill, hillock, mount

पहिया (nm) a wheel

पहिरावा (nm) see पहनावा

पहुँच (nf) access, arrival; reach; receipt

पहुँचना (v) to reach, to arrive

पहुँचा (nm) the wrist

पहेली (nf) riddle, puzzle, enigma

पाँख (nm) the wing of a bird

पांडित्य (nm) scholarship, wisdom

पांडु (a) yellow, yollowish white, pale; — रोग jaundice

पांडुलिपि (nf) a manuscript

पंति (nf) row, range, assembly

पाँव (nm) leg; foot

पाँसा (nm) a dice

पांसु (nm) dirt, dust

पाक (a) pure, clean, innocent

पाक (nm) the work of cooking

पाकदामन (a) chaste or morally good, virtuous lady

पाकशाला (nm) a kitchen

पाकिट (nf) a pocket

पाक्षिक (a) pertaining to a side or party; fortnightly

पाखंड (nm) heresy, humbug, false doctrine; hypocrisy

पाखंडी (a) vain, hypocrite, unbeliever

पाख (nm) a fortnight; a wing

पाख़ाना (nm) latrine

पाग (nm) a turban; any thing which is boiled in syrup

पागना (v) to boil in syrup

पागल (a) crazy, mad; foolish; (nm) a lunatic, mad person; — ख़ाना a lunatic asylum, mad house; — पन insanity, mania; lunacy

पाचक (a) aiding digestion; digestive; (nm) a cook

पाचन (nm) digestion, cooking on fire; (a) digestive; — शक्ति the power of digestion

पाचनीय (a) digestible

पाचिका (nf) a female cook

पाच्य (a) able to be cooked or digested

पाजामा (nm) trousers

पाजी (a) mean, vile, wicked; — पन scoundrelism, mean-ness

पाजेब (nf) an ornament which is worn on the ankles

पाटंबर (*nm*) silken cloth

पाटना (*v*) to cover with earth; to roof; to heap

पाटल (*a*) rose-coloured, red; (*nm*) the tree of trumpet flowers

पाठ (*nm*) reading, study, a chapter of a book; recital; —पढ़ाना to teach a lesson

पाठक (*nm*) a reader

पाठन (*nm*) the work of teaching, instructing

पाठशाला (*nf*) a school

पाठांतर (*nm*) variant, version

पाठार्थी (*nm*) a student

पाठित (*a*) taught, instructed

पाठ्य (*a*) worth studying; legible; —पुस्तक a text book; —क्रम syllabus prescribed for certain examinations

पाणि (*nm*) the hand, —ग्रहण act of marriage, a wedding

पातक (*nm*) guilt, sin, misdeed, crime

पातकी (*a*) sinful, peccable; a criminal

पाताल (*nm*) the lower regions, hades, hell

पातिव्रत्य (*nm*) chastity

पात्र (*nm*) a vessel, can, pot; character; a deserving person

पात्रता (*nf*) fitness, capacity, worthiness, propriety

पाथेय (*nm*) provisions stored up for a journey

पाद (*nm*) the foot; a leg; verse;

—तल sole of a foot; foot; —प a plant

पादरी (*nm*) padre, clergy, christian priest

पान (*nm*) drinking; liquid food; betel, betel-leaf

पानगोष्ठी (*nf*) a band of drunkers

पानदान (*nm*) a box of metal, in which betel leaf, lime etc. are kept

पाना (*v*) to acquire, to get, to obtain, to receive

पानी (*nm*) water; liquid substance; temper

पाप (*nm*) guilt, sin, evil; crime

पापकर्म (*nm*) a sinful act

पापग्रह (*nm*) an inauspicious planet

पापड़ (*nm*) a thin crisp cake which is made of several kinds of pulse

पापत्व (*nm*) impiety, criminality, sinfulness

पापदर्शी (*a*) one who sees with a wicked intention

पापबुद्धि (*a*) wicked, depraved, sinful

पापात्मा (*a*) unholy, sinful; (*nm*) a sinner, an unholy person

पापाशय (*a*) wicked, sinful

पापी (*a*) evil, immoral, sinful, criminal (*nm*) a sinner, a criminal

पाबंद (*a*) tied, bound, dependent

पाबंदी (*nf*) restriction, restraint

पामर (a) low, wicked, vile, sinful

पायजामा (nm) trousers, pantaloons

पायजेब (nf) an anklet, an ornament for the ankles (see पाजेब)

पायवार (a) strong, steady; durable

पायवारी (nf) stability, durability

पायल (nf) an ornament for the ankles

पाया (v) past tense of the verb पाना, to get, to obtain; (nm) a leg of a piece of furniture

पारंगत (a) conversant or versed in a subject; proficient

पार (nm) end, limit, extremity; opposite side of a river

पारखी (nm) an examiner

पारतंत्र्य (nm) dependence, subordination, reliance

पारदर्शक (a) clear, transparent; —ता transparence

पारदर्शी (a) seeing the opposite shore; farseeing, shrewd, skilful

पारमार्थिक (a) pertaining to spiritual object, immortal

पारलौकिक (a) relating to the next world, ultramundane

पारस (nm) the philosopher's stone which is believed to convert a baser metal into gold by a mere touch; (a) healthy

पारस्परिक (a) concomitant, mutual, reciprocal

पारा (nm) mercury, quicksilver

पारायण (nm) work of finishing, end, completion; reading a book from the beginning to the end

पारावार (nm) limit; boundary; the ocean

पारिजात (nm) the coral tree; a tree of Paradise obtained from the churning of the ocean

पारितोषिक (nm) reward, prize

पारिभाषिक (a) technical; —शब्द technology, technical terms

पारिवारिक (a) pertaining to the family

पारिश्रमिक (nm) remuneration, allowance

पारिषद (nm) a councillor, a senator

पारी (nf) turn, time; shift

पारू (nm) fire; the Sun

पारुष्य (nm) roughness of speech, abuse

पार्थक्य (nm) separation, difference

पार्थिव (a) earthen, made of earth; material

पार्श्व (nm) nearness; neighbourhood; part of the body below the armpit

पार्षद (nm) a servant, a courtier

पाल (nm) the process of ripening fruits by keeping

them under the layers of straw; the sail

पालक (nm) protector, a guardian; a kind of spinach

पालकी (nf) a sedan; —गाड़ी a coach

पालतू (a) domesticated, tame

पालन (nm) protection, cherishing, tending; —पोषण support, nurture

पालना (v) to tame; to foster; to feed; to bring up

पालना (nm) a swing, a cradle, a cot

पाला (nm) hoar frost; (a) brought up

पालिश (nf) polish

पाली (nf) shift; turn

पाँव (nm) leg; foot

पावक (a) purifying, pure; (nm) fire, heat, the Sun

पावन (a) holy, pure; —ता purification

पाश (nm) a net or noose, tie; snare, trap

पाशविक (a) beast-like, brutal, savage

पाश्चात्य (a) belonging to the west, western

पाषाण (nm) stone

पास (nm) side, nearness, proximity; —जाना to go near

पासा (nm) a die; dice

पाहुना (nm) a guest, a newcomer

पिंगल (a) yellow, tawny; (nm) science of prosody

पिंजड़ा (nm) a cage, trap

पिंजर (nm) a cage; skeleton of body

पिंड (nm) a round mass, lump

पिंडली (nf) the calf of a leg

पिघलना (v) to dissolve, to thaw, to be melted; to flow

पिघलाना (v) to dissolve, to cause to be melted

पिघलाव (nm) melting

पिचकना (v) to be squeezed, to be dented

पिचकारी (nf) a syringe, a pump

पिचपिचा (a) flabby, watery

पिछड़ना (v) to remain behind, to lag, to be left behind

पिछलगा (nm) the work of following a person

पिछला (a) hinder, hind; back, previous; latter

पिछवाड़ा (nm) back part of the house, the rear or hinder part

पिटना (v) to be defeated; to be beaten; to flop

पिटरिया (nf) a small box

पिटाई (nf) beating; stroke; work or wages for beating

पिटारा (nm) a large basket

पिटारी (nf) a small basket

पिट्ठू (a & nm) helper, follower, supporter; toady

पितर (nm) forefather, parents, ancestors

पिता (nm) father, dad

पितामह (nm) grand father

पितामही (nf) grand mother

पितृ (nm) father; —ऋण one of the three debts on a man from which he is freed when he begets a son; —कुल paternal family; —भक्ति filial attachment

पित्त (nm) gall, bile; bilious, humour

पिपासा (nf) craving, thirst; greediness; desire

पियक्कड़ (nm) a drunkard

पिरोना (v) to string, to thread

पिल्ला (nm) a puppy, a pup

पिशाच (nm) demon, devil, evil spirit

पिस्ता (nm) pistachio-nut

पिस्तौल (nf) revolver, pistol

पिस्सू (nm) a flea

पीकदान (nm) a cuspidor

पीछा (nm) the back; the rear; —करना to chase, to hunt, to follow; —छुड़ाना to get rid of

पीछे (adv) afterwards, after; in the absence of

पीटना (v) to thrash; to beat; to strike; to flog; to defeat

पीठ (nf) the back; (nm) a seat, bench

पीठिका (nf) background; seat, base

पीड़ा (nf) anguish, aching, woe, trouble, pain

पीड़ित (a) oppressed; sick; ill

पीतल (nf) brass

पीतांबर (nm) yellow silk cloth; yellow silk clothes worm at the time of worship; Lord Vishnu

पीना (v) to drink; to smoke; to conceal a secret; to absorb

पीप (nm) pus, purulent matter coming from a wound

पीपा (nm) tub, a cask, a barrel

पीपल (nm) the pipal tree

पीर (nf) pain, trouble, ache; (nm) a muslim saint

पीला (a) yellow; pale, pallid; ashen; —पन yellowness

पीलिया (nm) chlorosis, jaundice

पी लेना (v) to drink; to swallow

पीसना (v) to pound, to grind; to reduce to powder; to gnash the teeth

पीहर (nm) the father's family of a married woman, maternal kins-folk

पुंगीफल (nm) the betel-nut

पुं/ज (nm) mass; heap; collection; —जीभूत heaped together, massed together

पुंडरीक (nm) white lotus; a lion; a white elephant

पुंस्त्व (nm) manhood, virility

पुआ (nm) a sweet cake

पुआल (nm) straw of paddy

पुकार (nf) call; cry, shout; invitation

पुकारना (v) to call out; to exclaim, to shout

पुखराज (nm) topaz

पुख्ता (a) durable; strong; firm

पुचकार (nf) encouragement

पुचकारना (v) to produce a hissing sound from lips, to

fondle, to love

पुच्छल तारा (nm) a comet

पुजारी (nm) a worshipper, a Hindu priest

पुण्य (nm) meritorious action, happiness, merit, virtue; —काल auspicious moment; —कर्म meritorious action; —क्षेत्र a holy place

पुण्यात्मा (a) pious, virtuous, religious, saintly, holy

पुतला (nm) an idol, an image; an effigy, a lay figure

पुतली (nf) a doll, a puppet; pupil of the eye

पुताई (nf) white washing, the wages paid for white washing

पुत्र (nm) a son; —वधू son's wife, daughter-in-law of a person

पुत्री (nf) daughter

पुदीना (nm) garden mint, mint

पुन: (a) again, also, on the contrary, afterwards; —कथन repetition; —पुन: again and again; —स्थापना re-instatement

पुनरागमन (nm) recurrence, return

पुनरा/वृत्ति (nf) repetition, revision of statement; —वृत्त told a second time

पुनर्गठन (nm) reorganisation

पुनर्जागरण (nm) restoration; renaissance

पुनर्निर्माण (nm) reproduction, reconstruction

पुनर्वास (nm) rehabilitation

पुनीत (a) pure, clean; holy

पुरज़ा (nm) a piece, fragment; bill; part of a machine

पुरस्कार (nm) reward, prize

पुरस्कृत (a) rewarded, respected

पुराण (a) old, ancient; (nm) tale of by-gone ages; an ancient literature of Hindu mythology

पुरातत्त्व (nm) archaeology

पुरातन (a) old, ancient, aboriginal, mythological

पुराना (a) ancient, old, old-fashioned; antiquated

पुरी (nf) a city; the city of Jagannath

पुरुष (nm) male, man; mankind; —त्व manhood; virility, masculinity

पुरुषार्थ (nm) labour, energy, exertion

पुरुषार्थी (a) energetic; industrious; strong, vigorous

पुरुषोत्तम (nm) an epithet of the god Vishnu

पुरोहित (nm) a family priest of Hindus

पुरोहिताई (nf) the functions of a family priest

पुल (nm) a bridge

पुलक (nm) horripilation, thrill

पुलकित (a) rejoiced; —होना to thrill, to bristle

पुलटिस (*nm*) poultice

पुलाव (*nm*) a kind of dish made of rice boiled in soup and spices

पुलिंदा (*nm*) a bundle; a parcel; a sheaf of corn

पुलिया (*nf*) a culvert

पुलिस (*nf*) police; —मैन a constable

पुश्त (*nf*) back portion; back side of generation, ancestry

पुश्तैनी (*a*) ancestral, hereditary, traditional

पुष्कर (*nm*) a pond; a lotus; the fore part of an elephant's trunk, holy place of Hindus

पुष्टता (*nm*) lustiness, strength

पुष्टि (*nf*) nourishment; maintenance; confirmation

पुष्ट (*a*) able-bodied, strong; nourished, stiff

पुष्टिकर (*a*) causing growth, nourishing; —ओषधि nutriment

पुष्टिवर्धक (*a*) nutritious

पुष्प (*nm*) a flower, a blossom; —केसर stamen; —मय flowery; —राग pollen

पुष्पित (*a*) flowering, blossomed, filled with flowers

पुष्पाचयान (*nm*) a garden of flowers

पुस्तक (*nf*) a book

पुस्तकालय (*nm*) a library, —का अध्यक्ष librarian

पुस्तिका (*nf*) a pamphlet

पूँछ (*nf*) tail of a beast, the back part of an object

पूँजी (*nf*) capital; investment; —पति a capitalist

पूँजी/वाद (*nm*) capitalism; —वादी a capitalist

पूछ (*nm*) inquiry, investigation; respect; —ताछ investigation, inquiry

पूछना (*v*) to ask; to enquire; to question

पूजक (*nm*) a votary, worshipper, an adorer

पूजन (*nm*) worship, adoring

पूजना (*v*) to adore, to worship, to respect

पूजनीय (*a*) venerable, respectable, fit for being worshipped

पूजा (*nf*) homage, reverence, worship, —करना to adore, to worship, to glorify

पूजित (*a*) venerated, adored, respected, worshipped

पूज्य (*a*) worthy, sacred, respected, venerable; —पाद one whoose feet are worth adoring, very respectable

पूत (*nm*) a son; (*a*) clean, pure; sincere, true

पूतात्मा (*nm*) a saint, an ascetic, one who is purified by ablution

पूनी (*nf*) a roll of cotton prepared for spinning thread

पूरक (*nm*) a supplement; (*a*) completing, supplementary

पूरना (v) to complete, to fill; to make up a deficiency

पूरब (nm) the east quarter

पूरबी (a) eastern

पूरा (a) all, entire, complete; full; total

पूरी (nf) unleavened cake fried in clarified butter

पूर्ण (a) perfect; complete, whole; full; finished; —कालिक whole-timer; —विराम full stop; —काम having the desire fulfilled or satisfied

पूर्णत: (adv) fully, completely, entirely

पूर्णत्व (nf) completeness; perfection; totality

पूर्णांक (nm) maximum marks; an integer

पूर्णिमा (nf) a full-moon day

पूर्ति (nf) completion

पूर्व (nm) the east; (a) previous, fore, former; (adv) before; —अधिकार preoccupation; —अवस्था में लाना to renew; —कथित aforesaid; —कालीन whilom, formerly; —गामी preceding, prior; —ज ancestor (s), fore-father (s); —रूप previous form; —वर्ती previous, prior, happening before

पूर्वानुमान (nm) estimate; forecast

पूर्वार्द्ध/पूर्वार्ष (a) the first/former half

पूर्वावस्था (nf) pre-stage; initial stage

पूर्वी (a) eastern

पूर्वोक्त (a) mentioned above, aforesaid

पृथक् (a) irrespective; peculiar; separate; diverse; —भाग fragment; unit; —करण separation

पृथु (a) wide, large; innumerable

पृथ्वी (nf) the earth, ground, land; —नाथ a king

पृष्ट (a) asked, enquired

पृष्ठ (nm) page; the back; the rear, the hind part of anything; —भाग back surface, —त: from behind; —पोषक a helper, one who backs, supporter

पेंग (nf) oscillation of a swing; —मारना to be tossed from one side to the other, to swing

पेंडल (nm) a pendant

पेंदा (nm) base; the bottom

पेच (nm) coil, screw, part of a machine; intricacy

पेचदार (a) screwed; intricate, complex

पेचिश (nf) dysentery

पेचीदगी (nf) perplexity; intricacy; complexity

पेचीदा (a) coiled, twisted; difficult, intricate

पेट (nm) abdomen, belly, stomach; —भर (a) bellyfull; —भरना (*v*) to be satiated —पालना to subsist

पेटी (*nf*) a small box; a chest, a belt

पेटीकोट (*nm*) a petticoat

पेटू (*a*) varacious, ravenous, gluttonous; (*nm*) a glutton

पेठा (*nm*) a kind of gourd

पेड़ (*nm*) a tree; —पौधे trees and plants

पेड़ा (*nm*) a kind of sweetmeat made of milk; a globular mass of kneaded flour

पेय (*nm*) a beverage; (*a*) drinkable

पेरना (*v*) to press something in a machine, to crush; to torment

पेलना (*v*) to push, to thrust in; to press

पेश (*adv*) before, in front of; —करना to present

पेशगी (*nf*) advance, advance money

पेशतर (*ind*) formerly, before, heretofore

पे/शा (*nm*) trade; profession, a work, occupation; —शेवर an artisan, a workman

पेशानी (*nf*) brow, forehead; lot, fate

पेशाब (*nm*) urine, —खाना urinal

पेशी (*nf*) a muscle, hearing of a law suit

पैंतरा (*nm*) see पैतरा

पैग़म्बर (*nm*) a prophet, an apostle, a messenger of God

पैग़ाम (*nm*) a message, a mission

पैठ (*nf*) penetration; access; enterance

पैठना (*v*) to enter; to pierce; to rush in, to access

पैड़ी (*nf*) a ladder, a staircase

पैतरा (*nm*) the preparatory movements of a wrestler; counter move

पैतरे/बाज़ (*nm*) a strategist, dodger; —बाज़ी dodge, strategy

पैताना (*nm*) the foot part of any thing

पैतृक (*a*) paternal; ancestral, hereditary; —धन patri-mony; —भूमि fatherland; —सम्पत्ति inheritance

पैदल (*a*) walking on foot; (*nm*) infantry; —चलनेवाला pedestrian, —सिपाही kern, infantry; —यात्रा tramp

पैदा (*a*) born; produced; created; discovered; (*nm*) gain, income

पैदाइश (*nf*) birth, existence; production; creation

पैदाइशी (*a*) inborn, natural, innate, implanted by nature

पैदावार (*nf*) produce of land, crop, harvest; production

पैना (*a*) fine-pointed, sharp; (*nm*) the goad of a ploughman

पैबंद (*nm*) a patch

पैमाइश (*nf*) surveying, measurement or survey of land

पैमाना (*nm*) an instrument for measuring, a scale, a meter

पैयाँ (*nf*) the foot

पैर (*nm*) leg, foot; footprint; step

पैरवी (*nf*) pleading; advocacy; —करना to advocate; to pursue; to support; —कार a supporter, a follower

पैशाचिक (*a*) infernal, demoniacal, horrible

पैसा (*nm*) pice; wealth; पैसेवाला a wealthy person

पोंछना (*v*) to rub out; to wipe; to efface; to clean

पोच (*a*) mean, worthless, weak

पोटली (*nf*) a bale, a small bundle, a package

पोत (*nm*) a ship; a big boat

पोतना (*v*) to white-wash; to coat

पोता (*nm*) grandson, son's son; a white washing

पोती (*nf*) grand daughter. son's daughter

पोथा (*nm*) a book of large size; manuscript written on long separate leaves

पोथी (*nf*) a book

पोदीना (*nm*) mint

पोपला (*a*) toothless; (*nm*) a toothless person

पोर (*nm*) the space which lies between two joints, a gnarl; अंगुली का— knuckle

पोल (*nf*) an empty space, hollowness, agate; —खुलना disclosure of a secret

पोला (*a*) hollow, empty

पोशाक (*nf*) dress, clothes, raiment, garment, habiliment

पोशीदा (*a*) concealed, hidden

पोषक (*a*) a nourisher; a supporter

पोषण (*nm*) nourishing, cherishing, nutrition; assistance; supporting

पोषित (*a*) reared, nourished

पोसना (*v*) to pet, to rear, to nourish

पोस्त (*nm*) poppy plant; poppy seed

पोस्ती (*a*) one who intoxicates himself with infusion of poppy heads; idle (man)

पोस्तीन (*nm*) a garment which is made of leather covered with fine hairs

पौ (*nf*) early dawn; a ray of light

पौत्र (*nm*) a son's son, a grand son

पौत्री (*nf*) a son's daughter, a grand daughter

पौद (*nf*) a small plant; a transplanted seedling, a sapling

पौधा (*nm*) a young plant, a sapling

पौन (*nm*) three-fourth, three quarters

पौना (*nm*) a ladle with a long handle; (*a*) three quarters; three fourth

पौनी (*nf*) a low caste people who get tips on festive occasion; a small ladle

पौर (*a*) pertaining to a city

पौराणिक (*a*) old, pertaining to tradition; —कथा legend, mythological tales, —ता mythology

पौरुष (*nm*) manhood, masculinity; vigour

पौरुषेय (*a*) manly, performed by man; vigorous

पौष्टिक (*a*) tonic; nutritive

प्याऊ (*nf*) a waterbooth

प्याज़ (*nm*) onion

प्याज़ी (*a*) of light rosy colour

प्यादा (*nm*) a foot-soldier, a messenger

प्यार (*nm*) love; affection; attachment

प्यारा (*a*) dear, beloved, lovely

प्याला (*nm*) a cup

प्याली (*nf*) a small cup

प्यास (*nf*) thirst; eager, desire; —बुझाना to quench thirst; —लगना to be thirsty

प्यासा (*a*) thirsty, athirst

प्रकंप (*nm*) trembling, shivering

प्रकट (*a*) clear; manifest; apparent; evident

प्रकटित (*a*) displayed, manifested, evident

प्रकंपन (*nm*) quivering

प्रकंपित (*a*) quivered, trembled

प्रकरण (*nm*) subject, context; topic

प्रकर्ष (*nm*) superiority, excellence, eminence

प्रकांड (*a*) eminent; leading

प्रकार (*nm*) kind, quality; method, mode

प्रकारंतर (*nm*) a different method or manner

प्रकाश (*nm*) light; splendour, lustre

प्रकाशक (*nm*) an illuminator, discoverer; a publisher

प्रकाशन (*nm*) illuminating; publication

प्रकाशमान (*a*) shining, resplendent, brilliant, radiant

प्रकाशित (*a*) manifest; evident; apparent; published

प्रकाश्य (*a*) requiring to be manifested or published

प्रकीर्ण (*a*) extended, exposed; scattered; miscellaneous

प्रकीर्ति (*nf*) celebrity, fame

प्रकुपित (*a*) extremely angry; enraged; agitated

प्रकृत (*a*) true, real genuine; natural, —वादी a naturalist

प्रकृति (*nf*) nature; habit, disposition, temprament; —वाद naturalism; —वादी a naturalist; naturalistic; —शास्त्र the study of nature; —सिद्ध natural

प्रकोप (*nm*) excessive wrath;

agitation; disturbed condition of the body

प्रकोष्ठ (*nm*) a side room near, the main gate of a house, a big court yard; a bracket

प्रक्रम (*nm*) beginning; series

प्रक्रिया (*nf*) manner, observance, method of performance

प्रक्षालन (*nm*) cleansing, washing

प्रक्षालित (*a*) washed, cleansed

प्रक्षिप्त (*a*) cast forth; thrown; projected

प्रक्षेप (*nm*) throwing; scattering; mixing, adding

प्रखर (*a*) fierce, sharp; keen; hot

प्रख्यात (*a*) renowned, well-known, illustrious, famous, reputed

प्रगटना (*v*) to be manifested; to appear, to come to view

प्रगति (*nf*) development; progress; —वाद progressivism; —वादी progressivist, —शील progressive

प्रगल्भ (*a*) bold, impertinent, active

प्रगाढ़ (*a*) much, excessive, profound, deep

प्रचंड (*a*) furious, violent, terrible, fierce; daring, bold

प्रचंडता (*nf*) violence, fierceness

प्रचलन (*nm*) prevalence; custom; movement; usage

प्रचलित (*a*) prevailing, current, common, in usage

प्रचार (*nm*) propaganda; publicity; use

प्रचारक (*nm*) a propagator; a herald, a proclaimer

प्रचारित (*a*) proclaimed, made known

प्रचुर (*a*) abundant, plentiful, enough

प्रचुरता (*nf*) plenty, abundance

प्रचोदित (*a*) agitated; excited

प्रच्छन्न (*a*) concealed; covered, hidden; secret

प्रच्छादन (*nm*) a cover, covering; concealing

प्रच्छेद्य (*a*) fit to be lopped off

प्रजनन (*nm*) birth, midwifery

प्रजा (*nf*) a subject; public; —तंत्र democracy; —तांत्रिक democratic; —पति lord of creation; a king

प्रज्ञप्ति (*nf*) hint, suggestion

प्रज्ञा (*nf*) wisdom, intellect; understanding

प्रज्ञात (*a*) understood, known

प्रज्वलन (*nm*) the act of burning a thing

प्रज्वलित (*a*) blazing, burning

प्रण (*nm*) a pledge, vow; resolution, promise

प्रणम्य (*a*) fit to be reverenced

प्रणय (*nm*) love between man and woman, sexual love; affection

प्रणयी (*nm*) a lover, a husband

प्रणयन (*nm*) composition,

writing

प्रणव (nm) God, the holy monosyllable Om; absolutely new

प्रणाम (nm) salutation; bowing with respect; a term used in greeting elders

प्रणाली (nf) a method, system

प्रणेता (nm) creator; author

प्रताप (nm) dignity, glory; splendour

प्रतापी (a) glorious, powerful, famous, dignified

प्रति (nf) a copy; an inseparable prefix used in the following senses — instead of, each, every, equal, again, likeness

प्रतिकार (nm) retaliation, revenge; return

प्रतिकूल (a) opposite; contrary; inverted; unfavourable

प्रतिकृति (nf) an image, a picture; reflection

प्रति/क्रिया (nf) return, reaction; —क्रियात्मक reactivative; —क्रियावादी reactionary

प्रतिक्षण (adv) at every moment, constantly

प्रतिक्षेप (nm) obstruction

प्रतिघात (nm) a counter blow, concussion

प्रतिघाती (nm) foe, an enemy; a hostile person

प्रतिच्छाया (nf) a reflected image, shadow; a picture

प्रतिज्ञा (nf) a vow; promise;

resolution; —पत्र a bond, a written contract

प्रतिदान (nm) returning a thing deposited, an exchange

प्रतिदिन (ind) daily, every day

प्रतिद्वंद्व (nm) mutual struggle; contest; conflict

प्रतिद्वंद्वी (nm) a competitor; a rival; an opponent; an enemy

प्रतिध्वनि (nf) echo of a sound, repetition

प्रतिनिधि (nm) a deputy, an agent to a person; —त्व agency, substitution

प्रतिपक्ष (nm) rival side, opposition, contesting party

प्रतिपक्षी (nm) an adversary, an opponent, a competitor

प्रतिपादक (nm) one who makes a demonstration

प्रतिपादन (nm) ascertainment, thorough knowledge, proof, donation

प्रतिपादित (a) established; ascertained

प्रतिपालक (nm) a benefactor, a patron, a guardian

प्रतिपालन (nm) fostering, rearing, nourishing, protection

प्रतिफल (nm) result, conclusion

प्रतिबंध (nm) obstruction, impediment, restriction

प्रतिबिंब (nm) a shadow; an image; a reflection in a

looking glass

प्रतिभा (nf) intellect, sharpness of understanding, genius —शाली endowed with genius, most intelligent

प्रतिमा (nf) an image, an idol of a deity

प्रतिमान (nm) a pattern, example; standard

प्रतियोगिता (nf) rivalry, competition, emulation; contest; match

प्रतियोगी (nm) a competitor, rival

प्रतिरूप (nm) an image, a picture

प्रति/रक्षा (nf) defence; —रक्षात्मक defensive

प्रतिरोध (nm) obstruction, hindrance; opposition

प्रतिलिपि (nf) a copy of something, a facsimile

प्रतिलोम (a) inverted, reverse; opposite

प्रतिवाद (nm) a controversy, counter-statement

प्रतिशत (ind) percent

प्रतिशोध (nm) retaliation, revenge

प्रतिषेध (nm) rejection, prohibition, forbiddance

प्रतिष्ठा (nf) installation; honour; dignity, prestige

प्रतिष्ठित (a) established, respected

प्रतिस्पर्धा (nf) emulation, competition, rivalry

प्रतिस्पर्धी (nm) a rival, a competitor

प्रतिहिंसा (nf) retaliation, revenge

प्रतीक (nm) a mark, a sign; a symbol; —वाद symbolism; —वादी symbolical

प्रती/क्षा (nf) expectation; wait; —क्षालय a waiting room

प्रतीत (a) appeared; known

प्रत्यक्ष (a) cognizable by sight, visible, tangible; apparent

प्रत्यय (nm) credit; concept; suffix; —पत्र letter of credence

प्रत्याख्यान (nm) refutation, contradiction

प्रत्यावर्तन (nm) a return, a coming back

प्रत्याशा (nf) hope, expectation

प्रत्याशी (nm) an expectant; a candidate

प्रत्याह्वान (nm) recall, calling back

प्रत्युत (ind) but, contrary to, against

प्रत्युत्तर (nm) reply to an answer, a rejoinder, a retort

प्रत्युत्पन्न (a) reproduced, prompt

प्रत्युपकार (nm) return of service for a kindness

प्रत्येक (a) every, one by one

प्रथम (a) first, chief; initial; —त: firstly; previously

प्रथा (nf) custom, rule

प्रदक्षिणा (nf) walking round a

revered person or temple

प्रदत्त (a) granted, bestowed

प्रदर्शन (nm) display, exhibiting, demonstrating

प्रदर्शनी (nf) a public exhibition

प्रदर्शित (a) exhibited; displayed; showed

प्रदहन (nm) burning completely

प्रदाता (nm & a) a bestower, giver

प्रदान (nm) a gift, a giving in marriage

प्रदीप्त (a) lighted; resplendent

प्रदीप्ति (nf) light, brightness

प्रदेश (nm) a country; a territory, a region

प्रदोष (nm) evening, sunset; guilt or sin

प्रधान (nm) a chief, president; (a) principal, head; —मंत्री the prime minister

प्रधानता (nf) superiority; leadership; pre-eminence

प्रपंच (nm) fraud; the world, creation

प्रपंची (a) artful; deceitful, fraudulent, cunning

प्रपात (nm) a waterfall; a falling down of something

प्रपौत्र (nf) a great grandson

प्रबंध (nm) arrangement; management; —कर्ता a manager

प्रबल (a) strong, mighty; violent; powerful

प्रबुद्ध (a) awake, roused, expanded, wise, learned; —ता thorough knowledge

प्रबोध (nm) awakening from sleep, wakefulness

प्रभात (nm) the time of early morning, dawn

प्रभा (nf) light, lustre, radiance

प्रभाव (nm) effect; influence; might, power

प्रभावित (a) influenced; impressed

प्रभु (nm) lord, God, master, owner

प्रभुत्व (nm) superiority, lordship; dignity

प्रभूत (a) abundant, plentiful, over, much

प्रभृति (ind) the rest, and so forth

प्रभेद (nm) difference; sort, kind

प्रमाण (nm) proof; authority; —पत्र a certificate

प्रमाणित (a) authentically proved; certified

प्रमाद (nm) negligence, an error, a mistake; —पूर्ण careless

प्रमादी (a) negligent, careless; erring, confused

प्रमुख (a) first, best, chief

प्रमुदित (a) delighted, pleased, glad, very happy

प्रमेय (nm) fit to be used as a universal statement

प्रमोद (nm) pleasure, hilarity, delight, happiness

प्रयत्न (*nm*) an exertion; an effort; an action, attempt

प्रयाण (*nm*) voyage, departure; attack

प्रयास (*nm*) attempt; effort; labour, exertion

प्रयुक्त (*a*) used, applied

प्रयोक्ता (*nm*) user; an employer for a work

प्रयोग (*nm*) an experiment; exercise

प्रयोगत: (*adv*) practically

प्रयोजक (*nm*) one who performs an action, a stimulator

प्रयोजन (*nm*) motive, purpose; occasion

प्रयोज्य (*a*) suitable, fit to be used

प्रलंब (*a*) hanging, dilatory

प्रलय (*nf*) dissolution, final destruction of the universe

प्रलाप (*nm*) useless talk, useless gossip

प्रलेप (*nm*) an ointment

प्रलेपन (*nm*) the work of an ointing or besmearing

प्रलोप (*nm*) ruin, destruction

प्रलोभन (*nm*) temptation, allurement; attraction

प्रलोभित (*a*) enticed

प्रवंचना (*nf*) cheeting, fraud, deceipt

प्रवक्ता (*nm*) an eloquent speaker, a propounder of sacred texts

प्रवचन (*nm*) an explanation of the text

प्रवचनीय (*a*) explainable

प्रवर (*a*) eminent, chief, superior

प्रवर्त्तक (*nm*) a founder, an instigator

प्रवर्तन (*nm*) resolution, establishment, persuasion

प्रवर्तित (*a*) commenced, begun

प्रवाद (*nm*) rumour; false accusation

प्रवास (*nm*) residence in a foreign land, dwelling abroad; migration

प्रवासी (*nm*) a migrant

प्रवाह (*nm*) a stream of water, a current; flow

प्रविष्ट (*a*) entered, engaged in

प्रवीण (*a*) expert, competent, skilful

प्रवीणता (*nf*) proficiency

प्रवृत्त (*a*) inclined, determined; engaged in a work

प्रवृत्ति (*nf*) tendency; a continuous flow, inclination of mind; activity

प्रवेक्षण (*nm*) forseeing

प्रवेक्षित (*a*) anticipated

प्रवेश (*nm*) entrance, admission; —पत्र an admission ticket;—शुल्क admission fee

प्रशंसक (*nm*) one who praises; (*a*) praising

प्रशंसनीय (*a*) worthy of praise, laudable

प्रशंसा (*nf*) applause; praise; eulogy

प्रशस्त (*a*) vest; wide

प्रशस्ति (nf) praise, excellence; inscription on copper plates

प्रशांत (a) calm; peaceful, quiet

प्रशाखा (nf) a twig or small branch of a tree

प्रशास/न (nm) rule; administration; —क ruler; administrator

प्रशिक्षण (nm) training

प्रश्न (nm) a question; an enquiry; a problem; —कर्ता an interrogator; —पत्र a question paper; —माला questionnaire

प्रश्नोत्तर (nm) question and answer

प्रश्रय (nm) a place of shelter, an object of support

प्रष्टव्य (a) enquirable, enquiring

प्रसंग (nm) context, connection; occasion; sexual intercourse

प्रसक्त (a) attached, devoted

प्रसन्न (a) delighted, pleased, rejoiced

प्रसन्नता (nf) happiness, joy, pleasure

प्रसव (nm) child-birth, delivery, progeny

प्रसाद (nm) boon; blessing; gift, kindness

प्रसाधन (nm) make-up; cosmetics

प्रसार (nm) extent, scattering, expansion

प्रसारण (nm) spreading; broadcasting; extending outwardly

प्रसारित (a) spread, extended, broadcast

प्रसिद्ध (a) renowned, famous, well-known

प्रसिद्धि (nf) fame, reputation, renown

प्रसुप्त (a) sleeping, asleep

प्रसूत (a) born, delivered, produced

प्रसून (nm) a blossom, flower

प्रस्ताव (nm) a preliminary discourse, a suggestion, resolution; proposal

प्रस्तावना (nf) prologue to a play; introduction

प्रस्तावित (a) projected, proposed

प्रस्तुत (a) mentioned, declared; praised

प्रस्थान (nm) a journey, departure

प्रस्थापन (nm) establishment

प्रस्थापित (a) well-established

प्रस्फुटन (nm) manifest; blooming

प्रस्फुरण (nm) coming out, emanation

प्रहर (nm) the eighth part of a day, a period of three hours

प्रहरी (nm) a guard, watchman

प्रहर्षित (a) merry, delighted

प्रहसन (nm) a comedy; mockery

प्रहार (nm) a blow, a stroke

with fist; a kick

प्रहास (nm) a loud laughter

प्रहेलिका (nf) a riddle, an enigma

प्रांगण (nm) the courtyard in the middle of a house

प्रांजल (a) straight, plain; true; —ता clarity; refinement

प्रां/त (nm) territory; country; —तीय provincial, territorial

प्राकार (nm) a rampart; a surrounding wall

प्राकृत (a) low, unrefined, common

प्राकृतिक (a) nature made; unrefined

प्रागैतिहासिक (a) pre-historical

प्राची (nf) the east, the orient

प्राचीन (a) old, ancient; antique; outdated; —तर older; earlier; —तम most ancient; earliest; —ता antiquity, ancientness

प्राचुर्य (nm) abundance, plenty

प्राच्य (a) east, eastern; oriental

प्राज्ञ (a) intelligent, brilliant; prudent

प्राण (nm) one of the five vital-airs; breath, life; vitality; soul; —का ग्राहक a seeker after one's life; —दण्ड punishment of death; —दाता lifegiver; —धन beloved, as dear as life; —धारी a living being, a creature; —नाथ master of life; —शक्ति vitality; —हानि loss of life;

—हीन lifeless, inanimate

प्राणवान (a) animated, full of vitality; powerful

प्राणांत (nm) the end of life, death

प्राणी (nm) a sentient being, a creature; a man

प्राणेश्वर (nm) darling, beloved; husband

प्रात: (nm) dawn, early in the morning

प्राथमिक (a) elementary; primary, initial

प्रादुर्भाव (nm) appearance, coming into existence; manifestation; birth, rise

प्रादुर्भूत (a) born, manifested

प्रादेशिक (a) pertaining to a place or country; regional, territorial

प्रादेशिकता (a) regionalism

प्राधान्य (nm) superiority, supremacy

प्राध्यापक (nm) lecturer

प्रांत (nm) province; end, border

प्राप्त (a) gained, acquired, got, obtained

प्राप्ति (nf) gain; profit, benefit; income; receipt

प्राप्य (a) obtainable; attainable; available

प्राबल्य (nm) predominence; intensity

प्रामाणिक (a) reliable, authentic; established by proof; credible

प्राय: (*adv*) usually, often, generally; mostly

प्रायश्चित्त (*nm*) penance, atonement, expiation; —विधि rules prescribed in Shastra for expitation

प्रायोगिक (*a*) practical; experimental

प्रारंभ (*nm*) commencement; beginning; the starting point

प्रारंभिक (*a*) primary; first; elementary

प्रारब्ध (*nm*) fate, destiny, lot

प्रारूप (*nm*) a draft

प्रार्थना (*nf*) prayer; request, solicitation; petition; —पत्र an application

प्रार्थनीय (*a*) fit to be petitioned

प्रार्थित (*a*) solicited, requested; asked

प्रार्थी (*nm*) a petitioner; an applicant; one who submits a request

प्रासंगिक (*a*) pertaining to a topic under discussion; relevant; incidental; —ता relevance

प्रासाद (*nm*) a mansion, a palace

प्रियंवद (*a*) sweet speaking

प्रिय (*a*) darling, beloved, dear; pleasing, favourite; (*nm*) a lover; husband; —जन near and dear ones; —तम dearest; husband; —दर्शी showing love to all, —भाषी speaking sweet words; —वर much beloved, very dear

प्रिया (*a & nf*) darling, beloved; wife; sweet heart

प्रीतम (*nm*) husband, master, beloved person

प्रीति (*nf*) affection; love; enjoyment, satisfaction; —पूर्वक with love and kindness; —भाव courtesy, —भोज a feast in which friends and relatives dine together, a social party

प्रेक्षक (*nm*) a beholder; an onlooker; spectator

प्रेक्षण (*nm*) the work of seeing, looking, sight

प्रेक्षणीय (*a*) able to be seen or beheld

प्रेत (*nm*) a ghost, an evil spirit, a frightful person; —लोक the world of dead persons

प्रेतनी (*nf*) feminine form of प्रेत

प्रेम (*nm*) affection, love, kindness; —कहानी a love tale; —करना to love; —गीत a love song; —पत्र a love-letter; —पात्र beloved, dear; —भाव emotion of love, love

प्रेमालिंगन (*nm*) embracing in love

प्रेमाश्रु (*nm*) tears of joy falling in love

प्रेमिका (*nf*) a beloved

प्रेमी (*nm*) a lover

प्रेयसी (*nf*) darling, a beloved

प्रेरक (*nm*) a promptor, an

instigator, an inducer; inspirer

प्रेरणा (*nf*) drive; motive; inspiration, exitement; —शक्ति motive force, inspiration

प्रेरणार्थक क्रिया (*a*) a causative verb

प्रेरणीय (*a*) able to be impulsed or instigated

प्रेरित (*a*) induced, inspired; prompted

प्रेषक (*nm*) a sender, a dispatcher

प्रेषण (*nm*) the act of sending or dispatching a thing

प्रेषित (*a*) directed, dispatched, sent

प्रोक्त (*a*) declared; said, uttered

प्रोत्साहक (*nm*) an instigator

प्रोत्साहन (*nm*) instigation, stimulation

प्रोत्साहित (*a*) excited, stimulated, incited

प्रौढ (*a*) full grown, adult; mature

प्रौढता (*nf*) full growth, adulthood, maturity

प्रौढ़ा (*nf*) an elderly woman

प्लवन (*nm*) leaping, swimming, plunging

प्लेग (*nf*) plague

फ

फ the second member of the fifth pentad of consonants in Devnagri alphabet

फंदा (*nm*) a loop; a knot; noose;

फंदेदार (*a*) loopy; having a knot

फँसना (*v*) to be entrapped, to be involved in a difficulty

फँसाना (*v*) to entrap, to ensnare; to bait

फक (*a*) white, clean, pale, —पड़ना to turn pale; to be scared out of wits

फकीर (*nm*) a beggar, a hermit; a poor person

फकीरी (*nf*) beggary; poverty; the life of a hermit

फक्कड़ (*a*) carefree; a rough fellow, a base person, —पन carefreeness, carefree manner; indigence

फख (*nm*) pride

फज़ीहत (*nf*) infamy, disgrace, insult

फजूल (*a*) worthless, useless; futile; —खर्च dissipating; extravagant; —खर्ची dissipation; extravagance

फज़्ल (*nm*) favour, kindness, grace

फट (*adv*) at once; (*nf*) the

sound made by the fall of a light object, a crack; —फट an auto-rickshaw

फटकना (v) to knock off, to shake; to winnow

फटकार (nf) a reprimand, rebuke, chiding

फटकारना (v) to chide, to rebuke, to scold

फटना (v) to burst; to be torn; to be cracked; to be cut

फटफटाना (v) to make a fluttering noise; to flap

फय (a) rent; torn; —पुराना old and shattered, shabby

फटीचर (a) shabbily dressed, shabby

फट्टा (nm) a long piece of split bamboo, a plank

फड़क उठना (v) to be thrilled

फड़कन (nf) throbbing; palpitation, pulsation

फड़कना (v) to throb, to be thrilled; to pulsate

फड़फड़ाना (v) to flap, to flutter, to throb

फड़फड़ाहट (nf) flutter, flapping, throbbing

फणि (nm) the expanded hood of a snake, —धर snake

फणी (nm) a snake

फ़तवा (nm) a judicial judgement or decree passed by a Mohammedan judge

फ़तह (nf) victory, triumph, conquest; —करना (v) to conquer

फ़तूर (nm) defect, flaw; craze

फन (nm) snake's hood

फ़न (nm) skill; art, draft, artifice

फनकना (v) to move about in the air with a hissing sound

फ़नकार (nf) an artist

फ़ना (nf) ruin, destruction; died

फफूँदी (nf) mildew, fungus

फफोला (nm) a blotch, a blister; a scald

फबती (nf) a sarcasm, a jest, banter

फबना (v) to seem beautiful; to suit; to become an occasion

फ़र्जी (nm) the queen in the play of chess; a minister; (a) artificial, unnatural

फ़रमा (nm) a frame; a shoe-maker's last; a full sheet of paper folded several times on which book is printed

फ़रमाइश (nf) an order, a command; a royal edict; an imperative request

फ़रमाइशी (a) prepared or made according to order

फ़रमान (nm) a royal edict or command

फ़रमाना (v) to order, to command

फ़रशी (nf) a hubble-bubble

फ़रसा (nm) an axe, halberd, a poleaxe

फ़रार (a) absconding (person), a culprit at large; (nm) an

outlaw

फ़रियाद (nf) complaint; a petition; a request

फ़रियादी (a) a petitioner; a complainant

फ़रिश्ता (nm) a messenger of god, an angel

फ़रीक़ (nm) an opponent, an adversary, a section

फ़रेब (nm) duplicity, fraud, trick, wiliness

फ़रेबी (a) deceptive, fraudy, fraudulent

फ़र्क़ (nm) difference, distance

फ़र्ज़ (nm) moral duty; obligation; —करना to assume, to suppose

फ़र्ज़ी (a) fictitious; assumed; (nm) a minister, a vazir; the queen in the game of chess

फ़र्द (nf) a piece of cloth or paper, a roll, a catalogue

फ़र्राटा (nm) the sound of something fluttering in the air, rattling sound

फ़र्राश (nm) a servant who spreads carpets, lights, candles

फ़र्राशी (a) pertaining to the work of farrash

फ़रोश (nm) a seller, a vendor

फ़र्श (nm) a floor, a carpet

फ़र्शी (nf) a kind of large hubble bubble

फल (nm) a fruit; effect; gain; —त: therefore; thus; —दायक

fruitful, advantageous

फलक (nm) the sky

फलक (nm) a board, a bench, a sheet

फलना (v) to be fruitful, to bear fruit, to be useful; —फूलना to thrive

फलाँ (a) such and such; so and so

फलाहार (nm) fruitarian diet; subsisting on a diet of fruits alone

फलाहारी (nm) pertaining to fruitarian diet, one who subsists on fruits alone

फलालेन (nf) flannel

फलार्थी (nm) one who desires favourable consequences

फलित (a) full of fruits; successful, fulfilled; —ज्योतिष astrology

फली (nf) pod of a leguminous plant, a bean

फलीभूत (a) fructified, resulted in success

फव्वारा (nm) a fountain

फ़सल (nf) season time; crop, harvest; —काटनेवाला a harvester

फ़सली (a) pertaining to a season or crop; —बुख़ार seasonal fever

फ़साद (nm) revolt, agitation, quarrel, disturbance, dispute

फ़सादी (a) revolting, rowdy, quarrelsome, mischieveous, one who initiates an altercation

फ़साना (*nm*) a long narrative, a story

फ़सील (*nf*) battlement, parapet; a boundary wall

फहराना (*v*) to wave; to flutter in the air, to flap

फाँक (*nf*) a cleft; a cut slice, a slit, fragment; —करना to pare

फाँकना (*v*) to put something powdered into the mouth, to chuk some powdery thing into the mouth; धूल —to knock about, to run from pole to post

फाट (*nm*) the distance between the two banks of a river, the width

फाँटना (*v*) to divide something into equal parts

फाँद (*nf*) a leaping, spring; jumping

फाँदना (*v*) to leap over; to jump across; to skip; to spring; to cross

फाँस (*nf*) the splinter of a noose, a trap, knot

फाँसना (*v*) to catch in a trap, to ensnare

फाँसी (*nf*) a noose; execution, hanging; —चढ़ना to be hanged; —देना to hang by the neck; —देने वाला a hangman; —लगाना to commit suicide by means of hanging

फ़ाका (*nm*) a fast; starvation; —कशी starving

फ़ाका/मस्त (*a*) one who is merry even in extreme poverty, one whose spirit is not damped even though starved; carefree; —मस्ती carefreeness even though starved; maintenance of undamped spirit even in affliction

फ़ाख़्ता (*nf*) a dove

फाग (*nm*) the Holi festival; a typical song sung collectively during the Holi festival

फ़ाज़िल (*a*) proficient, extra; learned

फाटक (*nm*) main gate; entrance; door

फाट/का (*nm*) speculation; —बाज़ a speculator —केबाज़ी speculation

फाड़ना (*v*) to rend; to tear off; to crack; to split

फानूस (*nm*) large candles, a chandelier to burn candles

फ़ायदा (*nm*) profit; gain; use, utility; advantage

फ़ायदेमंद (*a*) useful; profitable; advantageous; beneficial

फ़ारखती (*nf*) the deed of release or acquittance

फ़ारसी (*nf*) the Persian languge; (*a*) persian

फ़ारिग़ (*a*) free from work, freed

फ़ार्म (nm) an agricultural farm

फाल (nm) a piece of betel nut; ploughshare; measure of one pace

फ़ाल (nm) a fall of sari

फ़ालतू (a) spare; sufficient; surplus, extra

फ़ालसई (a) brownish red

फ़ालसा (nm) a tree and its round tiny fruit — *Grewia asiatica*

फ़ालिज़ (nm) paralysis; palsy

फावड़ा (nm) a spade, mattock

फ़ाश (a) evident, exposed, uncovered; manifest; — करना to disclose a secret that undermines some-body's prestige

फ़ासला (nm) interval; space; a distance; gap; difference

फ़ाहा (nm) a flock of cotton used as a lint for dressing a wound, a plaster of medicine

फ़िकरा (nm) a sentence; taunt, phrase; — कसना to taunt

फ़िक्र (nf) care; anxiety, worry; thought; concern

फ़िक्रमंद (a) concerned; worried

फिटकिरी (nf) alum

फ़ितूर (nm) a defect, unsound-ness; craze

फिरंगी (a) English (man); (nm) a white man

फिर (adv) again; then; more-over, afterwards; in future; — आना to come back, to return; — जाना to go back; — कहना to encore; — से anew, afresh; — फिर again and again; — भी not with-standing; — क्या what then

फ़िरका (nm) a tribe, a sect; community; — परस्त a communalist; sectarian; — परस्ती communalism

फिरकी (nf) a spool; whirligig; a reel of thread

फिरना (v) to ramble; to walk about; to travel; to go round; to return

फ़िराक (nf) looking for, waiting for, keeping a watch for

फ़िलहाल (adv) for the present, for the time being

फ़िल्म (nf) a movie, film

फ़िल्मी (a) cinematographic

फिसड्डी (a) always lagging behind; doing nothing; sluggish

फिसलन (nf) the act of slipping, slipperiness; skid

फिसलना (v) to slide; to slip; to skid

फिसलाहट (nf) slipperiness

फ़ी (ind) every, each; — सदी percent, per hundred

फीका (a) insipid, tasteless; dull coloured; dim; — पन vapidity

फ़ीता (nm) a tape; tag; a lace; ribbon

फ़ीरोज़ी (a) violet-blue

फील (*nm*) an elephant; a piece in the game of chess

फीस (*nf*) tuition fee; fee

फूँकना (*v*) to burn, to be reduced to ashes, to be destroyed

फुंकार (*nf*) hiss of a snake

फुंसी (*nf*) a pimple, whelk

फुट (*nm*) a foot

फुटकर (*a*) miscellaneous; retail, — चीज़ें odds and ends, miscellaneous articles

फुदकना (*v*) to leap, to jump

फुनगी (*nf*) tip, top, summit, upper extremity

फुप्फुस (*nm*) a lung

फुफकार (*nf*) the hissing of a snake

फुफकारना (*v*) to hiss like a snake

फुर्ती (*nf*) quickness, smartness, promptness

फुर्तीला (*a*) quick, smart; prompt, alert

फुर्सत (*nf*) spare time; leisure; respite; — पाना to get time

फुलका (*nm*) a thin bread

फुलझड़ी (*nf*) a kind of fire-work which emits flower-like sparks

फुलवाड़ी (*nf*) a flower garden

फुलाना (*v*) to cause to swell; to cause to become proud; to inflate

फुलेल (*nm*) scented oil

फव्वारा (*nm*) a fountain

फुसफुसा (*a*) weak; hollow,

fragile; not sturdy

फुसफुसाना (*v*) to speak in a hushed up voice or low tone, to whisper

फुसफुसाहट (*nf*) a whisper

फुसलाना (*v*) to allure, to coax; to entice

फुसलाहट (*nf*) allurement

फुहार (*nf*) fine dense drops of rain, drizzle; spray

फुहारा (*nm*) a spray of water, a fountain, shower

फूँक (*nf*) a blowing; a puff

फूँकना (*v*) to burn; to blow; to set on fire

फूट (*nf*) enmity; disunion, disagreement, discord; — डालना to sow the seeds of a discord

फूटना (*v*) to crack; to break; to be broken, to burst; to sprout

फूफा (*nm*) husband of one's father's sister

फूफी (*nf*) father's sister

फूल (*nm*) a blossom, a flower; flower in embroidery; post-cremation ashes; a very light thing; — कारी embroidering of flowers; embroidery; — गोभी cauliflower; — दान a flower-pot; — दार embroidered; flowery; — माला a flower-garland

फूलना (*v*) to puff, to flower; to bloom; to feel proud; — फलना to flourish, to prosper

फूस (*nm*) dry grass, straw, hay

फूहड़ (*a*) unmannerly; (*nm*) a slattern

फूही (*nf*) a light shower of rain, drizzle

फेंकना (*v*) to cast, to throw; to waste; to toss

फेंटना (*v*) to beat up into froth, to batter, to mix by trituration

फेंटा (*nm*) a small turban; the part of the धोती rolled and tucked up round the waist

फेन (*nm*) froth, foam, lather

फेनिल (*a*) frothful, full of lather

फेफड़ा (*nm*) a lung

फेर (*nm*) a turning, a twist; doubt

फेरा (*nm*) a return, circuit, going round; coming and going back

फेरी (*nf*) round; going round; hawking

फेल (*a*) unsuccessful, plucked; (*nm*) action; misdeed; doings

फेहरिस्त (*nf*) an inventory, list

फैक्टरी (*nf*) a factory

फैलना (*v*) to spread, to expand; to extend; to be famous

फैलाव (*nm*) spread; scattering, dispersion

फैशन (*nm*) fashion; —परस्त fashionable; —परस्ती fashionableness

फैशनेबल (*a*) fashionable

फैसला (*nm*) decision; judgement, settlement

फोकट (*a*) worthless, of no value; —में without payment

फोटो (*nm*) a photograph; —ग्राफर a photographer

फोड़ना (*v*) to break; to split, to burst

फोड़ा (*nm*) an ulcer; a boil

फोरमैन (*nm*) a foreman

फौज (*nf*) a multitude; an army, regiment

फौजदार (*nm*) a military officer

फौजदारी (*nf*) a criminal court; —करना to commit a criminal offence

फौजी (*a*) pertaining to the army, martial; (*nm*) a soldier; —कानून martial law; —अदालत a military court

फौरन (*adv*) at once, immediately, there and then

फौलाद (*nm*) steel

फौलादी (*a*) made of steel, sturdy

फ्राक (*nm*) a frock

फ्रेम (*nm*) a frame

ब

ब the third member of the fifth pentad of consonants in Devnagri alphabet

बंकिम (*a*) curved, bent; oblique

बंका (*a*) bent, curved, powerful

बंगला (*nm*) a bungalow; (*nf*) the Bengali language

बंगाली (*a*) the language spoken in Bengal

बंजर (*a*) unproductive, barren, fallow

बंजारा (*nm*) nomad, a gypsy

बैंटवारा (*nm*) a division, partition, separation

बंटाढार (*nm*) devastation, undoing, ruination

बंडल (*nm*) a bundle

बंडी (*nf*) waistcoat, a jacket

बंद (*a*) shut; locked; stopped, discontinued; —गोभी cabbage

बंदगी (*nf*) salutation; service, worship, prayer

बंदनवार (*nf*) an ornamental arch, festoon of flowers and green leaves

बंदर (*nm*) harbour; monkey

बंदरगाह (*nf*) a harbour, port

बंदा (*nm*) a slave, servant; humble self used by a speaker for himself out of modesty

बंदिश (*nf*) forestalling; a restriction; musical pattern

बंदी (*nm*) a bard; prisoner; captive; —करना to catch, to arrest —गृह a prison, a jail

बंदूक (*nm*) a gun

बंदूकची (*nm*) a musketeer, a gunman, gunner

बंदोबस्त (*nm*) an arrangement, settlement; management

बंध (*nm*) a tie, a knot; a bond; —पत्र a bond

बंधक (*nm*) pawn; surety; —रखना to mortgage, to pawn

बंधन (*nm*) the act of binding; restriction; a bond

बँधना (*v*) to be bound; to be arrested; to be kept under restraint

बंधु (*nm*) a brother; a relation, kinsman; friend; —बांधव relatives, kinsfold; —त्व relationship, kinship, cognation

बंध्या (*nf*) a barren woman; childless woman; —पन barrenness; —पुत्र something which is impossible

बंब (*nm*) a bomb

बंबा (*nm*) waterpipe; a hydrant

बंसी (*nf*) a pipe, flute; fishing hook

बक (*nm*) a heron

बकझक (*nf*) gabble, babbling, —करना to jabber

बकना (v) to chatter, to babble, to make senseless talk

बकबक (nf) raving; twaddle

बकरा (nm) a he-goat

बकरी (nf) a she-goat

बकवाद (nf) chatter, twaddle, gabble

बकवादी (a) an idle talker, tattler, twaddler

बकसुआ (nm) fibula, a buckle

बक्स (nm) a box

बकाना (v) to cause some-one to gabble

बकाया (nm) amount of arrears, balance; (a) remaining, payable

बखान (nm) exposition; description; praise

बखानना (v) to relate, to dwell in details, to sing the praises

बखार (nm) a store-house, a barn in a village

बखिया (nf) back-stitching; a kind of strong stitching with needle; —उधेड़ना to expose thoroughly

बखुद (ind) by self, by oneself

बखूबी (ind) very well, in good manner, thoroughly

बखेड़ा (nm) complication; difficulty; broil

बखेरना (v) to scatter, to spread; to diffuse

बख्त (nm) fortune, fate; lot; कम — ill-fated, unfortune; नेक— fortunate, lucky

बख्तर (nm) an armour; —बंद armoured

बख्शाना (v) to grant, to bestow; to pardon

बख्शीश (nf) grant, gift; tip

बग़ल (nf) flank; an arm-pit; a side; (adv) by the side, closy by

बगला (nm) a heron —भगत a hypocrite

बगावत (nf) mutiny, rebellion, revolt

बगिया (nf) a small garden

बगीचा (nm) a garden, a small park

बगुला (nm) a heron

बगूला (nm) a whirlwind

बगैर (ind) excluding, without

बग्घी (nf) a four wheeled carriage drawn by horses

बघार (nm) spices which are used to season food

बघारना (शेखी) (v) to boast; to show off; to talk tall

बचकाना (a) fit for a child, puerile

बचत (nf) saving; gain

बचना (v) to escape; to recover; to be saved; to remain; बाल-बाल— to have a hair-breadth escape

बचपन (nm) childhood

बचपना (nm) childishness

बचाना (v) to defend; to save; to retain; to protect

बचाव (nm) defence, safety, protection

बच्चा (nm) a kid; a child; baby; infant; (a) inexperienced

बच्ची (nf) a small girl

बछड़ा (nm) a he-calf

बछिया (nf) a she-calf

बछेड़ा (nm) a colt

बछेड़ी (nf) a filly

बजना (v) to sound, to be struck

बजरंग (a) very stout and strong

बजरबट्टू (a & nm) stupid, fool, block-head

बजबाना (v) to cause a person to sound an instrument

बजा (a) fit, right, proper, true

बज्जाज (nm) a cloth merchant

बज्जाज़ा (nm) a cloth market

बज्जाज़ी (nf) the work of a draper

बजाना (v) to play on a musical instrument; to beat a drum; to accomplish a work

बजाय (ind) instead of, in place of

बटन (nm) switch; a button

बटना (v) to twist rope etc.

बटलोही (nf) a wide mouthed pot which is used for cooking food

बटवारा (nm) an assignation; partition; division

बटाई (nf) partition, division

बटाऊ (nm) a traveller

बटालियन (nf) a battalion

बटुआ (nm) moneybag, a purse

बटेर (nf) a quail; —बाज़ one who tames quails

बटोई (nf) a small cooking jar

बटोरना (v) to accumulate; to collect; to gather

बटोही (nm) a traveller, a wayfarer

बट्टा (nm) deficit, loss, damage; a stone pestle, a discount

बट्टाखाता (nm) dues which are unrealisable

बट्टी (nf) a small pestle or muller

बड़ (nm) a banyan tree; —पन greatness, eminence

बड़बोला (a) one who brags or boasts

बड़भागी (a) fortunate

बड़बड़ (nf) muttering, tattle, useless talk

बड़बड़ाना (v) to jabber, to grumble, to gabble, to babble

बड़बड़ाहट (nf) a rattle, a mutter

बड़वानल (nm) submarine fire

बड़ा (a) great; large; big; important, elder; grown up; (adv) very; (nm) ground pulse-formed into small round cakes and fried; —दिन the Christmas day; —बाबू head clerk; —बूढ़ा elderly

बड़ाई (nf) greatness, praise

बढ़ई (nm) a carpenter; —गीरी carpentry

बढ़ती (nf) abundance; growth; enhancement

बढ़ना (v) to grow; to surpass; to

proceed; to progress

बढ़ाना (v) to promote, to increase, to extend

बढ़ावा (nm) excitement, encouragement

बढ़िया (a) superior, nice, fine, excellent

बढ़ोतरी (nf) gradual increment; bonus; progress; addition

बतख़ (nf) a duck

बताना (v) to inform; to point out, to signify, to tell

बतासा (nm) a semi-spherical cake which is made of sugar and is very light and spongy

बतियाना (v) to talk, to converse with

बतौर (ind) just like; like; as

बत्ती (nf) a candle; a lamp, a light

बथुआ (nm) the common herb *chenopodium album*

बद (a) wicked, bad, mean, depraved; —अमनी disturbance, breach of peace; —इंतज़ामी bad management; —कार wicked, licentious; —कारी wickedness; —क़िस्मत unfortunate, unlucky, ill-fated; —ख़त bad hand-writing, —गुमान one who looks with suspicion at a person; —गुमानी a false suspicion; —चलन depraved, of immoral character, licentious; —चलनी bad

character; —ज़बान ill-speaking; —ज़ात mean, wicked, depraved; —ज़ायक़ा tasteless; —तमीज़ vulgar, uncivilised; —तर worse, more wicked; —दिमाग़ arrogant; —दुआ curse, malediction; —नसीब ill-fated, unfortunate; —नाम infamous, calumniated, notorious; —नामी a slander, a disrepute, a scandal; —नीयत of ill-intention; —नीयती a deception; —नुमा ugly, grotesque; —परहेज़ी an immoderate indulgence in diet, intemperance; —बख़्त unfortunate; —बू a foul smell, bad odour

बदन (nm) the body, physical frame

बदना (v) to settle, to bet

बदमाश (a) wicked; immoral; (nm) a man of bad character

बदमाशी (nf) wickedness, dissoluteness

बदमिज़ाज (a) of wicked nature

बदनसीबी (nf) lucklessness

बदल (nm) change, exchange

बदलना (v) to alter; to turn; to shift

बदला (nm) revenge, retaliation; return

बदली (nf) exchange; cloudiness; transfer, —करना to transfer

बदले में (*adv*) inspite of, in lieu of, instead of

बदशक्ल (*a*) deformed, ugly

बदसलूकी (*nf*) ill-behaviour

बदसूरत (*a*) deformed, ugly

बदस्तूर (*adv*) in the ordinary way; as usual; in the customary manner

बदहज़मी (*nf*) indigestion

बदहवास (*a*) in a fit of coma, perplexed, confused, thrown in disorder

बदा (*a*) fated, destined

बदी (*nf*) wickedness, evil, harm; the dark half of a lunar month

बदौलत (*ind*) by virtue of; by means of; for; due to; through; by the kindness of

बद्ध (*a*) tied up; bound; fixed

बधाई (*nf*) congratulation; —देना to congratulate, to felicitable

बधिक (*nm*) a slayer, a hunter

बधिया (*nm*) a castrated animal (bull)

बधिर (*a*) deaf, hard of hearing

बन (*nm*) a wood, forest

बनचर (*nm*) a wild beast, a forester

बनचारी (*a*) one who lives or wanders about in a forest

बनजारा (*nm*) a grain dealer, a grocer

बनना (*v*) to be made or prepared; to be constructed; to be fit for use; to seem beautiful

बनवास (*nm*) residing in forest, an exile

बनवासी (*a*) inhabiting in a forest

बनबिलाव (*nm*) a wild cat

बनमानुस (*nm*) a wild animal resembling a man

बनमाला (*nf*) a garland made of several kinds of flowers

बनराज (*nm*) a lion

बनवाई (*nf*) the work or wages paid for preparing a thing

बनाना (*v*) to construct; to make; to form

बनाम (*ind*) as against, versus

बनाव (*nm*) preparation, formation, ornamentation; —सिंगार make-up

बनावट (*nf*) construction; composition; frame, structure, get up

बनावटी (*a*) artificial, unnatural, showy, unreal; —बोली बोलना to mince; —रूप personation; —भक्ति sanctimony

बनिया (*nm*) a merchant, a grocer, a trader, a shop-keeper

बनियाइन (*nf*) a trader's wife; a kind of undergarment

बनैला (*a*) wild of forest

बपौती (*nf*) patrimony, heritage

बबर (*nm*) a lion; —शेर a lion

बबुआ (*nm*) a word of endearment used for a son, a child

बबूल (*nm*) mangrove, *acacia* tree

बबूला (*nm*) a bubble; आग — very enraged, fiery

बम (*nm*) a shell, a bomb

बया (*nm*) a weaver-bird, a tailor-bird

बयान (*nm*) a narration, a description or statement, an account

बयाना (*nm*) money which is given in advance, earnest money, advance money

बर/वर (*nm*) a bridegroom; (*a*) good, excellent, complete; (*ind*) on the other hand; beyond; on, upon; —करार fixed, established, effective; —ख्वास्त dismissed, discharged; dissolved; —ख्वास्तगी dismissal; dissolution; discharge

बरकत (*nf*) blessing, abundance, gain, profit

बरखा (*nf*) rain

बरगद (*nm*) a banyan tree

बरछा (*nm*) a lance, a dart

बरछी (*nf*) a pike, a spear, a dart

बरजना (*v*) to obstruct; to forbid, to prohibit

बरजोरी (*nf*) tyranny, force

बरत (*nm*) a fast

बरतन (*nm*) a pot, utensil

बरतना (*v*) to behave; to use

बरताव (*nm*) treatment, behaviour

बरदाश्त (*nf*) endurance; forbe-

arance; patience

बरफ़ (*nf*) ice

बरबस (*adv*) forcibly, all of a sudden

बरबाद (*a*) destroyed, ruined; wasted

बरमा (*nm*) an auger, a drill

बरस (*nm*) an year; —गाँठ birth-day

बरसना (*v*) to shower, to rain; to be spread all round

बरसात (*nm*) the rainy season; the rains

बरसाती (*a*) pertaining to rains; (*nm*) a raincoat

बरसी (*nf*) the first death anniversary

बरांडा (*nm*) a verandah

बरात (*nf*) a marriage party

बराती (*nm*) people comprising a marriage party

बराबर (*a*) level; equal, plain, matching; (*adv*) constantly; —करना to make even; to ruin; to leave nothing

बराबरी (*nf*) parity, equality, similarity

बरामद (*a*) recovered; exposed

बरामदा (*nm*) a balcony, a corridor, a gallery

बरौनी (*nf*) the eyelashes

बर्ताव (*nm*) treatment, behaviour

बर्फ़ीला (*a*) snowy, icy; glacial

बर्फ़ी (*nf*) a kind of rectangular sweetmeat, a lozenge

बर्बर (*a*) savage, barbarian;

—ता savagery

बल (nm) power; strength; vitality; —वान powerful; —हीन weak

बलगम (nm) phlegm

बलवा (nm) riot; rebellion; —ई a rioter; riotous

बलवान् (a) potent, vigorous, strong, stout

बलशाली (a) strong, powerful

बला (nf) calamity; an evil spirit

बलात् (ind) all of a sudden; forcibly

बलात्कार (nm) ravishment, rape; violence; oppression

बलि (nf) an oblation; an offering, sacrifice; the victim offered to a deity; —चढ़ाना to sacrifice

बलिदान (nm) offering a sacrifice to god, an immolation; —करना to sacrifice, to immolate

बलिष्ठ (a) very strong; strongest, having tremendous vigour

बलिहारी (nf) sacrifice

बली (a) powerful, robust, strong

बलैया (nf) trouble, disease, calamity

बल्कि (ind) moreover; on the contrary; but; rather

बल्लम (nm) a spear or lance; —दार a spearman

बल्ला (nm) racket; a bat

बल्ली (nf) a prop or pole

बवंडर (nm) a violent storm, a cyclone, a typhoon

बवासीर (nf) piles; खूनी— bleeding piles, haemorrhoids

बशर्ते (ind) —कि with the provision that, provided that, only if

बसंत (nm) the spring season

बस (nm) will; control; a bus; (adv) sufficient, enough; (ind) that's all, that'll do; enough; sufficiently

बसना (v) to live, to dwell, to settle, to stay

बसर (nf) maintenance

बसाना (v) to inhabit; to colonize; to rehabilitate

बसेरा (nm) a dwelling; an abode; short stay

बस्ता (nm) a bag; a bundle; a portfolio

बस्ती (nf) an inhabited place, a dwelling; colony

बहंगी (nf) a sling for carrying things on shoulders

बहक (nf) raving, rave

बहकना (v) to talk incoherently; to rave; to be intoxicated; to be enticed

बहकावा (nm) allurement, enticement; instigation

बहन (nf) a sister

बहना (v) to float, to flow, to glide, to blow

बहनोई (nm) the sister's

husband, brother-in-law

बहरहाल (*ind*) however, at any rate, nevertheless

बहरा (*a*) deaf, hard of hearing

बहलाना (*v*) to recreate, to amuse; to divert one's mind

बहलाव (*nm*) recreation, diversion, amusement, entertainment

बहलावा (*nm*) enticement, allurement; false hope

बहस (*nf*) an argument, a discussion, debate

बहादुर (*a*) brave, valiant; courageous; bold

बहादुरी (*nf*) bravery; courage; boldness

बहाना (*nm*) a pretence, false colours, an excuse; make believe; (*v*) to cause to flow, to set afloat; to ruin, to destroy

बहार (*nf*) the spring season; merriment; joviality

बहाल (*ind*) reinstated

बहाली (*nf*) restoration to former post

बहाव (*nm*) a flow, flood, ebb in water, outflow

बहिष्कार (*nm*) a proscription, reprobation, exile

बहिष्कृत (*a*) expelled from society, boycotted

बही (*nf*) an account book; —खाता a ledger

बहु (*a*) many, several, much; —ज्ञ well-informed, very experienced; master of many trades; —धंधी multipurpose; variously occupied; —मुखी multifarious; —मूल्य precious, invaluable; —रूपिया one who assumes various forms; —संख्यक majority

बहुत (*a*) very, abundant, too, plentiful

बहुतायत (*nf*) abundance, plenty

बहुतेरा (*a*) much, abundant; (*adv*) in various ways, fully

बहुतेरे (*a*) numerous, several

बहुदर्शी (*a*) learned, experienced

बहुधा (*ind*) in various ways; usually; generally, mostly

बहुभाषी (*a*) polyglot

बहुमत (*nm*) opinion of the majority

बहुलता (*nf*) amplitude, manifoldness

बहुवादी (*a*) very talkative

बहू (*nf*) a son's wife, a daughter-in-law; wife; a newly married woman

बहेड़ा (*nm*) the fruit of the tree —*belleric myrobalan*

बहेलिया (*nm*) a fowler, hunter

बाईं (*a*) left

बाँका (*a*) curved, crooked, foppish, dandy

बाँग (*nf*) the call of Mohammedans to worship; the crowing of a cock

बांचना (v) to read aloud; to read kestrel

बाँझ (nf) a barren woman; (a) barren, unfertile

बाँट (nf) allotment, division; deal; share

बाँटना (v) to divide; to distribute; to deal

बाँदी (nf) a bondmaid, a slave girl

बाँध (nm) a dike; dam; lock; barrage

बाँधना (v) to attach; to tie; to pack; to wrap around

बांधव (nm) relation, kindred; friend; brother

बांबी (nf) an ant-hill; a snake's hole

बाँस (nm) a bamboo; pole

बाँसुरी (nf) a flute, pipe; reed

बाँह (nf) a sleeve; an arm

बा a prefix to nouns meaning - having; —अदब respectful; humble; —क़ायदा regularly, duly; according to rules

बाक़ी (a) left over, remaining; (nf) balance; remainder

बाग (nm) a garden; (nf) the reins; —मोड़ना to turn in a direction; —डोर the reins, a halter

बाग़बान (nm) a gardener

बाग़बानी (nf) gardening, the act of cultivating, horticulture

बाग़ान (nm) gardens

बाग़ी (nm) a rebel; a mutineer

बाघ (nm) a tiger, a lion

बाज़ (nm) a hawk, falcon, kestrel

बाजरा (nm) Indian corn, millet

बाजा (nm) a muscial instrument of any kind

बाज़ार (nm) a market, market place; —भाव market-rate

बाज़ा/री —रू (a) belonging to the market place; vulgar; cheap

बाज़ी (nf) a wager, bet; play; turn

बाज़ीगर (nm) a conjurer; a juggler, a magician

बाज़ीगरी (nf) jugglery

बाजू (nm) the arm; overside; wing of bird; flank of an army

बाट (nf) way, path, course; (nm) a weight; —जोहना to wait for

बाड़ (nf) a hedge; a fence

बाड़ी (nf) an enclosure; a small orchard; house

बाढ़ (nf) freshet, a flood

बाण (nm) an arrow

बात (nf) talk; a discourse, a conversation, saying, statement; —काटना to interrupt

बातूनी (a & nm) talkative; great talker; a chatter-box

बाद (ind) subsequently, after, later

बादल (nm) a cloud; —फटनाthe clouds to be scattered; —छाना the sky to be overcast with clouds

बादशाह (nm) a ruler, a king

बादशाहत (nm) rule, kingdom, government

बादशाही (a) kingly, royal

बादाम (nm) an almond

बादामी (a) of the colour of almond

बादी (a) windy, flatulent; (nf) flatulence, fat; wind

बाधक (a) obstructing, troubling; hindering; —ता obstruction, impediment

बाधना (v) to obstruct, to impede

बाधा (nf) an impediment, **obstruction, hinderance**

बाधित (a) impeded, hindered obstructed

बाध्य (a) compelled, forced; obliged; —करना to obligate

बान (nm) an arrow; (nf) a structure, a custom

बानगी (nf) a sample, a specimen; an example

बानर (nm) a monkey; an ape

बाना (nm) dress

बानी (nf) speech

बाप (nm) father; —दादा forefathers, ancestors

बापुरा (a) mean, helpless; needy

बाबत (nf) connection, affair

बाबा (nm) father, dad, papa; grandfather; an old man; ascetic; —आदम the most primitive man

बाबुल (nm) father

बाबू (nm) a word used for a gentleman; father; middle class man

बायाँ (a) left, adverse

बायें (ind) to the left; in the opposite camp

बारंबार (ind) time and again, again and again; repeatedly

बार (nf) turn; time; (nm) a gate, a door, a place of shelter; —बार again and again

बारदाना (nm) the commodities of a trader, goods, wares

बारखड़ी (nf) the consonants of the Devnagri alphabet combined with the twelve vowels

बारहदरी (nf) a summer-house with several indoors

बारहमासा (nm) a kind of song which is sung in all the seasons of the year

बारहमासी (a) flowering all round the year; —पौधा a perennial plant

बारहसिंगा (nm) a reindeer, stag, gnu or wild beast

बारात (nf) a marriage procession; —सम्बन्धी processional

बाराती (a) member of a wedding party

बारिश (nf) the rainy season

बारिस्टर (nm) a barrister

बारी (nf) millet; a turn; (nm) a low Hindu caste in the traditional caste set up;

—बारी से in turns

बारीक (a) thin; slender; subtle; very small

बारीकी (nf) thinness; excellence; subtleness

बारूद (nf) gun-powder

बारे में (ind) with regards to

बाल (nm) a boy; hair; (a) young of tender age; not mature —बुद्धि childishness; childish; —ब्रह्मचारी a life-long celibate; —रोग children's disease; —विधवा child widow; —विवाह early marriage; —बराबर hair-breadth, very narrow

बालक (nm) a young child, a lad, a boy; —के सदृश boyish, —पन का juvenile; —त्व purility; —हत्या infanticide

बालकपन (nm) infancy, boyhood

बालकाल (nm) boyhood, infancy

बालचरित्र (nm) childish pranks and freaks

बालटी (nf) a bucket, pail

बाल-बच्चे (nm) children, family

बालभाव (nm) infancy

बालभोग (nm) offering made to Lord Krishna in the morning

बालम (nm) a lover; a husband, a beloved person

बालरोग (nm) diseases of children

बाललीला (nf) childish pranks

बालसूर्य (nm) Sun appearing in the sky in the early morning

बाला (nm) an ear-ornament; (nf) young woman; an adolescent girl

बालिका (nf) a girl, a daughter, a female child

बालिग़ (a) a youth who has attained the age of maturity; a major; adult; —होना to come of age

बालिग़ मताधिकार (nm) adult franchise

बालिश (nf) a pillow; (a) ignorant; stupid

बालिश्त (nm) a hand span

बाली (nf) an ear-ring; ear of corn

बालुका (nf) sand

बालू (nf) sand, gravel; —दानी a sand box

बालूशाही (nf) a kind of sweet-meat

बाल्य (nm) childhood, infancy, boyhood; (a) belonging to a boy; —काल childhood

बाल्यावस्था (nf) childhood, tender age, immaturity

बावड़ी (nf) a tank of water

बावजूद (adv) nevertheless, in spite of, against

बावरची (nm) a Mohammedan cook; —ख़ाना kitchen

बावला (a) insane; crazy, mad; —पन insanity; craziness

बावली (nf) an insane woman; a large well in which there

are flights of stairs to descend up to the water

बाशिंदा (nm) an inhabitant of a place, a resident

बाष्प (nm) vapour; tears

बास (nf) foul smell, bad adour

बासा (a) kept overnight, stale; (nm) a dwelling place

बासी (a) not fresh, stale, dried up

बाहर (ind) outside, without; beyond

बाहरी (a) exterior, outward; superficial, alien

बाहु (nf) an arm; —पाश an arm-embrace; —बल strength of one's arms, valour

बाहुल्य (nm) plenty, abundance

बाह्य (ind) beyond; outside; (a) external, outward, exterior; superficial

बिंदी (nf) a dot; a point; zero, cipher

बिंदु (nm) a spot; a point, dot; zero, cipher

बिंधना (v) to be entangled in something, to be pierced

बिंब (nm) a shade, reflection, glimmer, image; a shadow of something

बिकना (v) to be sold

बिकवाना (v) to cause to be sold

बिकाऊ (a) saleable, for sale

बिक्री (nf) sale, marketing; disposal

बिखरना (v) to be dispersed, to be scattered

बिखेरना (v) to scatter; to diffuse

बिगड़ना (v) to be spoiled; to be damaged; to be enraged, to lose temper

बिगाड़ (nm) friction, discord; quarrel

बिगाड़ना (v) to destroy; to spoil; to put out of order; to cause to go astray

बिगाना (a) foreign, alien

बिगुल (nm) a bugle

बिचकाना (v) to make mouths at, to balk, to wry the mouth

बिचरना (v) to loiter, to roam; to travel

बिचला (a) situated in the middle, mid; central

बिचारा (a) helpless, poor; —पन helplessness

बिच्छु (nm) a scorpion, a prickly plant

बिछना (n) the spreading of a bed

बिछना (v) to spread out a bed, to scatter, to extend

बिछावन (nm) a bed, bedding

बिछुड़ना (v) to be separate, to be separated from a person

बिछोह (nm) bereavement, deprivation

बिछौना (nm) a bed, bedding

बिजली (nf) lightning; electricity; thunderbolt; —घर a power-station

बिटिया (nf) a daughter

बिड़ाल (nm) a cat

बिताना (v) to spend time

बिता (nm) a span

बिदकना (v) to split asunder, to be provoked

बिदाई (nf) a farewell, a send off, an adieu

बिनती (nf) an earnest request, an entreaty

बिनना (v) to weave, to knit, to pick up, to select

बिना (ind) but, without, in the absence of

बिनाई (nf) work or wages for knitting, work of picking

बिनौला (nm) cotton-seed

बिफरना (v) to revolt, to be displeased, to be unhappy

बियाबान (nm) a desert, a wilderness, a jungle; (a) uninhabited; deserted

बिरता (nm) strength, power; capability

बिरला (a) rare, uncommon, scarce

बिरह (nm) separation from one's beloved; love-sickness

बिरही (a & nm) a lover who is suffering from the pangs of separation from his beloved

बिराजना (v) to take one's seat; to grace by one's presence

बिरादरी (nf) fraternity; brother-hood, community

बिराना (a) strange, alien; (v) to offend by making wry faces, to jeer, to make mouths at

बिरोज़ा (nm) tar, turpentine

बिल (nm) a hole; burrow; cavity; bill

बिलकुल (a & adv) all, quite, wholly, completely; utter, sheer

बिलखना (v) to sob, to weep, to lament

बिलग (a) separate

बिलगना (v) to be separated

बिलगाना (v) to detach, to disjoin, to separate

बिलगाव (nm) separation; detachment; aloofness

बिलटी (nf) a railway way-bill, railway receipt; —काटना to despatch

बिलबिलाना (v) to be tormented, to be restless with pain

बिला (ind) without, unless

बिलाना (v) to be ruined; to disappear, to vanish

बिलार (nm) a he-cat

बिलाव (nm) a tom-cat, big cat

बिलोना (v) to churn milk; to stir

बिलौटा (nm) a kitten

बिल्ला (nm) a tom-cat

बिल्ली (nf) a cat

बिल्लौर (nm) a pebble, a crystal

बिल्लौरी (a) pertaining to a crystal or pebble

बिवाई (nf) chilblain; —फटना to have chilblain

बिसात (nf) ability, capacity; a chess-board; —के बाहर beyond one's capacity

बिसातखाना (nm) a general

merchandise shop

बिसाती (*nm*) a pedlar, a haberdasher

बिसारना (*v*) to forget, not recollect or keep in mind

बिसूरना (*v*) to lament, to wail; to sob

बिस्कुट (*nf*) a biscuit

बिस्तर (*nm*) a bed; —बंद a hold-all

बिस्मिल्लाह (*nf*) beginning, commencement; (*ind*) with the name of God, a word used by Muslims at the commencement of a work; —करना to commence, to make a beginning; —ही गलत होना to misfire at the very outset, to have a wrong beginning

बिहा/र (*nm*) an eastern state of the Indian Union; a Buddhist monastery; —री belonging or pertaining to बिहार

बींधना (*v*) to bore a hole into, to pierce

बीघा (*nm*) a land measure which is five-eighths of an acre

बीच (*nm*) centre, middle part; —का intermediate; central; —बचाव mediation

बीचोंबीच (*adv*) exactly in the middle or centre of things

बीज (*nm*) seed; germ; origin; cause; nucleus

बीजक (*nm*) list; a bill of purchase, invoice

बीजगणित (*nm*) Algebra

बीट (*nf*) the dung of birds

बीड़ी (*nf*) a packet of betel leaves; crude form of a cigarette

बीतना (*v*) to be spent; to expire; to pass; to happen

बीन (*nf*) a lute, a flute; a classical Indian stringed instrument called वीणा

बीनना (*v*) to pluck; to choose; to pick up

बीबी (*nf*) a respectful word used by a woman for a younger sister of her husband; a respected lady

बीभत्स (*a*) loathsome, disgusting

बीमा (*nm*) an insurance

बीमार (*a*) diseased; ill; unwell; (*nm*) a patient

बीमारी (*nf*) illness; disease; sickness

बीर (*a*) intrepid; brave; (*nm*) brother

बीवी (*nf*) wife

बीहड़ (*a*) rugged; dense, thick; (*nm*) a dense forest

बुंदा (*nm*) an ornament in the form of a pendant which is worn in the ear

बुआ (*nf*) father's sister

बुखार (*nm*) fever

बुजदि/ल (*a*) timid, coward; —ली timidness

बुजुर्ग (a) old, elderly; venerable; (nm) fore-fathers, ancestors

बुजुर्गाना (a) befitting elders; elderly

बुझना (v) to be extinguished, to be quenched; to be dejected

बुझाना (v) to put out; to exting-uish; to quench; to talk in riddles

बुड़बुड़ाना (v) to murmur, to gabber

बुड्ढा (a) aged, old

बुढ़ापा (nm) old age

बुढ़िया (nf) an old woman

बुत (nm) a statue, an idol, image; (a) dumb and life-less; —परस्त idol-worship-per; —परस्ती idol-worship

बुदबुदाना (v) to jabber; to mutter

बुद्ध (nm) Lord Buddha

बुद्धि (nf) wisdom, intellect; sense; mind

बुद्धिमत्ता (nf) prudence, intel-ligence

बुद्धिमान (a) wise; intelligent; brilliant

बुद्धू (a) block-headed, stupid

बुध (a) wise

बुनकर (nm) a weaver

बुनना (v) to knit, to weave

बुनवाई (nf) charges for weaving

बुनाई (nf) wages paid for weaving

बुनिया/द (nf) base, foundation; basis; —दी fundamental

बुरका (nm) a mantle, a veil

बुरा (a) wicked; bad; evil; —व्यवहार misbehaviour; —भला bad and good, abuse; —मानना to feel bad

बुराई (nf) vice, evil; defect; fault

बुर्ज (nm) pinnacle; a tower

बुलं/द (a) lofty, high; —दी loftiness, height

बुलबुल (nf) a nightingale

बुलबुला (nm) a bubble; (a) transient, transitory

बुला/ना (v) to summon, to call, to invite; —वा call, invita-tion, summons

बुवाई (nf) sowing

बुहारना (v) to broom, to sweep

बुहारी (nf) a broom

बूँद (nf) a drop

बूँदाबाँदी (nf) light shower, a drizzle

बू (nf) foul smell; a disagre-eable odour

बूचड़ (nm) a butcher; —खाना butchery; a slaughter-house

बूझना (v) to make out; to enquire; to solve

बूट (nm) a boot; green pod of gram

बूटा (nm) a large sized embroidered

बूटी (nf) medicinal plant, a herb

बूढ़ा (a) aged, old

बूता (nm) capability; capacity

बूरा (*nm*) unrefined powdered sugar

बुह/त् (*a*) big; huge; large; —तर bigger

बेंत (*nm*) a stick, a cane

बे (*pref*) without, out of, void of, a vocative particle used to express contempts; —अक्ल foolish, stupid; —अदब rude, impudent; —आब without lustre, worthless; —आबरू disgraced; —इंसाफ़ी injustice, tyranny; —इज़्ज़त disgraced, dishonoured; —इज़्ज़ती dishonour, disgrace; —इल्म illiterate; —ईमान dishonest, treacherous; —ईमानी improbity; dishonesty, —कद्र disrespect; —करार restless, uneasy, perplexed; —करारी restlessness, perplexity; —कल disturbed in mind; —कली uneasiness, restlessness; —कस humble, mean, shelterless; —कसूर innocent, faultless; —काबू uncontrolled; —काम unemployed; idle; —कायदा contrary to rule or law, illegal; —कार useless, unemployed; idle; —कारी unemployment; —खटके without apprehension, freely; —ख़बर uninformed, senseless; —ख़बरी the state of being out of senses;

—गरज़ी carelessness; —गाना foreign, alien; —गार the act of forcing a person to work for less wages; —गुनाह fault-less, innocent; —घर home-less; —चारा helpless, poor; —चैन restless; —जान lifeless, feeble; —जोड़ unparalleled, matchless; —टिकिट ticket-less; —डौल ugly; —ढंगा silly; —ढब unmanageable; —तकल्लुफ़ informal; —तरतीब disorderly; —तहाशा at top speed; —तार wireless; —तुका absurd; —परदा unveiled, exposed; —फ़िक्र careless; un-worried; —फ़िक्री un-mindful; —बस helpless; —बसी helplessness; —मन unspirited; —मानी useless, —मेल mismatched; —रहम cruel; —रुख़ी disregard; —रोक-टोक without any hitch; —रोज़गार unemployed; —वफ़ा faithless, —शक of course; —शर्म shameless; —शुमार countless; —सब्री impatience; —सुध senseless, careless; —सुरा out of tune; —हया shameless; —हाल miserable; —हिसाब unlimi-ted, very much; —होश unconscious, fainted

बेचना (*v*) to sell; to dispose of

बेटा (*nm*) a son

बेटी (*nf*) a daughter

बेठिकाने (*a*) in the wrong place,

out of place

बेड़ा (nm) a raft; fleet

बेड़ी (nf) iron fetters for the legs, shackles

बेडौल (a) incongruous; ugly

बेतकल्लुफ़ (a) frank, without observing formalities

बेतमीज़ (a) rude, unmannerly

बेताब (a) perplexed

बेतौर (a) in a bad way

बेदख़ल (a) ejected, dispossessed from holdings

बेदर्दी (nf) hard-heartedness

बेघड़क (adv) fearlessly, unhesitatingly

बेधना (v) to pierce; to puncture

बेनसीब (a) unfortunate

बेपरवाह (a) unmindful, careless

बेबुनियाद (a) without a foundation

बेर (nm) a plum, a jujube

बेल (nm) the wood apple; (nf) a creeping plant, a flowery decoration made on walls

बेलदार (nm) a labourer who digs with a spade

बेलदारी (nf) working with a pick-axe; labour job

बेलन (nm) cylinder; a roller

बेलना (nm) a pastry roller; (v) to roll kneaded flour into flat bread

बेला (nm) a jasmine flower; a kind of violin, a house-hold utensil; (nf) time

बेवकूफ़ (a) foolish, unintelligent, stupid

बेवक़्त (adv) untimely, inopportunately

बेवा (nf) a widow

बेशक़ीमत (a) precious, costly

बेशक़ीमती (a) costly, of great value

बेसन (nm) gram flour

बेस्वाद (a) insipid, tasteless

बेहतर (a) better; (ind) very well

बेहतरी (nf) goodness, excellence

बेहद (a) boundless, unlimited

बेहूदा (a) rude, impolite, mean, uncivilised

बैंगन (nm) brinjal

बैंजनी (a) purple, reddish blue, violet-coloured

बैकुंठ (nm) the paradise

बैठक (nf) meeting; sitting; drawing room; base; —ख़ाना a drawing room

बैठना (v) to occupy a seat; to sit; to sink; to be adjusted; to appear; to ride on

बैरंग (a) bearing letter

बैर (nm) hostility, enmity, ill-will

बैरा (nm) a bearer

बैराग (nm) renunciation, disownment

बैरागी (nm) a recluse

बैरी (nm & a) a foe; an enemy; an opponent

बैल (nm) a bullock, an ox

बैसाखी (nf) a crutch

बोआई (nf) the work or wages

paid for sowing seeds in a field

बोझ (*nm*) load; a burden

बोझा (*nm*) same as बोझ

बोझिल (*a*) very heavy; burdensome

बोटी (*nf*) a slice of flesh

बोतल (*nf*) a bottle

बोदा (*a*) dull; lazy; timid; meek

बोदापन (*nm*) laziness; dulness

बोध (*nm*) sense; perception; knowledge; understanding

बोधक (*a*) informing, indicating

बोधगम्य (*a*) fit to be comprehended

बोधिसत्त्व (*nm*) an epithet of Gautama Buddha

बोना (*v*) to sow seeds, to set, to scatter

बोरा (*nm*) a canvas bag, a sack

बोरिया (*nf*) a small sack; a mat, a bedding

बोरी (*nf*) a small bag or sack

बोल (*nm*) speech; taunt

बोलचाल (*nf*) conversation, talk; friendly relation

बोलना (*v*) to speak, to utter; to pronounce

बोलवाना (*v*) to cause to speak up

बोलबाला (*nm*) overbearing influence, sway

बोली (*nf*) speech; dialect; language; a bid

बोवाई (*nf*) sowing

बोवाना (*v*) to cause seeds to be sown by another

बोहनी (*nf*) the first sale of the day of a trader

बौखला/ना (*v*) to be terribly enraged; to be insane or mad; —हट rage, fury

बौछार (*nf*) a shower, a splash; spray

बौड़म (*a & nm*) silly, stupid; hance —पना (*nm*)

बौद्ध (*a & nm*) a follower of Gautam Buddha, a Buddhist; —मत Buddhism; —विहार a Buddhist monastery

बौद्धिक (*a*) intellectual; —ता intellectuality

बौना (*a & nm*) pigmy; dwarf; dwarfish

बौर (*nm*) the small flowers that grow on mango or neem trees

बौरा (*a*) mad; ignorant; foolish; —ई madness; ignorance; foolishness; —या mad, insane

बौराना (*v*) to be mad or insance

ब्याज (*nm*) interest; —खोर a usurer; —खोरी usury; —दर-ब्याज compound interest

ब्याना to calf, to foal, to give birth to (in animals)

ब्यालू (*nf*) supper; dinner

ब्याह (*nm*) wedding, marriage ceremony

ब्याहता (*a & nf*) married to a person

ब्याहना (*v*) to wed, to marry; to

give or take in marriage

व्यौत (nf) an arrangement; a method; an opportunity; cutting of a cloth in tailoring

व्यौतना (v) to cut cloth for preparing garments

व्यो/रा (nm) detail; particulars; description; —रेवार systematic, detailed

व्यौरा (nm) see व्योरा

ब्रह्म (nm) God; the divine source of the universe; ego; —घाती killer of a Brahman. —ज्ञानी theologian —भोज the collective feeding of the Brahmans —विद्या theosophy

ब्रह्मचर्य (nm) celibacy, chastity

ब्रह्मचारिणी (nf) a woman who observes celibacy

ब्रह्मचारी (nm) a religious student who observes celibacy

ब्रह्मांड (nm) the universe, cosmos

भ

भ the fourth member of the fifth pentad of consonants in Devnagri alphbet

भंग (nm) fracture; dissolution; split; breach

भंगिम (nf) posture, pose; obliquity

भंगी (nm) a sweeper

भंगुर (a) brittle, perishable; —ता brittleness, perishableness

भंजन (nm) demolition, breaking; ruination

भंडा (nm) a secret; a utensil

भंडार (nm) a store house, a store; the place where household goods are stored

भंवर (nm) a whirlpool

भंवरा (nm) the black bee

भक्त (nm) a follower; devotee

भक्ति (nf) worship; devotion

भक्षक (nm) an eater, eating

भक्षण (nm) feeding; devouring; eating

भक्ष्य (a) eatable, edible

भगंदर (nm) fistula in the anus

भग (nf) the female genital

भगदड़ (nf) fleeing, stampede

भगवती (nf) a goddess, an epithet of Durga or Saraswati

भगवा (a) saffron (coloured)

भगवान् (nm) God, Lord

भगाना (v) to cause to run away, to drive off, to put to flight

भगिनी (nf) a sister, sisterly relation

भगोड़ा (*nm & a*) run away, deserter

भग्न (*a*) broken, defeated, vanquished

भग्नावशेष (*nm*) the broken fragments of something, the ruins of building

भजन (*nm*) a prayer; worship; adoration; a hymn

भजना (*v*) to adore; to worship; to repeat the name of God

भट (*nm*) a warrior, a soldier

भटकना (*v*) to lurk, to meander; to go astray

भटिया/र (*nm*) an innkeeper; —रिन (*nf*) a female inn-keeper

भट्ट (*nm*) a title of Brahmans,

भड़क (*nf*) show, pomp; gaud; splendour; —दार gaudy; splendid; shining

भड़कना (*v*) to be startled

भड़काना (*v*) to blow up into a flame; to excite

भड़कीला (*a*) showy; gaudy; —पन gaudiness, vividness

भड़मड़ाना (*v*) to tap, to thump

भड़भूँजा (*nm*) a man who parches grain

भड़ास (*nf*) accumulated grudge

भड़ुआ (*nm*) one who lives on the earnings of prostitutes

भती/जा (*nm*) a nephew (brother's son); —जी (*nf*) a niece (brother's daughter)

भत्ता (*nm*) an allowance

भदंत (*a*) reverend, honourable; adored

भदेस (*a*) unsophisticated; clumsy

भद्द (*nf*) humiliation, disgrace

भद्दा (*a*) gawky; ugly; vulgar; —पन deformity; vulgarity; ugliness

भद्र (*a*) educated; gentle; pious worthy, noble. —जन a gentle man

भनक (*nf*) a low sound; rumour, hearsay

भनभनाना (*v*) to buzz, to hum, to drone

भनभनाहट (*nf*) buzz, whizzing

भभक (*nf*) a sudden burst of flame, sudden blaze

भभकना (*v*) to inflame, to kindle fire

भभका (*nm*) a still, a retort

भभकी (*nf*) a threat

भभूका (*nm*) flame, blaze

भभूत (*nf*) the ashes of cowdung smeared on the forehead by ascetics

भयंकर (*a*) fierce, fearful, dreadful, terrible

भय (*nm*) a fright, fear; danger; risk. —ग्रस्त frightened; —शून्य dauntless

भयभीत (*a*) frightened, afraid; alarmed

भयाकुल (*a*) terrified, frightened

भयानक (*a*) fearful, frightened, dreadful, horrible

भयावह (*a*) terrible, fearful

भर (a) complete, full, entire, whole; —पाई quittance, payment in full, —पूर full, full to the brim; —पेट to the fullest satisfaction

भरण (nm) cherishing, nourishing, the act of bearing; —पोषण maintenance, support

भरती (nf) admission, an enlistment, a recruitment; enrolment

भरना (v) to fill; to load

भरम (nm) doubt, suspicion

भरमाना (v) to delude, to deceive, to create an illusion

भरमार (nf) plenty, abundance

भरसक (adv) to the best of one's ability

भराई (nf) the work or wages paid for filling a thing

भराव (nm) stuffing; filling

भरोसा (nm) hope; trust; confidence

भर्ता (nm) lord; husband; Vishnu

भर्त्सना (nf) reproach; abuse; denunciation

भर्राना (v) to be choked; to whizz; to turn hoarse

भलमनसाहत (nf) nobility

भला (a) good, well, gentle, noble; (nm) well-being; good; —चंगा healthy, in good health; —मानस a gentleman

भलाई (nf) goodness; weal, well-being

भव/तीय (ind) your, yours; —तीया feminine form of भवतीय

भवन (nm) mansion; a house, a palace

भवानी (nf) an epithet of Durga

भविष्य (nm) the future; —दर्शी, द्रष्टा a seer, one who can see through into the future; —वक्ता a prophet, an augur; —वाणी oracle, prediction

भविष्यत् (a) that is yet to come, future

भव्य (a) beautiful, grand; divine

भस्म (nf) ash; —सात् burnt to ashes

भस्मीभूत (a) burnt to ashes; ruined

भहराना (v) to crash down

भांग (nf) the intoxicating hemp; —खाना to be intoxicated; —छनना to drink भांग

भांजना (v) to fold; to twist something; to brandish

भांजी (nf) interruption, impediment; niece (sister's daughter)

भांड (nm) a jester, clown

भांड़ (nm) buffoon

भांड़ा (nm) a pot, utensil, equipment

भांडागार (nm) a treasure-house

भांडार (nm) a store-house, a

treasure-house

भाँति (nf) kind; mode; method

भाँपना (v) to look into; to guess the truth

भाँय-भाँय (nm) sound produced in a lonely place

भाई (nm) a brother; —चारा fraternity; —बंद्‌kith and kin; —भतीजावाद nepotism

भाग (nm) a share; a portion, a division

भाग-दौड़ (nf) strenuous effort; running about

भागना (v) to run away, to flee; to escape

भागी (a & nm) fortunate, lucky; —दार a sharer, partner

भागीरथी (nf) the river Ganga

भाग्य (nm) destiny, fate, fortune, lot, luck; —दोष fault of fortune; —परायण, वादी a fatalist; —लक्ष्मी god-dess of fortune; —वशात्‌ luckily; —वाद fatalism; —विधाता fortune-maker; —शाली fortunate; —हीनता star-crossed

भाग्य/वान् (a) happy, lucky; —वती fortunate lady

भाजक (nm) a divisor in mathematics; (a) dividing

भाजन (nm) a pot; a fit or suitable person

भाज्य (nm) a factor, divisor; (a) divisible

भाट (nm) a bard, a minstrel, a flatterer

भाटा (nm) low tide, falling tide

भाड़ (nm) a parcher's oven

भाड़ा (nm) fare; hire; rent; freight

भात (nm) boiled rice

भानजा (nm) the sister's son

भानजी (nf) sister's daughter

भाना (v) to fit, to suit; to be liked, to be pleasing

भाप (nf) steam; damp; fume; vapour

भाभी (nf) brother's wife, a sister-in-law

भामिनी (nf) a woman

भार (nm) load; burden; weight; —क्षमता carrying capacity; —वाहक a carrier; porter

भारत (nm) India; —माता Mother India; —वर्ष India, the Indian sub-continent; —वासी an Indian; —विद्या Indology

भारती (nf) speech, the name of the goddess Saraswati

भारतीय (a & nm) Indian; an Indian

भारी (a) big; heavy, weighty; —पन weight; heaviness; —भरकम of massive struc-ture

भार्या (nf) a married woman; wife, better half

भाल (nm) the forehead

भाला (nm) a spear, lance

भालू (nm) a bear

भाव (nm) rate; emotion, feeling; idea, —ताव bargain-

ing; —प्रधान emotional;
—व्यंजक expressive; —शून्य
unattached; —हीन cold

भावज (nf) brother's wife,
sister-in-law

भावना (nf) wish, fancy, desire,
motive

भावात्मक (a) emotional

भावबोधक (a) sentimental

भाववाचक (a) infinitive; (nm)
an abstract noun

भावानुवाद (nm) free translation

भावार्य (nm) purport; sense

भावी (a) future, coming

भावुक (a) emotional; sentimental; reflecting; hence—
ता (nf) emotion, sentiment

भाव्य (a) possible, probable

भावोत्कर्ष (nm) emotional
excellence

भावोन्मत्त (a) emotion-crazy,
overwhelmed by emotion

भावोन्मेष (nm) emergence of an
emotion or sentiment

भाषण (nm) talk, speech;
address; —कर्ता a speaker

भाषांतर (nm) rendition,
translation; —कार a tran-
slator; interpreter

भाषा (nf) speech, language,
tongue; —विज्ञान philology;
—शास्त्र glossology; —बद्ध
written in current dialect

भाषाई (a) linguistic

भाषित (a) spoken, uttered, told

भाषी (nm) a speaker

भाष्य (nm) a commentary,

annotation; —कार an-
notator

भास (nm) light, ray, —मंत
brilliant, —मान appearing

भासना (v) to glean; to appear,
to be known

भासित (a) glittering, appeared

भिंडी (nf) the vegetable called
lady's finger

भिक्षा (nf) begging; —वृत्ति a
beggar's occupation

भिक्षार्थी (nm) a beggar

भिक्षु (nm) a beggar; Buddhist
mendicant

भिक्षुक (nm) a beggar

भिखारिन (nf) a female beggar

भिखारी (nm) a beggar

भिगोना (v) to sop, to soak, to
drench

भिड़ंत (nf) clash; encounter,
confrontation

भिड़ (nf) a wasp; —का छत्ता a
cluster of wasps

भिड़ना (v) to quarrel, to collide,
to clash; to skirmish

भित्ति (nf) a wall; the board on
which a painting is made

भिदना (v) to enter into; to
penetrate; to be pierced

भिनकना (v) to hum as bees, to
create disgust, to buzz

भिनभिनाना (v) to make a
buzzing sound

भिन्न (a) separate, various;
—ता discordance, diversity,
difference

भिन्नार्थक (a) having a different

meaning or significance

मिन्नाना (*v*) to feel giddy

मिश्ती (*nm*) one who carries water in a large leather bag

मिषज् (*nm*) a physician

भींचना (*v*) to pull, to tighten

भी (*ind*) also; too; even

भीख (*nf*) begging; alms

भीगना (*v*) to be wet, to be drenched

भीड़ (*nf*) multitude; crowd; mob

भीड-मड़क्का (*nf*) hustle and bustle

भीत (*a*) terrified; afraid; (*nf*) a wall

भीतर (*ind*) in, within, inside, into; —ही भीतर within one-self

भीतरी (*a*) inner, inward; internal; secret

भीति (*nf*) terror; awe; trembling

भीनी (*a*) pleasant, sweet smell

भीम (*a*) awful, terrible

भीरु (*a*) coward; shy; timid

भीरुता (*nf*) timidity; cowardice

भील (*nm*) a wild mountainous tribe dwelling on the banks of the river Nurmada

भीषण (*a*) awful, terrible, fearful

भीषणता (*nf*) awfulness

भीष्म (*a*) terrible, frightful; —पितामह Grand-uncle of the Pandavas & Kauravas

भुक्खड़ (*a*) hungry, gluttonous; poor

भुक्त (*a*) eaten; enjoyed

भुक्ति (*nf*) food, meal; enjoyment

भुख/मरा (*a*) starved, hungry; gluttonous; —मरी famine; starvation

भुगतना (*v*) to suffer pain; to undergo

भुगतान (*nm*) payment in full settlement, decision

भुगताना (*v*) to finish; to pay; to deliver; to accomplish

भुजंग (*nm*) a snake, sarpent

भुजा (*nf*) arm; side

भुजिया (*nf*) dried and parched vegetable

भुट्टा (*nm*) maize-corn

भुनना (*v*) to be parched or fried

भुनभुनाना (*v*) to mutter, to speak in an indistinct way

भुनाना (*v*) to encash; to get parched; to change

भुरभुरा (*a*) friable; crisp; dry and powdery

भुलक्कड़ (*a*) forgetful; negligent

भुलाना (*v*) to cause to forget, to coax, to neglect

भुलावा (*nm*) deception, delusion

भुवन (*nm*) the universe; world

भुवनपति (*nm*) a king

भुस (*nm*) chaff, straw, husk

भूंकना (*v*) to bark, to yap, to bay, to yelp

भूंजना (*v*) to parch, to trouble

भू (nf) the earth; the world; ground; soil; —घर a mountain; —मंडलthe globe, the earth; —विद्a geologist; —विद्या geology

भूकंप (nm) an earthquake

भूख (nf) appetite, hunger; desire, necessity; —हड़ताल hunger strike

भूखा (a) hungry; needy, desirous

भूगर्भ (nm) the internal part of the earth

भूगोल (nm) geography, globe; —वेत्ता a geographer

भूघन (nm) material, matter

भूचर (nm) an animal living on the earth

भूचाल (nm) an earthquake

भूचित्र (nm) map of the world

भूटानी (a) pertaining to Bhutan; (nm) a resident of Bhutan

भूत (a) gone, past, bygone; (nm) an evil spirit, a ghost; —काल the past (tense); —पूर्व ex, previous, former

भूतल (nm) the surface of the earth, the world

भूदान (nm) gift of land

भूनना (v) to roast; to parch; to fry; to toast

भूपति (nm) an emperor, a king

भूपाल (nm) a king

भूमंडल (nm) the earth

भूमध्यरेखा (nf) equator

भूमध्यसागर (nm) the mediterranean sea

भूमि (nf) land; the earth, globe, soil; —गत underground

भूमिका (nf) foreward, preface; introduction; back-ground; —बाँधनाto prepare the back-ground

भूरा (a) brown, hoary, grey

भूरि (a) very much; —भूरि very much

भूल (nf) a mistake; negligence; slip, —करना to slip; —से amiss; —चूक a lapse, a miss; —सुधार correction

भूलना (v) to mistake; to err; to be forgotten

भूलभुलैयाँ (nf) a maze

भूलाभटका (a) stray

भूषण (nm) an ornament, jewels

भूषित (a) decorated, dight, adorned

भूसा (nm) chaff, husk, straw

भूसी (nf) chaff, bran, husk

भुंग (nm) the large black bee

भृकुटी (nf) eyebrow; a frown

भृत्य (nm) a slave; a servant; an employee

भेंगा (a) squint-eyed

भेंट (nf) an interview; meeting; gift, present; an offering

भेंटना (v) to visit

भेजना (v) to send; to transmit; to send forth

भेजवाना (v) to cause to despatch

भेजा (nm) the brain

भेड़ (nf) sheep; timid person

भेड़ा (nm) a ram

भेड़िया (nm) a wolf

भेद (nm) difference; secret

भेदक (a) piercing, breaking through

भेदभाव (nm) a difference

भेदिया (nm) a spy, an emissary

भेष (nm) an assumed appearance; a disguise; a counterfeit dress

भेषज (nm) medicine, medicament; remedy

भेस (nm) appearance; dress; guise; —बदलना to disguise

भैंस (nf) a female buffalo; an extra-fat woman

भैंसा (nm) a he-buffalo; stout and sturdy man

भैया (nm) a brother

भैरवी (nf) a Raga which is sung in the early morning

भोंकना (v) to pierce, to poke

भोंड़ा (a) ugly, illshaped; —पन insolence

भोंदू (a) stupid, foolish, silly

भोंपू (nm) a wind-instrument, horn, siren

भोक्ता (a) one who eats or enjoys; (nm) a licentious person

भोग (nm) the experience of pleasure or a pain; pleasure, enjoyment

भोगलिप्सा (nf) evil habit

भोगलोलुप (a) sybarite

भोगना (v) to suffer; to enjoy; to undergo

भोगी (nm) one who enjoys a thing, one who is always engaged in the pursuit of pleasure

भोग्य (a) worthy of being enjoyed or experienced, fit to be used

भोज (nm) a feast; banquet

भोजन (nm) meals, food; diet; —भट्ट a glutton

भोजनशाला (nf) a kitchen

भोजनालय (nm) a restaurant; mess

भोजपत्र (nm) the leaf and bark of birch tree

भोर (nm) the early morning, dawn

भोला (a) simple, innocent; foolish; —पन innocence, simplicity; —भाला very simple, artless

भौं (nf) an eyebrow

भौंकना (v) to bark like a dog; to talk too much

भौंरा (nm) a black bee, beetle

भौगोलिक (a) pertaining to the terrestrial globe, geographical; —ता geographicality

भौचक्का (a) non-plussed, dumb-founded

भौजाई (nf) brother's wife

भौतिक (a) material; physical, elemental; —वाद materialism; —वादी a materialist; —विज्ञान physics

भौतिकी (nf) physics

भौमवार (nm) Tuesday

भ्रंश (nm) falling, declining

भ्रम (nm) suspicion, confusion, —जाल illusion; चित्त— crack-brained

भ्रमण (nm) going round; excursion; travel

भ्रमर (nm) large black bee; beetle

भ्रष्ट (a) spoilt; corrupt; fallen

भ्रष्टता (nf) corruption, degradation

भ्रष्टाचार (nm) wantonness, depraved behaviour

भ्रष्टाचारी (a) of loose morals

भ्रांत (a) mistaken, fallen into error

भ्रांति (nf) a mistake, an error; delusion, a doubt

भ्राता (nm) a brother

भ्रातृत्व (nm) brotherhood

भ्रातृभाव (nm) brotherly affection

भ्रामक (a) causing to whirl, causing to err, deceiving

भ्रू (nm) an eyebrow; —भंगिमा attractive movement of eyebrows

भ्रूण (nf) a child in the womb; —हत्या murder of a foetus

म

म the fifth member of the fifth pentad of consonants in Devnagri alphabet

मंगता (nm) a beggar

मंगनी (nf) engagement; a borrowed thing

मंगल (nm) auspiciousness; Mars; welfare; Tuesday; (a) auspicious; —कामना good wishes; —कार्य an auspicious ceremony; —सूचक auspicious; —सूत्र the lucky thread worn by a married woman

मंगलाचरण (nm) the worship of Ganesha at the commencement of an undertaking, a benediction

मंगाना (v) to ask for, to send for, to cause to bring

मंगेतर (nm & nf) fiance or fiancee; (a) one to whom a man or a women is betrothed (for marriage)

मंच (nm) a bed; a dais, a raised platform

मंजन (nm) tooth-powder

मंजना (v) to be cleansed, to be rinsed

मंजरी (nf) a new shoot, a sprout

मँजाई (nf) act of cleansing

मंज़िल (nf) a halting-place in a journey; a storey of a house; destination

मंजु (a) good, beautiful, pleasing, lovely; —भाषी sweet-speaking (man) —भाषिणी sweet-speaking (women)

मंजुल (a) see मंजु

मंजूर (a) accepted; granted; bestowed; approved

मंजूरी (nf) acceptance; approval; sanction

मंजूषा (nf) a small chest, a case, a box

मंझधार (nf) see मझधार

मंझला (a) intermediate; middle

मंझोला (a) middling, of average size

मंडन (nm) ornamentation, decoration; support through argumentation

मंडप (nm) a shelter; a canopy raised for ceremonial purposes; a pavilion

मंडराना (v) to hover, to circumambulate, to flutter about

मंडल (nm) circumference; ring; territory; board; orbit

मंडलाकार (a) circular, annular

मंडली (nf) corporation, association, party, society; ring

मंडलेश्वर (nm) a ruler over twelve kingdoms

मंडवा (nm) canopy

मंडित (a) ornamented; decorated; filled

मंडी (nf) a big market; a bazar

मंडूक (nm) a frog

मंतव्य (nm) a view, opinion

मंत्र (nm) advice; a counsel; a secret consultation

मंत्रणा (nf) a counsel; advice; view, opinion

मंत्रविद्या (nf) the science of spells; magic, jugglery

मंत्रसंहिता (nf) part of the Veda which contains hymns

मंत्रालय (nm) ministry

मंत्रिमंडल (nm) cabinet, ministry

मंत्री (nm) a minister; a secretary; an adviser; a counsellor

मंथन (nm) agitating, stirring; churning, a churning stick

मंथर (a) slow, lazy, stupid, dull

मंद (a) feeble, idle, dull

मंदता (nf) slowness, tardiness, lassitude

मंदप्रकाश (nm) dimlight, glimmer

मंदबुद्धि (a) dull, blunt

मंदभाग्य (a) wretched, ill-fated; unlucky, unfortunate

मंदमति (a) feather-brained

मंदा (a) slow, tardy; weary, bad

मंदाकिनी (nf) celestial Ganga

मंदाग्नि (nf) indigestion

मंदिर (nm) a temple

मंदी (nf) a fall in price

मंशा (nf) wish, desire; wild

intention; purpose

मंसूख (a) repealed, cancelled

मँहगा (a) costly, expensive, high in price; see also महँगा

मकई (nf) Indian corn, maize

मकड़ी (nf) a spider

मकनातीस (nm) a loadstone, a magnet

मकबरा (nm) a large building containing a tomb

मकसद (nm) desire, intention

मकान (nm) a house, a residence, a dwelling place; —मालिक house-owner, landlord

मकोड़ा (nm) any small insect

मक्का (nm) maize, corn

मक्कार (a) deceitful, crafty, cunning

imposture

मक्खन (nm) butter; —बाज़ a flatterer; —बाज़ी flattery

मक्खी (nf) a fly; a bee; —मारन idle fellow

मक्खीचूस (nm) skinflint, miser, a niggardly person

मखमल (nm) velvet, plush

मखमली (a) velvety

मखाना (nm) a kind of dry fruit

मखौल (nm) a joke, a jest

मगज़ (nm) brain; kernel; pith; —पच्ची too much of brain-taxing

मगज़ी (nf) welter, edging, hem, frill

मगर (nm) a crocodile; (ind)

but, except

मगरमच्छ (nm) a crocodile

मग़रूर (a) proud, arrogant

मग्न (a) drowned, sunk, engaged

मचलना (v) to persist, to insist

मचला (a) insisting, obstinate

मचली (nf) nausea; —आना to feel like vomitting, to nauseate

मचान (nm) a raised platform, a stage, a scaffold; —बाँधना to prepare a scaffold

मच्छर (nm) a mosquito; gnat

मच्छरदानी (nf) a mosquito net

मछंदर (nm) a buffoon, a dunce

मछली (nf) a fish; pisces

मछुआ (nm) a fisherman, a fishmonger

मज़दूर (nm) a labourer, worker; —वर्ग the working class; —दल the Labour Party

मज़दूरी (nf) price which is paid for work or labour, wages; remuneration; stipend

मजनूँ (nm) the celebrated lover of Laila; a mad or insane man

मज़बूत (a) strong, compact, firm, vigorous, sturdy

मज़बूती (nf) firmness, strength, vigour; durability

मजबूर (a) helpless; obliged; compelled

मजबूरी (nf) helplessness, compulsion

मजबूरन (ind) under pressure,

being compelled

मज़मून (nm) subject, topic; article; composition

मजलिस (nf) an assembly, a meeting, a congregation

मज़हब (nm) sect, creed, religion

मज़हबी (a) religious

मज़ा (nm) flavour, relish; taste; pleasure

मज़ाक़ (nm) a joke, jest, humour

मज़ाकिया (a) humorous, witty, pranky; (nm) a jester, buffoon

मजाल (nf) power, strength

मजिस्ट्रेट (nm) a magistrate

मज़ेदार (a) relishing, tasteful; giving pleasure; delicious

मज्जन (nm) a bathing, a bath

मज्जा (nf) marrow

मझधार (nf) the current in the middle of a river

मझला (a) intermediate; middling

मझोला (a) middle, middle-most, of average size

मटकना (v) to conquect, to strut, to swagger

मटकाना (v) to cause to twinkle, to conquect

मटका (nm) a large earthen pitcher

मटकी (nf) a small pitcher

मटकीला (a) moving the body in ogling or winking eyes

मटमैला (a) muddy, dusty, dusky

मटर (nm) a pea

मटरगश्ती (nf) a stray walking, a ramble, a stroll

मटियामेट (a) almost destroyed or ruined

मटियाला (a) muddy, dusty, dirty

मट्ठा (nm) churned curd, butter milk

मट्ठी (nf) a kind of small bread which has been cooked in oil or clarified butter

मठ (nm) a monastery, a hermitage; —धारी the head of a monastery, an ascetic

मढ़ना (v) to envelop; to wrap, to frame; to impose

मणि (nf) a jewel, a gem, a precious stone

मणिधर (nm) a snake

मणिबंध (nm) the wrist, the corpus

मतंग (nm) an elephant; cloud

मत (nm) dogma, belief; an opinion; faith; vote; —दान poll, polling, casting of votes; —दाता a voter, an elector

मतभेद (nm) disagreement

मतलब (nm) purport, meaning; relation

मतलबी (nf) selfish, self-concerned

मतलाना (v) to feel like vomitting, to feel sick

मतली (nf) nausea, a feeling like vomitting

मतवाला (a) drunk, intoxicated; insane

मताधिकार (nm) a right to vote, suffrage, franchise; वयस्क— adult franchise

मताधिकारी (nm) one who is authorised to vote

मतानुयायी (nm) the follower of a tenet, a theorist

मति (nf) sense, intellect; understanding; opinion; —हीन stupid, foolish; — भ्रम confusion

मतैक्य (nm) agreement; unanimity

मत्त (a) drunk, mad, intoxicated; happy

मत्था (nm) the forehead; head

मत्स्य (nm) a fish

मत्स्यावतार (nm) an incarnation of Vishnu in the form of a fish

मथना (v) to churn, to batter; to agitate

मद (nm) passion; intoxication, arrogance; —मत्त intoxicated; passionate

मदद (nf) aid; help; assistance, support; relief

मददगार (nm) a helper; a supporter; an assistant

मदन (nm) the god of love

मदरसा (nm) a school

मद/होश (a) dead drunk; rendered senseless; —होशी drunkenness; intoxicatedness

मदारी (nm) a snake-charmer, a juggler

मदिरा (nf) wine, spirit

मदोन्मत्त (a) intoxicated; arrogant

मद्धिम (a) dim; slow; moderate

मद्य (nm) liquor, spirit, wine; —निर्माणशाला a distillery; —पान drinking

मधु (nm) honey; juice of flowers; liquor; the spring; —कोष a honey comb, —कर the large black bee; —करी alms given in the form of cooked food only; —मक्खी honey-bee, bee; —मेह diabetes; —शाला a bar

मधुर (a) pleasant; sweet; —ता sweetness; melodiousness

मधुरिमा (nf) sweetness, softness, melodiousness

मध्य (a) central, middle; intermediate; (nm) the middle part, the centre; —काल interval; mediaeval period; —भाग heart; —युग the Middle Ages; —पूर्व middle-east; —वर्ग middle class; —वर्ती central

मध्यम (a) middle, intermediate of moderate strength or size

मध्यमा (nf) the middle finger

मध्यस्थ (a) intermediate, medial; (nm) a mediator; —ता mediation

मध्यांतर (nm) an interval

मध्याह्न (nm) midday, noon

मन:शास्त्र (nm) psychology

मन (nm) heart; mind; desire; disposition; a weight equal to forty seers; —गढ़ंत imaginary; —चाहा desired, wished for, favourite; —बहलाव amusement, entertainment, recreation; —भावन beloved; attractive; —माना arbitrary; self-willed; —मौजी self-willed

मनका (nm) a bead

मनन (nm) brooding; meditation; thinking deeply over something; —शील thoughtful

मनश्चिकि/त्सा (nf) psychological treatment; —त्सक a psychotherapist

मनसूबा (nm) design; plan; intention; idea

मनस्ताप (nm) mental agony, regret, remorse, sorrow

मनस्वी (a) wise, strong-minded

मनहू/स (a) inauspicious, ill-fated; gloomy; —सियत (nf) gloominess, sombreness, inauspiciousness

मनहूसी (nf) gloominess, sombreness

मना (a) prohibited, forbidden

मनाही (nf) a prohibition, a restraint, forbiddance

मनाना (v) to persuade

मनिहार (nm) one who sells or makes glass bangles

मनीऑर्डर (nm) a money order

मनीषी (a) wise, learned

मनुष्य (nm) a man, human being; —लोक the world

मनुष्यत्व (nf) humanity

मनुहार (nf) persuasion

मनोकामना (मन:कामना) (nf) desire, wish

मनोगति (nf) mental disposition

मनोज (nm) an epithet of cupid—the god of love

मनोनीत (a) approved; nominated

मनोबल (nm) morale, moral strength

मनोयोग (nm) concentration

मनोरंजक (a) attractive, pleasing to the mind

मनोरंजन (nm) recreation, amusement

मनोरथ (nm) wish, desire; longing

मनोरम (a) attractive, beautiful, lovely

मनोवांछित (a) desired, wished

मनोविकार (nm) emotion of mind, feeling

मनोविज्ञान (nm) psychology

मनोविनोद (nm) amusement, pastime; hobby

मनोविलास (nm) musing, fancy

मनोविश्लेषण (nm) psycho-analysis

मनोवृत्ति (nf) mentality; mental attitude

मनोवेग (nm) impulse; a

passion

मनोवैज्ञानिक (a & nm) psychol - ogical; a psychologist

मनोव्यथा (nf) mental agony; affliction

मनोव्यापार (nm) thought, conception, mental work

मनोहर (a) beautiful, lovely

मनौती (nf) an assurance, a vow to offer something to a deity after the fulfilment of one's desire

मंतव्य (nm) thought

मन्नत (nf) same as मनौती

मन्मथ (nm) cupid

मम/ता (nf) —त्व (nm) affec - tion, attachment

मयूर (nm) a peacock

मयूरी (nf) a peahen

मरकत (nm) emerald

मरघट (nm) a cremation ground, a place for burning the dead

मरज़ (nm) a disease, a malady, a bad habit

मरण (nm) death, dying, mortality, expiration

मरणासन्न (a) on the death bed

मरतबा (nm) an order; a turn

मरदानगी (nf) bravery, valour, courage

मरदाना (a) masculine, male

मरना (v) to die, to decease, to pass away

मरम्मत (nf) mending, repair

मरहम (nm) an ointment; an unction; —पट्टी bandage

मरहूम (a) deceased, late, dead

मराल (nm) a goose, swan

मरियल (a) lean and thin, weak

मरीचिका (nf) mirage, sunbeam

मरीज़ (a) sick; ill; diseased; (nm) an ailing person, a patient

मरीना (nm) a kind of soft fine woollen cloth

मरु (nm) a desert, a barren soil

मरुत् (nm) wind, the deities of the wind

मरुद्वीप (nm) a fertile land in a desert, an oasis

मरुस्थल (nm) a desert

मरोड़ (nm) sprain, wrench, twist

मरोड़ना (v) to wring, to twist, to tease

मरोड़ा (nm) a gripe in the stomach

मर्कट (nm) a monkey, an ape

मर्ज़ (nm) a disease; ailment

मर्तबान (nm) an enamelled earthen pot which is used for holding oil or ghee

मर्ज़ी (nf) will, desire; pleasure

मर्त्य (a) dying, earthly; (nm) a mortal; —लोक the earth; —धर्म mortality, human nature

मर्द (nm) a man; a brave person

मर्दन (nm) rubbing; massage

मर्दानगी (nf) bravery; masculi - nity

मर्दाना (a) masculine; male

मर्म (nm) a secret, core, a vital organ

मर्मज्ञ (a) having a deep insight into a subject; (nm) a learned man, one who knows the secret

मर्ममेदक (a) fatal

मर्ममेशी (a) stinging, heart-rending

मर्म/पीड़ा (nf) intense mental agony; —स्पर्शी touching, poignant, heart-rending

मर्मर (nm) rustling; marble; —ध्वनि rustling noise

मर्यादा (nf) limit, dignity; rank

मल (nm) rubbish, filth; dirt; —मूत्र urine and faeces, excrement

मलना (v) to press hard; to rub; to smear; to massage

मलबा (nm) rubbish, debrish

मलमल (nf) muslin, linen

मलहम (nm) see मरहम

मलाई (nf) the cream of milk

मलाल (nm) sadness, dejection

मलिन (a) foul, dirty, filthy, sad; —पदार्थ filth

मलिनता (nf) nastiness, pollution

मलेरिया (nm) malaria

मल्ल (nm) an ancient tribe of wrestlers; an athlete; —भूमि a place for wrestling; —युद्ध a duel, a hand to hand fight

मल्लाह (nm) a boatman; a sailor, mariner, seamar

मवाद (nm) purulent matter, pus secreted from body

मवेशी (nm) cattle, quadrupeds, beast; —खाना a cattle pond

मशक (nm) a mosquito; (nf) a leathern water bag

मशक्कत (nf) labour, toil, pains

मशगूल (a) busy, engaged, employed

मशविरा (nm) counsel, advice, consultation

मशहूर (a) well-known, famous, celebrated

मशाल (nf) a torch; —ची a torch-bearer

मश्क (nf) exercise; practice

मस (nf) ink; the hairs on the upper lip appearing in early youth

मसकना (v) to split, to press, to tear asunder

मसखरा (a) humoursome; waggish; funny (nm) a joker, a buffoon, jester, funnyman

मसखरी (nf) a joke, a jest

मसजिद (nf) a mosque

मसनद (nf) a very big pillow

मसल (nf) a fable, an allegory, an example

मसलन (adv) pressing; rubbing; crushing; (ind) for example, for instance

मसलना (v) to crush, to press hard, to rub

मसला (nm) a proverb, a maxim, a saying

मसविदा (nm) a plaint of a suit, draft

मसहरी (nf) a mosquito curtain, a bedstead which is fitted with such a curtain

मसा (nm) a wart, mole

मसान (nm) a place for burning the dead, a cremation ground

मसाला (nm) spices; condiments; मसालेदार spiced

मसि (nf) writing ink; — शोषक blotting paper; — दानी an inkpot

मसीहा (nm) Jesus Christ; a religious leader

मसुड़ा (nm) the gum of the teeth

मसूर (nf) lentil, a kind of pulses

मसोसना (v) to repress; to subdue

मसौबा (nm) a draft

मस्जिद (nf) see मसजिद

मस्त (a) intoxicated, drunk, happy

मस्तक (nm) the head; forehead

मस्ताना (a) intoxicated, drunk; (v) to be lustful, to be overjoyed

मस्तिष्क (nm) head, brain, cerebrum

मस्ती (nf) intoxication, drunkenness, carefreeness

मस्तूल (nm) the mast of a boat or ship

मस्सा (nm) a wart

महँगा (a) expensive; dear; costly, high-priced

महँगाई (nf) dearness; expensiveness; costliness

महंत (nm) head priest of a temple, a monk; self-willed leader

महक (nf) odour, fragrance, scent, perfume; — दार sweet-smelling, fragrant

महकना (v) to give out fragrance or sweet smell, to perfume

महकमा (nm) the department for the performance of a work

महज़ (a) mere, pure, unmixed, only; (adv) only, entirely, merely, wholly

महताब (nm) the moon; (nf) moonlight

महतारी (nf) mother

महत् (a) big; great; excellent

महत्तर (a) greater, bigger

महत्ता (nf) significance, importance; greatness

महत्व (nm) greatness; — पूर्ण important, significant

महत्त्वाकां/क्षा (nf) ambition; — क्षी ambitious

महफ़िल (nf) a private assembly, recreational assembly

महबूब (a) dear, beloved

महर्षि (nm) a great saint

महल (nm) a palace, a stately mansion

महसूल (nm) custom, duty,

levy

महसूस (a) felt; experienced; perceived

महा (a) great, large, very, most; —कवि a great poet; an epic poet; —काल an epithet of Shiva; —काव्य a poetical composition of great length, an epic; —देव an epithet of Lord Shiva; —देवी an epithet of goddess Parvati; —नगर/नगरी cosmopolitan city; —पातक a great sin; —पातकी a great sinner; —पुरुष a great man; —प्रलय the great deluge; —प्रस्थान death; the final journey; —रथी a great warrior

महा/जन (nm) money lender; —जनी money lending

महात्मा (a) lofty-minded, high-souled; noble, generous; (nm) a great sage

महादान (nm) a great gift which attains heaven

महाद्वीप (nm) a continent, a mainland

महान् (a) great; eminent; big; —ता nobility; greatness

महानुभाव (a) illustrious, glorious, grand, eminent

महापुरुष (nm) a great personage, a saint

महाप्रलय (nm) the total destruction of the world

महाबली (a) extremely powerful, very strong

महाबाहु (a) having very long arms; very powerful

महामारी (nf) plague, an epidemic

महायज्ञ (nm) a great sacrifice

महायुद्ध (nm) a world-war, a war

महारत (nm) practice, expertise

महा/राज (nm) a great king; a term of respect used for Brahmans; a cook; —राजा a ruler, king; —राजाधिराज a king of kings; —रानी the queen

महावत (nm) the driver of an elephant

महावर (nm) red colour which is prepared from lac with which ladies whose husbands are alive paint their feet

महाविद्यालय (nm) a college

महावीर (a) lion-hearted, a very brave, heroic

महाशय (a & nm) a term of respect, sir, master, mister

महाशालीन (a) very humble and meek

महिमा (nf) dignity, greatness, worship, magnitude

महिला (nf) a lady

महिष (nm) a he-buffalo

महिषी (nf) a she-buffalo; a queen

महीन (a) thin, fine, not coarse, soft

महीना (nm) a month; menses;

महीने से in menses

महोत्सव (nm) great festival, a big celebration

महोदय (a) sir; hence महोदया madam

माँ (nf) mother, mamma

माँग (nf) a demand, a request, requirement

माँगना (v) to demand, to call for; to claim; to invite

मांगलिक (a) prosperous, auspicious

माँजना (v) to cleanse, to scrub; to polish

माँझी (nm) a seaman, a boatman, sailor

माँड (nm) boiled rice-water, rice-starch

माँडना (v) to rub, to knead flour

माँद (nf) a lair, den, barrow

माँदा (a) tired, ill, sick

मांस (nm) flesh; meat; —पेशी a muscle; —ल fleshy

मांसाहारी (nm) non vegetarian

माई (nf) a maid servant; an old woman; mother

माचिस (nf) a match-box, safety matches; match stick

मातम (nm) mourning; grief; —पुरसी expression of condolence

मात/हत (a) subordinate, under; hence —हती

माता (nf) mother; small-pox

मातामह (nm) mother's father, maternal grandfather

मातृ (nf) mother; —त्व motherhood; —भाषा mothertongue; —भूमि mother land

मात्र (ind) merely; only; barely; sheer

मात्रक (a) a certain size, magnitude or measure

मात्रा (nf) quantity, magnitude, a dose; scale

मात्सर्य (nm) jealousy, malice

माथा (nm) the forehead; forepart

मादक (a) inebriant; intoxicating; fascinating

मादकता (nm) drunkenness

मादा (a) female, of female sex

मादा (nm) essence; capability; pith; element

माधुर्य (nm) sweetness, gracefulness

माध्यम (a) medium, middle, central

माध्यमिक (a) intermediary; secondary

मान (nm) weight; measure, dignity; —चित्र a map; —दंड a standard; —पत्र an address of welcome

मान/क (a & nm) standard, norm, —कीकरण standardization

मानता (nf) recognition; importance

मानना (v) to accept; to agree, to confess; to respect; to suppose

माननीय (a) respectable;

honourable; revered; worthy

मानव (*nm*) human being, a man; mankind

मानवता (*nf*) mankind; humanity; —**वाद** humanism; —**वादी** a humanist

मानवीय (*a*) humane

मानस (*nm*) the mind; thought, the psyche; heart

मानसरोवर (*nm*) a large lake in the north of the Himalayas

मानसिक (*a*) mental, fanciful, psychic

मानहानि (*nf*) defamation

मानिनी (*a*) amorously sulking

मानी (*a*) haughty, proud, arrogant; (*nm*) purport

मानीटर (*nm*) a monitor

माने (*nm*) meaning, purport

मानो (*ind*) as though, as if, supposing

मान्य (*a*) respectable; considerable; —**ता** recognition

माप (*nm*) size; measurement; dimensions; —**दंड** touchstone; standard

मापक (*nm*) measurer, one who measures a quantity

मापना (*v*) to measure; to weigh

माफ (*a*) pardoned; forgiven; excused

माफ़िक (*a*) suitable; agreeable, favourable

माफ़ी (*nf*) pardon; forgiveness; exemption; rent-free land

मामला (*nm*) a business; an affair; a case; matter

मामा (*nm*) a maternal uncle, mother's brother

मामी (*nf*) a maternal aunt; mother's brother's wife

मामूली (*a*) common; ordinary; usual

मायका (*nm*) maternal house of a married woman

माया (*nf*) illusion, unreality; riches; phantom; —**मोह** illusion and attachment

मायावी (*a*) deceitful, illusive, phantasmic

मायूस (*a*) disappointed, frustrated

मार (*nm*) thrashing, beating, the cupid; —**काट** bloody encounter; —**धाड़** fighting and killing

मारक (*a*) destroying, killing, putting to death

मारकीन (*nm*) a kind of coarse jaconet, unbleached cloth

मारना (*v*) to beat; to kill; to hit, to strike; to punish

मारफ़त (*ind*) through; by; care of

मार्का (*nm*) a sign, a mark, a trade-mark

मार्ग (*nm*) a path, passage, way; road, route; —**प्रदर्शक** a guide; pioneer; —**प्रदर्शन** guidance

मार्गरक्षक (*nm*) a watch, a sentry

मार्जक (*nm*) a cleaner,

washerman

मार्जनी (nf) a broom

मार्फ़त (ind) by; through; C/o (care of)

मार्मिक (a) affecting the vital parts, influential to a great degree, touching

मार्मिकता (nf) the quality of having a thorough knowledge; heart-touching

माल (nm) goods; commodity; merchandise; stock; produce; riches; —ख़ाना a store house, a ware house; —गाड़ी a goods train; —गुज़ारी rent paid for land;—गोदाम the store house at a Railway station; —दार rich, wealthy; —पुआ a sweet cake; —मत्ता assets, riches, wealth

माला (nf) a row, series; a garland of flowers

मालाकार (nm) a garland-maker

मालामाल (a) immensely rich, very rich or wealthy

मालिक (nm) owner; master; a proprietor; husband

मालिकिन (nf) a matron, a mistress, housewife

मालिकाना (nm) ownership, a landed property; (a) proprietary

मालिकी (nf) ownership

मालिन (nf) wife of a gardener

मालिन्य (nm) dirtiness, impurity, foulness

मालिश (nf) rubbing oil on the body, massage

माली (nm) a gardener; garlander

मालूम (a) known

मावा (nm) essence, pith

माश (nm) black gram

माशा (nm) a weight of eight Rattis or eighteen grains

माशूक़ (nf) a beloved

मास (nm) a month

मासिक (a) monthly; per mensem; (nm) menstruation; a monthly magazine; —धर्म menstruation, monthly course

मासी (nf) the mother's sister

मासूम (a) harmless; innocent; hence —मियत

माह (nm) a month; —ताब the moon; —वार monthly, —वारी pertaining to every month, monthly

माहात्म्य (nm) glory, greatness

माहिर (a) expert

मिकदार (nf) quantity

मिचकाना (v) to wink, to blink

मिचना (v) to close, to shut

मिचलाना (v) to feel sick, to nauseate

मिचली (nf) feeling like vomitting, nausea

मिज़ाज (nm) temperament, habit; pride

मिज़ाजदार (a) arrogant, proud

मिज़ाज़ी (a) arrogant; fastidious

मिटना (v) to be erased, to be destroyed; to be ruined

मिट्टी (nf) earth; dust; soil; —का तेल kerosene oil; —के मोल damn cheap

मिट्ठू (nm) a parrot

मिठबोला (nm) a sweet-speaking person

मिठाई (nf) sweets, sweetmeat; confectionery

मिठास (nf) sweetness

मितभाषी (nm) one who is moderate in speech

मितव्यय (nm) economy, frugality

मितव्ययी (a) spending sparingly, frugal

मिताई (nf) friendship

मित्र (nm) a friend; an ally; —ता friendship; intimacy

मित्रद्रोही (nm) one who is on bad terms with his friends

मिथ्या (a) false, untrue, sham; (nm) untruth, falsehood; illusion

मिनमिनाना (v) to speak through nasal sounds

मिन्नत (nf) supplication; entreaty, request

मिमियाना (v) to bleat as sheep or goats

मियाँ (nm) master; husband; sir; a Mohammedan; —बीवी husband and wife; —मिट्ठू a sweet-spoken person; a parrot

मिरगी (nf) epilepsy

मिर्च (nf) pepper; chillies

मिलता-जुलता (a) resembling, having resemblance, like

मिलन (nm) union; a meeting; contact; —सार sociable

मिलना (v) to meet; to be mixed; to encounter; to merge

मिलान (nm) a comparison; verification, authentication

मिलाना (v) to compare; to unite; to mix

मिलाप (nm) an agreement, meeting; union

मिलावट (nf) blend, mixing; alloy adulteration

मिल्कियत (nf) estate; property; landed property

मिश्र (a) blended; mixed; combined; —ण a mixture, blend; combination

मिश्रित (a) mixed, compounded, complex

मिश्री (nf) sugar candy

मिश्रीकरण (nm) an admixture

मिष्टान्न (nm) sweetmeat, confectionery

मिसरी (nf) sugar candy

मिसाल (nf) an example, a comparison, a maxim

मिस्त्री (nm) a mechanic, mistry; technician; artisan

मींचना (v) to close, to shut

मीठा (a) pleasant; sweet; (nm) sweetmeat

मीन (nm) a fish; the twelfth sign of zodiac

मीना (*nm*) a valiant tribe of Rajputana; a kind of precious stone of blue colour

मीनाक्षी (*nf*) having eyes like those of a fish

मीनार (*nf*) a tower, a spire

मीमांसक (*nm*) one who reflects deeply on a subject

मीमांसा (*nf*) one of the six systems of Hindu Philosophy

मीर (*nm*) a leader, a chieftain, a religious promulgator

मीरासी (*nm*) a sect of Mohammedans who earn their living by buffoonery and singing

मील (*nf*) a mile

मुँगरा (*nm*) a wooden hammer, mallet

मुंज (*nf*) a kind of stiff grass which is used in making ropes (see also मूँज)

मुंडन (*nm*) the shaving of the head, the shaving of hairs of a child's head for the first time

मुंडना (*v*) to be head shaven; to be robbed

मुंडेर (*nm*) a parapet

मुंदना (*v*) to be closed or covered, to be shut up

मुंशी (*nm*) a scribe, a writer, a clerk; —गीरी the work or profession of a clerk/scribe

मुसिफ़ (*nm*) a judge of the civil court who is subordinate to a civil judge

मुँह (*nm*) the mouth; face; forepart; an opening; outlet; source; —काला disrespect, infamy; —ज़बानी verbal, oral; —दर-मुँह face-to-face; —देखी superficial; —फट loose-tongued; —बोला adopted; —माँगा fully answering one's wish; —लगा allowed too much liberty

मुहाँसा (*nm*) the pimples which appear on the face on the advent of youth

मुअत्तल (*a*) suspended from work for some time

मुअत्तली (*nf*) suspension

मुआ (*a*) dead; good-for-nothing

मुआफ़िक (*a*) suitable; agreeable, favourable (see also माफ़िक)

मुआयना (*nm*) inspection; visit

मुआवज़ा (*nm*) compensation; remuneration

मुकदमा (*nm*) a law suit; a case

मुकदमेबाज़ (*nm*) a litigant

मुकद्दर (*nm*) luck, fate, destiny

मुकद्दस (*a*) pure, holy

मुकम्मल (*a*) finished; ready

मुकर्रर (*a*) fixed, appointed, employed

मुकाबिला (*nm*) an opposition; competition; a comparison

मुकाम (*nm*) a halting place,

halt; a place, site

मुकुट (*nm*) a diadem, crown

मुकुर (*nm*) a looking-glass, a mirror

मुकुल (*nm*) a bud, a blossom

मुकुलित (*a*) blossoming, half-opened and half-shut; twinking of eyes

मुक्का (*nm*) a blow with the fist, buffet, thump

मुक्केबाज़ (*nm*) a boxer

मुक्केबाज़ी (*nf*) boxing

मुक्त (*a*) liberated, released from bondage, set free, let loose; —कंठ one who speaks very loudly, one who speaks up without any reserve; —चेता one who is desirous of attaining salvation; —वसन naked; —संशय whose doubts have been removed

मुक्ता (*nf*) a pearl

मुक्तावली (*nf*) a string of pearls

मुक्ति (*nf*) salvation; redemption, release, deliverance

मुख (*nm*) the mouth; face; forepart; entrance; —ज produced from mouth; —पृष्ठ the cover-page; —मंडल the face

मुखड़ा (*nm*) the mouth, face

मुख़्तार (*nm*) an agent, a deputy, an attorney; —नामा power of an attorney

मुख़्तारी (*nf*) the profession of a Mukhtar, attorneyship

मुखप्रक्षालन (*nm*) the washing of the mouth

मुखबंध (*nm*) a preface, an introduction or foreword to a book

मुख़बिर (*nm*) an informer

मुख़बिरी (*nf*) the work of a reporter or informer

मुखमंडल (*nm*) face, look, countenance, visage

मुखर (*a*) talkative, noisy

मुखरित (*a*) resonant, outspoken

मुख़ातिब (*a*) with whom a person talks, conversable

मुखापेक्षी (*nm*) one who is dependent on others

मुख़ालिफ़ (*a*) opposing, an enemy, a foe

मुख़ालिफ़त (*nm*) enmity

मुखिया (*nf*) a leader, a chief, the headman of a village

मुखौटा (*nm*) a mask

मुख्य (*a*) premier, chief; main, capital; —त: primarily, chiefly, mainly

मुख्यालय (*nm*) headquarters

मुगदर (*nm*) a club which is used in physical exercise

मुग़ालता (*nm*) illusion, mistake; misconception

मुग्ध (*a*) beautiful, infatuated; charmed

मुचलका (*nm*) a bond, binding agreement

मुजरा (*nm*) a deduction, allowance, salutation

मुजरिम (*nm*) an offender, a criminal

मुज़ायका (*nm*) worry, anxiety; obstruction

मुजाहिद (*nm*) a crusader

मुझ (*pron*) an inflective case of मैं

मुझे (*pron*) to me

मुटाई (*nf*) sturdiness; thickness

मुटापा (*nm*) plumpness, fatness

मुट्ठी (*nf*) a clutch, a grip; fist; a handful

मुठभेड़ (*nf*) conflict; an encounter, a confrontation

मुड़ना (*v*) to be turned back; to be bent; to be twisted

मुतआल्लिक (*a*) concerning, belonging to

मुताबिक़ (*ind*) agreeable to, corresponding, in accordance with

मुदित (*a*) delighted, pleased, rejoiced, happy

मुद्दई (*nm*) a complainant; a plaintiff, a prosecutor

मुद्दत/त (*nf*) a space of time, duration, time-limit; —ती old, antiquated

मुद्दा (*nm*) intention, theme, purport

मुद्रक (*nm*) a printer

मुद्रण (*nm*) the act of printing; —कला typography

मुद्रांकित (*a*) stamped, sealed

मुद्रालय (*nm*) a printing press

मुद्राक्षर (*nm*) a printing type

मुद्रा (*nf*) a seal; stamp; money, coin

मुद्रित (*a*) stamped; printed; sealed

मुनक्का (*nm*) a large-size dried grape, big currant

मुनसिफ़ (*nm*) a judge, an administrator of justice

मुनादी (*nf*) a proclamation by beat of drum

मुनाफ़ा (*nm*) a profit, deal, a bargain, gain; —ख़ोर a profiteer; —ख़ोरी profiteering

मुनासिब (*a*) proper, suitable, fit, convenient

मुनि (*nm*) a pious and religious person, an ascetic, a saint

मुनीम (*nm*) an assistant, an accountant, a syndic

मुफ़लिस (*a*) indigent, poor, penniless

मुफ़लिसी (*nf*) poverty, indigence

मुफ़स्सल (*a*) detailed; (*nm*) the suburb of a town

मुफ़ीद (*a*) beneficial, profitable, useful

मुफ़्त (*a*) without price, free of charge; —ख़ोर one who enjoys the wealth of others

मुबारक (*a*) auspicious, blessed, happy; —बाद congratulations

मुमकिन (*a*) feasible, possible

मुमुक्षु (*a*) wishing salvation

मुरझाना (*v*) to fade, to wither; to lose lustre

मुरदा (*nm*) a dead person, a

corpse; (a) lifeless, dead,
—दिल lifeless, melancholic

मुरब्बा (nm) a jam, candy, a
preserve, a sweetmeat, (a)
square

मुरली (nf) a pipe, flute

मुरव्वत (nf) politeness, benevolence, affability

मुराद (nf) a desire, wish;
purport, craving

मुरीद (nm) a follower, a pupil,
a disciple

मुर्गा (nm) a cock, fowl

मुर्गी (nf) a hen

मुर्दनी (nf) a death-like stillness

मुर्दा (nm) corpse, dead body;
—घर mortuary

मुलज़िम (nm) a convict, an
accused

मुलम्मा (nm) the covering of an
article with gold or silver

मुलहठी (nf) liquorice

मुलाकात (nf) a visit, a meeting,
an interview

मुलाकाती (nm) an acquaintance

मुलाज़मत (nf) employment,
service

मुलाज़िम (nm) a servant, an
attendant

मुलायम (a) soft; tender, gentle

मुलायमियत (nf) softness,
gentleness, tenderness

मुलाहज़ा (nm) notice, inspection, regard

मुल्क (nm) a country, kingdom,
realm

मुल्की (a) belonging to one's

country, civil, national

मुल्तवी (a) postponed; adjourned

मुल्ला (nm) a Muslim priest

मुवक्किल (nm) a pleader's
client

मुशायरा (nm) a poetic
symposium

मुश्किल (a) difficult, intricate,
(nf) difficulty, hardship

मुसकराना (v) to smile, to titter

मुसकराहट (nm) smile, a laugh,
a beam

मुस्कान (nf) a smile

मुसन्निफ़ (nm) the compiler or
writer of a book

मुसम्मात (nf) a woman, a
female; a title which is
affixed to the name of a
female

मुसलमान (nm & a) a Moham-
medan; Muslim

मुसाफ़िर (nm) a traveller, a
passenger; —खाना a halting
place for passengers; an
inn; a waiting room at a
railway station

मुसीबत (nf) misery, misfortune,
disaster, —का मारा afflicted

मुस्टंडा (a) stout, robust,
wicked

मुस्तकिल (a) firm, strong,
settled, permanent

मुस्तैद (a) prompt, ready

मुस्तैदी (nf) promptness,
readiness

मुहताज (a) needy, poor,

necessitous, indigent

मुहताजी (nf) poverty, indigence

मुहब्बत (nf) love, affection, fondness

मुहर (nf) seal; a gold coin; stamp; — बंद sealed

मुहरा (nm) the front part, face

मुहर्रम (nm) the first month of the Arabic year-which is held sacred by Moham- medans

मुहर्रमी (a) pertaining to Moharrum; melancholy

मुहर्रिर (nm) a scribe, a clerk

मुहर्रिरी (nf) the work of a scribe or clerk, the work of writing

मुहल्लत (nf) grace period; extra time

मुहल्ला (nm) a locality

मुहाना (nm) the mouth of a river

मुहाफ़िज़ (a) a protector, guard, keeper

मुहाल (a) impossible, difficult; (nf) facade

मुहावरा (nm) idiom; practice, phraseology

मुहिम (nf) an arduous task, an expedition, compaign

मुहर्मुहु (ind) again and again

मुहूर्त (nm) a division of time, auspicious moment

मुहैया (a) available, procured

मूँग (nm) the kidney-bean or black gram, green lentil

मूँगफली (nf) ground nut

मूँगा (nm) coral

मूँगिया (a) of dark-green colour

मूँछ (nf) moustaches, whiskers

मूँज (nf) a kind of red long reed of which ropes are made

मूँड़ना (v) to shave, to shave the hair of one's head

मूँदना (v) to cover, to shut up, to close the upper portion of a thing

मूक (a) speechless, dumb, wordless

मूठ (nf) a staff, stock, a handle

मूढ़ (a) ignorant, stupid, foolish, silly; — ता foolish- ness, stupidity; silliness

मूत्र (nm) urine, piss

मूत्राशय (nm) urinary bladder

मूर्ख (a) foolish, stupid, idiot, silly; — मंडली an assembly of fools, a group of idiots

मूर्खता (nf) folly, ignorance, stupidity

मूर्च्छा (nf) fainting, fit; state of unconsciousness

मूर्च्छित (a) fainted, swooned; unconscious

मूर्त (a) tangible; formal

मूर्ति (nf) statue, an idol; image; — कला sculpture; statuary; — कार sculptor, statuary

मूर्तिमान (a) incarnate, personi- fied

मूर्धन्य (a) pertaining to the head, top-ranking

मूल (nm) the root of a tree; an edible tuber; principal; origin, source; the original

text; (a) chief, original;
—त: basically, fundamen-
tally, primarily; essentially;
—तत्त्व the essential; —धन
the principal; —पाठ text,
original text; —भूत fundamental, essential, basic;
original; —स्रोत main source

मूली (nf) a radish, rootlet

मूल्य (nm) price; rate;
worth

मूल्यवान (a) precious, costly;
valuable, expensive

मूल्यांकन (nm) assessment,
evaluation

मूषक (nm) a mouse, a rat

मूसल (nm) a pestle; a pounder;
a rammer

मूसलाधार (a) heavy rain

मूसली (nf) a plant, the roots of
which are used in medicine

मूसा (nm) the founder of
Jewish religion

मृग (nm) a beast of the forest,
a deer; —चर्म the skin of an
antelope; —छाला deer-skin;
—जल waves seen in a
mirage; —तृष्णा mirage;
—नाभ musk

मृगया (nm) sport, hunting

मृगलोचना/नी (a) deer-eyed or
fawn-eyed (women)

मृगांक (nm) the moon

मृणाल (nf) the root of a lotus
plant

मृणालिनी (nf) a lotus plant

मृत (a) dead, late, no more

मृतक (nm) a dead person, a
corpse, a defunct person;
—कर्म funeral rites

मृतकल्प (a) almost dead

मृतगृह (nm) a cemetery, a
burying place

मृतजीवनी (nf) the art of
restoring a dead body to
life

मृत्तिका (nf) clay, earth

मृत्युंजय (nm) one who has
conquered death; (a)
deathless; an epithet of
Lord Shiva

मृत्यु (nf) death, demise,
decease; quietness, the end

मृत्युलोक (nm) the world of the
dead, the mortal world

मृत्युशय्या (nm) death-bed

मृत्युशोक (nm) mourning

मृदंग (nf) a drum, a tabor, a
timbrel

मृदु (a) cool; soft, mild; sweet;
tender; gentle

मृदु/ता (nf) softness; sweetness,
tenderness; —भाषी soft-
spoken; —हृदय pitiful,
tender-hearted

मृदुल (a) sweet; soft; tender;
mild; —ता softness; sweetness; mildness

मृषा (ind) falsely, uselessly, in
vain; (a) false, untrue

में (ind) in, into; among; between

मेंगनी (nf) the orbicular dung
of sheep or goat

में-में (nf) the bleating of sheep or goat etc.

मेंढक (nm) a frog; toad

मेंह (nm) rain

मेंहदी (nf) myrtle

मेख (nf) a peg; nail

मेखला (nf) a girdle, waist bend, a sword-belt

मेघ (nm) a cloud, a musical mode

मेघनाद (nm) the rumbling of clouds, thunder

मेज़ (nf) a table

मेज़पोश (nm) a table-cover

मेज़बान (nm) one who entertains a guest, a host

मेट (nm) a supervisor of labourers in a factory

मेथी (nf) a small plant the leaves of which are used as vegetable

मेदा (nm) the stomach

मेधा (nf) sense, intellect, prudence, understanding

मेधावी (a) wise; sagacious, intelligent

मेम (nf) an European lady, madam

मेमना (nm) a lamb, a kid, a species of horse

मेरा (pron) my, mine

मेरी (pron) faminine form of मेरा

मेरु (nm) a mythological mountain which was supposed to be made of gold

मेरुदंड (nm) backbone, spine; spinal cord

मेल (nm) connection; treaty; relation; match; mixture —जोल intimacy; union

मेला (nm) crowd, assemblage; fair; procession

मेवा (nm) dry fruit

मेह (nm) rain, rainfall; diabetes (see also मेंह)

मेहतर (nm) a sweeper of public lanes, a scavenger

मेहतरानी (nf) a female sweeper

मेहनत (nf) toil, labour; hard work; —कश a labourer

मेहनताना (nm) wages, price paid for a work

मेहनती (a) hardworking; laborious; industrious

मेहमान (nm) a guest; —खाना a guest house; —दार a host; —दारी hospitality, kindness to strangers

मेहमानी (nf) hospitality

मेहर (nf) kindness, compassion, favour

मेहरबान (a) kind, compassionate

मेहरबानी (nf) favour, kindness

मेहराब (nm) an arch, vault

मेहरी (nf) a woman who works as household utensil cleaner

मैं (pron) I; — स्वयं myself

मैका (मैके) (nm) a woman's paternal house

मैत्री (nf) friendship, cordiality

मैथुन (nm) sexual intercourse

मैदा (*nm*) fine flour

मैदान (*nm*) an open field; plain; battle-field

मैदानी (*a*) pertaining to plains; even

मैना (*nf*) blackbird

मैया (*nf*) mother

मैल (*nm*) filth, dirt, dross

मैलख़ोरा (*a & nm*) absorbing dirt, an apron

मैला (*a*) dirty, foul, unclean

मैला-कुचैला (*a*) filthy, dirty, dingy

मोढ़ा (*nm*) a stool which is made of basket

मोक्ष (*nm*) final liberation, salvation

मोच (*nf*) sprain, twist

मोची (*nm*) a shoe-maker, a cobbler, a saddler

मोज़ा (*nm*) stocking, socks

मोटर (*nf*) a motor-car

मोटा, (*a*) fat, plump; coarse, rough; —ई fatness, thickness; —ताज़ा fleshy; robust; मोटे तौर पर roughly speaking

मोटापा (*nm*) fatness, plumpness

मोड़ (*nm*) a bend, a twist; the winding of a river

मोड़ना (*v*) to twist; to turn back or in another direction

मोतिया (*nm*) a kind of jasmine flower; (*a*) light red or yellow, pearly-coloured

मोतियाबिंद (*nm*) a disease of the eye, cataract

मोती (*nm*) a pearl; —झरा typhoid

मोदी (*nm*) a grocer; —ख़ाना a provision store

मोम (*nf*) wax; —जामा oil-cloth; —बत्ती a candle-stick

मोमी (*a*) made of wax

मोर (*nm*) a peacock; —नी a peahen; —पंख a peacock-feather

मोरचा (*nm*) rust on iron; a battle front; —बंदी entrenchment

मोल (*nm*) price

मोह (*nm*) ignorance; delusion, illusion; affection; spell; —पाश the snare of worldly illusion; —भंग disillusionment; —ममता affection and attachment

मोहक (*a*) charming, fascinating; producing ignorance

मोहन (*a*) attractive, charming; tempting; (*nm*) enchantment; an epithet of Lord Krishna

मोहनी (*nf*) enchantment; delusion; a spell

मोहब्बत (*nf*) love, affection

मोहर (*nf*) a seal; a stamp; a guinea, gold coin

मोहल्ला (*nm*) a locality, ward, street

मोहलत (*nf*) fixed time

मोहित (*a*) charmed, spellbound; fallen in love; deceived

मोहिनी (*a*) charming, bewitching, fascinating; (*nf*) delusion, an incarnation of the god Vishnu

मौका (*nm*) occasion; chance; situation; location; site of occurrence; मौके पर at the appropriate time; on the spot; मौके से duly, just in time

मौखिक (*a*) oral, verbal; —परीक्षा *viva voce*

मौज (*nf*) caprice, a whim; delight; a wave

मौज़ा (*nm*) a village

मौजी (*a*) working according to one's whim, whimsical, merry

मौजूद (*a*) existing; present; ready, at hand

मौजूदगी (*nf*) presence; existence

मौजूदा (*a*) present, ready, current, existing

मौत (*nf*) demise, death, mortality

मौन (*a*) silent, taciturn, mum, quiet, speechless; (*nm*) quiescence; —व्रत a vow to keep quiet, to adopt silence

मौनी (*a*) taciturn, reticent

मौर (*nm*) a crown which is worn by a bridegroom during the marriage ceremony; blossom of a mango tree

मौलवी (*nm*) a learned Mohammedan

मौलिक (*a*) ultimate, original; fundamental; essential; —ता originality

मौली (*nf*) untwisted red coloured thread which is used in worship

मौसम (*nm*) season; weather

मौ/सा (*nm*) the husband of mother's sister; —सी mother's sister; —सेरे born of mother's sister

म्याऊँ (*nf*) mewing of a cat

म्यान (*nf*) a sheath

म्लान (*a*) faded, weak, withered; dirty; —ता state of being faded

म्लेच्छ (*nm*) a barbarian, a man of low birth; (*a*) unclean, shabby

य

य the first of the य, र, ल, व series of Devnagri alphabet, traditionally called अंत:स्थ (semi-vowels.)

यंत्र (*nm*) an engine, a machine; an instrument; mystical diagram; —चालित mechanized; —वत् like a machine; —कार a machinist, an engineer

यंत्रणा (*nf*) torment, torture

यंत्रशाला (*nf*) an observatory

यंत्रीकरण (*nm*) mechanization

यकीन (*nm*) faith; confidence; trust

यकृत (*nm*) the liver

यक्ष (*nm*) a kind of demi-god, attendant on Kuvera

यक्ष्मा (*nm*) tuberculosis, consumption

यजमान (*nm*) a host, one who performs a sacrifice

यजुर्वेद (*nm*) the third of the four Vedas

यज्ञ (*nm*) a religious sacrifice, an oblation; —कुण्ड the alter on which a sacrifice is made; —करने वाला a sacrificer; —कर्म a sacrificial ceremony; —पति he who makes a sacrifice; —पशु an animal which is slain in a sacrifice; —पुरुष an epithet of the God Vishnu; —भूमि the place where a sacrifice is performed

यज्ञोपवीत (*nm*) the sacred thread which is mostly worn by three upper classes of Hindus, the initiation ceremony among Hindus

यति (*nf*) a pause, check; (*nm*) an ascetic, an anchorite who has completely subdued his passions

यतीम (*nm*) an orphan, a foundling or deserted infant; —खाना an orphanage

यतीन्द्रिय (*a*) one whose passions and senses are under his control

यत्किंचित (*adv*) somewhat, a little

यत्न (*nm*) effort; exertion; attempt; labour

यत्नवान् (*a*) making effort; laborious; energetic; strenuous

यत्र (*adv*) where; —यत्र wheresoever; —तत्र hither and thither; —तत्र-सर्वत्र here, there and everywhere

यथा (*adv*) in whatever manner, as for example, for instance, as per; thus; —अवसर according to opportunity; —क्रम systematically, in order; —तथा in every way, by some means or other; —तथ्य as it is; —नियम as per rule; —निर्दिष्ट as directed; —पूर्व as existed before; —योग्य proper, suitably; —रुचि according to one's liking or taste; —वत as before; —विधि according to rule; —शक्ति according to one's capacity or power; —शीघ्र as early as possible; —संभव as far as possible; —समय in due course; —स्थान at the proper place

यथार्थ (*a*) actual, real

यथार्थता (*nf*) really, actually;
—वाद realism; —वादिता
realism; —वादी a realist;
realistic

यथेच्छ (*adv*) according to one's
wishes or desire

यथेष्ट (*a*) enough, sufficient;
adequate

यथोक्ति (*a*) as already stated,
above mentioned

यथोचित (*a*) proper; rightful;
reasonable; due; (*adv*)
justly; properly; duly

यदा (*a*) while, when, —कदा
sometimes or other

यदि (*ind*) provided that, if, in
case

यद्यपि (*ind*) although, though,
however

यदृच्छा (*nf*) free will

यम (*nm*) the god of death;
—दूत the messenger of
Yama, the god of death;
—लोक hell

यमक (*nm*) an alliteration in
different meanings

यमुना (*nf*) one of the most
important Indian rivers

यवन (*nm*) a Mohammedan; a
Greek

यवनिका (*nf*) a curtain; drop
scene

यश (*nm*) reputation, fame;
name; glory

यशस्वी (*a*) renowned, reputed;
glorious

यष्टि (*nf*) a stick, a twig, the
branch of a tree

यह (*pron*) it, this

यहाँ (*adv*) here, hither

यहीं (*adv*) at this very place

यहूदी (*nm*) a Jew

या (*ind*) or, whether

याचक (*nm*) a suppliant; a
beggar

याचना (*nf*) solicitation,
begging; asking for some-
thing

याचिका (*nf*) a petition

याजक (*nm*) one who performs
a sacrifice, a sacrificing
priest

यातना (*nf*) agony, anguish,
torment, torture

यातायात (*nm*) traffic

यात्रा (*nf*) a travel, journey; trip;
tour

यात्री (*nm*) a pilgrim; a traveller;
a passenger; a tourist

याद (*nm*) recollection;
remembrance, memory

यादगार (*nf*) a monument;
memorial; memento

याददाश्त (*nf*) memory

यादव (*nm*) a descendant of
Yadu

यान (*nm*) vehicle; a van

यानी (*ind*) that is, that is to say

यापन (*nm*) spending time,
passing away of time

यामिनी (*nf*) night

यार (*nm*) a companion; a
friend; a lover; —बाश a
friend of friends, good

companion

यराना (*nm*) friendship

यारी (*nf*) friendship; illegal love affair

यावत् (*adv*) until, as long as, as far as

यीशु (*nm*) Jesus Christ; —मसीह Jesus Christ

युक्त (*a*) combined, united; joined; fit, proper

युक्ति (*nf*) tact, skill, device; argument; —संगत reasonable, logical

युग (*nm*) era; period; times; age; epoch; couple

युगांत (*nm*) the end of a Yuga, cosmic destruction

युगांतर (*nm*) a new era, another age; —कारी revolutionary

युग्म (*nm*) couple; pair; (*a*) two

युद्ध (*nm*) a war, warfare, battle; fight; hostilities; —क्षेत्र battle-field; —नीति strategy; —पोत warship, —बंदी a prisoner of war; —विराम cease-fire

युयुत्सा (*nf*) an intention to wage war

युवक (*nm*) a young man; a youth

युवती (*nf*) a young woman, a youthful lady

युवराज (*nm*) a prince

युवराज्ञी (*nf*) a princess

युवा (*a*) young, vigorous; —अवस्था prime of life, youth

यूँ (*adv*) in this way, in this manner

यूथ (*nm*) a group, company, band

यूनिवर्सिटी (*nf*) a university

यूनानी (*a*) Greek; (*nm*) a Greek

ये (*pron*) these

येन-केन-प्रकारेण (*adv*) somehow, by fair or foul means; by hook or by crook

यों (*adv*) thus, in this way, like this, in this manner

योग (*nm*) sum, total; combination; addition; joining together; mixture; —क्षेम possessions, —तत्त्व the name of an Upanishad; —दर्शन one of the six schools of Hindu philosophy; —दान contribution; —निद्रा Vishnu's sleep which comes after the annihilation of the world —फल the sum total of numbers; —बल the power which is derived from continuous meditation; —रुढि a compound word which is used in a sense quite different from the meanings of its component parts

योगात्मा (*nm*) an ascetic

योगाभ्यास (*nm*) the practice of योग

योगासन (nm) posture of body which is proper for profound meditation of a Yogi

योग्य (a) suitable, fit; qualified; eligible

योग्यता (nf) eligibility; talent; aptitude; capacity

योजक (a) uniting, joining; (nm) one which combines

योजन (nm) union, joining, uniting; a measure of distance

योजना (nf) joining, uniting; a planning scheme; —आयोग Planning Commission

योद्धा (nm) a combatant, warrior, fighter, soldier

योनि (nf) source, origin; vagina, female organ of generation

यौगिक (a) pertaining to the practice of yoga; proper, suitable

यौवन (nm) youth, manhood, youthfulness

र

र the second amongst the series य, र, ल, व of Devnagri alphabet, traditionally called as अंत:स्थ (Semi vowels)

रंक (a) penniless, poor, pauper; (nm) a beggar, penniless person

रंग (nm) dye; colour; complexion; paint; beauty; influence; whim; kind; stage; —ढंग ways, manners; —बिरंगा multi-coloured; —भूमि theatre; —मंच stage; —रंगीला colourful; —रूप physical appearance; —शाला theatre; —साज़ a painter; —साज़ी painting

रंगत (nf) complexion; colour, delight; colour of face

रंगना (v) to dye; to paint, to colour

रंगरूट (nm) a newly recruited soldier or police man

रंगरेज़ (nm) a dyer of clothes

रंगवाई (nf) the price paid for colouring or dyeing

रैग/रेली —रेलियाँ (nf) (usually used in plural form) rejoicing, merriment

रँगाई (nf) dying charges; dyeing

रंगावट (nf) colouring, dyeing

रंगीन (a) coloured, dyed; painted; gay; luxury-loving; —मिज़ाज gay, colourful; mirthful; luxury loving

रंगीनी (nf) mirthfulness;

colourfulness

रैंगीला (a) gaudy, showy; beautiful, colourful, gay

रंचक (a) a little, slight; a small quantity (of a thing)

रंज (nm) grief, sorrow; anxiety; trouble

रंजक (a) delighting, glad-dening; a dyer; a painter

रंजित (a) painted; dyed; coloured; happy, delighted

रंजिश (nf) enmity; displeasure; ill-feeling

रंजीदा (a) sorry, grieved; sad, gloomy

रंजीदगी (nf) sadness, sorrow, displeasure

रैंडापा (nm) widowhood

रंडी (nf) a harlot, prostitute

रैंडुआ (nm) a widower

रंदना (v) to smoothen with a plane

रंदा (nm) a carpenter's smoothing instrument

रँधना (v) to cook food

रंध्र (nm) a hole, an aperture

रंभा (nf) the name of a fairy; (nm) a crow-bar, a lever

रैंभाना (nm) the bellowing of a cow or bull

रका/र (nm) the letter र (ra) and its sound; —रांत (word) ending in र

रईस (nm) a noble man; a rich person; (a) rich, wealthy; hence —ज़ादा

रईसी (nf) wealthiness; nobility;

richness

रकम (nf) an amount, a sum, wealth

रकाब (nm) a stirrup

रक्त (nm) blood; (a) red, saffron; attached; —क्षीपता anaemia, —पात a bloodshed, a bloody fight, slaughter; —पिपासा blood-thirst; —पिपासु blood-thirsty; —रंजित bloody; causing bloodshed

रक्षक (nm) a guard; a rescuer, defender; protector; (a) preventive

रक्षण (nm) a defence, protec-tion; an insurance

रक्षणीय (a) tenable

रक्षा (nf) protection; safety; care; defence; guarding; —सेना defence force

रक्षात्मक (a) safeguarding; defensive; protective

रख/ना (v) to set; to put; to hold; to keep; to possess; to employ; —रखाव mainte-nance; safe-keeping

रखवाला (nm) a guard, a guardian; a watchman

रखवाली (nf) care, guardianship, custody; protection

रखाना (v) to cause to keep, to give in charge

रग (nf) a vein, an artery, a nerve

रगड़ (nm) a rub, friction, concussion

रगड़ना (v) to rub, to chafe, to scrub, to bruise

रगड़ा (nm) friction; toil, a rub

रचना (nf) work; production; structure; composition; (v) to create; to form, to construct

रचयिता (nm) an author; creator; composer

रचित (a) composed; made; compiled; formed

रजक (nm) a washerman

रजत (nf) silver; (a) silvery; white; bright; —जयन्ती silver jubilee

रजनी (nf) night

रजवाड़ा (nm) a former princely state of India

रज(स) (nm) menstruation; —कण dust particle

रज़ा (nf) consent, permission; will; —मंद consenting, willing; —मंदी will; consent, agreement

रज़ाई (nf) a quilt

रजिस्ट्री (nf) registration

रजोगुण (nm) the passion of love and pleasure, one of the three constituent qualities of living-beings which is the cause of vice

रज्जु (nf) a rope; a cord; a string

रट (nm) repetition, iteration

रटना (v) to repeat, to iterate; to learn by heart

रण (nm) a combat; a war; a battle; —क्षेत्र the battle-field; —नीति strategy; —बाँकुरा a great fighter

रति (nf) the wife of Cupid; affection, love, beauty; a very pretty woman

रतौंधी (nf) night-blindness, the disease called nyctalopia

रत्ती (nf) a weight equal to eight grains of rice

रत्न (nm) a gem, jewel, precious stone, ruby

रत्नाकर (nm) the ocean; a heap of jewels

रत्नावली (nf) a necklace of gems

रथ (nm) a chariot; —यात्रा the chariot festival of Jagannath

रथी (a) riding a chariot; (nm) a fighter, warrior

रद्द (a) refuted, rejected; cancelled

रद्दी (a) worthless, of inferior quality; rough; (nf) waste paper

रद्दोबदल (nf) alteration, change; modification

रनिवास (nm) an apartment allotted to females in a palace, a harem

रपट (nf) hard labour; slipperiness; a report

रपटना (v) to slide, to slip, to skid

रफ़ा (a) removed, settled; pacified —दफ़ा settled

रफू (*nm*) darn; —गर a darner

रफूचक्कर (*a*) disappeared, run away

रफ्तार (*nf*) speed, pace

रफ्ता-रफ्ता (*adv*) by degrees, slowly

रबड़ (*nm*) a rubber

रबड़ी (*nf*) milk which is thickened by boiling and mixing sugar in it

रबी (*nf*) the crop reaped in the spring season

रब्त (*nm*) practice, custom; —ज़ब्त intimacy, acquaintance

रमज़ान (*nm*) the ninth month of the Mohammedan year in which they observe fast from early morning to sunset

रमषी (*nf*) a young woman, a pretty woman; —क beautiful

रमषीय (*a*) pretty, beautiful, charming

रमता (*a*) wandering, moving about

रमना (*v*) to make merry, to enjoy; to roam, to wander about

रम्य (*a*) pretty, beautiful, elegant, pleasant, delightful

रम्यता (*nf*) elegance, amenity

रड़कना (*v*) to smart, to produce a painful sensation

रव (*nm*) noise, cry, tumult

रवानगी (*nf*) a setting out, a departure, a start

रवाना (*a*) proceeded, departed, sent out; —होना to depart, to set out

रवि (*nm*) the Sun

रवैया (*nm*) attitude, behaviour; practice, custom

रश्क (*nm*) malice, jealousy, spite

रश्मि (*nf*) a ray or beam of light; a horse's rein

रस (*nm*) taste, flavour, juice; —दार juicy, tasty, relishing; —भरी raspberry; —भीना full of flavour

रसगुल्ला (*nm*) a kind of Bengali sweetmeat

रसज्ञ (*a*) competent in appreciating literature; a poet who understands the various sentiments; one who appreciates the beauty of literature

रसद (*nf*) provision, supplies

रसना (*nf*) the tongue; relish; cord

रसवंत (*a*) full of relish; juicy; having aesthetic sense

रसा (*nf*) tongue; soup; juice

रसातल (*nm*) the nether world, hell

रसायन (*nm*) chemistry; (*a*) chemical; —ज्ञ well versed in chemistry; —विज्ञान/शास्त्र chemistry

रसास्वाद (nm) relish, emotive, relish

रसिक (nm) admirer, lover, one who appreciates beauty or excellence; (a) amorous, sharp, humorous

रसिकता (nf) taste, joviality

रसिया (nm) amorist, having aesthetic relish

रसीद (nf) the acknowledgement of a sum, receipt

रसीदी (a) regarding to a receipt

रसीला (a) tasteful; juicy; delicious; inspired by love

रसूल (nm) divine messenger, prophet

रसोइया (nm) a cook

रसोई (nf) cooked food; kitchen; —घर a kitchen

रसौली (nf) a disease attended with glandular swellings, a tumour

र/स्म (nf) a custom; practice; a ceremony; formality; —स्मी formal

रस्सा (nm) a thick rope; a cable; —कशी tug of war

रस्सी (nf) a cord; rope

रहट (nf) an appliance for lifting water from a well, a water-wheel

रहन (nm) manner, a pawn, mortgage; —सहन living

रहना (v) to reside; to remain; to stay; to live; to continue

रहम (nm) mercy, pity; compassion, kindness, —दिल merciful

रहमत (nf) pity, compassion

रहस्य (nm) a secret; a mystery

रहस्योद्घाटन (nm) disclosure of mystery

रहित (adv) without, devoid of, destitute of

राँड (nf) a widow; a term of abuse

राई (nf) mustard; a very small quantity

राक्षस (nm) monster, a demon; a wicked person

राक्षसी (nf) monstress; (a) monstrous

राख (nf) ashes

राग (nm) mental affectation, desire, —द्वेष love and hatred

रागिनी (nf) modification or a musical mode

राज (nm) rule, administration; government; kingdom; —काज affairs of the state; —कुमार a prince; —कुमारी a princess; —कीय royal, regal, —गद्दी the royal throne; —गृह a royal palace; —तिलक the coronation ceremony of a king; —दूत a royal ambassador; —द्रोह sedition; —द्रोही disloyal; —द्वार the door of a palace; —धर्म the duties of a sovereign or king; —पथ a highway; —पाट reign, royal throne; —प्रासाद a palace; —भक्त a loyalist; —भक्ति

loyalism; —मर्मज्ञ a statesman; —यक्ष्मा tuberculosis;
—वंश a dynasty; —वैद्य royal
physician; —व्यवस्था polity;
—सत्ता royal authority;
—सभा a royal court; —सिंहा-
सन the royal throne

राज़ (nm) a secret

राजकीय (a) royal; official

राजधानी (nf) a capital

राजनीति (nf) politics

राजनैतिक (a) political

राजनीतिज्ञ (nm) a politician

राजनीतिशास्त्र (nm) political
science

राजप/त्र (nm) a gazette; —त्रित
gazetted

राजभवन (nm) governor's
house; palace

राजभाषा (nf) the official
language

राजसी (a) royal, kingly,
princely

राजस्व (nm) a royal tax or duty,
revenue

राजहंस (nm) a male swan

राजा (nm) a king, lord, a
monarch, darling; —बेटा
good boy

राजाज्ञा (nf) the order of a king,
a royal mandate

राजाधिराज (nm) an emperor,
overlord

राज़ी (a) willing; healthy,
happy; —खुशी welfare;
—नामा agreement; writ of
compromise which is filed

in a court

राजीव (nm) a lotus flower

राजेश्वर (nm) a king of kings, an
emperor

राज्ञी (nf) a queen

राज्य (nm) kingdom; state;
—च्युत dethroned; —त्याग
abdication; — द्रोह sedition;
—पाल a governor; —सभा
the Upper House of the
Indian Parliament

राज्याभिषेक (nm) accession to
the throne

राज्याधिकार (nm) the right to a
kingdom

रात (nf) the night; —का राजा an
owl; —दिन day and night;
always

रातिब (nm) food for cattle

रात्रि (nf) night

रानी (nf) a queen; a king's wife;
beloved

राम (nm) the eldest son of
Dasharath, God; —कहानी
narration of events of one's
own life; —लीला the folk
drama in which the deeds
of king Rama are enacted
for a number of days;
—बाण very efficacious

राय (nf) view, opinion; advice;
(nm) a king

रायता (nm) vegetables pickled
and spiced in curd

रार (nf) a quarrel, a dispute;
wrangling

राशन (nm) ration

राशि (nf) a sum; amount; heap; sign of the zodiac; —चक्र the zodiac

राष्ट्र (nm) a kingdom; a nation; —गीत the national anthem; —चिह्न the national emblem; —ध्वज the national flag; —नीति national policy; —पति President; —भाषा the national language; —वाद nationalism; —वादी a nationalist; —संघ the United Nations Organisation —हीन stateless

राष्ट्रिक (a & nm) national

राष्ट्रीय (a) national; —करण nationalisation; —ता nationality

रास (nm) the circular dance performed by Krishna

रासघारी (nm) a person who acts in रासलीला

रासलीला (nf) the amorous pastime of Lord Krishna with cowherdesses

रासायनिक (a) chemical; (nm) a chemist

रास्ता (nm) a path; street; road; route, course; passage

राह (nf) a way, a path; a road; method; manner; —खर्च travelling expenses; —गीर a traveller; —ज़नी robbery on the highway; —चलता a stranger

राहत (nf) relief; comfort, ease; —कार्य relief operations

राहदारी (nf) duty which is imposed on roads, toll-tax

राही (nm) a traveller, wayfarer

राहु (nm) one of the nine principal planets, the mythological dragon's head which is supposed to devour the Sun during an eclipse

रिंगाना (v) to cause to crawl, to help a child to walk

रिंद (nm) a freewilled person, (a) passionate, intoxicated

रिंदा (a) unrestrained, impudent, rash, headstrong

रिआयत (nf) concession; favour, softness

रिआयती (nm) a favoured person; concessional

रिआया (nf) a subject

रिकार्ड (nm) a record; gramophone record; —तोड़ना to break a record

रिक्त (a) empty, void; evacuated; —ता vacancy; vacuum

रिक्थ (nm) legacy

रिक्शा (nm) a rickshaw

रिझाना (v) to please, to entice, to captivate, to charm

रिझाव (nm) the act of being happy or pleased

रिटायर (a) retired

रिपु (nm) a foe, an enemy

रिमझिम (nf) the drizzling of rain

रियाज़ (*nm*) exercise; practice

रियासत (*nf*) dominion, estate, a state

रिरियाना (*v*) to whimper, to cry as a child

रिवाज (*nm*) custom; practice

रिश्ता (*nm*) affinity; relation - ship; connection

रिश्तेदार (*nm*) a relation, a relative; kith and kin

रिश्तेदारी (*nf*) relationship, kinship

रिश्वत (*nf*) a bribe; —ख़ोर a bribee; —ख़ोरी bribery

रिसना (*v*) to leak in drops, to drizzle

रिसवाना (*v*) to cause to get angry

रिसालदार (*nm*) an officer of Indian infantry

रिसाला (*nm*) a journal; cavalry

रिहा (*a*) set at liberty, released, discharged

रिहाई (*nf*) release, deliverance, liberation

रिहाइ/श (*nf*) residence; —शी residential

री (*ind*) a vocative particle used in addressing a female

रीछ (*nm*) a bear

रीझना (*v*) to be pleased; to be charmed to be satisfied

रीठा (*nm*) soap-wart, soap- nut

रीढ़ (*nf*) the backbone, spine

रीता (*a*) empty; void

रीति (*nf*) method; manner;

custom; —रिवाज **traditions**

रील (*nf*) a reel

रुँधना (*v*) to be choked; to be obstructed

रुआँ (*nm*) fuzz; wool

रुई (*nf*) cotton

रुकना (*v*) to halt; to stop; to stay; to stand

रुकावट (*nf*) obstacle, hurdle, hindrance; blockade; bar; resistance

रुक्का (*nm*) a small letter, a note; a chit, slip; promis- sory note

रुक्षता (*nf*) harshness, rough- ness

रुख़ (*nm*) direction; attitude; face; (*a*) in the direction

रुख़सत (*nf*) permission; departure; leisure from work

रुख़सती (*nf*) a departure

रुख़ाई (*nf*) indifference, harshness, roughness

रुग्ण (*a*) sick, unwell; ill

रुचना (*v*) to be gratifying, to be agreeable

रुचि (*nf*) taste; liking; relish; wish, desire; —कर full of taste; interesting; relishing; —कारक relishing

रुचिर (*a*) beautiful; agreeable, pleasing

रुचिवर्धक (*a*) appetising, increasing relish or hunger

रुझान (*nm*) proclivity; natural tendency

रुतबा (*nm*) dignity; rank; respect

रुदन (*nm*) weeping, wailing

रुद्ध (*a*) obstructed, hindered; choked

रुधिर (*nm*) blood

रुनझुन (*nf*) the tinkling of small bells

रुपया (*nm*) wealth; money; rupee; —पैसा money; रुपये वाला rich, wealthy

रुपहला (*a*) silvery, made of silver

रुलाई (*nf*) weeping, a cry

रुष्ट (*a*) angry, displeased; vexed; enraged

रुष्टता (*nf*) anger, displeasure, sulkiness

रू (*nm*) face; —ब-रू face to face; —रियायत consideration; leniency

रूखा (*a*) dry; crude; rough; inconsiderate; —सूखा plain and simple

रूखापन (*nm*) roughness, acrimony, indifference

रूठना (*v*) to be displeased

रूढ़ (*a*) established; popular; traditional

रूढ़ि (*nf*) usage, convention, —वाद conventionalism; —वादी a conventionalist

रूप (*nm*) form, shape, appearance; beauty

रूपरेखा (*nf*) a synopsis, an outline

रूपवान (*a*) good looking, handsome

रूपसी (*nf*) a beauty

रूपांतर (*nm*) transformation; variation; adaptation

रूपी (*a*) similar to

रूमानी (*a*) romantic

रूमाल (*nm*) a handkerchief

रूह (*nf*) soul; spirit; essence

रेंकना (*v*) to bray, to sing badly, to shout hoarsely

रेंगना (*v*) to crawl; to creep

रेंड़ी (*nf*) the castor seed

रेखा/कन (*nm*) lineation, lining, under-lining; —कित lined, under-lined

रेखा (*nf*) a straight line, lineament; mark; —गणित geometry; —चित्र a sketch

रेगिस्तान (*nm*) a sandy desert

रेचक (*a*) laxative, purgative; (*nm*) a purgative

रेज़गारी (*nf*) smaller coins

रेड़ (*nf*) destruction; ruination

रेणु (*nf*) dust, dirt, sand

रेत (*nm*) sand

रेतना (*v*) to file, to polish by rubbing or filing

रेताई (*nf*) the work or wages paid for filing an object

रेती (*nf*) sandy soil; a file, a rasp

रेतीला (*a*) sandy, gritty

रेल (*nf*) a railway train or carriage; —पेल (*nf*) plenty; abundance, overcrowding; rush

रेला (*nm*) a rush, a flood,

huge wave, influx

रेवड़ (*nm*) a flock of sheep or goats

रेवड़ी (*nf*) a kind of crisp sweetmeat

रेशम (*nm*) silk; —का कीड़ा silk-worm

रेशमी (*a*) made of silk, silken, silky

रेशा (*nm*) fibre, filament, crude fibre; grain

रेहन (*nm*) pawn, mortgage

रैयत (*nf*) a subject; a tenant

रोंगटा (*nm*) the hairs on the entire body

रोआँ (*nm*) small and soft hair on the body

रोक (*nf*) restraint, bar, ban, check; barrier; —टोक restriction; obstruction; —थाम prevention; check

रोकड़ (*nf*) ready money, cash; —जमा opening balance; —बाकी cash balance in hand

रोकड़िया (*nm*) a cashier, a treasurer; a financier

रोकना (*v*) to stop; to shut; to detain; to prevent; to ban; to forbid

रोग (*nm*) a disease; sickness; illness; —ग्रस्त ailing, diseased, ill; sick

रोगन (*nm*) paint, varnish; oil; polish

रोगी (*nm*) a patient, diseased; (*a*) ailing

रोचक (*a*) pleasing, interesting

रोज़ (*nm*) day; (*adv*) every-day; —ब-रोज़ everyday, daily; —मर्रा everyday, daily

रोज़गार (*nm*) an occupation, a profession; trade; a business; employment

रोज़नामचा (*nm*) a book of daily accounts, diary, journal

रोज़मर्रा (*a*) daily, always

रोज़ा (*nm*) the fast observed by Mohammedans in the month of Ramzan

रोज़ाना (*a*) daily

रोज़ी (*nf*) livelihood; living; —रोटी livelihood

रोटी (*nf*) bread; loaf; meals; food; —कपड़ा means of sustenance; —दाल plain and simple food

रोड़ा (*nm*) a fragment of stone or brick-bat; a pebble

रोदन (*nm*) weeping, lamentation

रोना (*v*) to weep, to cry, to lament; (*nm*) weeping, crying, lamenting; —धोना/पीटना to weep and wail

रोपना (*v*) to plant, to sow, to obstruct

रोब (*nm*) dignity, influence; terror; —दाब awe, influence; sway

रोबदार (*a*) imposing; awe-inspiring; commanding

रोम (*nm*) the small hair on the body; —रोम से throughout the body; —रोम में with heart and soul

रोमकूप (nm) the pores on the surface of the skin

रोमांच (nm) titillation, standing of hairs on the end

रोमांचित (a) thrilled in rapture; horripilant

रोयाँ (nm) the small hair on the body

रोली (nf) a powder prepared from a mixture of turmeric and lime used in painting the forehead

रोवेंदार/रोएँदार (a) fleecy, fluffy, feathery

रोवाँसा/रोआँसा (a) about to weep

रोशन (a) burning; lighted, bright; shining, glittering,

—दान ventilator

रोशनाई (nf) ink

रोशनी (nf) brightness, light, illumination

रोष (nm) rage, wrath, anger, resentment

रोषी (a) angry, wrathful

रौंदना (v) to trample, to tread, to crush

रौ (nf) flow of water, impulsive mood

रौद्र (a) formidable, terrible, fearful, violent

रौनक (nf) splendour, elegance, brightness; —दार gay, splendid

रौला (nf) noise

ल

ल the third of the semi-vowel series य, र, ल, व of Devnagri alphabet

लँगड़ा (a) lame, crippled, limp; (nm) a lame person

लँगड़ाना (v) to limp, to walk lamely or limpingly

लँगड़ा-लूला (nm) crippled

लंगर (nm) an anchor; an alms-house

लंगूर (nm) an ape, a kind of black-faced monkey with a stiff long tail

लँगोट (nm) loin cloth, a piece

of cloth tucked to the waist to cover the privities

लंघन (nm) passing beyond limit, jumping over, fast

लंठ (a) foolish, impertinent

लंपट (a) sensual, licentious, wanton, lustful

लंपटता (nf) wantonness, sensualism

लंबा (a) lenghty, long; tall; large; huge; —चौड़ा vast, tall and well-built; —तड़ंगा tall and tough

लंबाई (nf) length; tallness;

largeness

लंबी (a) tall; long; great

लँहगा (nf) a gown, petticoat

लकड़बग्घा (nm) a hyena

लकड़हारा (nm) a woodcutter

लकड़ी (nf) wood; timber; firewood; stick

लकवा (nm) palsy, paralysis

लकीर (nf) a line

लक्ष (a) one hundred thousand

लक्षण (nm) a characteristic mark, a symbol, sign

लक्षणा (nf) a metaphor

लक्षित (a) observed, marked, seen

लक्ष्मी (nf) the goddess of wealth, prosperity, fortune

लक्ष्य (nm) a mark; an aim; objective; (a) indicated, implied

लक्ष्यार्थ (nm) the metaphorical meaning or significance

लखना (v) to behold, to see, to look

लखपती (nm) a very wealthy person, a millionaire

लगन (nf) an attachment, love, devotion; —पत्री a letter sent by the bride's father to the father of the bridegroom for informing the day of marriage

लगना (v) to be attached; to be applied; to be affixed to, to be employed; to seem, to appear; to be engaged

लगभग (ind) about, almost, thereabouts, nearly, approximately; roughly

लगवाना (v) to cause to be placed or applied, to cause to be fixed

लगा (a) attached, occupied in, connected with, related

लगातार (adv) continuously, consecutively, incessantly; (a) continuous; continual

लगान (nm) land revenue, the work of fastening or attaching one thing to another

लगाना (v) to attach; to apply; to stick; to join; to engage; to employ

लगाम (nf) reins, bridle, check

लगालगी (nf) affection, attach-ment; love; a connection

लगाव (nm) attachment; love; affection; connection

लगे (ind) until

लग्गा (nm) a long bamboo, a pole used to propel a boat, the commencement of a work

लग्घी (nf) a rod, a fishing rod

लग्घड़ (nm) a kind of hawk; a kind of leopard

लग्न (nm) the rising of a sign of the zodiac above the horizon, the sun's entrance into a sign of the zodiac; an auspicious moment for the performance of a work; (a) attached, connected with, —पत्र (see लगनपत्री)

लधिमा (*nf*) smallness, little-
ness

लघु (*a*) short; small; light; low;
mean; —तम minimum,
lowest; —तर smaller; lower

लघुता (*nf*) insignificance; smallness; meanness

लघुमति (*a*) foolish, a fool

लघुशंका (*nf*) urinating, urine;
making water

लघुकरण (*nm*) reduction in
weight, commutation

लचक (*nf*) flexibility, elasticity;
—दार flexible, elastic

लचकना (*v*) to bend; to spring

लचकाना (*v*) to bend; to jolt

लचर (*a*) week, loose; (*nm*) a
foolish person

लचीला (*a*) elastic, flexible,
limp, soft; —पन spring,
elasticity

लच्छा (*nm*) a bundle of thread,
a hank; बालों का— tress

लच्छी (*nf*) a small skein of
thread

लच्छेदार (*a*) pleasant to hear
interesting; fascinating

लजाना (*v*) to feel shy, to put to
shame, to be ashamed

लजीला (*a*) shy

लजीज़ (*a*) tasty, tasteful

लज्ज़त (*nf*) deliciousness; taste;
relish

लज्जा (*nf*) dishonour, shame,
shyness; modesty

लज्जालु (*a*) sheepish, shy

लज्जावती (*a*) bashful woman

लज्जावान् (*a*) modest, bashful,
shy

लज्जित (*a*) bashful; blushing;
ashamed

लट (*nf*) tangled hair, a lock of
hair, a ringlet.

लटक (*nf*) the work of hanging,
a bend; an affected motion

लटकना (*v*) to overhang, to
hang; to lop; to suspend, to
be in a suspense; to be
delayed

लटका (*nm*) tip; device; trick

लटकाना (*v*) to suspend; to hang

लट्टू (*a*) top; bulb

लट्ठ (*nm*) a long stick, —बाज a
cudgel, player, a fencer;
—मार one who fights with a
cudgel; harsh and cruel
person

लट्ठा (*nm*) a long, raft, pile

लठैत (*a & nm*) skilled in
wielding cudgel

लड़ (*nf*) a string of pearls;
chain

लड़कपन (*nm*) boyhood; childhood; frivolity

लड़का (*nm*) a boy, a lad; male
child; son; an inexperienced person

लड़की (*nf*) a girl; a daughter

लड़खड़ाना (*v*) to falter; to
stagger; to stutter

लड़खड़ाहट (*nm*) stagger; totter

लड़ना (*v*) to fight; to quarrel; to
struggle; —भिड़ना to pick up

quarrel

लड़ाई (*nf*) a war; fight; a quarrel; encounter; enmity; —झगड़ा quarrel

लड़ाका (*a*) quarrelsome, hostile

लड़ना (*v*) to cause to fight or quarrel

लड़ी (*nf*) chain; row

लडू (*nm*) comfit, a sweetmeat of the shape of a ball

लत (*nf*) a bad habit, whim, addiction

लता (*nf*) a creeping plant, tender branch of a tree; vine

लताड़ (*nf*) insult, scolding

लताड़ना (*v*) to rebuke; to trample under feet

लतीफ़ा (*nm*) a joke, jest, anecdote

लत्ता (*nm*) a scrap of cloth, rag

लथपथ (*a*) wet, drenched

लदना (*v*) to be laden, to be loaded

लपक (*nf*) flash, radiance, flame; swiftness

लपकना (*v*) to stretch out the hand for snatching; to rush

लपट (*nf*) flame; a blast of fragrance

लपलपाना (*v*) to be bent; to glitter

लपेट (*nf*) a fold, twist; envelopment

लपेटना (*v*) to coil; to roll up; to fold; to involve

लपेटवाँ (*a*) folded; rolled up; twisted

लप्पड़ (*nm*) a slap with the hand

लफंगा (*nm*) a loafer, a vaga-bond, a man of loose character

लफंगेबाज़ी (*nf*) roguery

लफ्ज़ (*nm*) a word or expression

लब (*nm*) a lip; brim; edge

लबड़ना (*v*) to speak a lie, to speak absurdly

लबादा (*nm*) a gown, a cloak; a heavy overall

लबार (*nm*) a liar; a babbler

लबालब (*adv & a*) brimful, spil-ling; full to the brim

लब्ध (*a*) obtained, got, received; —प्रतिष्ठ renowned, honoured

लब्धपुत्र (*nm*) an adopted son

लब्धि (*nf*) acquirement, achievement

लभ्य (*a*) attainable, available, within the reach of

लमहा (*nm*) a moment

लय (*nf*) tune; rhythm; —बद्ध rhythmic, attuned

ललक (*nf*) intense desire; ardour; longing, yearning

ललकना (*v*) to desire intensely, to long for, to be greedy

ललकार (*nf*) a challenge, bawl

ललकारना (*v*) to call out insultingly, to challenge, to hold out

ललचना (v) to feel greedy, to be enticed, to be impatient owing to an intense desire

ललचाना (v) to allure, to temp, to charm; जी— to feel tempted

ललना (nf) a woman

लल्ला (nm) a beloved son

ललाई (nf) redness

ललाट (nm) the forehead, front part, bow; fortune; —पटल the surface of the forehead; —रेखा lines on the forehead supposed to indicate good or bad fortune

ललित (a) lovely, beautiful, attractive, pretty; elegent, —कला fine arts

लल्ला (nm) a boy

लब (nm) a very small division of time; a bit, a portion, a particle; —लीन absorbed; —लेश a very small quantity

लवण (nm) salt

लश्कर (nm) an encampment; a crowd

लश्करी (adv) pertaining to an army or navy

लसलसा (a) adhesive, viscous; glutinous

लसीला (a) adhesive, viscous, glutinous

लस्सी (nf) a drink made of churned curd and water with sugar or salt added to it

लहकना (v) to wave, to quaver, to blow, to flash

लहजा (nm) tone of voice, speech, accent

लहमा (nm) a moment

लहर (nf) a large wave, surf, ripple; caprice, whim; —दार wavy, sinuate

लहराना (v) to fluctuate; to wave

लहरिया (nm) the total effect of wavy lines

लहलहाना (v) to be full of green leaves, to be verdant, to be pleased, to be delighted

लहसुन (nm) garlic

लहसुनिया (nm) a precious stone of grey colour; cat's eye

लहू (nm) blood; —लुहान covered with blood, blood-stained

लाँघना (v) to pull through, to go over, to cross, to jump over

लांछन (nm) a stigma, stain, blemish, blame

लांछित (a) blamed, reproached

लाइलाज (a) irremediable, incurable

लाइसेंस (nm) a licence; —दार licensed, licence holder

लाक्षणिक (a) symbolic; metaphorical; allegorical

लाक्षा (nf) lac; —गृह a house which is made of lac

लाख (nf) sealing lac; lac; (nm) the number one lac; (a) a hundred thousand, a large number

लाग (nf) competition; hostility;

connection, —बट rancour, rivalry; competition

लागत (*nf*) expenditure, prime cost of a commodity; cost

लागू (*a*) adhering to, applicable, desirous, enforceable

लाघव (*nm*) minuteness, skill; smartness

लाचार (*a*) forlorn; helpless; compelled; obliged; (*adv*) being helpless

लाचारी (*nf*) helplessness, pressing necessity

लाज (*nf*) shyness; shame; —वंत/वंती a very sensitive plant called 'touch me not'

लाजवाब (*a*) matchless; silent, speechless

लाज़िमी (*a*) inevitable, essential, compulsory

लाट (*nm*) a lord, governor; a thick lofty pillar

लाठी (*nf*) a stick, a club, a cudgel; —चलना fighting with sticks

लाड़ (*nm*) endearment, fondling, affection

लाड़ला (*a*) dear, a darling

लात (*nf*) leg, foot, a kick; —मारना to kick, to spurn; to abandon

लादना (*v*) to burden, to load; to freight; to heap one upon another

लानत (*nf*) reproach, reproof, censure, condemnation; rebuke

लाना (*v*) to fetch; to bring; to present; to introduce

लापता (*a*) disappeared; missing, gone underground

लापरवाह (*a*) listless, careless, negligent; headless

लापरवाही (*nf*) negligence, carelessness

लाभ (*nm*) an advantage; profit; gain; benefit; dividend

लाभकारी (*a*) beneficial; gainful; profitable

लाभांश (*nm*) bonus; dividend

लाम (*nm*) a host, an army; war-front; —बंदी mobilisation

लामा (*nm*) a Buddhist monk of Tibet or Mongolia

लायक (*a*) fit, able; competent; proper, capable

लायकी (*nf*) nobility; ability

लार (*nf*) saliva, sputum

लारी (*nf*) a lorry

लाल (*a*) red, angry; communist; (*nm*) darling, dear boy; ruby

लालच (*nm*) temptation, greed, greediness, covetousness; avarice

लालची (*a*) covetous, greedy, avaricious

लालटेन (*nm*) lantern

लालन (*nm*) coaxing, caressing, fondling; —पालन nurturing

लालमिर्च (*nf*) pepper, chilly

लालसा (*nf*) longing, an ardent desire, yearning

लालसी (a) wishful, desirous, eager

लाला (nm) a term of address used for a Kayastha and certain other Hindu castes, like Bania

लालायित (a) coveted, eager; tempted

लालित्य (nm) beauty, gracefulness, delicacy

लालिमा (nf) redness; ruddiness

लाली (nf) redness, ruddiness; honour, respect

लाव (nf) —लश्कर an array of followers, army with civilian support and material

लावण्य (nm) saltness; loveliness, grace, extreme beauty

लावा (nm) parched rice, fried gram; lava, hot mud of a volcano

लावारिस (a) heirless

लाश (nf) a dead body, a carcass

लासा (nm) a glutinous substance

लिंग (nm) a sign, a mark; male genital organ

लिप् (ind) with a view to, for the sake of, for, on account of; (a) carrying, bearing

लिखना (v) to write; to note down; to record; —पढ़ना to study; writing and reading, studying

लिखाई (nf) work of writing, composition; —पढ़ाई study, education

लिखा-पढ़ी (nf) written agreement; correspondence

लिखावट (nf) handwriting; writing

लिखित (a) written; recorded

लिटाना (v) to cause to lie down, to lay on bed

लिपटना (v) to adhere to, to embrace, to coil around

लिपाई (nf) the act of smearing or plastering; —पुताई plastering and whitewashing

लिपि (nf) writing; a script; —बद्ध recorded; written

लिपिक (nm) a clerk

लिप्त (a) absorbed; deeply attached; involved

लिप्यंतरण (nm) transcription; transliteration

लिप्सा (nf) greed, lure, an earnest desire for a thing

लिफ़ाफ़ा (nm) a wrapper; an envelope; cover

लिफ़ाफ़िया (a) showy

लिबास (nm) garment, dress, attire, clothes

लिबासी (a) false, counterfeit

लियाकत (nf) merit; ability, fitnes, skill; qualification

लिहाज़ (nm) sense, respect, considerateness; point of view

लिहाज़ा (ind) therefore, thus, accordingly

लिहाफ़ (nm) a quilt

लीक (*nf*) mark, track, track-way; rut

लीचड़ (*a*) slow, sluggish, mean, one who is not prompt in the payment of dues

लीची (*nf*) the fruit of the tree *seytalia lichi*

लीडर (*nm*) a leader

लीद (*nf*) dung of horse

लीन (*a*) immersed, absorbed, rapt; merged

लीपना (*v*) to coat; to plaster; to smear; —पोतना to clean and tidy up

लीलना (*v*) to gulp, to swallow

लीला (*nf*) a sport, play; amorous sport; fun and frolic

लुंगी (*nf*) a piece of cloth which is wrapped round the waist

लुंज (*a*) without hand and feet, crippled; leafless tree; —पुंज having no muscles

लुंठन (*nm*) robbing, plunder-ing; the act of stealing

लुगदी (*nf*) pulp

लुगाई (*nf*) a woman; wife

लुच्चा (*a & nm*) wanton; vile, a scoundrel, black sheep

लुटना (*v*) to be robbed; to be undone; to be sacked

लुटिया (*nf*) a small jug

लुटेरा (*nm*) a plunderer, a bandit, a robber

लुढ़कना (*v*) to tumble down, to roll down

लुत्फ़ (*nm*) pleasure, fun

लुनाई (*nf*) beauty

लुप्त (*a*) concealed, hidden, disappeared, missing

लुभाना (*v*) to charm; to lure; to attract; to captivate

लू (*nf*) the hot wind of summer, warm air; sunstroke; —लगना to have a sunstroke

लूट (*nf*) a spoil; a plunder; booty; —खसोट plunder, pillage; —मार plundering and killing or murder

लूटना (*v*) to rob, to plunder, to spoil, to maraud

लूला (*a*) maimmed, crippled, handless; —लँगड़ा crippled, disabled

लेई (*nf*) paste, starch, mortar

लेकिन (*ind*) but; on the other hand

लेख (*nm*) writing; an essay, an article; writ

लेखक (*nm*) an author, a writer

लेखन (*nm*) the work or art of writing, writing, —कला art of writing; —शैली style of writing; —सामग्री stationery, writing material

लेखनी (*nf*) a pen

लेखा (*nm*) record, account; —जोखा calculation; estimate

लेखिका (*nf*) a female author

लेटना (*v*) to lie down; to rest

लेन (*nm*) the act of taking or receiving anything; —दार a creditor; a money-lender; —देन transaction, exchange; dealings

लेना (v) to accept; to take, to receive; to borrow; to buy, to hold

लेप (nm) a plaster, an ointment; a paint; smearing

लेपना (v) to apply plaster to, to coat; to smear

लेश (a) very small; (nm) a small portion, smallness, a whit; —मात्र a shadow of

लैंगिक (a) phallic; sexual

लैस (a) ready, equipped

लोंदा (nm) a ball of wet powder etc.

लोक (nm) the world, the universe; people, folk; public; (a) popular, public; —कथा a folk tale; —कल्याण public welfare; —गीत a folk song; —तंत्र democracy; —तांत्रिक democratic; a democrat; —निंदा public slander; —नृत्य folk dance; —प्रिय popular; —मत public opinion; —सभा House of the People; —सम्मत enjoying popular support; —सेवा public service; —हित public welfare

लोकाचार (nm) a popular custom, fashion; convention; popular tradition

लोकाचारी (nm) a man of the world; (a) worldly wise

लोकापवाद (nm) a public slander

लोकोक्ति (nf) a popular saying, a proverb

लोकोत्तर (a) supernatural, extraordinary

लोग (nm) the public; people; men; —बाग people; men in general

लोच (nf) elasticity, flexibility; tenderness

लोचन (nm) the eye

लोट (nf) lying, rolling; —पोट rolling; resting; bursting with laugh

लोटना (v) to lie in bed; to roll; to toss

लोथ (nf) a carcass; a corpse

लोथड़ा (nm) a lump of flesh

लोन (nm) salt; charm, beauty

लोप (nm) disappearance; elimination

लोभ (nm) greed, attraction; avarice, lure; covetousness

लोभी (a) covetous, greedy

लोम (nm) the hair on the body

लोमड़ी (nf) a fox

लोरी (nf) an Indian lullaby; —देना to lull a baby to sleep

लोलुप (a) greedy, voracious, covetous

लोहा (nm) iron; (a) very hard, very strong

लोहार (nm) a hammersmith, an ironsmith, a blacksmith

लोहारी (nf) the blacksmith's profession

लोहित (a) red, reddened

लोहिया (nm) an iron-monger

लोहू (nm) blood

लौंग (*nf*) the clove; an ornament in the form of a pin or stud worn on the nose

लौंडा (*nm*) a boy, a lad, a slave boy

लौंडी (*nf*) a servant girl, a slave girl, a girl

लौंडिया (*nf*) a girl

लौ (*nf*) the flame, the light of a lamp; glow; attachment; —लगाना to be deeply attached to

लौकिक (*a*) earthly, secular; worldly

लौकी (*nf*) a pumpkin

लौट (*nf*) returning; —फेर substantial change; modification

लौटना (*v*) to return, to come back

लौटाना (*v*) to send back, to return, to refund, to withdraw

लौह (*nm*) iron; (*a*) made of iron; —पुरुष an iron man; —युग iron age

व

व the last of the traditional semi-vowel set य, र, ल, व of Devnagri alphabet

वंग (*nm*) the province of Bengal, Indian state of Bengal

वंचना (*nf*) a deception, a fraud, sham

वंचित (*a*) cheated, deceived

वंदन (*nm*) adoration, obeisance

वंदना (*nf*) salutation, obeisance, worship

वंदनीय (*a*) adorable, fit to be worshipped

वंध्या (*a*) unfertile, barren; unproductive

वंश (*nm*) a bamboo, family; stock; dynasty; —गत pertaining to family

वंशज (*nm*) a descendent

वंश-परंपरा (*nf*) lineage, family tradition

वंश-वृक्ष (*nm*) a bamboo tree, lineage

वंशी (*nf*) a pipe, a flute; a fishing hook

वकालत (*nf*) delegation, pleadership, advocacy; —नामा a writ for the appointment of a lawyer to plead in a case, power of attorney

वकील (*nm*) pleader, a lawyer, an advocate

वक्त (*nm*) time; opportunity; circumstance; —का पाबंद punctual

वक्तव्य (*nm*) a speech, a statement (*a*) proper to be

spoken or told

वक्ता (*nm*) spokesman; speaker

वक्तृता (*nf*) a speech, an oration

वक्तृत्व (*nm*) eloquence, art of speaking

वक्र (*a*) crooked, curved, oblique; cunning; —गति crooked gait, zigzag motion; —गामी a fraudulent person; —दृष्टि an angry look; —रेखा curved line

वक्रता (*nf*) crookedness; dishonest dealings

वक्ष (*nm*) the breast, chest

वगैरह (*ind*) and so forth, etcetera

वचन (*nm*) speech, utterance; number (in grammar) commitment, pledge; —तोड़ना to break a promise; —देना to make a promise, —बद्ध committed; —ग्राही obedient, submissive

वजन (*nm*) weight; burden; value; —दार heavy; important, weighty

वजनी (*a*) weighty, heavy; important

वजह (*nf*) reason, cause

वज़ीफ़ा (*nm*) stipend; scholarship

वज़ीर (*nm*) a minister of state; the queen in chess

वज़ीरी (*nf*) the office of a minister

वजूद (*nm*) presence; existence

वज्र (*nm*) the thunderbolt of Indra, lightning; a fatal weapon; (*a*) very hard

वज्रपात (*nm*) the stroke of lightning

वज्राघात (*nm*) an astounding calamity or misery

वट (*nm*) a banyan tree

वटी (*nf*) a pill, tablet

वणिक् (*nm*) a merchant, a trader, a shopkeeper

वतन (*nm*) the native country

वत्स (*nm*) a calf; dear boy

वत्सल (*a*) tender, affectionate, child-loving

वत्सलता (*nf*) fondness, tenderness

वदन (*nm*) the mouth, face

वध (*nm*) slaughter; murder, killing

वधिक (*nm*) a hunter; a murderer

वधू (*nf*) wife, a bride; son's wife

वध्य (*a*) fit to be killed or murdered

वन (*nm*) a wood, jungle, forest; —चर a woodman, —राज a lion; —रोपण afforestation; —लक्ष्मी forest-goddess; —वास dwelling in a forest; —स्थली a heath

वनस्पति (*nf*) a tree or plant, vegetable; —घी hydrogenated oil of groundnut etc.; —विज्ञान Botany

वनिता (*nf*) a beloved woman;

mistress; wife

वनौषधि (nf) the herbs of a forest

वन्य (a) produced in a forest; wild, savage

वपु (nm) the body

वफ़ा (nf) the fulfilment of a promise, fidelity, sincerity; —दार faithful, loyal

वबाल (nm) a curse, calamity

वमन (nm) puke, vomitting

वय (nm) the duration or period of time; age

वयस्क (a) pertaining to age, adult; major

वयस्कता (nf) adulthood

वयस्य (nm) a friend, a companion

वयोवृद्ध (a) old, aged

वर (nm) a blessing; bride-groom; (a) excellent, beautiful, better

वरक़ (nm) the leaf of a book, a gold or silver leaf

वरज़िश (nf) physical exercise

वरण (nm) selecting or choosing; a promise of marriage

वरदान (nm) a boon

वरदी (nf) the uniform

वरन् (ind) on the other hand

वराह (nm) pig, a boar

वरिष्ठ (a) best, most preferable or excellent, respected, senior; most preferable

वरीय (a) senior; —ता seniority

वरुण (nm) the deity of the waters

वरुणालय (nm) the ocean

वर्ग (nm) a multitude of similar objects, a class, a kind, group; a square; a square number; निम्न— the lower class; निम्नमध्य — lower middle class; —फल square; —भेद class distinction; —संघर्ष class-struggle; —हीन classless

वर्गीकरण (nm) a classification; —करना to square, to classify

वर्गीकृत (a) classified

वर्जन (nm) inhibition, prohibition

वर्जनीय (a) fit to be avoided; wicked

वर्जित (a) avoided, inhibited, prohibited

वर्जना (nf) a taboo, an inhibition; (v) to inhibit, to taboo

वर्ण (nm) colour; caste; dye; a letter of the alphabet; —क्रम colour scheme, alphabetical order; —माला the alphabet; —विचार orthography; —विन्यास spelling; —व्यवस्था the caste system; —संकर a mixture of castes; —हीन casteless; colourless

वर्णन (nm) narration, description

वर्णनातीत (a) indescribable

वर्णनीय (a) describable

वर्णाश्रम (nm) the caste to which

a person belongs

वर्ण्य (a) fit for being described; (nm) the topic of a description

वर्तनी (nf) spelling

वर्तमान (a) present, existing, living; current; (nm) the present

वर्तुल (a) round, circular, spherical

वर्धन (a) increasing, growing, growth

वर्ष (nm) a year

वर्षण (nm) the falling of rain

वर्षा (nf) rain, rainfall

वलय (nm) circle, a ring; fold

वली (nm) a master; a ruler; a guardian; — वारिस guardian or heir, kith and kin

वल्कल (nm) the bark of a tree, cloth made of bark

वल्गा (nf) a rein, a bridle

वल्लरी (nf) a creeper

वल्लभ (a) dear, beloved; (nm) a lover; husband

वश (nm) control; power

वशीकरण (nm) conjuration, bewitchment, glamour

वशीभूत (a) subdued, overpowered, fascinated

वसंत (nm) the spring season

वसीयत (nf) a testament, a will, a legacy; — नामा a will

वसुंधरा (nf) the earth

वसूल (a) obtained, realised, collected; — करना to collect

वसूली (nf) the realisation or

collection of dues

वस्तु (nf) an item, an article, a substance, an object

वस्तुत: (ind) strictly, in fact, rather, actually

वस्त्र (nm) cloth, textile; fibre

वस्ल (nm) lover's union

वह (pron) that; he; she; it

वहन (nm) carrying, conveying, bearing

वहम (nm) false notion, doubt, suspicion

वहमी (a) whimsical, suspicious

वहशत (nf) rudeness, savagery; incivility

वहशी (a) rude, uncivilised, savage; — पन savagery, barbarousness

वहाँ (adv) there, thither

वहीं (ind) at that very place, on the spot

वही (pron) the same

वह्नि (nm) fire

वांछनीय (a) desired, desirable, worth wishing for

वांछित (a) desirable, wished

वा (ind) or; or else; either, whether

वाक़ (nm) a word, speech, language

वाकई (ind) actually, infact

वाकिफ़ (a) conversant; acquainted

वाकफ़ियत (nf) conversance; knowledge, acquaintance

वाकया (nm) event, incident

वाक़ (nf) voice, speech;

goddess of speech; —पटु eloquent in speech

वाक्य (nm) a sentence, —रचना syntax, construction of sentence; —शैली a mode of expression

वाक्यार्थ (nm) the meaning of a sentence

वाग्जाल (nm) an equivocation, circumlocution, an empty talk

वाग्दान (nm) betrothal, engagement

वाग्देवी (nf) the goddess Saraswati, the power of speech

वाड.मय (nm) literature

वाचक (nm) a speaker, a reader

वाचन (nm) speaking; reading

वाचनालय (nm) a reading room

वाचाल (a & nm) talkative, gobbling, chattering

वाच्य (a) expressible in words, predicable; (nm) voice (in grammar)

वाच्यार्थ (nm) the denotative meaning

वाजिब (a) fit, suitable, proper

वाजिबी (a) reasonable, necessary

वाटिका (nf) a garden

वाणिज्य (nm) trade, commerce

वाणी (nf) voice; speech; an epithet of the goddess Saraswati

वात (nm) wind; air; breeze; one of the humours of the body; —प्रकोप the disorder of wind which creates diseases of various kinds

वातानुकूल (nm) airconditioning

वातायन (nm) a ventilator

वातावरण (nm) atmosphere

वात्सल्य (nm) fondness, affection, a parent's love towards progeny

वाद (nm) cause, a suit; discussion; dispute; theory; —प्रतिवाद controversy; —विवाद dispute, discussion

वादा (nm) a promise, an agreement (see also वायदा)

वादी (nm) a speaker, an arguer, a disputant, a plaintiff in a suit, a prosecutor; —प्रतिवादी the plaintiff and the defendant

वाद्य (nm) a musical instrument; —वृंद the orchestra

वानर (nm) a monkey; an ape

वापस (a) given back; returned; come back; reverted

वापसी (a) returned; (nf) a withdrawl, refund

वाम (a) left; reverse; inverted, opposite

वामन (nm) dwarfish, a dwarf; a pigmy

वायदा (nm) commitment; a promise; —खिलाफी breach of a promise

वायस (nm) a crow

वायवीय (a) windy, airy; aerial

वायु (nf) air, wind; windy

humour; —मंडल atmos-
phere; —मार्ग airways; —
सेना air force

वायुयान (*nm*) an aeroplane,
aircraft

वारंट (*nm*) a warrant; voucher

वारंबार (*ind*) again and again;
repeatedly

वार (*nm*) a stroke; an assault; a
day of the week; —पार full
expanse; this side and the
other

वारदात (*nf*) unfortunate event;
a mishap

वारना (*v*) to dedicate, to
sacrifice; to make an
offering of

वारनिश (*nf*) varnish

वारांगना (*nf*) a prostitute, a
harlot

वाराणसी (*nf*) the old name of
Kashi or Banaras

वारा-न्यारा (*nm*) decision, a
settlement, gain

वारि (*nm*) water

वारिज (*nm*) lotus, conch

वारिस (*nm*) a successor, an
heir

वारुणी (*nf*) wine, liquor

वार्डन (*nm*) a warden

वार्ता (*nf*) talks, a talk;
negotiation; —कार a talker;
negotiator

वार्तालाप (*nm*) conversation, a
dialogue, a discourse,
parley

वार्तिक (*nm*) an explanatory,
commentary, gloss

वार्धक्य (*nm*) old age, senility

वार्षिक (*a*) yearly, annual; per
annum

वार्षिकोत्सव (*nm*) anniversary

वालंटियर (*nm*) a volunteer

वालिद (*nm*) father

वालिदा (*nf*) mother

वाबैला (*nm*) uproar, turmoil,
weeping, lamentation

वाष्प (*nm*) vapour; tears

वास (*nm*) residence, habitation; odour, fragrance; —
स्थान a house

वासना (*nf*) passion, intense
desire, fancy

वासर (*nm*) a day

वासी (*nm*) an inhabitant, a
dweller

वास्तव (*a*) real, factual;
genuine; substantial

वास्तविक (*a*) factual, real, true,
solid, bonafide; —ता reality,
truth

वास्ता (*nm*) connection,
relation

वास्तु (*nm*) the site of a building,
house, a building, —विद्या
the science or art of building
a house; —कला/शिल्प
architecture

वास्ते (*ind*) for the purpose of,
for the sake of, in order to;
in the name of

वाह (*int*) denoting admiration
or contempt, Well done!
Ah! Bravo! excellent!

fine ! hurrah

वाहक (nm) a porter, carrier, bearer; a charioteer, horse-man

वाहन (nm) a conveyance of any kind, a vehicle

वाहवाही (nf) praise, applause

वाहिनी (nf) an army; —पति the commander of any army

वाहियात (a) worthless, useless; nonsense; ridiculous

विकट (a) huge, horrible, ghastly, frightful; difficult

विकराल (a) terrible, horrible, dreadful; frightful; hideous; monstrous

विकर्षण (nm) repulsion; detachment

विक/ल (a) agitated, restless, mutilated; —लांग crippled, disabled

विकल्प (nm) an option, alter-native

विकसित (a) opened; bloomed; developed

विकार (nm) a defect, alterna-tion, deformation, defile-ment; disorder

विकास (nm) expansion, development, evolution, growth; —वाद theory of evolution; —शील develop-ing

विकीर्ण (a) scattered, diffused, renowned

विकृत (a) altered, changed, deformed, mutilated,

disordered; oblique

विकृति (nf) a change of form or nature, a defect, a deform-ed appearance

विक्रम (nm) heroism, strength, mettle; (a) best, excellent

विक्रमी (a) pertaining to Vikramaditya; heroic, valiant

विक्रय (nm) sale, selling

विक्रयी (nm) a seller, vendor

विक्रांत (a) valiant, heroic, mighty

विक्रेता (nm) a seller, vendor

विक्षत (a) injured, wounded

विक्षिप्त (a) crazy, mad; perplexed

विक्षिप्तता (nf) madness

विक्षुब्ध (a) bewildered, perplexed, confused

विक्षेपण (nm) scattering, confusion, disturbance

विक्षोभ (nm) the agitation of mind

विख्यात (a) notable, renowned, famous, distinguished

विख्याति (nf) fame, renown, celebrity

विगत (a) gone away, passed, departed, disappeared

विग्रह (nm) a struggle, strife, quarrel, form

विग्रही (nm) a fighter, one who quarrels with another

विघटन (nm) a breaking up, destruction, disintegration, disorganisation; decomposition

विघ्न (nm) an obstacle, an interruption; meddling, interference

विचक्षण (a) far-sighted, extremely sagacious

विचर (a) wandered, strayed; — ण wandering, strolling, movement; variation

विचल (a) unsteady, movable, unfixed

विचलन (nm) deviation; moving about

विचलित (a) unsettled, unsteady, not fixed

विचार (nm) thinking, thought; idea; observation; pondering; reflection; — क a thinker; — गोष्ठी a seminar, —विमर्श discussion; — धारा ideology; —शील thoughtful

विचारणीय (a) noteworthy, noticeable, dubious, questionable

विचारना (v) to think, to consider

विचाराधीन (a) under consideration, under trial

विचित्र (a) surprising; strange; wonderful; curious

विचित्रता (nf) strangeness, diversity

विच्छिन्न (a) cut off; divided, separated

विच्छेद (nm) disjunction; separation, division; breaking up

विच्छेदन (nm) separation, destruction

विछोह (nm) separation

विजय (nf) mastery; victory, conquest, triumph; —देवी the goddess of victory; —ध्वज the banner of victory; —लक्ष्मी the goddess of victory

विजया (nf) an intoxicating herb 'भाँग'— दशमी Dushahra

विजयोत्सव (nm) the festival on the विजयादशमी or Dushahra day

विजाति (nf) another caste or class

विजेता (nm) a conqueror

विज्ञ (a) wise, clever; skilful, experienced; learned

विज्ञता (nf) wisdom; learning, knowledge

विज्ञप्ति (nf) an information, notification, a communique

विज्ञान (nm) science; —वेत्ता a scientist, man of science;

विज्ञानी (nm) a scientist

विज्ञापन (nm) an advertisement; announcement; a poster

विटप (nm) a tree; a plant

विडंबन (nm) mimicry, disguise

विडंबना (nf) mockery

विडंबित (a) troubled, distressed; mocked

वितरण (nm) a gift, a donation; a distribution; delivery

वितर्क (nm) reasoning, discussion; a doubt

वितृष्णा (nf) repulsion, repugnance

वित्त (nm) wealth, riches; property

वित्तीय (a) financial

विदग्ध (nm) a libertine, a clever person

विदग्धता (nf) cleverness, shrewdness, learning

विदा (nf) a taking leave, farewell, adieu; a departure

विदाई (nf) sending off, farewell; departure

विदित (a) known, understood

विदीर्ण (a) split, torn, opened; killed

विदुषी (nf) a learned woman

विदूषक (nm) a jester, a buffoon; a humorous companion of the hero in a sanskrit drama

विदूषण (nm) reviling, corruption

विदेश (nm) a foreign country, a distant land

विदेशी (a) foreign, alien; (nm) a foreigner

विद्यमान (a) extant, present, still existing

विद्यमानता (nf) presence

विद्या (nf) knowledge, learning, study; —दान teaching, imparting knowledge; —देवी Saraswati, the goddess of learning; —पीठ a school

विद्याभ्या/स (nm) pursuit of learning; study; —सी stu-

dious

विद्यार्थी (nm) a pupil, a student; a scholar

विद्यालय (nm) a school

विद्युत (nm) lightning, electricity

विद्रूप (a) ugly, distorted, hideous, monstrous; (nm) monstrosity; irony

विद्रोह (nm) revolt, uprising, rebellion, insurrection

विद्रोही (a) mutinous, revolting, a rebel

विद्वत्ता (nf) learning, knowledge; scholarship

विद्वान् (a & nm) learned, wise, well-read, a scholar

विद्वेष (nm) enmity; hatred, contempt; malice

विद्वेषी (a) inimical, malicious, spiteful

विधना (nm) the god Brahma, Providence

विधर्म (nm) a religion different from one's own; heresy; (a) unjust, inequitable

विधर्मी (nm) a man who follows a religion different from one's own

विधवा (nf) widow

विधवाश्रम (nm) a refuge or home for widows

विधा (nf) form, type; device

विधाता (nm) the creator — Brahma

विधान (nm) an arrangement, legislation, rule; methold; —परिषद् legislative council;

—सभा legislative assembly

विघायक (*nm*) a legislator, a prescriber, a manager

विघायी (*a*) legislative

विधि (*nf*) an order, command; manner, process; law; method, system; direction; rule; —पूर्वक duly; methodically, systematically; —वत duly, methodically, systematically; —विधान method and manner; —वेत्ता a juris-consultant; —शास्त्र jurisprudence; —शास्त्री a jurisprudent

विघु (*nm*) the moon

विघुर (*nm*) widower; (*a*) widowed

विघेय (*a*) what is required; to be accomplished, governable

विघेयक (*nm*) a bill

विघ्यात्मक (*a*) positive

विघ्वंस (*nm*) ruin, destruction, devastation

विघ्वंसी (*nm*) one who ruins or demolishes, a destroyer

विघ्वस्त (*a*) destroyed, demolished

विनत (*a*) bent, humble, bowing, modest

विनती (*nf*) request; prayer; humility; solicitation

विनम्र (*a*) bent, humble, modest, meek; respectful, courteous

विनय (*nf*) politeness, modesty, humility, humbleness; good behaviour

विनयी (*a*) mild, courteous, humble, modest, polite

विनश्वर (*a*) transitory, not lasting for ever, perishable

विनष्ट (*a*) ruined, destroyed, spoiled; dead, perished

विनायक (*nm*) an epithet of the god Ganesha

विनाश (*nm*) ruin, destruction, down fall, disaster, wreck

विनाशक (*nm*) a spoiler, a destroyer annihilator

विनाशी (*a*) destructive, baneful

विनिमय (*nm*) exchange, substitution, permutation; —करना to exchange, to permute

विनियोग (*nm*) the use of an object for attaining a special end or purpose

विनीत (*a*) gentle, humble, modest; polite, submissive, meek

विनोद (*nm*) fun, amusement, recreation, entertainment; a joke; wit, humour

विनोदी (*a*) jovial, witty, jolly, humorous

विन्यास (*nm*) laying down, an adjustment; structure, disposition, arrangement

विपक्ष (*nm*) the opposition

विपक्षी (*a*) opposition; rival; hostile; (*nm*) an opponent, an enemy

विपत्काल (*nm*) the time of distress or disaster, misfortune

विपत्ति (nf) a calamity, a disaster; misfortune, hardship; —ग्रस्त afflicted, distressed

विपथ (nm) a bad road

विपद् (nf) affliction, distress, hardship, calamity, crisis; —ग्रस्त in distress, afflicted

विपन्न (a) fallen into a calamity; distressed, afflicted

विपरीत (a) contrary; opposed; reverse

विपर्यय (nm) a change, perverseness of disposition, reversal

विपिन (nm) a jungle, a forest

विपुल (a) broad, large, big, deep, extensive; mammoth

विपुलता (nf) magnitude, plentitude

विप्र (nm) a Brahman

विप्रलंभ (nf) separation of lovers; deception, a trick

विप्रलब्ध (nm) the man whose desires are not fulfilled; separated

विप्लव (nm) disorder, insurrection; insurgency, revolt

विफल (a) vain, useless, failed, unsuccessful; fruitless, futile

विभंजन (nm) the act of breaking up into component parts

विभक्त (a) separated, partitioned; divided

विभक्ति (nf) a separation, partition; division

विभव (nm) wealth, riches, dignity

विभाग (nm) division, department; portion, part

विभागीय (a) departmental

विभाजक (a) dividing, parting; (nm) a division

विभाजन (nm) partition, division

विभाजित (a) divided; distributed

विभाज्य (a) divisible, fit to be divided or distributed

विभावरी (nf) night

विभिन्न (a) various; quite different; disunited; —ता variety, diversity

विभीषण (a) terrible, fearful; a brother of Ravana

विभीषिका (nf) a show of fear, a dreadful sight; horror, terror

विभु (a) huge, powerful; (nm) God, Vishnu

विभूति (nf) majesty; ash

विभूषित (a) decorated; adorned, ornamented; beautified

विभेद (nm) separation, division

विभ्रम (nm) doubt; blunder, error; motion

विभ्रांति (nf) an error; a confusion; mistake

विमंडन (nm) ornamentation, decoration

विमंडित (a) decorated; beautified

विमत (a) contrary opinion,

counter principle

विमर्दन (*nm*) crushing, killing

विमर्श (*nm*) a trial, an investigation; consultation, consideration, examination

विमल (*a*) clean; clear; dirtless; pure

विमाता (*nf*) step-mother

विमान (*nm*) aircraft, an aeroplane; — चालक a pilot; — पत्तन airport; — परिचारिका air-hostess

विमार्ग (*nm*) an evil course

विमुक्त (*a*) released, liberated, set free

विमुक्ति (*nf*) liberation

विमुख (*a*) disinclined, indifferent, having a sense of aversion

विमुग्ध (*a*) fascinated, attracted, charmed

विमूढ़ (*a*) very foolish or stupid; senseless, unconscious

विमोक्ष (*nm*) release, salvation

विमोचन (*nm*) untying, liberation, acquittal

विमोह (*nm*) ignorance, suspicion, seduction

विमोही (*a*) alluring, fascinating; cruel, hard-hearted

वियुक्त (*a*) abandoned, separated, deserted

वियोग (*nm*) disunion, a separation; bereavement

वियोगिनी (*nf*) a woman separated from her husband or lover

वियोगी (*nm*) a lover/husband separated from his beloved/wife

विरंचि (*nm*) creator, Brahma

विरक्त (*a*) free from worldly attachment; disaffected; indifferent

विरचित (*a*) prepared; composed; written

विरत (*a*) free from worldly attachment; indifferent, stopped

विरति (*nf*) the absence of desire, indifference

विरल (*a*) fine; rare, scarce

विरलता (*nf*) tenuity; scarcity

विरह (*nm*) parting, separation

विरहिणी (*nf*) one separated from her lover/husband

विरहित (*a*) deserted, exempt, devoid

विराग (*nm*) absence of desire or passion, renunciation, detachment

विरागी (*a*) averse to worldly pleasures

विराजना (*v*) to enjoy oneself, to grace; to take seat

विराजमान (*a*) shining, brilliant, handsome; seated, looking glorious

विराट् (*a*) very big, huge, colossal, gigantic

विराम (*nm*) interval, pause; stop; stoppage; rest; halt; — चिह्न punctuation mark

विरासत (*nf*) inheritance, legacy

विरुद्ध (a) contrary; against; opposite; adverse, hostile

विरुद्धता (nf) hostility, opposition

विरूप (a) variegated, multi-coloured, ugly, ill-shaped

विरेचक (a) purgative

विरेचन (nm) a purgative medicine, purging

विरोध (nm) hostility, opposition, antagonism; resistance; objection; protest

विरोधाभास (nm) a paradox

विरोधी (a) hostile, inimical, disputant, an adversary, rival; opponent

विलंब (nm) tardiness, delay; lag

विलंबित (a) hanging, late, delayed, tardy

विलंबी (a) tardy, laggard

विलक्षण (a) uncommon; queer, strange, wonderful; remarkable, extra-ordinary, fantastic

विलक्षणता (nf) imparity, queerness

विलग (a) separated, detached

विलय (nm) merger; annihilation; dissolution

विलाप (nm) crying, weeping, lamentation

विलायत (nm) a foreign country, a distant land

विलायती (a) foreign, European

विलास (nm) merriment, enjoyment; luxury; amorous, playfulness

विला/सी (a & nm) amorous, playful, lustful; luxury-loving; —सिता debauchery; —सिनी a beautiful woman, a harlot, a flirt

विलीन (a) hidden, vanished, disappeared, invisible

विलोकन (nm) the act of seeing

विलोकित (a) beheld, looked at, viewed

विलोचन (nm) the eye

विलोड़न (nm) stirring, whirling, moving

विलोम (a) converse; reverse; contrary; antonym

विलोल (a) unsteady; beautiful

विवक्षित (a) desired, intended, signified

विवरण (nm) explanation, description, statement

विवरणिका (nf) a brochure

विवर्ण (a) of low caste; of bad colour, faded; colourless

विवर्त (nm) illusion, falsity

विवश (a) compelled, helpless; under compulsion; forced

विवस्त्र (a) devoid or destitute of clothes, naked

विवाद (nm) dispute, argument; quarrel, altercation; discussion

विवादास्पद (a) controversial

विवादी (nm) a wrangler

विवाह (nm) wedding, marriage, matrimony; —संबंध matrimonial relation

विवाहित (*nm*) married man

विवाहिता (*nf*) married woman

विविध (*a*) various, different, multiform; —ता variety, variation

विवृत (*a*) expanded, opened

विवेक (*nm*) discretion, reason; wisdom, intelligence

विवेकी (*a*) judicious, prudent, wise

विवेचन (*nm*) a thorough investigation, judgement, critical appreciation

विवेचित (*a*) discussed; critically appreciated; evaluated, investigated

विशद (*a*) elaborate, detailed; clear-cut

विशारद (*nm*) a very learned man; (*a*) learned, wise, clever, competent

विशाल (*a*) extensive; huge, large, big; grand; gigantic

विशिष्ट (*a*) special; particular; prominent; typical

विशिष्टता (*nf*) speciality, qualification

विशुद्ध (*a*) pure, unmixed, unadulterated; true, genuine

विशुद्धि (*nf*) greater purity, genuineness

विशूचिका (*nf*) the disease called cholera

विशृंखल (*a*) disorderly, disintegrated, disarrayed

विशेष (*a*) special, peculiar, specific, distinctive, chara- cteristic; typical

विशेषज्ञ (*nm*) an expert, a specialist; (*a*) skilful; —ता specialisation

विशेषण (*nm*) attribute; adjective; —पद attributive

विशेषता (*nf*) peculiarity

विशेषांक (*nm*) a special number of a newspaper or a magazine

विशेषाधि/कार (*nm*) privilege; —कारी a special officer; privileged person

विशेष्य (*nm*) a substantive, that which is qualified

विश्रब्ध (*a*) calm and quiet; confidential; fearless

विश्रांत (*a*) calm; at ease; reposed

विश्रांति (*nf*) rest, repose, recess

विश्राम (*nm*) recreation, repose, relaxation, rest

विश्रुत (*a*) famous, renowned

विश्लिष्ट (*a*) analysed, disunited, separated

विश्लेषण (*nm*) analysis

विश्लेषित (*a*) analysed

विश्व (*nm*) the world, universe; —कोश an encyclopaedia; —विद्यालय a university; —विख्यात world known; —विजयी world-conqueror; —व्यापी pervading the universe

विश्वसनीय (*a*) trustworthy, bonafide, reliable, dependable, believable, credible

विश्वस्त (a) reliable, confidential; solid, responsible, truthful

विश्वास (nm) trust, credit, belief, faith; confidence; assurance; —घात betrayal, treachery, violation of trust; —घाती treacherous, a traitor; —पात्र a reliable person; —भंग a breach of faith

विश्वासी (a) honest, faithful, steady

विष (nm) poison, venom; —धर a snake; —मंत्र a charm for curing snake-bite

विषण्ण (a) gloomy, melancholic

विषम (a) uneven, rough, odd; adverse, dissimilar; disagreeable

विषमता (nf) irregularity, disproportion, enmity

विषय (nm) topic, a subject; matter; content; an affair; object; —रत sexy; —लोलुप lustful, sexy, sensual; —वासना sexuality and lust; sensuality; —वस्तु theme; —सुख sexual pleasure; —सूची a list of contents, table of contents

विषयक (ind) concerning, relating to

विषयांतर (nm) another topic; digression

विषयासक्त (a) lustful, sensual, given to sexual indulgence

विषयी (nm & a) a sensualist, an amorous person, rich, wealthy

विषाक्त (a) poisonous, toxic

विषाद (nm) sorrow, sadness, gloom, dejection, melancholy

विषैला (a) poisonous, venomous, viperous

विसंग/त (a) illogical, irrelevant; —ति irrelevance

विसर्जन (nm) departure; dispersion

विसर्जित (a) dispersed

विस्तार (nm) spread, elaboration, expanse, span; extent; enlargement; details; volume; —पूर्वक extensively; in details; elaborately

विस्तीर्ण (a) spread wide, extended; spacious; elaborate

विस्तृत (a) expanded; voluminous; elaborate, detailed; lengthy

विस्था/पन (nm) displacement; —पित displaced

विस्फारित (a) spread

विस्फोट (nm) explosion, blast; burst

विस्फोटक (nm) a poisonous boil, an explosive substance

विस्मय (nm) astonishment, wonder, surprise

विस्मयाकुल (a) wonderstruck

विस्मयादिबोधक (nm) an interjection

विस्मरण (nm) forgetting,

oblivion; —शील forgetful;
—शीलता forgetfulness

विस्मित (a) amazed, astonished, surprised

विस्मृत (a) forgotten

विस्मृति (nm) forgetting, oblivion

विहंगम (nm) a bird

विहंगावलोकन (nm) a bird's eye view

विहग (nm) a bird

विहसित (nm) a laugh which is neither too loud nor too slow

विहान (nm) day-break

विहार (nm) pastime, merry-making; wandering, roaming; a Buddhist monastery

विहित (a) arranged; instituted, performed

विहीन (a) abandoned, deserted; deprived of; (adv) without

विह्वल (a) confused, agitated; perplexed; impatient

वीक्षण (nm) the act of seeing

वीचि (nf) a wave, ripple

वीणा (nf) Indian lute, lyre; —वादिनी an epithet of goddess सरस्वती, —वादक a lute player

वीत (a) abandoned, left off, released; —राग one who is free from worldly attachment

वीथि, वीथी (nf) a path, passage, way, a road

वीर (a) brave, valiant, plucky, daring; —गति the attainment of heaven which a warrior slain in war is supposed to get; —पूजा hero-worship; —हृदय stout-hearted

वीरता (nf) bravery, valiancy, heroism, daring

वीरा/न (a) devastated, desolate; uninhabited; —नी desolateness, desertedness

वीरासन (nm) a special posture of body befitting a warrior

वीर्य (nm) semen; potency, valour; virility; heroism

वुजूद (nm) existence, being

वृंत (nm) nipple, leaf

वृंद (nm) an assembly, multitude, a collection; —गान chorus; —गायक the chorus

वृक्ष (nm) a tree

वृत्त (nm) ring; circle; account; news; verse, meter

वृत्तांत (nm) a report, narrative, account; news

वृत्ति (nf) subsistence, instinct; mentality; vocation; stipend; —कार a commentator

वृथा (a) fruitless, useless; ineffective; (adv) vainly, in vain

वृद्ध (a) aged, old; (nm) aged man, oldman

वृद्धता (nf) senility, old age

वृद्धा (nf) an old woman

वृद्धावस्था (*nf*) old age

बुद्धि (*nf*) progress, increase; growth; enlargement; magnification

वृषभ (*nm*) a bull, bullock

वृष्टि (*nf*) rain, shower; —काल rainy season

वृहत् (*a*) large, great, much, big

वे (*pron*) they, those

वेग (*nm*) momentum, speed

वेगवान् (*a*) swift, rapid, quick, hasty

वेणी (*nf*) a woman's braided hair falling down on her back like a tail

वेणु (*nf*) bamboo, a flute, a pipe

वेतन (*nm*) wages, salary; —भोगी salaried; —वृद्धि increment

वेताल (*nm*) a sentinal, a porter, a goblin

वेत्ता (*nm*) one who knows, (*a*) understanding, knowing, acquainted with

वेद (*nm*) the most ancient and sacred scripuptures of the Hindus; the divine know-ledge; —ज्ञ one who knows the Vedas, conversant with the scriptures

वेदना (*nf*) pain, ache, agony, distress, affliction, torment

वेदांग (*nm*) the six subordinate branches of Vedas; —शिक्षा rules for correct pronunci-ation of Vedic Mantras; —कल्प details of religious ceremonies

वेदांत (*nm*) one of the six systems of Hindu philoso-phy which is particularly based on the Upanishads, theology; —सूत्र the ophorisms on Vedanta compiled by the sage Vadarayan

वेदांती (*nm*) a follower of the Vedanta philosophy, a theologian

वेदाभ्यास (*nm*) the study of the Vedas

वेदी (*nf*) an altar, a platform; terrace

वेदोक्त (*a*) enjoined by the holy writ, scriptural, taught in the scriptures, or Vedas

वेध (*nm*) a hole, perforation, piercing; the observation of planets by means of a telescope

वेला (*nf*) time; an hour; coast, shore

वेश (*nm*) dress, costume, guise; —भूषा apparel; get-up, appearance

वेश्या (*nf*) a harlot, a prostitute; —वृत्ति profession of prostitution

वेष्टन (*nm*) enclosure, fence

वेष्टित (*a*) enclosed, surroun-ded

वैकल्पिक (*a*) alternative, optional

वैकुंठ (*nm*) paradise, heaven

वैचित्र्य (nm) queerness, peculiarity, strangeness

वैजयंती (nf) a banner; a garland of five colours of Lord Vishnu

वैज्ञानिक (nm) a scientist; (a) scientific

वैतनिक (a) salaried, on salary-basis

वैतालीय (a) pertaining to a goblin

वैदेशिक (a) foreign, external

वैद्य (nm) a physician; —शास्त्र medical science, medicine

वैद्यक (nm) the Indian system of medical science, Ayur-veda

वैध (a) legal, valid; tenable, regular

वैधर्म्य (nm) heresy, atheism

वैधव्य (nm) widowhood

वैभव (nm) greatness, majesty; wealth; grandeur, glory

वैभवशाली (a) rich, magnificent, royal

वैमनस्य (nm) enmity, hostility, malice, rancour

वैयक्तिक (a) personal; individual; private; —ता individuality

वैयाकरण (nm) a grammarian

वैर (nm) enmity, hostility, opposition

वैरागी (a & nm) detached; one who has subdued his passions

वैराग्य (nm) freedom from worldly desires; renunciation

वैरी (nm) a foe, an enemy, an adversary

वैरूप्य (nm) difference of form

वैवाहिक (a) matrimonial, married

वैशिष्ट्य (nm) peculiarity; speciality

वैषम्य (nm) difference, irregularity

वैषयिक (a) pertaining to a subject

वैष्णव (nm) a devotee of Vishnu; (a) pertaining to Vishnu

वैष्णवी (nf) the personified energy of Vishnu

वैसा (adv) so, such, like that; (a) of that kind, such as that

वैसे (ind) in that manner, that way; in the same manner

व्यंग्य (nm) joke, irony, sarcasm, caricature; —चित्र a cartoon; —चित्रकार a cartoonist

व्यंग्यार्थ (nm) suggestion; connotative meaning

व्यंजक (a) making clear or manifest; (nm) a mark, a symbol

व्यंजन (nm) a consonant; rich cooked food

व्यंजित (a) conveyed through suggestion, suggested

व्यक्त (a) manifest, apparent,

clear; expressed

व्यक्ति (nm) a person, an individual; subject; —गत subjective; individual, personal; —त्व personality; individuality; —वादी an individualist; individual - istic

व्यग्र (a) impatient, restless; concerned

व्यग्रता (nf) perplexity, solici - tude, anxiety

व्यतिक्रम (nm) contrariety, converse

व्यतिरेक (nm) negation, exclu - sion, an exception

व्यतीत (a) gone, passed; past

व्यथा (nf) anguish, pain, suffering, misery, distress

व्यथित (a) troubled, distressed pained, afflicted

व्यभिचार (nm) following an improper or sinful course, debauchery; adultery

व्यभिचारिणी (nf) a wanton woman, an adulteress

व्यभिचारी (a & nm) uncnaste, immoral; a debauchee; an adulterer; lewd

व्यय (nm) expense, cost, expenditure; consumption

व्यर्थ (a) to no purpose, fruit - less, useless; futile, in - effective; unprofitable

व्यवच्छेद (nm) separation, division, contrast

व्यवधान (nm) hindrance, interruption

व्यवसाय (nm) an occupation; profession; vocation; practice

व्यवसायी (nm) a man of business

व्यवस्था (nf) form; an adjustment, order, system, arrangement; provision

व्यवस्थापक (nm) a regulator; a director; an organiser; a manager

व्यवस्थित (a) regular, systematic; settled; provi - ded

व्यवहार (nm) dealings, treat - ment; behaviour; transac - tion; practice; usage, use

व्यवहार्य (a) usual, practicable, feasible

व्यवहृत (a) followed in practice, employed, used, applied; adjusted

व्यष्टि (nm) individual

व्यसन (nm) calamity, misfortune, addiction

व्यसनी (a & nm) vicious; (nm) a person who is addicted to a vice

व्यस्त (a) perplexed, engaged in some work, busy, occupied

व्याकरण (nm) grammar

व्याकुल (a) upset, perturbed, restless, distempered

व्याकुलता (nf) distraction, agitation, confusion

व्याख्या (nf) a description, interpretation; explanation; commentary; exposition; —कार a commentator

व्याख्याता (nm) a speaker, a lecturer

व्याख्यान (nm) an explanation, speech, lecture; interpretation

व्याघात (nm) an obstacle, interruption; hindrance, obstruction

व्याघ्र (nm) a lion, a tiger

व्याज (nm) fraud, deception, interest

व्याघ (nm) a fowler, a hunter

व्याधि (nf) a malady, disease, an ailment

व्यापक (a) extensive, comprehensive, circumambient

व्यापकता (nf) prevalence, diffusion, extensiveness

व्यापार (nm) profession, trade, business; traffic; function; phenomenon

व्यापारिक (a) mercantile, commercial

व्यापारी (nm) a trader, merchant, business man

व्याप्त (a) diffused; pervaded, spread; extended

व्याप्ति (nf) pervasion, omnipresence

व्यामोह (nm) ignorance, illusion, bewilderment

व्यायाम (nm) exercise, physical exercise; gymnastics; —शाला a gymnasium

व्यावसायिक (a) vocational, professional

व्यावहारिक (a) customary; practical

व्यास (nm) calibre, diameter; diffusion; —शैली diffused style

व्युत्क्रम (nm) irregular arrangement of a thing, disorder

व्युत्पत्ति (nf) origin, derivation, etymology of words

व्युत्पन्न (a) literate, well-read, learned

व्यूह (nm) a military array, an army; —रचना logistic strategy

व्योम (nm) the sky

व्रण (nm) a tumour, boil, wound

व्रत (nm) a fast; vow; pledge

व्रती (nm) one who observes a religious vow, an ascetic, a devotee

ब्रीडा (nf) bashfulness; shyness

श

श the first of the conventional sibilant trio (श, ष, स) of Devnagri alphabet

शंका (nf) suspicion; mistrust; doubt; —शील suspicious

शंकालु (a) mistrustful; of suspicious nature

शंकित (a) filled with doubt; alarmed

शंकु (nm) a cone

शंख (nm) conchshell; a number equal to 10,000,000,000 crores

शऊर (nm) decency; manner-liness

शक (nm) suspicion, doubt

शक संवत् an era introduced by emperor Shalivahan of India (in 78 A.D.)

शक्ति (nf) strength, energy; power, —मान strong

शक्ल (nf) form; shape, —सूरत appearance; looks

शख़्स (nm) a human being; an individual; person

शख़्सियत (nf) individuality; personality

शगल (nm) recreation; a pastime, hobby

शत (nm) one hundred; —प्रति शत cent percent

शतक (nm) one hundred, a century

शता/ब्दि, ब्दी (nf) century

शती (nf) a century

शत्रु (nm) an enemy, a foe; —ता enmity, hostility

शनि (nm) Saturn —वार Saturday

शनै: (ind) slowly; gradually, —शनै: little by little

शपथ (nf) swearing; an oath, —पत्र an affidavit

शफ़ा (nf) health; recovery; curative power; —ख़ाना a dispensary, clinic

शबनम (nf) dew

शब्द (nm) a word; voice, sound; noise; tone, —कोश a dictionary; —रचना word-formation, —सूची concor-dance

शब्दश: (ind) word by word

शमन (nm) quenching; suppres-sion; pacification

शमा (nf) a candle, flame (of fire)

शयन (nm) sleep, (the act of) sleeping, —कक्ष a bedroom

शय्या (nf) a bed, bedstead

शरण (nf) protection; shelter, refuge

शरणार्थी (nm) a refugee

शरद् (nf) the autumn

शरबत (nm) syrup; beverage

शराफ़त (nf) nobility; civility, politeness

शराब (nf) wine, liquor; —ख़ाना

a bar, wine shop

शराबी (*nm & a*) a drunkard, intoxicated, drunk

शरारत (*nf*) wickedness; mischief

शरीफ़ (*n*) a gentleman; noble, virtuous, pure, holy

शरीर (*nm*) physique, body; —और आत्मा body and soul; —क्रिया विज्ञान Physiology; —रचना शास्त्र Anatomy

शर्त (*nf*) provision; bet; a condition; term

शर्तिया (*a & adv*) positively, definitely, without fail; sure

शर्म (*nf*) shame; shyness; —नाक shameful, disgraceful

शर्माना (*v*) to feel shy, to blush; to be ashamed

शर्मि/न्दा (*a*) ashamed; —दगी shame

शर्मीला (*a*) shy, modest, bashful —पन shyness, modesty

शल्य (*nm*) a surgical instrument; a thorn; —क्रिया/ चिकित्सा surgery/surgical operation

शव (*nm*) a corpse, dead body; —दाह cremation; —परीक्षा post-martem

शशि (*nm*) the moon

शस्त्र (*nm*) an arm, weapon; tool

शस्त्रागार (*nm*) an armoury

शहंशाह (*nm*) a king of kings

शहद (*nm*) honey

शहर (*nm*) a town; city

शहादत (*nf*) martyrdom; evidence

शहीद (*a & nm*) martyr

शांत (*a*) peaceful; still; slient, quiet

शांति (*nf*) peace; calmness, quiet; silence

शाक (*nm*) vegetable

शाकाहा/र (*nm*) vegetarian diet; —री a vegetarian

शाखा (*nf*) a branch; sect

शागिर्द (*nm*) a pupil, disciple; an apprentice

शादी (*nf*) wedding, marriage

शान (*nf*) splendour, pomp, magnificence, grandeur —दार grand; splendid, pompous; magnificent —शौकत pomp and show

शाप (*nm*) a curse

शाबा/श (*int*) bravo! well-done!, excellent; —शी praise, applause

शाम (*nf*) evening, dusk

शामत (*nf*) misfortune, ill-luck, affliction

शामियाना (*nm*) a canopy

शामिल (*a*) included; connected, associated; united

शाय/र (*nm*) a poet; —राना poetic —री poetry

शारीरिक (*a*) physical, bodily; concrete

शाला (*nf*) a house, residence

शालीन (a) modest, gentle; cultured, well-behaved

शाश्वत (a) permanent, eternal, immortal

शास/क (nm) a ruler; king; —कीय governmental

शासन (nm) administration, government; rule; command

शासित (a) administered, governed; ruled

शाहंशाह (nm) an emperor, a monarch; (a) very liberal

शाही (a) regal, majestic, royal

शिकंजा (nm) a clamp, pressing appliance; clasp

शिकस्त (nf) defeat

शिकायत (nf) a complaint; grievance; accusation

शिकार (nm) a prey; victim

शिकारा (nm) a long, partly covered boat

शिकारी (a & nm) hunting; huntsman, a hunter

शिक्षक (nm) a teacher

शिक्षण (nm) teaching, education; instruction; —कला the art of teaching

शिक्षा (nf) teaching; moral; education; instruction

शिक्षार्थी (nm) a pupil, student

शिक्षालय (nm) a school, educational institution

शिखर (nm) a peak; top; summit, pinnacle

शिथिल (a) loose; slow; slack; weary; —ता looseness; weariness; slackness

शिनाख्त (nf) indentification

शिला (nf) a rock, foundation stone; cliff; —न्यास laying of the foundation stone

शिल्प (nm) architecture; craft; —कला technology; craft; —कार a craftsman

शिव (nm) one of the divine trio of the Hindus; welfare; well-being

शिविर (nm) a camp, tent

शिशिर (nm) the winter

शिशु (nm) an infant; a baby, child; —ता childhood

शिश्न (nm) penis, male genital organ

शिष्ट (a) civilised, polite, courteous, civil

शिष्टता (nf) civility, gentleness, decency

शिष्टाचार (nm) etiquette; courtesy, decency

शिष्य (nm) a pupil, disciple; student

शीघ्र (adv) soon, urgently; immediately, quickly, hurriedly, speedly; —ता quickness, rapidity, hurry

शीतल (a) cold, frigid; cool; —ता coldness, frigidness; coolness

शीतला (nf) small-pox

शीतोष्ण (a) moderate, temperate

शीर्ष (nm) the head; top, summit

शीर्षक (*nm*) a heading, title

शील (*nm*) modesty; virtue, piety

शीलवान् (*a*) well-behaved; modest; hence शीलवती feminine form

शीश (*nm*) the head; the front part of the head

शीशा (*nm*) a mirror, looking glass; glass

शीशी (*nf*) a small bottle

शुक्र (*nm*) semen; venus; Friday

शुक्र (*nm*) thanks, an expression of gratitude —गुज़ार grateful, thankful; —गुज़ारी gratefulness

शुक्रिया (*nm*) gratefulness, gratitude, thankfulness

शुक्ल (*a*) white; —पक्ष the bright half of a lunar month

शुगल (*nm*) hobby; fun

शुचि (*a*) free from fault; pure, virtuous; sacred

शुद्ध (*a*) pure; sacred; unadulterated; uncorrupt; correct; amended; clean; —ता, —त्व purity; sacredness; correctness; cleanliness

शुभ (*a*) auspicious; good; (*nm*) the good, well-being; —कामनाएँ good wishes; —चिंतक a well-wisher; —मुहूर्त an auspicious moment

शुभाकांक्षी (*a*) well-wisher

शुभागमन (*nm*) welcome

शुभाशुभ (*a*) good and evil

शुमार (*nm*) accounting; counting

शुरू (*nm*) beginning, commencement

शुरुआत (*nf*) beginning, commencement

शुल्क (*nm*) fee; subscription; duty

शुश्रूषा (*nf*) attendance, nursing

शुष्क (*a*) dried; withered; tedious (as काम); dull; hard

शून्य (*a*) empty, void; zero; (*nm*) the empty space

शूर (*a & nm*) brave, gallant, heroic, mighty; a warrior; hero

शृंखला (*nf*) a chain, fetters; order; belt; —बद्ध systematic, orderly

शृंग (*nm*) peak; pinnacle; horn of an animal

शृंगार (*nm*) elegant make-up; adornment

शेखी (*nf*) boasting, bragging; —बाज़ boastful; —बाज़ी boastfulness

शेरवानी (*nf*) a typical long-tight coat

शेष (*a & nm*) rest, remaining; balance; remainder

शेषांश (*nm*) the remaining part; remainder; residue

शैक्षिक (*a*) academic, educational

शैतान (nm) devil, the Satan; a mischief-monger; (a) mischievous, naughty

शैतानी (nf) mischievousness, wickedness; naughtiness

शैल (nm) a rock; mountain

शैली (nf) style; —कार a stylist

शोक (nm) sorrow, grief; condolence; —संदेश a condolence message; —सभा a condolence meeting

शोख (a) insolent; bright, of deep shining colour

शोखी (nf) insolence; playfulness, brightness

शोचनीय (a) critical; miserable

शोणित (nm) blood; (a) bloody, red

शोध (nf) research; purification, refinement; setting right; cleaning; correction

शोधना (v) to purify; to correct; to refine

शोभा (nf) grace, glory, beauty; splendour

शोभित (a) splendid; adorned; beautiful

शोर (nm) noise; tumult, hue and cry

शोरबा (nm) soup, broth

शोला (nm) a flame of fire

शोषक (nm) an exploiter, an absorbent

शोषण (nm) exploitation; soaking

शोहरत (nf) celebrity, fame

शौक (nm) an eager desire; hobby; fondness

शौकिया (a & adv) amateurish; fondly, fashionably; as a hobby

शौकी/न (a) fashionable; fond of fine things; —नी fashionableness, fondness

शौच (nm) toilet; cleanliness

शौचालय (nm) a latrine, lavatory

शौर्य (nm) valour, heroism, bravery

शौहर (nm) husband

श्याम (a) black, dark-coloured; dark-blue

श्याम/ल (a) dark-coloured, of blue-black colour; hence —लता (nf)

श्रद्धांजलि (nf) homage, tribute

श्रद्धा (nf) faith, trust, veneration; reverence

श्रद्धालु (a) having faith, trustful

श्रद्धास्पद (a) venerable, deserving faith

श्रद्धेय (a) venerable, worthy of faith

श्रमण (nm) a Buddhist monk

श्रमिक (nm & a) a labourer; labour

श्रमी (a & nm) hard-working, laborious

श्रव/ण (nm) an ear; audition; —णीय audible, hearing

श्रव्य (a) audible; able to be heard

श्रांत (a) exhausted; fatigued,

tired, wearied

श्री (a) Mr.; (nf) the goddess of wealth — Lakshmi

श्रेष्ठ (a) good; —तर, better; —तम best, topmost

श्रोता (nm) a listener; —गण audience

श्लथ (a) loose, weary, languid, slothful; feeble

श्लाघा (nf) praise, applause

श्लील (a) clean, nice, not vulgar

श्लेष्मा (nm) mucus, phlegm

श्वास (nm) breath, respiration; —क्रिया the act of breathing

श्वेत (a) white; bright; spotless

ष

ष the second of the sibilant-trio (श ष स) of Devnagri alphabet

षट् (a) six; (nm) the number six; —कोण six angled

षट्पद (nm) a large black bee; having six legs

षट्पदी (nf) a female bee

षट्शास्त्र (nm) the six schools of Indian philosophy (viz न्याय, सांख्य, योग, वैशेषिक, पूर्व-मीमांसा and उत्तरमीमांसा)

षड् (a) an allomorph of षट् (six) appearing as the first member in some compound words —अंग the six supplementary branches of sacred science (viz शिक्षा, कल्प, व्याकरण, निरुक्त, छंद and ज्योतिष); the six parts of body (viz. two arms, two legs, the head and the waist); —ऋतु the six seasons of the year (viz. ग्रीष्म, वर्षा, शरत् हेमन्त, शिशिर, वसंत)

षड्भुज (nm) a hexagon

षड्रस (nm) six prominent tastes (viz salt, sour, astringent, pungent, bitter and sweet —लवण, अम्ल, तिक्त, कषाय, कटु और मधु)

षड्राग (nm) the six main ragas in Indian music (viz. भैरवी मल्हार, श्रीराग, हिंडोल, मालकोस and दीपक)

षड्रिपु (nm) the six internal enemies of man according to Indian tradition (viz. काम, क्रोध, मद, लोभ, मोह, मत्सर)

षड्यंत्र (nm) a conspiracy, an intrigue; —कारी a conspira-tor, an intriguer, plotter

षष्टि (a) sixty; (nm) the number sixty

षष्ठ (a) sixth

षष्ठी (nf) the sixth day of a fortnight, the sixth day from the day of child birth

षोडश (a) sixteen (nm) the number sixteen

षोडशी (nf) a girl of sixteen years of age

स

स the last of the sibilant trio (श, ष, स) of Devnagri alphabet

संकट (nm) misfortune, risk, crisis; hazard, danger

संकर (nm) hybrid; a mixed caste; intergrade; —ता (nf) hybridization

सैंकरा (a) narrow

संकर्षण (nm) attraction; ploughing; Balram, brother of Krishna

संकलन (nm) a collection; compilation; —कर्ता a compiler

संकलित (a) compiled, collected; assembled

संकल्प (nm) resolve, determination; solemn promise, will; vow —करना to resolve

संकीर्ण (a) narrow; mean; crowded; —ता narrowness

संकुचित (a) narrow; mean; limited

संकुल (a) confused; congested; crowded

संकेत (nm) a sign; signal; hint; symbol; —करना to hint, to suggest

संको/च (nm) hesitation, hitch; shame, shyness; contraction; —ची shy, hesitant, reserved, bashful

संक्रमण (nm) motion, transition; —काल transition period

संक्रामक (a) contagious, infectious; —रोग an epidemic

संक्षिप्त (a) abridged; short, brief; —करना to abbreviate; —रूप में summarily

संक्षेप (nm) brief, summary; brevity; —करना to shorten, to summarize, to curtail; to abbreviate

संक्षेपत: (a) briefly, in short

संखिया (nm) arsenic

संख्या (nf) a number; numeral; figure; —की गणना score, बड़ी — multitude; सैनिकों की — strength; —सूचक numerical

संग (nm) a union, association, company, attachment; stone; —तराश a stone-carver; —तराशी stone-carving —मरमर marble

संगठन (nm) a league; an organization; an act of organization

संगठित (a) organised

संगत (nf) company, party; (a) logical; relevant; appropriate, harmonious; —करना to keep company with; —होना to hold good

संगति (nf) association, company; relevance, relation; sexual intercourse; —प्रिय social

संगम (nm) junction, union, meeting; federation

संगिनी (nf) a female companion

संगी (nm) a comrade, a friend, an ally, a companion and associate; —साथी companions and friends

संगीत (nm) the art of music and dancing; playing on musical instruments; —नाटक a musical drama, an opera; —शास्त्र music

संगीतज्ञ (nm) a musician

संगीताचार्य (nm) a master of music

संगीन (nf) a bayonet; (a) serious; —भोंकना to bayonet

संगृहीत (a) gathered; amassed; collected; compiled

संग्रह (nm) collection; compilation; storage; deposit; —करना to gather; to amass; to collect; to compile, to store —कर्ता collector

संग्रहण (nm) collection

संग्रहणी (nf) a chronic disorder of bowels, acute form of chronic diarrhoea, sprue

संग्रहणीय (a) worthy of collecting, fit to be acquired

संग्रहालय (nm) a museum

संग्राम (nm) battle, war; fight; —योग्य warlike

संग्राह्य (a) worthy of collecting, fit to be acquired

संघ (nm) a club, society; corporation, federation; union, league; an assembly

संघटन (nm) formation; constitution; organization

संघटक (a) constituent, component

संघर्ष (nm) rubbing; conflict, struggle, strife

संघीय (a) federal; union

संचय (nm) collection; deposit, reserve; hoard; —करना to hoard; to deposit

संचरण (nm) act of going; movement of a body etc.; —करना to go, to move

संचार (nm) motion, movement; communication; transmission

संचालक (nm) a leader, director; conductor

संचालन (nm) management; direction; conduction

संचित (a) collected, gathered; hoarded; —करना to gather

संजी/दा (a) serious; sober; wise, intelligent —दगी

intelligence

संजीवनी (*a*) reanimating, restoring; (*nf*) a kind of medicine which is supposed to restore a dead man to life

सँजोना (*v*) to arrange; to put things in order

संज्ञा (*nf*) a noun (gram); name; consciousness; sign; जातिवाचक— a common noun; भाववाचक— an abstract noun; व्यक्तिवाचक— a proper noun; —हीन unconscious, senseless

सँझला (*a*) younger than the middle brother

संडास (*nm*) a latrine, lavatory, sink

संत (*nm*) a saint; saintly; a devotee

संतत (*adv*) perpetually, continuously, ever, eternally

संतति (*nf*) descendant, progeny, generation succession, issue

संतप्त (*a*) grieved, troubled; burnt; afflicted

संतरण (*nm*) swimming; salvation, emancipation

संतरा (*nm*) an orange

संतरी (*nm*) a watchman, a sentry, a door-keeper

संतान (*nm*) children, progeny, issue

संताप (*nm*) sorrow, torment, distress, grief

संतु/लन (*nm*) equilibrium, balance; —लित balanced

संतुष्ट (*a*) complacent, content, satisfied, gratified, acquiescent, —करना to satisfy, to suffice, to meet, to gratify

संतृ/प्त (*a*) gratified, saturated; hence —प्ति gratification

संतोष (*nm*) satisfaction; contentment; —जनक satisfactory

संतोषी (*a & nm*) a contented person

संदर्भ (*nm*) a context, reference, —ग्रंथ a reference book

संदल (*nm*) sandal wood

संदिग्ध (*a*) dubious, uncertain, doubtful; ambiguous, suspicious

संदूक (*nm*) a chest, a box; —चा a box; —ची a little box (feminine form)

संदूकड़ी (*nf*) a small box or chest

संदेश (*nm*) a message; information, word; a kind of Bengali sweet; —भेजना to send word

संदेह (*nm*) suspicion, doubt; distrust

संधि (*nf*) union; joint; a treaty; articulation; —पत्र a treaty

संध्या (*nf*) evening, twilight

संन्यास (*nm*) asceticism, renunciation

संपत्ति (nf) wealth, richness, property, estate

संपदा (nf) property, wealth

संपन्न (a) rich, prosperous; —ता prosperity, wealthiness

संपर्क (nm) contact

संपादक (nm) one who performs a certain action; an editor; —त्व act of editing

संपादकीय (nm & a) an editorial

संपादन (nm) performing; executing, editing

संपूर्ण (a) all, total; completed

सँपेरा (nm) a snake-charmer

संप्रदाय (nm) a religious society, a community; sect

संप्रेष/ण (nm) communication; —णीय communicable

संबंध (nm) connection, relation, link; terms; association, —रखना to regard, to belong

संबंधित (a) related; affiliated; connected

संबद्ध (a) attached to, jointed, connected; bound; related; affiliated

संबल (nm) backing, support

सँभलना (v) to be alert; to maintain; to save one self from a fall

संभव (a) probable, possible; practicable

संभवत: (adv) probably, possibly; perhaps

सँभालना (v) to help; to support; to manage; to take care of; to hold

संभावना (nf) probability, possibility, likelihood

संभावित (a) likely, probable

संभाव्य (a) possible, probable

संभाषण (nm) conversation, dialogue, talk

संभ्रांत (a) respectable

संभ्रांति (nf) confusion

संयत (a) suppressed, tied up, guarded; controlled, restrained; sober

संयम (nm) a check, restraint; moderation, control

संयुक्त (a) joint; united; mixed

संयुत (a) fitted, mixed together

संयोग (nm) chance, coincidence; luck; mixture

संयोजक (nm) a convener

संयोजन (nm) composition; conjugation; attachment

संरक्षक (nm) protector, patron; guardian

संरक्षण (nm) safeguard, protection; guardianship

संलग्न (a) joined; attached; engaged; enclosed

संवत् (nm) an era, a year

संवत्सर (nm) a year

सँवरना (v) to be mended; to be arranged; to be tip-top; to be decorated

संवर्धन (nm) increase; protection; nourishment

संवाद (nm) conversation;

dialogue; news; message;
—दाता a pressman, a
correspondent

सँवारना (v) to adorn; to dress;
to make up; to decorate; to
arrange; to mend

संवेग (nm) emotion, passion,
momentum

संवेदन (nm) feeling, sensation
—शील sensitive

संवेदना (nf) sensibility,
sensation, feeling

संशय (nm) doubt, suspicion;
uncertainty

संशयी (a) doubting, sceptic,
uncertain

संशोधक (nm) a mender;
purifier

संशोधन (nm) correction,
amendment; purification;
revision

संशोधित (a) amended, cor-
rected; improved; revised

संश्रय (nm) alliance; refuge,
protection

संश्रयण (nm) taking refuge;
shelter, protection

संश्लेषण (nm) uniting, joining
together; synthesis

संस/द (nf) parliament; —दीय
parliamentary

संसर्ग (nm) connection,
relation, contact; company,
association

संसार (nm) the world; the
mortal world; domestic life

संसारी (nm & a) a mortal being;
belonging to the world

संसृष्ट (a) joined together,
mixed up, muddled

संसृष्टि (nf) an intermixture

संस्करण (nm) correction; an
edition of a printed book

संस्कर्ता (nm) the person who
corrects or purifies

संस्कार (nm) ceremony, rite;
sacrament; purification

संस्कृत (a) purified, cleansed,
refined; (nf) Sanskrit
language

संस्कृति (nf) purification;
culture; civilisation

संस्था (nf) an organisation,
institution; concern

संस्थान (nm) an organisation,
institute

संस्थापक (nm) a founder

संस्थापन (nm) setting up,
establishing

संस्मरण (nm) memoirs

संहत (a) collected, gathered

संहति (nf) union, collection

संहार (nm) completion;
destruction, slaughter

संहारक (nm) destroyer;
slaughterer, murderer

सइयां (nm) husband; lover

सकना (v) may; can; to be
competent

सकपकाना (v) to wonder, to be
amazed; to hesitate, to
totter

सकर्मक (a) transitive; —क्रिया a
transitive verb

सकल (*a*) all, whole, entire

सकाम (*a*) inspired by a desire; desirous, lustful

सकुचाना (*v*) to intimidate, to hesitate

सक्षम (*a*) capable; competent

सखा (*nm*) a friend, an associate

सखी (*nf*) a female friend

सखी (*a*) liberal, open-handed

सख्त (*a*) hard; strong; stiff; strict

सख्ती (*nf*) strictness; stiffness; hardness; harshness

सगा (*a*) born of the same parents

सगाई (*nf*) an engagement, betrothal

सगापन (*nm*) near relationship

सगोत्र (*a*) allied by blood; a kin, relative

सघन (*a*) thick, dense, cloudy

सच (*a*) real, true; right; —मुच actually; truly, really

सचाई (*nf*) truthfulness; truth; integrity

सचित्र (*a*) illustrated, pictorial

सचिव (*nm*) secretary

सचिवालय (*nm*) secretariat

सचेत (*a*) wakeful; careful, alert; attentive

सचेतक (*nm*) a whip

सचेतन (*a*) conscious

सचेष्ट (*a*) active, zealous, alert; energetic

सच्चरित्र (*a*) honest, virtuous, of moral character

सच्चा (*a*) genuine; loyal; real, sincere

सचाई (*nm*) sincerity, reality, truth

सच्चिदानंद (*nm*) an epithet of the supreme soul of Brahma

सजग (*a*) cautious; careful; watchful, alert

सजधज (*nf*) paraphernalia, ornamentation

सजन (*nm*) a respectable person, a gentleman; a husband; a lover

सजना (*v*) to prank; to be made up; to be decorated; to be neatly arranged, (*nm*) a lover/husband

सजनी (*nf*) sweetheart; wife; beloved

सजल (*a*) containing water; full of tears, tearful

सजवाई (*nf*) the work or wages paid for decorating

सज़ा (*nf*) penalty; punishment; —देना to punish; —पाना to be chastised or punished; —याफ्ता convicted

सजाति (*a*) belonging to the same class, homogeneous

सजातीयता (*nf*) homogeneity

सजान (*a*) knowing, clever, adept

सजाना (*v*) to adorn, to decorate; to furnish; to arrange; to dress neatly

सजाव/ट (*nf*) ornamentation,

decoration; make up; display; —टी decorative

सजीला (a) beautiful; handsome, graceful, attractive

सजीव (a) lively, quick, living, active

सज्जन (nm & a) noble, gentle; a gentleman; —ता nobility

सज्जा (nf) equipment; decoration

सज्जित (a) adorned, decorated; equipped

सज्ञान (a) intelligent, wise; careful, sagacious

सटना (v) to stick; to be in close proximity

सटपट (nf) astonishment, suspense; doubt; wonder

सटपटाना (v) to be surprised, to wonder

सट्टा (nm) a written agreement or contract; speculation

सड़क (nf) a road; street; lane

सड़न (nm) decay; rottenness, rot

सड़ना (v) to rot; to decay; to perish, to fall in misery

सड़ाना (v) to addle, to rot; to decompose

सड़ाँघ (nf) stench; rot, rottenness; mustiness

सड़ियल (a) rotten; decomposed; bad, good for nothing, worthless

सत (nm) juice, essence; strength; truth; virtue

सतगुना (a) sevenfold, septuple

सतगुरु (nm) a good preceptor; God

सतजुग (nm) the golden age or period

सतत (adv & a) always; continuous, incessant, incessantly

सतफेरा (nm) the ceremony of going round the sacred fire seven times at the time of wedding

सतर्क (a & adv) cautions, alert, careful

सत/ह (nf) upper surface; level; —ही superficial

सताना (v) to torment, to oppress, to torture

सती (nf) a faithful woman, a woman who willingly burns herself on her husband's funeral pyre; daughter of Daksha who was married to Shiva

सत् (a) pious, good; virtuous; true

सत्कार (nm) welcome; hospitality; salute

सत्कार्य (nm) virtue, a pious action

सत्कीर्ति (nf) fame, reputation

सत्कुल (nm) a high family, a person of noble birth

सत्त्व (nm) extract, essence; truth

सत्ता (nm) existence, being; power, authority

सत्ताधारी (*nm*) an officer of state, administrator

सत्पथ (*nm*) a good way; virtuous action

सत्पात्र (*nm*) a worthy person, a man of good character

सत्फल (*nm*) good result

सत्य (*a*) veritable, true, real, right, (*nm*) truth, virtue, —काम a lover of truth; —त: really, truly

सत्यपुरुष (*nm*) a gentleman

सत्ययुग (*nm*) the first of the four Hindu ages, the golden age

सत्यवान (*nm*) the husband of Savitri

सत्याग्रह (*nm*) civil disobedience

सत्यानाश (*nm*) total destruction, complete ruin

सत्यानाशी (*a*) ruining devastating; destructive

सत्वर (*ind*) soon, immediately, swiftly; —ता quickness

सत्संग (*nm*) intercourse with pious men

सदन (*nm*) dwelling, a house; place of rest, chamber

सदमा (*nm*) a stroke, emotional stroke; sorrow, a blow

सदय (*a*) kind, merciful, compassionate

सदर (*a*) chief, principal; (*nm*) president

सदस्य (*nm*) a fellow, a member; —ता membership

सदा (*adv*) constantly, always,

ever; (*nf*) echo, voice, call; —चरण good behaviour

सदाचार (*nm*) probity, morality, virtuous conduct

सदाबहार (*a*) evergreen

सदी (*nf*) a century

सदुपयोग (*nm*) good or proper use

सदृश (*a*) alike, similar, like

सदेह (*a*) with a body, in an embodied form

सदैव (*adv*) ever, always

सद्गति (*nf*) salvation; emancipation

सद्गुरु (*nm*) a good tutor; God

सद्भाव (*nm*) courtesy, amiability, kind feeling

सद्य: (*adv*) immediately; recently; afresh

सधना (*v*) to be completed; to be habituated, to be tamed; to hit the mark

सधवा (*a* & *nf*) a woman whose husband is alive

सन (*nm*) year; ईस्वी— the christian era

सनक (*nf*) caprice; craze

सनकी (*a* & *nm*) crazy; capricious

सनद (*nf*) a certificate, testimonial; deed

सनसनाना (*v*) to rustle; to tingle; to faint, to thrill

सनसनी (*nf*) excitement; thrilling sensation

सनातन (*a*) continual; ancient; eternal

सनेह (*nm*) love, (see also स्नेह)

सन्न (*a*) stupefied, stunned, dumb-founded

सन्नद्ध (*a*) tied up, attached; ready, equipped

सन्नाय (*nm*) loneliness, silence, still

संन्या/स (*nm*) renunciation, monasticism; —सी a monk

सपत्नीक (*a*) along with wife

सपना (*nm*) a dream

सपरिवार (*a & adv*) with family

सपरेटा (*a & nm*) separated (milk)

सपाट (*a*) smooth, even; flat

सपूत (*nm*) a dutiful son, the son who performs his filial duty

सप्तद्वीप (*nm*) the seven continents of the world

सप्ता/ह (*nm*) a week; —हांत week-end

सफर (*nm*) journey, travel; —नामा a travelogue

सफल (*a*) effective; successful; fruitful; —ता success; achievement; —होना to succeed

सफा (*a & nm*) clean, a page; —चट perfectly clean

सफाई (*nf*) purity; cleanliness; defence; clarification

सफाया (*nm*) a clean sweep, end; ruination

सफीर (*nm*) an envoy, ambassador

सफेद (*a*) blank, not written upon; white; —पोश dressed in white

सफेदा (*nm*) white lead

सफेदी (*nm*) whitewash; whiteness

सब (*a*) entire, whole, total; all —कुछ all; all in all, —डिवीज़न a sub-division

सबक (*nm*) a moral; a lesson

सबब (*nm*) a cause; reason

सबर (*nm*) patience, (see also सब्र)

सबल (*a*) forcible; strong, powerful

सबूत (*nm*) testimony, evidence, a proof

सबेरे-सबेरे (*adv*) in the early morning

सबेरा (*nm*) dawn, the time of early morning

सब्ज़ (*a*) green; good

सब्ज़ी (*nf*) herbage; vegetable; —मंडी a vegetable market

सब्बल (*nm*) a crowbar

सब्र (*nm*) contentment, patience

सभा (*nf*) association, assembly; meeting; society; —गार/गृह an assembly hall; —पति chairman; —सद member of an assembly

सभ्य (*a*) civilised; polite, genteel, decent; —ता civilization, courtesy, decency

समंजन (*nm*) co-ordination,

adjustment

सम (a) equal; level, even; similar; —कक्ष equal, similar

समकालिक (a) contemporary; contemporaneity

समकालीन (a) contemporary, living, —ता contemporaneity

समकोण (nm) a right angle; (a) having equal angles

समक्ष (adv) in front of, before

समग्र (a) entire, whole, total; all

समझ (nf) intellect, understanding; —दार intelligent; sensible; wise

समझ/ना (v) to grasp, to know, to understand, to catch, to follow; —बूझकर deliberately

समझाना (v) to persuade; to explain; —बुझाना to persuade

समझौता (nm) the settlement of a dispute; compromise, understanding; an agreement

समतल (a & nm) even, level, plain

समता (nf) similarity, likeness; equality

समतुल्य (a) equivalent; hence —ता equivalence

समदर्शी (a) impartial, dispassionate; equanimous

समधिन (nf) mother-in-law of son or daughter

समधी (nf) father-in-law of son or daughter

सम/न्वय (nm) harmony, coordination; —न्वित harmonized, co-ordinated

समय (nm) period; time; occasion; leisure

समर (nm) a battle; a war; conflict; —नीति strategy; —भूमि field of battle

समरस (a) harmonious, equanimous; —ता harmony, equanimity

समर्थ (a) competent, capable

सम/र्थक (nm) vindicator, supporter; —र्थन vindication, support; —र्थित supported

समर्पक (nm) assigner, dedicator

सम/र्पण (nm) surrender; sacrifice; dedication, assignment; —र्पित surrendered, dedicated

समवा/य (nm) Company, collection; concomitance, —यी concomitant, inseparable

समवेत (a) collective

समवेदना (nf) condolence

समशीतोष्ण (a) temperate, moderate

समशक्ति (nf) equal power

समष्टि (nf) aggregate, collectiveness

समसामयिक (a) contemporary

समस्त (a) whole, entire, complete; all

समस्या (nf) a problem

समाँ (nm) time; season, weather; occasion

समागत (a) arrived, approached

समाचार (nm) information; message; news; report

समाज (nm) community; society; —वाद socialism; —वादी a socialist; —सेवी a social worker

समादूत (a) honoured, respected

समाधान (nm) solution, answer

समाधि (nf) a tomb; intense meditation, devotion

समान (a) alike, similar; equal, —ता equality, similarity

समानांतर (a) parallel, equidistant

समाना (v) to penetrate; to fill, to fit, to enter

समानार्थक (a) of similar meaning, synonymous

समापन (nm) work of finishing, completion, conclusion

समाप्त (a) completed, ended, finished; concluded; terminated; —प्राय almost finished

समाप्ति (nf) termination; conclusion; completion

समारोह (nm) function, celebration

समालोचक (nm) a critic, reviewer

समालोचन (nm) criticism

समाविष्ट (a) entered, included; pervaded

समावेश (nm) entry, inclusion, pervasion

समास (nm) abridgment, a compound, curtailment, contraction; —शैली terse style

समाहित (a) concentrated, collected

समिति (nf) a committee; meeting; society

समीकरण (nm) the act of equalizing, equation, —करना to equate

समीक्षक (nm) a reviewer

समी/क्षा (nf) a review; search; commentary; —क्षाकार a reviewer

समीप (a) beside; near; about

समीपता (nf) proximity, congruity; vicinity

समीर (nf) wind, breeze, air

समुचित (a) right; proper, useful, fit

समुच्चय (nm) collection, assemblage, heap

समुदाय (nm) collection; group, assemblage; community

समुद्र (nm) sea, brine, ocean

समुद्री (a) marine, maritime, oceanic

समूचा (a) whole, entire; all

समूह (nm) community; collection; group

समृ/द्ध (a) wealthy, rich; prosperous, successful; flourish; —द्धि prosperity;

richness

समेटना (v) to collect; to wind up; to rally; to wrap up

सम्रेत (a & adv) mixed up, with, together with, along with

सम्मत (a) approved, agreed upon

सम्मति (nf) consent; opinion; advice

सम्मान (nm) honour, respect; prestige

सम्माननीय (a) respectable, honourable

सम्मानित (a) respected, revered, esteemed, honoured

सम्मिलित (a) mixed; united; included; —करना to intermix; to interblend; to federate

सम्मुख (a) in front of, before; facing; opposite

सम्मेलन (nm) meeting; conference; assembly

सम्मो/ह (nm) fascination; hypnosis; —हन fascinating, hypnotising

सम्यक् (adv & a) wholly; duly, thoroughly

सम्राझी (nf) an empress

सम्राट् (nm) an emperor

सयाना (a) clever; grown up

सरंजाम (nm) arrangements; preparations; accomplishment

सरकना (v) to glide; to slip; to creep; to slide

सरकस (nm) circus

सरकार (nf) government, administrator

सरकारी (a) governmental; official; administrative

सरपट (a & adv) apace; galloping

सरमा/या (nm) capital; —येबार a capitalist; —येबारी capitalism

सरल (a) simple easy; direct; straight; light; —ता simplicity; easiness

सरस (a) sweet; juicy; tasteful, delicious; relishable

सरसना (v) to prosper, to flourish; to be in full bloom

सरसरी (a) hurried, cursory

सरसों (nf) mustard

सरस्वती (nf) name of a river; speech; the goddess of learning

सरह/द (nf) border, boundary; frontier; —बी pertaining to boundary

सरा/फ (nm) a dealer in gold and silver jewellery; —फा gold and silver exchange market

सराफी (nf) banking, money changing

सराबोर (a) quite wet, drenched with water; soaked

सरासर (adv) entirely, altogether; sheer

सराह/ना (v) to laud, to applaud, to praise, to commend.

(nf) praise, applause, appreciation; —नीय praise-worthy

सरिता (nf) stream, a river

सरीखा (a) resembling, like

सरोवर (nm) a large pond, pool; a lake

सर्दी (nf) cold weather, winter; coldness; catarrh

सर्प (nm) snake, serpent

सर्पिणी (nf) a female snake

सर्व (a) whole, complete, entire; all; —गत eternal —नाश complete ruin; —प्रिय dear to all; —व्यापक omnipresent; universal; —व्यापी omnipresent; universal; —शक्तिमान omnipotent; —श्रेष्ठ the best, —साधारण the common man

सर्वत्र (ind) always, every-where; in very case

सर्वथा (ind) thoroughly, entirely

सर्वदा (ind) at all times, always

सर्वस्व (nm) entire property, everything

सर्वहारा (nm) the proletariat

सर्वात्मा (nm) the supreme spirit; the god Brahma

सर्वाधिकार (nm) full power; general control

सर्वेक्ष/ण (nm) survey; —क surveyor

सर्वेसर्वा (a) all powerful, all-in-all

सर्वोत्तम (a) paramount, foremost, excellent, the best

सर्वोदय (nm) uplift of all

सर्वोपरि (a) above all, on the whole, supreme, ahead of all

सर्वोच्च (a) highest, best, supreme; —ता supremacy

सलज्ज (a) modest; shy, bashful

सलहज (nf) wife's brother's wife

सलाई (nf) thin wire; needle; stick, a knitting needle

सलाख (nf) a rod

सलाम (nm) good bye, salutation; adieu

सलामी (nf) salute, salutation

सलाह (nf) counsel, advice; opinion, reconciliation

सलाहकार (nm) counsellor; an adviser

सलीका (nm) manners; etiquette

सलीब (nm) cross

सलूक (nm) conduct, behaviour, favour

सलोना (a) winsome, charming; saltish; —पन winsomeness, charm; saltishness

सवर्ण (a) homogeneous, of the same caste or colour

सवार (nm) horseman; rider

सवारी (nf) riding, carriage, vehicle; passenger

सवाल (nm) a question; an exercise; demand; —जवाब question and answer

सविनय (a) courteous, modest, polite, civil

सवेरा (nm) dawn, morning, daybreak

सशंक (a) sceptic, suspicious

सशक्त (a) strong, forceful, powerful

सशस्त्र (a) equipped with arms, armed

ससुर (nm) father-in-law

ससुराल (nf) father-in-law's house

सस्ता (a) of little value, cheap; trivial; trash

सस्ती (a) cheap

सस्य (nm) crop; —क्रांति green revolution

सह (ind) together, along with, with; —कारिता co-operation, —कारी co-operative

सहज (a) easy, simple, natural

सहधर्म (nm) congeniality

सहधर्मी (a) congenial

सहन (nm) tolerance, forbearance; —शक्ति forbearing; endurance; tolerance, —शील tolrant, enduring, forbearing

सहपाठी (nm) a fellow student

सहभोज (nm) taking food together

सहम (nm) dread, fear, terror, hesitation

सहम/त (a) of one mind, agreed; —ति agreement, consent

सहयोग (nm) help, co-operation, assistance; —करना to co-operate with others

सहयोगी (nm) a helper, an assistant; a co-operator, one who works with others

सहल (a) simple, easy

सहलाना (v) to rub-to tickle; to rub gently

सहसा (ind) all of a sudden, suddenly, unexpectedly

सहानुभूति (nf) sympathy, fellow-feeling, —शील sympathetic

सहायक (nm) a helpmate, an assistant, a supporter

सहायता (nf) assistance; help; aid; relief; —करना to contribute; —देना to assist, to support

सहार (nm) endurance, tolerance —ना to endure, to tolerate

सहारा (nm) backing; support, help

सहित (ind) together with, along with, with

सहिष्णु (a) enduring, patient; tolerant; —ता endurance tolerance, forbearance

सही (a) right; accurate; correct; true; —सलामत safe and sound, hale and hearty; faultless

सहूलियत (nf) facility; convenience

सहृदय (a) kind, gentle, humane; considerate

सहेजना (v) to keep with care; to

entrust

सहेली (nm) a female companion

सहोदर (nm) a real brother

सह्य (a) endurable, tolerable

सांकेतिक (a) allusive; token; nominal

साँझ (nf) dusk, evening

साँझा (nm) partnership, share in business

साँड़ (nm) a bull

साँड़नी (nf) a she-camel used for riding

सांत्वना (nf) pacification, solace, consolation

साँप (nm) a serpent, a snake

सांप्रदायिक (a) communal; —ता communalism

साँवला (a) blue-black, dark complexioned

साँस (nf) breath; sigh; asthma

साँसत (nf) affliction, trouble, distress

सांसारिक (a) earthly, worldly, mundane

साकार (a) concrete, formal

साक्षर (a) literate; —ता literacy

साक्षात् (adv) within sight of, before, visibly; —कार an interview

साक्षी (nm) an eye-witness, evidence, deponent

साक्ष्य (nm) testimony, evidence

साख (nf) credit; reputation; trust; —पत्र credit-note

साग (nm) greens; vegetable; —पात vegetables and herbs;

—सब्ज़ी vegetables

सागर (nm) sea, the ocean

साज़ (nm) musical instruments

साजन (nm) lover, husband, lord

साज़िश (nf) plot, conspiracy

सा/झा (nm) partnership; share; —झेदार a partner, shareholder; —झेदारी partnership

साड़ी (nf) a sari

साढ़ू (nm) the husband of wife's sister

साढ़े (a) plus half

सातत्य (nm) continuity

सात्त्विक (a) righteous, virtuous; —ता righteousness

साथ (adv) together, with, along with, by, (nm) association, company, support

साथी (nm) an associate, friend; a fellow, a companion

सादगी (nf) simplicity, plainness

सादर (adv) with regards, respectfully

सादा (a) plain, simple; artless; —पन simplicity, plainness; artlessness

साधन (nm) means; medium, device; equipment

साधना (nf) practice; devotion; spiritual endeavour; (v) to aim; to practise

साधारण (a) simple; ordinary; common; usual

साधु (nm) saintly person; a saint; hermit; (a) noble, good, virtuous

साधुवाद (nm) applause

साध्य (nm) the end; —ता feasibility

साध्वी (a) chaste woman, virtuous wife

सानंद (a & adv) happy with pleasure, happily

सान (nf) whetting; whetstone

सानी (nf) food for cattle consisting of chaff and oilcake mixed together with water

सान्निध्य (nm) nearness, proximity

सापराध (a) guilty, faulty; offending; criminal

सापेक्ष (a) conditional, qualified; relative; —ता relativity

साप्ताहिक (nm) a weekly journal; (a) weekly

साफ (a) pure; clean; frank; —करना to purify, to cleanse, to kill; —कहना to speak plainly; —सुथरा prim, trim

साफल्य (nm) success; fruitfulness

साबित (a) complete, entire, unbroken; proved; steady

साबुत (a) complete, entire

साबुन (nm) a soap

साबूदाना (nm) sago

साभार (adv) gratefully

सामंजस्य (nm) harmony

सामंत (nm) a warrior, landlord; —वाद feudalism

सामंती (a) feudal

साम (nm) Sam (Veda)—one of the four Vedas; conciliation

सामग्री (nf) material; matter; stuff, things; —जुटाना to provide; —भंडार में रखना to put in store

सामना (nm) meeting; encounter; opposition, confrontation —करना to face; to confront, to oppose

सामने (ind) before, face to face; —का frontal, opposite; —से from before one's face

सामयिक (a) timely, temporal, provisional; modern; upto date; —पत्र a newspaper

सामरिक (a) pertaining to war; strategic; military

सामर्थ्य (nf) capacity; competence; strength

सामवेद (nm) the third Veda

सामवेदीय (adj) pertaining to Samaveda; (nm) one who has studied this Veda

सामाजिक (a) pertaining to an assembly, social; —जीवन social life; —स्थिति status

सामाजिकता (nf) sociability

सामान (nm) luggage, goods; stock, stuff, tools; —घर luggage-office

सामान्य (a) ordinary, general; common; normal; usual; —प्रकृति का of the common nature —बातचीत table talk; —बुद्धि mother wit; —भोजन simple diet; —मूल्य से अधिक above par; —मूल्य से कम below par; —रूप से usually —वार्ता common talk; —व्यक्ति common man; —वर्णन an outline

सामान्यत: (ind) usually, generally; normally; ordinarily, on an average

सामिष (nm) non-vegetarian

सामीप्य (nm) nearness; proximity

सामुवायिक (a) pertaining to an assembly; collective

सामूहिक (a) collective

साम्य (nm) similarity, equality; resemblance, identity

साम्राज्य (nm) reign, sovereignty, empire; —वाद the theory of imperialism

सायं (a) pertaining to the evening; (nm) the evening; —काल the eve, the evening, dusk

सा/या (nm) shelter, shade; influence, —येवार shady

सारंग (nm) a hawk; a peacock; a deer; a snake, a sword; —पाणि an epithet of Vishnu

सारंगी (nf) a lute, a typical stringed Indian musical instrument

सार (nm) gist, substance; essence; —गर्भित full of pith or marrow; —तत्त्व extract, substance; —भूत essential; substantial; —वान significant, useful, substantial, meaningful

सारणी (nf) schedule; a table

सारथि, सारथी (nm) a charioteer

सारस (nm) a crane, species of heron

सारना (v) to complete, to finish, to mend

सारनाथ (nm) a place near Banaras where lord Buddha first preached his new religion

सारस्वत (nm) sub-sect of Brahmans originally inhabiting in the punjab

सारांश (nm) gist, abstract, summary, purport, substance

सारा (a) all; whole, entire

सारिका (nf) an Indian (मैना) bird

सारूप्य (nm) identity; likeness, similarity, uniformity

सार्थक (a) meaningful; effective, useful; —ता meaningfulness

सार्ध (a) one and a half

सार्वकालिक (a) pertaining to all times, everlasting, eternal; universal

सार्वजनिक (a) public, relating to people in general

सार्वत्रिक (a) universal

सार्वदेशिक (a) pertaining to all countries, universal

सार्व/भौम, भौमिक (a) universal

सार्वलौकिक (a) cosmopolitan, universal

साल (nm) pain; year; the sal tree

सालगिरह (nf) birthday

सालना (v) to tease, to torment, to pierce

सालस (nm) an arbitrator or umpire

सालसी (nf) arbitratorship, arbitration

साला (nm) wife's brother, brother-in law; a term of abuse (directed to man)

सालाना (a) annual, yearly

सालिम (a) whole, complete, entire

साली (nf) wife's sister, sister-in-law; a term of abuse (directed to women)

सालू (nm) a kind of red sari

सावधान (a) aware, alert; attentive, careful; (ind) attention

सावन (nm) the fifth month of the Hindu year

सावनी (a) pertaining to the month of sawan or shravan

साष्टांग (a) in conjunction with eight limbs; —प्रणाम prostration before a person on the ground as a mark of high esteem

सास (nf) mother-in-law, mother of (one's) wife or husband

साहचर्य (nm) company, association

साहब (nm) lord, the master, gentleman, —जादा son of a gentleman —जादी daughter of a gentleman

साहबी (nf) sway, eminence, grandeur, lordliness

साह/स (nm) rashness, boldness; courage, —सिक/—सी courageous, daring; adventurous, enterprising; —सहीन courageless; coward

साहि/त्य (nm) literature, —त्यकार writer, a litterateur; —त्यिक literary —त्यिकता literariness

साहिब (nm) see साहब

साहूकार (nm) a capitalist, money-lender; a richman;

साहू/कारा, कारी banking, money lending business

साहेब (nm) see साहब

साहेबा (nf) a mistress; a lady

सिंकना (v) to roast on open fire

सिंगार (nm) ornamentation; make up

सिंगी (nm) a kind of trumpet; a kind of pipe with which village surgeons suck up bad blood from the body

सिंघाड़ा (nm) water chestnut, a waternut

सिंचन (nm) irrigation; sprinkling of water

सिंचना (v) to sprinkle water on an object; to irrigate a field

सिंचाई (nf) irrigation

सिंचाना (v) to cause to be irrigated

सिंचित (a) drenched; irrigated

सिंदूर (nm) vermilion red lead; minium; —रंग scarlet; —वृक्ष oak

सिंदू/रिया, री (a) deep red, scarlet; very red in colour

सिंध (nm) the province of Sindh. (nf) the Sindh river which flows in the Punjab

सिंधी (a) belonging or pertaining to Sindh

सिंधु (nm) a river; sea, ocean; the province of Sindh; —जा the goddess of wealth

सिंह (nm) a lion; leo, the fifth sign of the zodiac; —द्वार the main gate of a palace —नाद the roaring of a lion, war cry

सिंहल द्वीप (nm) name of an island in the south of India

सिंहवाहिनी (nf) an epithet of the goddess Durga

सिंहावलोकन (nm) a retrospect

सिंहासन (nm) a throne

सिंहिनी (nf) a lioness

सिकंदर (nm) Alexander

सिकता (nf) sand, sandy soil

सिकुड़न (nf) wrinkle; shrinkage, shrivel

सिकु/ड़ना (v) to shrink; to wrinkle; —ड़ा हुआ shrunk; —ड़ने योग्य shrinkable

सिकोड़ना (v) to contract, to draw, to compress, to shrivel

सिक्का (nm) a medal; a coin, coinage

सिक्ख, सिख (nm) a sikh, a follower of Guru Nanak

सिक्त (a) wet, drenched; irrigated; watered

सिखलाना, सिखाना (v) to teach; to school; to train; to instruct; to show, to guide; to educate

सिगरा, सिगरी (a) entire, full, complete; all

सिजदा (nm) salutation, prostration

सिटपिटाना (v) to hesitate, to be stupefied, to be in a flux

सिटटी (nf) bragging

सिड़ (nf) insanity, madness, eccentricity, whim

सिड़ी (a) mad, insane, eccentric

सित (a) white; clear, shining, bright; —ता whiteness, brightness

सितम (nm) violence; injustice, tyranny, oppression; —गर tyrannical, unjust, troublesome

सितार (nm) a kind of guitar

सितारा (nm) planet, star, fate

सिद्ध (a) accomplished; proved, perfect; (nm) a saint, one who has acquired supernatural powers

सिद्धांत (*nm*) theory, principle, rule, doctrine

सिद्धांती (*a & nm*) dogmatic, theoretician; a demonstrator

सिद्धार्थ (*a*) whose desires are attained; (*nm*) Gautama Buddha

सिद्धि (*nf*) success, proof; fulfilment, acquisition

सिद्धेश्वर (*nm*) a great saint, an epithet of Shiva

सिधाना (*v*) to help acquire practice; to tame

सिधारना (*v*) to depart; to expire, to die

सिनकना (*v*) to expel mucus from the nose; to snot

सिपहसालार (*nm*) the commander of an army

सिपाही (*nm*) sepoy, a constable, a policeman; a soldier

सिपुर्द (*a*) entrusted

सिप्पा (*nm*) approach; influence; means; —जमाना to make an approach, to fulfil an aim

सिफ़त (*nf*) quality, nature; characteristic

सिफर (*nm*) zero; a cipher; blank

सिफा/रिश (*nf*) recommendation; —रिशी recommendatory

सिमटना (*v*) to contract; to shrink; to shrivel; to be complete

सिमेटना (*v*) to gather; (*adv*) together

सियन (*nf*) a stitch, seam

सियापा (*nm*) weeping over a death, mourning

सियार (*nm*) a jackal; cunning fellow

सियाह, स्याह (*a*) black

सिया/सत (*nf*) politics; —सतवां (*nm*) a politician

सिर (*nm*) head; top, highest part or point; —के बल headlong; —खपाई (too much of) mental exertion; —ताज crown; —नामा form of address

सिरकटा (*nm & a*) with head cut off; one who does evil to others

सिरका (*nm*) vinegar

सिरजन (*nm*) creation; —हार the creator

सिरजना (*v*) to produce, to create

सिरमौर (*nm*) a coronet

सिरा (*nm*) head; extremity; end, beginning

सिर्फ़ (*a*) only, merely, alone, mere, unmixed

सिलना (*v*) to sew, to stitch

सिलवाना (*v*) to cause to be sewn or stitched by some body

सिलसि/ला (*nm*) series; a chain; line; system; —लेवार serial, systematic

सिलाई (*nf*) stitching charges,

the act or process of sewing

सिलाना (v) same as सिलवाना

सिल्ली (nf) a whetstone

सिवा (ind) except, but, without

सिवाय (ind) without, but, save

सिसकना (v) to sob

सिसका/रना (v) to hiss, to produce a hissing sound; —री hissing sound

सिसकी (nf) sobbing, a sob

सिहरन (nf) shiver, thrill

सिहरना (v) to shiver; to be thrilled, to be afraid

सींक (nf) wicker, spit

सींकचा (nm) window-bars

सींग (nm) a horn

सींचना (v) to drench, to wet; to irrigate

सी (ind) similar; equal; hissing sound

सीकर (nm) a drop of water, sweat

सीख (nf) counsel, 'teaching, advice; instruction; moral

सीखना (v) to acquire knowledge; to learn

सीझना (v) to be roasted or fried; to boil

सीटी (nf) a pipe, whistle; a whistling sound

सीठा (a) tasteless, insipid

सीठी (nf) dregs, a worthless object

सीढ़ी (nf) a ladder

सीता (nf) a furrow made by a plough; the daughter of Janaka who was married to Ram

सीताफल (nm) the custard-apple

सीध (nf) straightness; alignment

सीधा (a & adv) simple, straight, direct, gentle, good, upright, plain, calm and quiet

सीधी (a & adv) feminine form of सीधा; —राह a straight path

सीधे (adv) without a halt; straight

सीना (v) to stitch, to sew, to seam; (nm) the chest —पिरोना stitching etc

सीप (nf) mother pearl

सीमंत (nm) the parting of hairs on the head

सीमा (nf) a landmark; extremity; limit; —चिह्न landmark, terminus; —प्रांत verge; —रहित limitless, —रेखा border line

सीमित (a) limited, restricted, bounded

सीरा (nm) molasses

सील (nf) damp/dampness; a seal

सीलन (nf) moisture, dampness

सीवन (nm) sewing, stitching, a seam, a joint

सीसमहल (शीश महल) (nm) a house which is fitted with mirrors

सीसा (nm) lead

सुँघनी (*nf*) a snuff

सुँघाना (*v*) to cause to smell

सुंदर (*a*) pretty; lovely; beautiful; fancy; —ता beauty; prettiness

सु (*pref*) a prefix showing the meanings of good, excellent beautiful, easy, well etc. (just as in सुप्रभात, सुभाष, सुकुमारी, सुगम etc.)

सुअर (*nm*) a pig, a boar, a swine

सुकर (*a*) easy, practicable

सुकर्म (*nm*) a pious action, a good deed

सुकुमा/र (*a*) delicate, tender, gentle, soft; —री of tender body

सुकून (*nm*) comfort; peace, consolation

सुकृत (*a*) pious, virtous, auspicious

सुकोमल (*a*) soft, very delicate;

सुख (*nm*) pleasure; comfort; happiness; contentment; —चैन happiness and comfort; —द pleasant, happy, pleasurable; —दा a female who affords pleasure; —दायक affording pleasure; —पूर्वक comfortably, happily; —शांति happiness and peace; —से at ease, happily —सौभाग्य pleasure and plenty

सुखी (*a*) well; glad; pleasant; happy; contented

सुख्यात (*a*) famous, reputed

सुगंध (*nf*) perfume, scent, smell

सुगंधि (*nf*) fragrance, perfume

सुगंधित (*a*) fragrant, odourous, sweetscented

सुगठित (*a*) wellbuilt, muscular; well-organised

सुगति (*nm*) happy condition, salvation

सुगम (*a*) plain, practicable, easy, accessible, simple

सुगम्य (*a*) easily accessible, attainable

सुघड़ (*a*) beautiful, elegant, clever, competent, dextrous; —ता elegance, beauty; —पन competency, cleverness, ability

सुघड़ाई (*nf*) shapeliness, elegance; dexterousness

सुचारु (*a*) very beautiful, pretty, charming

सुचेत (*a*) careful, attentive, clever, alert

सुजन (*nm*) a respectable person, a gentleman

सुजान (*a*) intelligent, wise, learned

सुझाना (*v*) to propose, to suggest, to show

सुझाव (*nm*) proposal, suggestion

सुड़कना (*v*) to sniff up; to drink noisily

सुडौल (*a*) shapely, well-shaped, well-built

—पन symmetry

सुत (nm) a son

सुतली (nf) thin rope, twine

सुता (nf) a daughter

सुथरा (a) pure, clean; neat; tidy —पन neatness and tidiness; cleanliness; refinement

सुदर्शन (a) elegant, beautiful, attractive

सुदी (nf) the bright half of a lunar month

सुदूर (a) at a long distance, far

सुदृढ़ (a) very firm, very strong, very powerful

सुदेश (nm) a beautiful country; (a) elegant, beautiful

सुध (nf) attention; conscious-ness, senses, care; memory; —बुध memory; conscious-ness, senses

सुधरना (v) to be corrected; to be mended; to be reformed

सुधर्मी (a) pious, virtuous

सुधांशु (nm) the moon

सुधा (nf) nectar, ambrosia water

सुधाकर (nm) the moon

सुधार (nm) reform; correction; repair; improvement, amendment; —कa reformer

सुधारना (v) to refine; to amend; to adjust; to improve; to correct, to reform, to revise

सुधि (nf) see सुध

सुधी (a) wise, learned, pious; (nm) a learned man

सुनना (v) to listen, to hear; to pay heed

सुनवाई (nf) listening, hearing, hearing of a law-suit

सुनसान (a) lonely; desolate; barren

सुनह/रा, —ला (a) golden; —रापन goldenness

सुनाना (v) to relate, to cause to hear; to recite; to read out

सुनाम (nm) fame, reputation, good name

सुना/र (nm) a goldsmith; —रिन a goldsmith's wife

सुनारी (nf) the profession of a goldsmith

सुनीति (nf) name of Dhruva's mother; good policy, morality

सुन्न (a) benumbed; senseless, lifeless

सुपच (a) easily digestible

सुपथ्य (a) salubrious; (nm) salubrious diet

सुपरिचित (a) intimate

सुपात्र (nm) a worthy person, a respectable man

सुपारी (nf) the betel nut

सुपुर्द (a) entrusted, committed, —गी trust; charge, care

सुप्त (a) asleep, shut up

सुप्रतिष्ठित (a) very respectable, far renowned, highly distinguished

सुप्रसिद्ध (a) very famous reputed, renowned

सुफल (nm) good result

सुबह (nf) dawn, early morning

सुबास (nf) fragrance, sweet smell (see also सुवास)

सुबुद्धि (nf) wisdom, good sense; (a) intelligent, wise

सुबूत (nm) proof, authenticity

सुबोध (a) intelligent, intelligible

सुभ/ग (a) beautiful, fortunate, beloved, —गा beautiful woman, having her husband alive

सुभट (nm) a great warrior

सुभद्रा (nf) name of lord Krishna's sister married to Arjuna; an epithet of goddess Durga

सुभाषित (a) well-said, well-spoken, eloquent

सुभीता (nm) opportunity, convenience, leisure

सुमति (nf) good understanding

सुमन (nm) a flower; (a) beautiful, benevolent, kind

सुमुखी (a & nf) pretty faced, beautiful

सुयोग (nm) a happy chance, good opportunity

सुयोग्य (a) able, worthy

सुरंग (nf) mine, a tunnel

सुर (nm) a god; a note in music; tone, —मिलाना to tune

सुर/क्षण (nm) क्षा (nf) protection, security —क्षित protected, safe; reserved

सुरख्राब (nm) an ostrich

सुरख्री (nf) brick-dust which is used in masonry; redness; lipstick

सुरभि (nf) aroma, fragrance, scent, purfume; —त fragrant, aromatic, scented

सुरमा (nm) antimony ground into fine powder, collyrium

सुरा (nf) liquor, wine

सुराख्र (nm) an aperture, hole

सुराग (nm) trace, clue

सुराही (nf) longnecked earthen water-pot, pitcher

सुरीला (nm) melodious, sweet; lyric, —पन symphony, sweetness

सुरुख्र, सुर्ख़ (a) red; happy, compassionate

सुरुचि (nf) good taste, refined taste

सुरूपा (a) beautiful (woman)

सुर्ख़ी (nf) a headline, redness, lipstick

सुर्ता (a) clever, wise, intelligent

सुल/क्षण (a) auspicious; fortunate, lucky, —क्षणा beautiful female, attractive

सुलगना (v) to burn, to be kindled; to be sorry

सुलगाना (v) to light, to kindle fire, to inflame

सुलझना (v) to be solved, to be unravelled

सुलझाना (v) to disentangle a thing, to unravel

सुलझाव (nm) disentanglement, solution

सुलटा (a) straight, unopposed

सुलतान (nm) an emperor, king

सुलभ (a) accessible; handy, —ता feasibility

सुलह (nf) treaty, agreement, truce; —नामा a deed of compromise

सुलाना (v) to cause to sleep, to put to sleep, to lull

सुलूक (nm) treatment, behaviour

सुलेख (nm) calligraphy

सुलेमान (nm) Solomon, the name of a mountain situated in the west of Punjab

सुवर्ण (nm) good colour; higher caste; gold

सुवा/स (nm) sweet smell, fragrance, —सित fragrant

सुविधा (nf) comfort, facility, convenience, benefit, gain

सुव्यव/स्था (nf) orderliness, good organisation; —स्थित well-organized

सुशिक्षित (a) well-educated

सुशील (a) good, gentle, modest, polite

सुशोभित (a) graceful, adorned

सुश्री (a) very beautiful, very rich (used for ladies)

सुषमा (nf) exceptional prettiness, beauty, charm, excellent beauty

सुषु/प्त (a) fast or sound asleep, in deep slumber —प्ति deep sleep

सुष्ठु (a) appropriate, elegant

सुसंगति (nf) good society, good company

सुसंस्कृत (a) refined, cultured

सुसज्जित (a) well-equipped, well-adorned

सुसमय (nm) season of plenty, good times

सुसमाचार (nm) the gospel, good news

सुसर, सुसरा (nm) (see ससुर) a term of abuse (directed to man)

सुसाध्य (a) easily accomplished

सुस्त (a) indolent; languid; lazy; spiritless

सुस्ताना (v) to rest, to relax

सुस्ती (nf) laziness; depression; idleness; indolence

सुस्थिर (a) stable, resolute, firm

सुस्पष्ट (a) very intelligible, distinct or clear

सुस्वादु (a) delicious, flavoury

सुहबत (nf) association, company

सुहाग (nm) good fortune; husband

सुहागा (nm) borax

सुहागिन (nf) a female whose husband is alive

सुहाना (v) to look charming, to be pleasing

सुहावना (a) charming, pleasing

सुहृत, सुहृद् (nm) a friend (a) friendly, loving

सूंघना (v) to scent; to smell; to sniff

सूंघनी (nf) a snuff

सूंड (nf) the trunk of an

elephant

सुअर (*nm*) pig, boar, swine, a word of abuse

सुआ (*nm*) a parrot; big needle

सुई (*nf*) the hand of a watch, a needle

सुक्ति (*nf*) an epigram, maxim, good saying

सूक्ष्म (*a*) thin; subtle, minute; fine; —ता subtlety, fineness, thinness; —दर्शक यंत्र a microscope; —दर्शी nice-sharp-sighted

सुखना (*v*) to parch, to dry, to wither, to fall away

सूचक (*a*) a pointer, an informant

सूचना (*nf*) notice; information; intimation, —पत्र a notification, circular; —देने वाला an informer, a reporter

सूचिका (*nf*) a needle; the trunk of an elephant

सूचित (*a*) intimated; informed; indicated, —करना to refer, to attribute

सूची (*nf*) list; —पत्र a catalogue; —बनाना to list

सूजन (*nf*) a swelling, —संबंधी inflammatory, फेफड़े की— bronchitis

सूजना (*v*) to swell

सुज़ाक (*nm*) the veneral disease called gonorrhoea

सूजी (*nf*) coarse ground flour

सूझ (*nf*) vision, insight, perception; —बूझ imagina-

tion, intelligence

सूझना (*v*) to appear, to be visible; to be understood; to be intelligible

सूत (*nm*) thread, yarn, —कातना to spin yarn

सूतिका गृह (*nm*) a lying-in-chamber

सूत्र (*nm*) a thread, fibre, formula —मय thready; —पात beginning

सूथनी (*nf*) trousers

सूद (*nm*) interest; —खोर usurer; —खोरी usury; —दर सूद compound interest

सूना (*a*) lonely; empty; —पन loneliness; emptiness

सूप (*nm*) a cook; broth; a winnowing basket

सूबा (*nm*) a province

सूबेदार (*nm*) the governor of an Indian province

सूम (*a*) miser; niggardly; (*nm*) a miser; the hoof of a horse

सूर (*a*) blind; brave; (*nm*) the sun; a wise man; blind man

सूरज (*nm*) the Sun; —मुखी the sunflower, *albino*

सूरत (*nf*) looks, face; appearance; means; method; figure

सूरमा (*nm*) a hero, warrior

सूराख़ (*nm*) a hole; a puncture; a passage

सूर्य (*nm*) the Sun; —कांत a magnifying glass; —ग्रहण

solar eclipse; —घड़ी a sun dial; —पूजा heliolatry; —मणि jasper; —मुखी a sunflower

संक्रांति (nf) the enterning of the Sun from one sign of zodiac to the other

सूर्यास्त (nm) the time of sunset, the evening

सूर्योदय (nm) the time of sunrise, the morning

सूली (nf) gibbet, gallows

सृजन (nm) the work of creation, creation; —शील creative

सृष्टि (nf) creation; the World; construction; —कर्ता the creator

सेंकना (v) to roast; to foment; to bake

सेंध (nf) a hole made in a wall by a thief; burglary

सेंधना (v) to make a hole in the wall of a house as a burglar

सेंवई (nf) vermicelli

सेज (nf) richly decorated bed; sofa; a bed

सेठ (nm) a great merchant; a wealthy person; lender

सेतु (nm) a bridge; causeway

सेना (v) to hatch an egg

सेना (nf) an army; a troop; a regiment; military, —ध्यक्ष, the commander of an army, —नायक a brigadier —नायक (समुद्री) an admiral

सेब (nm) an apple; खट्टा—

crab

सेम (nf) kidney -bean, bean

सेमल (nm) the silk -cotton tree

सेव (nm) a sweet meat prepared from the meal of gram

सेवक (nm) a servant; attendant; a worshipper; —गण suite

सेवकाई (nf) service; attendance

सेवन (nm) use; serving; taking (as medicine etc.)

सेवा (nf) service; attendance; homage; —टहल service, servitude; —धर्म servitude; —वृत्ति servitude

सेविका (nf) a female servant

सेवित (a) used, enjoyed; served; employed

सेवी (a) serving, enjoying

सेव्य (a) deserving to be served; worthy of being protected —सेवक the master and the servant

सेहत (nf) good health; relief from illness; comfort; happiness

सैंधव (nm) rock salt; a resident of Sindh; (a) pertaining to Sindh

सैकड़ा (nm) a group of hundred; one hundred

सैकड़ों (a) several hundred; numerous

सैद्धांतिक (a) theoretical; (nm) a learned man

सैनिक (nm) a soldier; troop; sentry; —क्रांति military

revolution — शासन martial law

सैन्य (a) an army; military; — दल platoon; — समूह lavy of warriors

सैयाँ (nm) lord; master; husband; lover

सैर (nf) rample; a walk for the sake of amusement; stroll

सैलानी (nm) wanderer; tourist; (a) roaming at pleasure

सैला/ब (nm) flood. — बी wet, drenched, damp

सैलून (nm) a saloon; barber's shop

सोंटा (nm) a truncheon, mace, baton

सोंठ (nf) dry ginger

सोंधा (a) fragrant, odorous; sweet-smelling

सो (adv) thus, therefore; (pron) that, he

सोखना (v) to absorb, to merge, to dry up

सोख्ता (nm) blotting paper

सोच (nm) thought; anxiety; reflection; repentence; regret; — विचार consideration, pondering, reflection

सोचना (v) to consider; to suppose, to think, to ponder, to imagine, to conceive, to reflect

सोजिश (nf) swelling; inflammation

सोटा (nm) same as सोंटा

सोता (nm) a spring, a fountain,

brook; current; source, (see स्रोत)

सोधना (v) to amend, to correct; to purify, to refine; to investigate

सोधाना (v) to cause to be amended, purified or refined

सोनहला (a) see सुनहला or सुनहरा

सोना (nm) gold; an excellent thing; (v) to lie, to sleep; — चढ़ाना to gild; — चाँदी gold and silver; wealth

सोनार (nm) goldsmith

सोपान (nm) a staircase, stair

सोफ़ा (nm) a sofa; — सेट a sofa set

सोफ़ियाना (a) attractive, gaudy; fashionable; sophisticated

सोम (nm) the moon; Yama; nectar; — पान the drinking of the Soma juice — पायी one who drinks Soma juice — रस the juice of the Soma plant; — वार Monday

सोयाबीन (nm) soyabean

सोहन हलवा (nm) a kind of nice sweetmeat

सोहना (v) to look attractive or beautiful, to be pleasing, to shine; to be glorious

सोहनी (nf) a broom; (a) beautiful

सोहबत (nf) intercourse, coition, copulation; company, association

सोहम् (phr) (Sanskrit) I am

the same i.e. I am none
other but the Brahma

सोहागिन (*nf*) see सुहागिन

सोहागा (*nm*) borax

सोहना, सोहावना (*v*) to be
agreeable or pleasant

सौंदर्य (*nm*) beauty, charm,
attractiveness, prettiness

सौंधा (*a*) odorous, pleasing,
excellent

सौंपना (*v*) to give in charge, to
hand over, to give; to
surrender, to assign

सौंफ (*nf*) anise; fennel;
aniseed

सौंह (*nf*) an oath, swearing

सौ (*nm*) the number hundred,
century; (*a*) hundred;
—गुना hundred times —वाँ
hundredth —वर्ष century

सौकुमार्य (*nm*) youth; delicacy,
tenderness

सौख्य (*nm*) happiness, pleasure;
comfort, relief; ease,
joy, delight; good health

सौगंध (*nf*) an oath, swearing;
—खाना to take a vow, to
swear; —टूटना breaking of a
vow

सौगात (*nf*) a present, gift; a
present for a friend etc;
brought from a distant place

सौगाती (*a*) given to someone as
a gift or present

सौजन्य (*nm*) goodness;
courtesy; generosity;
compassion, kindness,
gentility

सौ/त (*nf*) a rival wife, co-wife;
—तिया डाह malice as
between co-wives

सौते/ला (*a*) begotten from a
step-mother

सौतेला भाई a step-brother

सौतेली बहन a step-sister; —ली
माता a step-mother

सौदा (*nm*) a bargain; negotiation; goods; commodity;
—गर a merchant, trader

सौदाई (*nm & a*) mad; insane

सौदामिनी (*nf*) lightning

सौभाग्य (*nm*) fortune, good
luck, prosperity, auspiciousness —वती fortunate in
having one's husband alive

सौम्य (*a*) gentle; amiable, mild,
lunar, auspicious

सौर (*a*) produced by the Sun;
solar; —परिवार solar system
— मास a solar month
a solar month

सौर/भ (*nm*) aroma, saffron,
fragrance —भित odorous;
fragrant

सौष्ठव (*nm*) elegance, excellence, shapeliness

सौहार्द (*nm*) friendship; amity;
attraction, love

स्ख/लन (*nm*) stumbling; a
mistake, a slip, —लित fallen,
slipped, dropped down,
mistaken

स्तंभ (*nm*) a pillar, a column;
—लेखक a columnist

स्तंभन (nm) stoppage, retention, obstruction

संभित (a) stupefied, wonder-struck; benumbed

स्तन (nm) the breast; udder; —पान sucking of breast

स्तब्ध (a) stupefied; stilled, stagnant; —ता stupefaction, firmness

स्तर (nm) level; a fold; grade; standard

स्तरीय (a) stratified; levelled

स्तव (nm) a hymn of praise spoken to a deity

स्तवक (nm) a bunch of flowers

स्तव/न (nm) praise; eulogy —नीय praise worthy

स्तुति (nf) invocation; praise, prayer, orison

स्तुत्य (nm) praiseworthy, laudable, admirable

स्तूप (nm) a Buddhistic tope

स्तोत्र (nm) a hymn of praise, eulogism

स्त्री (nf) a woman; female; wife, dame; (pron) she. —गमन sexual intercourse; —जाति fair sex; —त्व womenhood; —रोग a female disease; —सुख sexual enjoyment; —हरण kidnapping of a woman

स्त्रैण (a) effeminate; womanish

स्थ/गन (nm) adjournment; postponement; —प्रस्ताव adjournment motion; —गित adjourned, postponed, suspended

स्थल (nm) place, site; spot, region; opportunity; —डमरु-मध्य isthmus; —मार्ग roadway —सेना army

स्थली (nf) dry land, soil

स्थविर (nm) a Buddhistic monk

स्थान (nm) a place; space, room, site; post; —च्युत/ —भ्रष्ट displaced; demoted

स्थानांत/र (nm) different place, situation or position. —रण displacement; translocation; transfer —रित displaced; translocated; transferred

स्थानापन्न (a) officiating, acting; substitute

स्थानीय (a) local; colloquial; positional

स्थापक (a) founder, erector, moulder

स्थापत्य (nm) architecture; —कला architecture

स्था/पन (nm) foundation, erection; —पित founded, erected, situated; settled

स्थापना (nf) founding, establishing; propounding

स्थायित्व (nm) permanency; durability; stability

स्थायी (a) permanent; lasting; stable; stationary. —करण confirmation; stabilisation; —कृत confirmed

स्थावर (a) stationary;

immovable; —जंगम immovable and movable

स्थित (a) residing; situate; —प्रज्ञ firm in judgment

स्थिति (nf) condition; status; location; position

स्थिर (a) motionless; firm; steady; inflexible; stable —ता motionlessness; firmness, steadiness; stability

स्थूल (a) thick; fat; bulky; gross; rough. —ता thickness; fatness; bulkiness; grossness; roughness

स्नात/क (nm) a graduate; —कोत्तर postgraduate

स्नान (nm) bath, bathing —गृह bathroom, a bath

स्नानागार (nm) bathroom, a bath

स्नायविक (a) nervous, ligamentary

स्नायु (nm) nerves, ligament

स्निग्ध (a) oily, greasy, lubricant; affectionate; —ता oiliness, greasiness, lubricity; affection

स्नेह (nm) love, liking, affection; —पात्र object of love

स्नेहिल (a) of loving disposition, loving

स्नेही (a) loving, kind; (nm) a friend; a lover

स्पं/दन (nm) trembling; vibration, pulsation; —दित vibrated, pulsated

स्पर्धा (nf) rivalry; competition

स्पर्धी (a) rival; competitor

स्पर्श (nm) touch; contact

स्पष्ट (a) clear; simple, vivid; obvious; apparent; plain, —त: clearly; simply; obviously etc.;—तयावividly; apparently etc.;—ताclarity; obviousness; vividness; —वक्ता straight forward

स्पष्टीकरण (nm) clarification; explanation; ellucidation

स्पृश्य (a) touchable

स्पृहणीय (a) desirable, coveted

स्फटिक (a) crystal, quartz

स्फुट (a) miscellaneous, apparent, obvious; separate

स्फुटन (nm) becoming apparent; blossoming

स्फु/रण (nm) pulsation; spurt —रित pulsating; spurting

स्फूर्ति (nf) promptness; inspiration —दायक imparting promptness

स्फोटक (a) explosive —ता explosiveness

स्मरण (nm) recollection; memory; —शक्ति memory

स्मरणीय (a) notable; memorable

स्मारक (nm) memorial, a monument; (a) reminding

स्मारिका (nf) a souvenir

स्मित (nf) a smile; (a) smiling

स्मिति (nf) a smile

स्मृति (nf) remembrance, memory

स्यापा (nm) mourning

स्यार (nm) jackal

स्याह (a) black; dark

स्याही (nf) ink; darkness, blackness

स्रष्टा (nm) creator of the universe (i.e. Brahma)

स्राव (nm) secretion; abortion

स्रोत (nm) source, a current, stream; resource

स्व (pron) personal; self; —त्व one's due; —शासन self-rule

स्वगत (a) to oneself; —कथन/भाषण aside, soliloquy

स्वचालित (a) automatic

स्वच्छंद (a) free; independent; spontaneous; unobstructed; —ता freedom; spontaneity; —तावाद Romanticism

स्वच्छ (a) clean; clear; pure; transparent; —ता cleanliness; clarity; purity; transparency

स्वजन (nm) a kinsman, a relative ।

स्वजातीय (a) co-racial

स्वतंत्र (a) free, independent; self-willed; separate —ता freedom, independence; —लेखन free lance writing

स्वत: (adv) voluntarily, spontaneously; —सिद्ध self evident

स्वत्व (nm) ownership; monopoly; copyright

स्वदेश (nm) country, homeland motherland; —त्याग emigration; —प्रेम patriotism; —भक्ति patriotism

स्वदेशी (a) pertaining to one's own country

स्वनाम (nm) one's own name

स्वप्न (nm) a dream; —दर्शी a dreamer; —दोष emission; —मय dreamy

स्वप्निल (a) dreamy

स्वभाव (nm) nature; habit; —त: naturally; habitually

स्वयंवर (nm) self-choice of her husband by a bride

स्वयं/सेवक (nm) a (male) volunteer; —सेविका (nf) a female volunteer; —सेवा self-service

स्वयम् (pron) self (adv) personally; by oneself

स्वर (nm) voice; tone, note; a vowel; —बद्ध rhythmic —भंग hoarseness of throat; —मधुरता melody

स्वराज्य (nm) autonomy, home-rule, self-government

स्वराष्ट्र (nm) one's own country, home land

स्वरूप (nm) form, shape; appearance; nature

स्वर्ग (nm) heaven, paradise, abode of gods —वास heavenly abode i.e. death; —वासी late; —सिधारना to die

स्वर्गिक (a) divine, paradisaic,

celestial

स्वर्गी/य (a) late, dead; divine; — या (fem. form) late, dead

स्वर्ण (nm) gold; — कार goldsmith; — जयंती golden jubilee — मुद्रा a gold coin; — युग the golden age

स्वर्णाक्षर (nm) a golden letter

स्वर्णिम (a) golden, of gold

स्व/ल्प (a) very small, very little; — ल्पाहार light refreshment

स्वशासन (nm) self-government, home-rule

स्वस्थ (a) hale, healthy; sound; — चित्त sane; — चित्तता sanity — ता healthiness; health; ease

स्वाँग (nm) mimicry; sham; — बनाना to mimic

स्वागत (nm) reception, welcome; acceptation; — कक्ष reception room — समिति reception committee — समारोह a reception

स्वातंत्र्य (nm) liberty, independence; freedom — सेनानी a freedom fighter

स्वाद (nm) taste, savour; flavour; swallow

स्वादिष्ट (a) tasty, delicious, relishable

स्वाधीन (a) independent, free — ता independence, freedom

स्वाध्या/य (nm) study; regular study; — यी studious

स्वाभाविक (a) natural; inborn; — ता naturality

स्वाभिमा/न (nm) self-respect; — नी self-respecting

स्वामित्व (nm) proprietorship, ownership

स्वामिनी (nf) a female master; the mistress of a house

स्वा/मी (nm) master, owner; lover, — मिभक्त loyal, faithful — मिभक्ति loyalty, faithfulness

स्वायत्त (a) under one's control, autonomous

स्वार्थ (nm) self-interest; — परायण selfish; self-seeking; — परता selfishness — साधक a self-seeker; — हीन liberal

स्वार्थी (a) self-seeking; selfish; interested

स्वावलंबन (nm) self-reliance

स्वास्थ्य (nm) health; sound state of body; — प्रद useful to health; — संबंधी regarding to health

स्वी/करण (nm) granting; sanctioning; — कर्ता one who grants or sanctions

स्वीकार (a) granted; accepted; agreed; admitted; (nm) grant; acceptance; agreement — ना to accept; to admit; to agree; to acknowledge; to accede

स्वीकृ/त (a) accepted; approved; acknowledged;

confessed; —ति acceptance; confession; consent

स्वेच्छया (*adv*) voluntarily

स्वेच्छ (*nf*) free will; —चारिता autocracy —चारी wilful, arbitrary; —पूर्वक voluntarily

स्वेद (*nm*) prespiration, sweat

स्वैच्छिक (*a*) voluntary; arbitrary

स्वैर (*a*) free, sluggish; —चारिता self-willedness; —चारी a self-willed person

स्वैराचा/र (*nm*) self-willed conduct; —री a self-willed person

स्वैरिणी (*nf*) a wanton woman

ह

ह the thirty third letter of Devnagri alphabet

हंगामा (*nm*) tumult, uproar

हंडिया (*nf*) a small earthen pot

हंता (*nm*) a murderer, a slayer

हंस (*nm*) a swan, goose; a duck; —गामिनी a female with a graceful gait; —वाहिनी the goddess Saraswati

हंस/ना (*v*) to laugh, to smile; to joke; to ridicule; —ने योग्य amusing, laughable

हंसमुख (*a*) cheerful, jolly; having a smiling face

हंसली (*nf*) collar-bone

हंसाई (*nf*) ridicule; —कराना to cause ridicule

हंसाना (*v*) to tickle, to make to laugh

हंसिनी (*nf*) a female goose

हंसिया (*nm*) a sickle

हंसी (*nf*) laughter; joke; ridicule; —खुशी happily —खेल fun

हंसोड़ (*a*) merry; humarous, jolly

हक (*nm*) right, due; —दार a claimant; —नाहक right and wrong

हकबकाना (*v*) to be confused

हकला (*nm*) a stammerer; —हट stammering

हकलाना (*v*) to falter in speech, to stutter, to stammer

हकारत (*nf*) contempt

हकीकत (*nf*) reality, fact; —बयानी statement of truth

हकीकतन (*ind*) in fact

हकीकी (*a*) factual; real

हकीम (*nm*) a (Unani) physician

हकीमी (*nf*) the Unani system of medicine

हक्का-बक्का (*a*) confused, thunderstuck

हगना (*v*) to go to stool, to

discharge faeces

हगाना (v) to cause to evacuate

हचकोला (nm) a jolting

हज (nm) a pilgrimage to Mecca (by Muslims)

हज़म (a) digested; —करना to digest; to mis-appropriate

हज़रत (nm) an eminent person; a naughty person

हजामत (nf) shaving; hair-cutting; —करना to shave

हज़ार (a) one thousand; innumerable

हजूर (nm) same as हुजूर

हज्जाम (nm) a barber

हटक (nf) prevention, obstruction

हटकना (v) to prohibit, to forbid, to restrain

हटना (v) to step back, to withdraw; to give way; to move away

हटवाना (v) to cause to be removed

हटाना (v) to remove; to push aside; to obstruct

हट्टा-कट्टा (a) vigorous, strong, robust

हट्टी (nf) same as हाट

हठ (nm) obstinacy; disobedience; stubbornness

हठधर्मी (a) obstinate, fanatic; (nm) a bigot

हठात् (ind) all of a sudden, suddenly

हठी (a) obstinate, wilful, arrogant, headstrong, stiff-necked

हठीला (nm) same as हठी

हठीली (nf) same as हठी

हड़कंप (nm) a great agitation

हड़ंक (n) eager; longing, yearning

हड़काना (v) to estrange

हड़ताल (nf) a strike; —करना to strike

हड़ताली (nm) a striker

हड़प (a) swallowed; illegaly taken

हड़पना (v) to swallow up, to gulp, to misappropriate

हड़बड़ (nf) a confusion

हड़बड़ाना (v) to be perplexed, to be in a hurry; to cause some-one to be in a hurry

हड़बड़िया (a) hasty, rash

हड़बड़ी (nf) haste, rashness; confusion; uproar

हड्डी (nf) a bone

हतक (nf) disrespect, dishonour —करना to dishonour, to defame

हतबुद्धि (a) stupid, foolish, unintelligent

हतभागा (a) unlucky, unfortunate, ill-fated

हतभाग्य (a) unfortunate

हताश (a) hopeless

हताहत (a) slain and wounded

हतोत्साह (a) disheartened, depressed, discouraged

हत्था (nm) the handle of an instrument

हत्थी (nf) the (small) handle

of a small instrument

हत्थे (ind) in hand —आना to be under subjugation

हत्या (nf) murder, slaughter, assassination

हत्या/रा (nm) a murderer, an assassin —री (nf)

हथ contraction of हाथ used as a prefix; —कड़ sleight of hand; —कड़ी handcuff; —गोला a hand-grenade; —चक्की a hand-mill; —बुना hand-woven

हथियनी (nf) a female elephant

हथियाना (v) to seize, to occupy, to pocket

हथियार (nm) a tool; a weapon, arms

हथेली (nf) the palm, the palm of hand

हथौड़ा (nm) a hammer

हथौड़ी (nf) a small hammer

हद (nf) limit; boundary; limitation; —बंदी delimitation

हदीस (nf) the traditional saying of Mohammad

हद्द (nf) (see हद)

हनन (nm) murder, killing, assassination

हनुमान् (a) having big jaw-bones; (nm) the Monkey God

हफ्ता (nm) a week

हबशी (nm) a negro

हम (pron) we, plural form of first person मैं

हम (a) similar, equal; —जोली a companion; —दर्द sympathetic; —दर्दी sympathy; —नाम name sake; —पेशा co-professional; —राज़ a confidant; —राही a co-traveller; —वतन a compatriot; —सफ़र a co-traveller —साया a neighbour

हमला (nm) attack, assault —वर an assailant

हमवार (a) even, level

हमारा (pron) our, ours

हमें (pron) to us

हमेशा (ind) always, ever

हया (nf) shame, modesty

हयात (nf) existence, life

हर (a) each, every; (nm) Lord Shiva; —दम always; —रोज़ daily

हरकत (nf) movement, motion, action; naughtiness; wickedness

हरकारा (nm) a postman

हरगिज़ (a) at any time, ever; —नहीं never

हरज (nm) see हर्ज

हरजाई (a) a wanderer, flirt; (nf) disloyal (woman)

हरज़ाना (nm) damages, compensation; —देना to compensate

हरण (nm) carrying off, taking away by force

हरना (v) to take away by force

हरम (nm) female apartments; (nf) a kept women, wife, a

handmaid

हरमज़दगी (nf) wickedness; misbehaviour

हरबाना (v) to cause to lose money in gambling

हरषाना (v) to please; to be pleased

हरा (a) green; fresh; unripe (fruit) —पन viridity —भरा fresh, verdant

हराना (v) to defeat, to beat; to counteract

हराम (a) polluted; unlawful; improper —खोर lazy —खोरी slothfulness; —ज़ादा bastard, rascal

हरामी (a & nm) wicked; rascal

हररत (nf) slight fever; feverishness; warmth

हरिजन (nm) an untouchable

हरि/ण (nm.) a deer; an antelope, –णी a hind

हरित (a) green

हरियाना (v) to turn green; to be delighted; (nm) one of the northern states of the Union of India

हरियाली (nf) verdure; green grass

हर्ज़ (nm) obstruction; harm; loss

हर्ता (nm) kidnapper; stealer

हर्ष (nm) joy, pleasure, glee, delight, mirth, gladness, happiness

हर्षित (a) joyous, pleased, delighted, glad, happy, cheerful

हल्, हलंत (nm) a consonant

हल (nm) a plough; solution; —जोतना to plough a field

हलक़ (nm) throat

हलकई (nf) lightness; silliness; meanness

हलकना (v) to toss about

हलक़ा (a) light in weight; cheap; careless; —पन (nm) lightness; cheapness

हलकान (a) perplexed, disturbed; tired

हलचल (nf) tumult, commotion; agitation, turmoil, —मचना commotion to be caused

हलबी (nf) turmeric

हलधर (nm) the farmer having a plough

हलफ़ (nm) an oath —उठाना to take an oath; —नामा an affidavit, a declaration on oath

हलवा (nm) a kind of sweet-meat

हलवा/ई (nm) a confectioner —इन a female confectioner

हलवाह (nm) a ploughman

हलाक (a) murdered, killed; —करना to murder, to kill; to torment

हलाल (a) lawful, right, sanctioned by law

हलाहल (nm) a very deadly poison

हल्दी (nf) see हलदी

हवन (nm) a fire sacrifice, an

offering

हवस (nf) yearning, longing; thirst; desire

हवा (nf) wind, air, breeze; reputation; —खोरी a walk; —पानी climate; —बाज़ an airman; —बाज़ी airmanship, —भर/सा very flimsy

हवाई (a) airy, aerial; false; —अड्डा aerodrome; —किला imaginary things; —छतरी an air umbrella; —जहाज़ an aeroplane; —डाकairmail; —मार्ग airways —यात्रा air journey

हवा/ला (nm) reference; example; custody, trust; —ले करना to yield, to hand over (to)

हवा/लात (nf) (police) custody —लाती under (police) custody

हवास (nm) senses (used as होश-हवास)

हवेली (nf) a mansion

हम्र (nm) ultimate result

हसद (nf) jealousy, malice; envy

हसरत (nf) craving, longing; desire; —भरा wistful

हसीन (nm) pretty, beautiful, charming

हस्त (nm) the hand; the hand-writing; —कला handicraft; —क्रिया masturbation; —कौशल manipulation; —क्षेप interference; —मैथुन

masturbation; —रेखा the line appearing on hand; —रेखा-विशेषज्ञ a palmist

हस्तलिखित (a) handwritten

हस्तलिपि (nf) handwriting

हस्ताक्षर (nm) signature; autograph; —करना to sign; to endorse; to initial; —करने वाला signatory; —युक्त signed

हस्तिनी (nf) a female elephant

हस्ती (nm) an elephant

हस्पताल (nm) a hospital; an asylum

हहरना (v) to tremble; to be embarrassed

हहराना (v) to tremble; to terrified

हाँ (adv) yea, yes; indeed; —करना to assent, to agree

हाँक (nf) calling aloud; —लगाना to call aloud

हाँकना (v) to drive; to push away; to goad

हाँडी (nf) a small earthern pot

हाँपना, हाँफना (v) to heave, to breathe heavily

हाकिम (nm) a governor, ruler; an officer

हाजत (nf) desire; need; pressure in the bowels

हाज़मा (nm) digestion, digestive power

हाज़िर (a) present; ready; —जवाब ready-witted; —करना to cause to appear; —रहना to be present; —होना

to attend a court

हाज़िरी (nf) presence; atten-dance; —लेना to take attendance

हाजी (nm) one who has made a pilgrimage to Mecca

हाट (nf) a market, bazar; a periodic market; —करना to go for shopping

हाड़ (nm) a bone; —मांस bones and flesh

हातिम (a) competent, proficient; (nm) an ancient chief of Arab, a generous person

हाथ (nm) a hand; handle —खर्च personal expenses

हाथा-पाई (nf) a tussle, scuffle

हाथी (nm) an elephant; —दाँत ivory

हादसा (nm) an accident, mishap, calamity

हानि (nf) a loss, harm; an injury; damage; —कर/कारक/कारी harmful, inhygienic; —पहुँचाना to injure, to damage, to harm

हाफ़िज़ (nm) the Mohammedan who learns the whole of the Quran by heart; a protector

हामिला (a) pregnant (woman)

हामी (nf) acceptance, assent; (nm) supporter; —भरना to give assent

हाय (int) alas! alack! lack-a-day; —तोबा uproar, havoc; —हाय करना to be afflicted

हार (nf) defeat, loss; (nm) necklace, wreath; —मानना to acknowledge defeat; —जीत defeat and victory

हारना (v) to lose, to fail, to be unsuccessful

हार्दिक (a) affectionate, hearty, cordial

हाल (nm) condition, state; news, narratives; (a) re-cent, current; —चाल general condition; —का fresh, recent

हालत (nf) condition, state

हालात (nf) circumstances, conditions (plural of हालत)

हालाँकि (adv) though, although

हाला (nf) wine, liquor

हालाहल (nm) a deadly poison

हाव-भाव (nm) blandishments; gestures

हावी (a) dominant; —होना to dominate

हाशिया (nm) margin, border

हास (nm) laughter, fun; joke; ridicule; —परिहास fun and humour

हासिल (a) obtained, acquired; what is carried forward; —जमा total; —करना to obtain; —होना to be acquired

हास्य (nm) laughter, a laugh; joke; ridicule; —जनक humorous; —चित्र a cartoon; —चित्रकार cartoonist —व्यंग्य humour and satire

हास्यास्पद (a) funny, ridiculous

हाहा (nf) loud laughter; — हीही fun and humour

हाहाकार (nm) sound of distress, an uproar

हिंग, हिंगु (nf) same as हींग

हिंडो/रा/ला (nm) a sway, cradle

हिंद (nm) India, Hindustan

हिंदवी (nf) Hindi language

हिंसा (nm) a number, digit

हिंदी (a) Indian, pertaining to India; (nm) a resident of Hindustan; (nf) Hindi language

हिंदुत्व (nm) Hinduism

हिंदुस्तान (nm) India

हिंदुस्तानी (nm) Indian

हिंदुस्थान (nm) same as हिंदुस्तान

हिंदू (nm & a) Hindu

हिंदोस्तान (nm) same as हिंदुस्तान

हिंसक (a) murderous, savage; (nm) a murderer — जंतु fierce animal; — पक्षी carnivorous bird

हिंसा (nf) violence, murder, slaying, slaughter; — त्मक destructive; — रत violent

हिंस्र (a) fierce, violent; murderous; hard-hearted

हिकमत/त (nf) Unani medical practice; method; — ती clever, dexterous

हिकायत (nf) a tale, a narration

हिकारत (nf) contempt, scorn

हिचक्का (nf) hiccup

हिचक (nf) hitch, hesitation; suspense, doubt

हिचकना (v) to hitch, to hesitate; to shrink

हिचकिचा/ना same as हिचकना; — हट hitch, hesitation

हिचकी (nf) hiccup

हिचकोला (nm) a jolt, jerk

हिजड़ा (nm) eunuch; (a) impotent

हिजरी (nf) the Mohammedan era

हिज्जे (nm) spelling; — करना to spell a word

हिज्र (nm) separation

हित (a) well-being; benefit, gain; — कर/कारक/कारी beneficial, advantageous; — चिंतक well-wisher; — चिंतन well-wishing

हिताहित (nm) good and bad

हितेच्छा (nf) well-wishing

हितेच्छु (a & nm) well wishing; a well-wisher

हितैषी (a & nm) same as हितेच्छु

हिदायत (nf) instruction — नामा a letter of instructions

हिनहिना/ना (v) to whinny, to neigh — हट whinnying, neighing

हिफ़ाज़त (nf) safety, protection; — करना to protect, to safeguard

हिब्बा (nm) a present, gift

हिम (nm) ice, snow; frost; — कण icicle; — कर the moon; — गिरि Himalaya; — नदी a glacier; — पात snow-fall; — मानव snow-man; — युग

the ice-age; —वर्षा snow-fall; —शिखर ice-cap — सागर ice-sea

हिमवान् (*nm*) the Himalayas

हिमांशु (*nm*) the moon

हिमाक़त (*nf*) stupidity, foolishness

हिमाचल (*nm*) the Himalayas; —प्रदेश a northern state of India

हिमानी (*nf*) a glacier

हिमाय/त (*nf*) support, backing; help, protection; —ती protector, helper, supporter

हिमालय (*nm*) the Himalaya mountains

हिम्मत (*nf*) courage; bravery; boldness

हिम्मती (*a*) courageous; brave; bold

हिया (*nm*) heart; courage; breast, bosom

हिरण्मय (*a*) of gold, golden

हिरण्य (*nm*) gold

हिरन (*nm*) a deer, an antelope

हिराना (*v*) to disappear; to forget

हिरासत (*nf*) custody; imprisonment

हि/स (*nf*) ambition, ardent desire; envy; —सी ambitious; envious

हिलकोर (*nf*) हिलकोरा (*nm*) a wave, billow

हिलना (*v*) to rock, to move; to swing; —डोलना to wander;

to move; —मिलना to have intimate connection with

हिलाना (*v*) to move, to wave, to quaver, to shake, to swing

हिलोर (*nf*) हिलोरा (*nm*) a wave, billow

हिल्लोल (*nf*) a wave, billow

हिसाब (*nm*) calculation; account; rate; arithmetic; —किताब accounts —करना to account, to work out; —चुकाना to clear off the old dues

हिसाबी (*a*) calculative

हिस्सा (*nm*) share; part; portion; lot

हिस्से/दार (*nm*) shareholder, partner; —दारी partnership; participation

हींग (*nf*) *asafoetida*

हीं-हीं (*nf*) sound of laughter

ही (*ind*) only, alone, solely; none but

हींक (*nf*) a slight bad smell

हीन (*a*) inferior, low; deprived; free from; —ग्रंथि inferiority complex; —चरित of bad character; —ता inferiority; —भावना feeling of inferiority

हीरक (*nm*) a diamond; —जयंती diamond jubilee

हीरा (*nm*) adamant, a diamond

हीला (*nm*) pretence; pretext; evasion; —हवाला pretence; evasion

ही-ही (*nf*) laughing loudly

हुँ (*int*) a word of assent, yes

हुँकार (nm) roar, bellowing

हुंडी (nf) a bill of exchange, draft; cheque; —सकारना to honour a bill

हुकुम (nm) same as हुक्म

हुकूमत (nf) government, rule, authority; —करना to govern, to rule; —चलाना to run a government

हुक्का (nm) a hubble-bubble; —भरना to flatter

हुक्म (nm) permission; order; command; —उदूली dis-obeyance; —नामा a decree; —बरदार a loyal servant; —बरदारी loyalty; —रान ruling authority

हुजूम (nm) a crowd

हुजूर (nm) sir, a title of respect, your majesty, presence

हुजूरी (nm) a special attendant

हुज्ज/त (nf) controversy, argument; —ती fractious, altercating

हुड़क (nf) longing, pining

हुड़कना (v) to fret, to pine

हुड़द/ग (nm) tumult, uproar, riot; —गी riotous, commotive

हुतात्मा (nm) a martyr

हुनर (nm) skill; craft, art; —मंद skilful; crafty

हुमकना (v) to stretch forward, to leap

हुलसना (v) to look pretty

हुलसाना (v) to cause to be made

merry

हुलास (nm) delight, joy, hilarity

हुलिया (nf) appearance, shape; —बिगाड़ना to harass

हुल्लड़ (nm) uproar, outbreak, tumult; —बाज़ tumultuous; —बाज़ी tumultuousness; —मचाना to make a tumult

हुश (int) be silent ! hush !

हुस्न (nm) beauty, elegance, prettiness; —परस्ती love of beauty

हूँ (ind) yes; (v) am

हूक (nf) pain, ache, sorrow

हूबहू (a) similar, alike

हूर (nf) a fairy of paradise; a fairy, beautiful woman

हृत (a) stolen, taken away; —बुद्धि stupefied

हृदयंगम (a) understood

हृदय (nm) the heart; core (of the heart); mind; —ग्राही attractive; —स्थ taken to heart; —स्पर्शी heart-touching; —हारी bewitching, charming —हीन hard-hearted

हृदये/श, श्वर (nm) the dear one; husband; lover —श्वरी (nf) the beloved; dear wife

हृद्गत (a) internal, pertaining to the heart

हृद्रोग (nm) heart disease

हृष्ट (a) delighted, glad, pleased; —पुष्ट lusty, robust, stout

हें-हें (*nm*) the low sound of laughter

हे (*ind*) a vocative particle O !

हेकड़ी (*nf*) rudeness, arrogance; —दिखलाना to show arrogance

हेच (*a*) insignificant, mean, trifling

हेठा (*a*) mean, low, trivial; —पन meanness, lowness

हेठी disrespect, insult, humiliation; —होना to insult, to humiliate

हेतु (*nm*) purpose, motive, cause, reason

हेमंत (*nm*) cold season, winter

हेम (*nm*) gold; —गिरि the Sumeru mountain

हेमाद्रि (*nm*) the Sumeru mountain

हेय (*a*) fit to be abandoned, insignificant, worthless

हेरना (*v*) to search; to persue; to spy

हेर-फेर (*nm*) disorder; interchange —करना to make unlawful changes; to make amendments

हेराफेरी (*nf*) interchange; manipulations; —करना to interchange; to make unscrupulous changes

हेलमेल (*nm*) intimacy; familiarity; friendship

हैं (*v*) are, plural of है (*ind*) a particle showing wonder or negation

है (*v*) is

हैजा (*nm*) cholera

हैरत (*nf*) astonishment, wonder; —अंगेज़ astonishing

हैरान (*a*) disturbed; perplexed, worried

हैरानी (*nf*) disturbance; perplexity, weariness, harassment

हैवा/न an animal; foolish person; —नियत brutality —नी rustic, brutal

हैसियत (*nf*) ability; status; capacity

हों (*v*) plural of the verb होना (in condition)

होंठ (*nm*) the lip, same as ओठ

होठ (*nm*) see ओठ

होड़ (*nf*) bet; race; competition; —लगाना to bet; to compete, to contest

होनहार (*nm*) fate; destiny, ultimate lot; (*a*) promising, hopeful

होना (*v*) to be; to born; to pass; to happen; to occur; to exist; to become

होनी (*nf*) destiny, a would-be incident

होम (*nm*) a burnt offering, a sacrifice

होलिका (*nf*) the festival of Holi; —दहन burning of the heap of wood on Holi

होली (*nf*) a great Hindu festival; —खेलना to throw coloured water on each other

होश (*nm*) sense, sensibility, consciousness; —आना to come to senses; —करना to be alert; —में आना to come to senses; —रखना to be watchful; —हवास see होश

होशियार (*a*) attentive; cautious; smart, clever; intelligent, careful

होशियारी (*nf*) attentiveness; caution; smartness, cleverness; intelligence, carefulness

हौंस (*nf*) longing

हौआ (*nm*) a bugbear, a bogey; a word used to frighten children

हौज़, हौद (*nm*) a reservoir of water etc.

हौल (*nm*) dread, fear; —दिली terrified; —नाक dreadful

हौले-हौले (*adv*) slowly; gently; quietly

हौवा (*nm*) same as हौआ

हौसला (*nm*) courage; dare; morale; enthusiasm —पस्त होना loss of energy, —अफ़ज़ाई encouragement

ह्रद (*nm*) a lake, large pond

ह्रस्व (*a*) small; short; worthless (*nm*) a short vowel

ह्रास (*nm*) decrease; decline; deficiency; downfall; —मान decreasing; decaying

ह्रसोन्मुख (*a*) decaying —ता decadence

ह्वेल (*nf*) a whale fish

हिन्दी लोकोक्तियाँ

अंत भला तो सब भला—All is well that ends well.

अंधों में कनवा राजा—A figure among cyphers.

अकल बड़ी कि भैंस — Knowledge is more powerful than mere strength.

अधजल गगरी छलकत जाए, भरी गगरिया चुपके जाए—Deep rivers move with silent majesty. Shallow brooks are noisy.

अपने पूत सबको प्यारा—Every potter praises his own pot.

अपनी इज़्ज़त अपने हाथ—Respect yourself and you will be respected.

अपनी गली में कुत्ता भी शेर होता है—Every cock fights best on his own dunghill.

अपने दही को कोई खट्टा नहीं कहता—Every potter praises his own pot.

अपने मुँह मियाँ मिट्ठू—Self-praise is no recommendation.

अभी दिल्ली दूर है—Make not your sauce till you have caught your fish.

अशर्फियाँ लुटें, कोयले पर मुहर—Penny wise, Pound foolish.

आगे दौड़ पीछे छोड़—Haste makes waste.

आदत प्रकृति बन जाती है—Habit is the second nature.

आप भला तो जग भला—Good mind good find.

आप मरे जग लोप—Death's day is Doom's day.

आम के आम गुठली के दाम—Earth's joys and heaven's combined.

आवश्यकता में सभी कुछ उचित है—Necessity knows no law.

इलाज से परहेज अच्छा—Prevention is better than cure.

इस हाथ दे, उस हाथ ले—Early sow early mow.

उतावला सो बावला—Merry in haste repent at leisure.

उतने पाँव पसारिए जितनी चादर होए—Cut your coat according to your cloth.

उधार स्नेह की कैंची है—He that does lend does lose a fore-friend.

उल्टे बाँस बरेली को—To carry coal to New Castle.

ऊँची दुकान फीका पकवान—Great cry little wool.

ऊँट के मुँह में जीरा—A drop in the ocean.

एक अनार सौ बीमार—One post and one hundred candidates.

एक पंथ दो काज—To kill two birds with one stone.

एक परहेज़ सौ इलाज—Diet cures more than doctors.

एक म्यान में दो तलवारें नहीं समातीं—Two of a trade seldom agree.

एक हाथ से ताली नहीं बजती—It takes two to make a quarrel.

एक ही थैले के चट्टे-बट्टे—Cast in the same mould.

एका बड़ी शक्ति है—Union is strength.

ओस चाटे प्यास नहीं बुझती—A fog cannot be dispelled by a fan.

औरत की बात का क्या विश्वास—A winter's wind and a woman's heart oftenest change.

कर बुरा हो बुरा—Do evil and look for the like.

कल किसने देखा है—Tomorrow never comes.

कहीं बूढ़े तोते भी पढ़ते हैं—Can you teach an old woman to dance ?

काठ की हँडिया एक ही बार चढ़ती है—It is the silly fish that is caught with the same bait.

कानी के ब्याह को सौ सौ जोखिम—There is many a slip between the cup and the lip.

काम प्यारा होता है चाम नहीं—Handsome is that handsome does.

काम ही कारीगर बनाता है—Practice makes perfect.

कुछ न होने से थोड़ा अच्छा है—Something is better than nothing.

कूड़े के भी दिन फिरते हैं—Every dog has his day.

कोई सुख ऐसा नहीं जिसमें दुख न होय—No joy without alloy.

कौन है जिससे ग़लती नहीं होती—Even a good horse stumbles.

क्या अक्ल चरने गई है—Wits have gone wool-gathering.

क्या बूढ़े तोते भी पढ़ते हैं—An old dog will learn no tricks.

खाने में भी क्या शर्माना—Never feel shy to eat your meal.

खेती खसम सेती—The master's eye makes the mare fat.

गँवार गन्ना न दे भेली दे—Penny wise Pound foolish.

गया वक़्त फिर हाथ नहीं आता—Time and tide wait for no man.

ग़रीब की जोरू सबकी भाभी—A light purse is a heavy curse.

ग़रीबी में आटा गीला—Misfortunes seldom come alone.

गेरुए वस्त्रों से साधु नहीं बनता—Cowl does not make a monk.

गेहूँ के साथ घुन भी पिस जाता है—When the buffaloes fight crops suffer.

घर का जोगी जोगना आन गाँव का सिद्ध—A prophet is not honoured in his own country.

घर का भेदी लंका ढाए—Traitors are the worst enemies.

घर की आधी भली, बाहर सारी नहीं—Dry bread at home is better than sweetmeat abroad.

घायल की गति वैद्य क्या जाने —The wearer best knows where the shoe pinches.

चार दिन की चाँदनी फिर अँधेरी रात—A nine day's wonder.

चोर का साथी गिरहकट—Birds of same feather flock together.

चौबे गए छब्बे होने दूबे होकर आए—An ass went to ask for horns but lost his ears.

जब अपनी उतारी तो दूसरे की उतारते क्या देर—Beware of him who regards not his reputation.

जब तक साँस तब तक आस—As long as there is life, there is hope.

ज़बाने ख़ल्क नक्कारा-ए-ख़ुदा—Public voice is God's voice.

ज़र, ज़मीन और औरत लड़ाई की जड़ है—Money, women and land are the roots of all troubles.

ज़रूरत के वक़्त गधे को बाप बनाना पड़ता है — The needy stoops to every-thing however mean.

जल्दी का काम अच्छा नहीं होता—Quick and well do not go well together.

जहाँ चाह वहाँ राह—Where there is a will, there is a way.

जहाँ फूल वहाँ काँटा—No rose without a thorn.

जाको राखे साइयाँ मार सके ना कोय—Whom God keeps, no frost can kill.

जितना धन उतनी चिंता—Much coin, much care.

जिसके पैर न फटी बेवाई, वह क्या जाने पीर पराई—He laughs at scars who never felt a wound.

जैसा आया वैसा गया—Evil got, evil spent.

जैसा देश वैसा भेष—When you go to Rome, do as the Romans do.

जैसा बाप वैसा बेटा—Like father like son.

जैसा राजा वैसी प्रजा—As the king so are the subjects.

जैसी करनी वैसी भरनी—As you sow, so shall you reap.

जैसे काली कामरी चढ़ै न दूजो रंग—Black will take no other hue.

जैसे को तैसा — Tit for tat.

जो आता है अपना सिक्का चलाता है—New lords, new laws.

जो गरजते हैं वे बरसते नहीं—Barking dogs seldom bite.

डंडा सबका पीर—Rod tames every brute.

डौला-डौल की मिट्टी खराब—A rolling stone gathers no moss.

तुरत दान महा कल्याण—He gives thrice who gives in a trice.

तेते पाँव पसारिए जेती लाम्बी सौर—Cut your coat according to your cloth.

तेल देखो तेल की धार देखो—See which way the wind blows.

थोथा चना बाजै घना—Empty vessels make much noise.

दान की बछिया का दाँत नहीं देखा जाता—Beggars and borrowers could not be choosers.

दाम करावे काम—Money makes the man run.

दीवाल के भी कान होते हैं—Hedges have eyes and walls have ears.

दुःख भोगे बिना सुख कहाँ—No meat without some sweat.

दुर्बल में क्रोध अधिक होता है—A little pot is soon hot.

दुविधा में दोनों गए माया मिली न राम—Between two stools one falls to the ground.

दूध का जला छाछ फूँककर पीता है—A burnt child dreads the fire.

देखिए ऊँट किस करवट बैठता है—Let us see which way the wind blows.

दो मुल्लाओं में मुर्गी हराम—Too many cooks spoil the broth.

धूप में बाल नहीं पकाए हैं—Wisdom is the daughter of old age.

नक्ल में अक्ल क्या!—Imitation has no intelligence.

न नौ नगद न तेरह उधार—A bird in hand is worth two in bush.

न नौ मन तेल होगा न राधा नाचेगी—If the sky falls, we shall gather larks.

नाच न जाने आँगन टेढ़ा—A bad workman quarrels with his tools.

निरन्तर कार्यशील जीतता है—Slow and steady wins the race.

नीम हकीम खतर-ए जान—A little knowledge is a dangerous thing.

नेकी कर दरिया में डाल—Do good and cast it into the river.

नौकरी की क्या जड़—Service is no inheritance.

पढ़े न लिखे नाम विद्यासागर—An ignorant man keeping a great fuss.

पहिले अपने को सम्हालो—Sweep before your own door.

पहिले तौलो फिर बोलो—Think before you speak.

पाँचों अँगुलियाँ घी में—Bread is buttered on both sides.

पानी में रहकर मगर से वैर—To live in Rome and strife with the Pope.

पूत कपूत पालने में ही पहचाने जाते हैं—The child is the father of the man.

पेट की खातिर टोकरी उठानी पड़ती है—Want goads to industry.

प्रत्येक कार्य मनुष्य नहीं कर सकता—No living man can do all things.

प्रश्न गेहूँ उत्तर जौ—Your answer is besides the question.

प्राण बचे लाखों पाए—Life is better than bags of gold.

फ़जूल खर्ची पर कमर कसी है—He burns the candles at both ends.

बग़ल में छुरी मुख में राम राम—A wolf in lamb's skin.

बड़ी है चिंता जो जीते जी भी खाती है—Anxiety is the canker of the heart.

बड़े मियाँ सो बड़े मियाँ छोटे मियाँ सुभान अल्ला—The younger is even worse than the elder.

बद अच्छा बदनाम बुरा—A bad man is better than a bad name.

बातों से पेट नहीं भरता—It is money that buys the land.

बिन बुलाये मान नहीं होता—Uninvited guests sit on thorns.

बिना सेवा मेवा नहीं मिलता—No pain, no gain.

बिल्ली ने शेर पढ़ाया बिल्ली को खाने को आया—My foot my tutor.

बीती ताहि बिसार दे—Let the past bury its dead.

बुरा कर हो बुरा—Do evil and look for the like.

बूँद-बूँद से तालाब भर जाता है—Many a pickle makes a mickle.

बेकार से बेगार भली—Forced labour is better than idleness.

बेकारी में शैतानी सूझती है—An idle brain is a workshop of devil.

बोए पेड़ बबूल का आम कहाँ से खाय—Gather thistles and expect pickles.

भय और प्रेम एक जगह नहीं रहते—Dread and affection never exist together.

भलाई से न चूको—Never be weary of doing good.

भाग्य के लिखे को कौन मेट सकता है—What is lotted, cannot be blotted.

भिड़ों के छत्तों को मत छेड़ो—Let sleeping dogs lie.

भूख में चने भी बादाम—Hunger is the best sauce.

भूखा सो रूखा—A hungry man is an angry man.

मक्खी खांड पर गिरती है—Daub your mouth with honey and you will get plenty of flies.

मरता क्या न करता—The desperate man does all things.

मरे-मुर्दे मत उखाड़ो—Let by-gones be by-gones.

महँगा रोए एक बार, सस्ता रोए बार-बार—The cheaper buyer takes no meat.

माया को माया मिले कर-कर लम्बे हाथ—Money begets money.

माया बादल की छाया—Riches have wings.

माले-मुफ्त दिले बेरहम (हराम का माल बेकार चला जाता है)—Ill-got, ill-spent.

मित्र वही जो समय पर काम आए—A friend in need is a friend indeed.

मुँह पर झूठ नहीं बोला जाता—Face to face, the teeth comes out.

मुल्ला की दौड़ मस्जिद तक—The priest goes no further from the church.

मेहनत का फल मीठा होता है—No roses without thorns.

मौन आधी स्वीकृति है—Silence is half consent.

यथा राजा तथा प्रजा—As king, so are his subjects.

यहाँ तुम्हारी दाल नहीं गल सकती—Your schemes won't take here.

राई को पर्वत बनाना—To make a mountain of a mole hill.

राम राम जपना, पराया माल अपना—A robber in the garb of a saint.

लातों के देवता बातों से नहीं मानते—Rod is the logic of fools.

लालच बुरी बला है—No vice like avarice.

लोहे को लोहा काटता है—Diamond cuts diamond.

वीरता का काम न चाहे नाम—Good deeds need no show.

वे दिन गये जब जनाब फाख्ता उड़ाते थे—Gone is the goose that was golden.

शक्करखोरे को ईश्वर शक्कर देता है—Spend and God will send.

सबको अपना ही मतलब प्यारा है—Every one knows his interest best.

समझदार को इशारा काफी—Word to the wise is enough.

समय को दुर्लभ जानो—Make hay while the Sun shines.

साझे की हँडिया चौराहे पर फूटती है—A common horse is worst shod.

सारा जाता देखिए आधा लीजे बाँट—Better give the wool than the whole sheep.

सावन के अंधे को हरा ही हरा दिखाई देता है—Everything looks yellow to a jaundiced eye.

स्याना कौवा कूड़े पर—Positive men are often in error.

हथेली पर सरसों नहीं जमती—Rome was not built in a day.

हरफन मौला, हरफन अधूरा—Jack of all trades and master of none.

होनहार बिरवान के होत चीकने पात—Coming events cast their shadows before.

हिंदी मुहावरे

अंग-अंग मुस्कराना to be beaming and buoyant.

अंग फूले न समाना to be in a rapture.

अंग लगाना to embrace.

अंगारे उगलना to be fierce in speech.

अंगारे बरसना to be excessively hot (weather).

अंगारों पर पैर रखना to invite trouble.

अंगारों पर लोटना to burn within (on account of jealousy).

अंगूठा दिखाना to reject forcibly.

अंगूर खट्टे होना to decry something that has proved inaccessible.

अंतिम साँसें गिनना to be breathing one's last.

अंधा होना to be lost to realities.

अंधे की लाठी a helpless man's only support.

अँधेरे में छलाँग लगाना to leap into the dark.

अँधेरे में रखना to keep in dark.

अक़्ल के घोड़े दौड़ाना to indulge in mental gymnasium.

अक़्ल चरने जाना to be out of one's head.

अक़्ल ठिकाने लगाना to set one right.

अक़्ल पर पत्थर to be out of one's head.

अधर में लटकना to hang in mid-air.

अनसुना करना not to pay any attention.

अपना-सा मुँह लेकर रह जाना to face discomfiture.

अमली जामा पहनाना to put into practice.

अरमान रह जाना not to have one's aspirations materialised.

आँख का तारा darling.

आँख का पानी उतर जाना to be lost to shame.

आँख चुराना to avoid being sighted by.

आँख बदलना to withdraw favour or regard all of a sudden.

आँख लड़ाना to meet stare with stare.

आँखें दिखाना to look at angrily.

आँखें बिछाना to give a very cordial welcome.

आँखों पर परदा पड़ना to be under an illusion.

आँखों में धूल झोंकना to cheat.

आकाश-पाताल एक करना to make a Herculean attempt.

आकाश से बातें करना to be as lofty as the sky.

आग बरसाना to bombard.

आग में घी डालना to add fuel to the fire.

आगे-पीछे कोई न होना to be without any kith and kin.

आटे के साथ घुन पिसना to undergo an undeserved.

आटे-दाल का भाव मालूम होना to be confronted with unwelcome realities of practical life.

आड़े वक़्त पर काम आना to do a good turn when one is in difficulty.

आपे से बाहर होना to lose self-control.

आफ़त मोल लेना to own unnecessary botheration.

आवाज़ कसना to pass unwelcome remarks.

आशाओं पर पानी फिरना to have one's hopes shattered.
आस टूटना to be disappointed.
आसन डोलना to be allured or tempted.
आस बँधाना to extend assurances.
आसमान पर थूकना to puff against the wind.
आसमान सिर पर उठा लेना to create a tumult.
आसमान से बातें करना to vie with the sky.
आस लगाना to look hopefully to.

इघर–उघर की हाँकना to gossip.
इघर की उघर लगाना to indulge in back-biting.

उड़न छू होना to disappear all of a sudden.
उन्नीस-बीस होना to be slightly better or worse.
उफ न करना to endure quietly.
उम्मीदों पर पानी फेरना to dash all hopes to the ground.
उल्टा पाठ पढ़ाना to misguide.
ऊँचा सुनना to be hard of hearing.
ऊपर होना to be senior in status or office.

एक न चलना all efforts to prove in vain.
एहसान मानना to feel obliged.

ऐसी की तैसी करना let it go to hell.

ओखली में सिर देना to take up a difficult challenge.

कंधा देना to lend a shoulder in carrying a dead body.
कंधे से कंधा छिलना to be over-crowded.
कंधे से कंधा मिलाना to lend full co-operation.
कंधों पर उठाना to give a rousing welcome.
कच्चा पड़ना to prove ineffective.
कच्ची गोली नहीं खेलना to have learnt the tricks of the trade.
कटे पर नमक छिड़कना to add insult to injury.
कठघरे में खड़ा करना to bring before the bar.
कदम उठाना to make progress.
कन्नी काटना to fight shy of.

कबाड़ा होना to be ruined.

कमर कसना to be all set for action.

कमर झुकना to become old.

कमर तोड़ना to break one's back.

कमर सीधी करना to relax for a while.

करम फूटना to be unfortunate.

करबट बदलते रात बीतना to spend a restless night.

कलई खुलना to be exposed.

कलम तोड़ना to work wonders in (one's) writing.

कलम फेरना to strike out or delete what is written.

कलेजा कड़ा करना to prepare oneself for a shock.

कलेजा ठंडा होना to be fulfilled.

कलेजा मुँह को आना to be restless on account of grief.

कलेजे पर साँप लोटना to be struck with jealousy.

कलेजे से लगाना to embrace fondly.

कसर न उठा रखना to leave no stone unturned.

काँटे बोना to sow seeds of misfortune.

काठ का कलेजा होना to be hard-hearted.

काठ मार जाना to be stunned.

कान खड़े करना to get alert.

कान धरना to listen attentively.

कान न देना to turn a deaf ear to.

कान पर जूँ न रेंगना to turn a deaf ear to.

काम तमाम करना to put an end to.

काम रखना to mind one's (own) business.

कायल करना to convince (by argument).

कायल होना to be convinced.

किए-कराए पर पानी फेरना to undo what has been achieved.

किया-कराया मिट्टी में मिलाना to undo what has been accomplished.

कुएँ में धकेलना to ruin the life of.

कुछ कहना to show anger on.

कुछ न सूझना to be in a fog.

कुर्सी तोड़ना to occupy a chair idly.

कैंची-सी ज़बान चलना to talk nineteen to the dozen.

कोई कसर उठा न रखना to leave no stone unturned.

कोठे पर बैठना to turn into a prostitute.

कौड़ी के मोल damn cheap.

खतरे से खेलना to play with fire.

खरी-खरी सुनाना to call a spade a spade.

खरी-खोटी सुनाना to take to tasks.

खस्ता हाल हो जाना to go to grass.

ख़ाक में मिलना to fall to the ground.

खाट से लगना to be reduced to skeleton.

खाते में डालना to debit to the account (of).

खाने के लाले पड़ना to be hard up for each meal.

(अपनी) खिचड़ी अलग पकाना to go one's own queer way.

खिलवाड़ करना to treat lightly.

खिल्ली उड़ाना to ridicule.

खुलकर खेलना to indulge in misdeeds openly.

खुशी से पाँव ज़मीन पर न पड़ना to be over-whelmed with joy.

खून चूसना to exploit.

खून सफ़ेद होना to become inhumane.

खेल बिगड़ना to have a business spoilt.

गड़े मुर्दे उखाड़ना to rake up the long lost past.

गत बनाना to give a thorough beating.

गधे को बाप बनाना to flatter a fool for expediency.

गप मारना to indulge in boastful gossip.

गरदन नापना to insult.

गरदन फँसना to be involved in a difficulty.

गला दबाना to exercise undue pressure.

गवारा करना to tolerate.

गाँठ बाँधना to make a note of.

गाली खाना to endure foul language.

गुज़र जाना to pass away.

गुज़र होना to sustain.

गुस्सा थूक देना to forgive and forget.

गोद सूनी होना to lose the only child.

गोली मारना to ignore.

घड़ियाँ गिनना to await keenly.

घर के घर रहना to be even in a bargain.

घर भरना to amass wealth.

घात लगाना to lie in ambush.

घाव पर नमक छिड़कना to add insult to injury.
घी-शक्कर होना to become inseparably.
घोड़े बेचकर सोना to go into a deep care-free sleep.
चकमा खाना to be tricked.
चकमा देना to play a trick.
चपेट में आना to sustain injury/loss.
चमड़ी उधेड़ना to beat bare.
चलता बनना to slip away.
चाँद-सा मुखड़ा lovely face.
चार आँखें करना to come face to face.
चार सौ बीस deceitful.
चिड़िया का दूध a non-existent commodity.
चीं बोलना to accept defeat.
चूल्हे में जाना to go to hell.
चेहरे पर हवाइयाँ उड़ना to be dispirited.

छक्के छुड़ाना to put out of gear.
छप्पर फाड़कर देना to give as a windfall.
छाती ठंडी करना to assuage one's feelings.
छाती ठोककर कहना to take a pledge.
छाती पर पत्थर रखना to endure patiently.
छाती पर साँप लोटना to burn with jealousy.
छाती से लगाना to embrace.
छू-मंतर होना to vanish.

ज़ख्म पर नमक छिड़कना to add insult to injury.
ज़बान पर ताला लगाना to be rendered speechless.
ज़बान हिलाना to make an utterance.
ज़मीन चटाना to throw flat.
जले पर नमक छिड़कना to add insult to injury.
जान के लाले पड़ना to be under the shadow of death.
जान छुड़ाना to get rid of.
जान निकालना to be in great agony.
जान पर खेलना to put one's life in peril.
जान में जान आना to feel relieved.
जी खट्टा होना to be disgusted.
जी चुराना to shirk work.

जी छोटा होना to lose heart.
जी बहलाना to recreate.
जोर पर होना to be in full swing.

झंडा गाड़ना to achieve a victory.

टका-सा जवाब देना to say a flat 'no'.
टक्कर लेना to set one's face against.
टुकड़ों पर पलना (किसी के) to thrive on leavings.
टेक निभाना to fulfil one's resolve.
टोपी उछालना to expose publicly.

ठंडी साँस लेना to heave a sigh.
ठोकर खाते फिरना to wander aimlessly.

डंडे बजाना to idle away time.
डकार न लेना to assimilate another's due quietly.
डकार लेना to assimilate another's due.
डेरा डालना to come to stay.
डोरे डालना to allure.

ढिंढोरा पीटना to proclaim aloud.
ढेर हो जाना to pass away.

नकदीर खुलना to be in luck.
नकदीर फूटना to be under the spell of ill-luck.
तकल्लुफ में पड़ना to be formal.
नड़ी मारना to give oneself airs.
नबियत आना to fall in love with.
तलवे चाटना to fawn upon.
तशरीफ ले जाना to depart.
नहलका मचाना to cause a havoc.
नाना मारना to taunt.
तारीख पड़ना a date to be fixed.
नौरे गिनना to keep awake the whole night.
तालू से जीभ न लगाना to go on chattering.
तिनका तक न तोड़ना not to stir even a finger.

निल का नाड़ करना to make a mountain of a mole.
नीर निशाने पर बैठना to hit the mark.
नीसमारखाँ a sham hero.
तुक होना to make a sense.
तुक्का लगाना to take a chance.
तूफ़ान खड़ा करना to work havoc.
तेवर बदलना to frown.
तैयारी पर होना to be in form.
तैश में आना to be provoked.
तोता पढ़ाना to teach over and over again.
नौबा करना to vow never to repeat.

थककर चूर होना to be dead tired.
थप्पड़ जड़ना to slap on the cheek.
थाह लेना to unearth the reality.
थूककर चाटना to eat one's own words.

दत्तचित्त होकर सुनना to be all ears.
दबी ज़बान से कहना to say in a hushed manner.
दबाव डालना to influence.
दम घुटना to be suffocated.
दम घोटना to suffocate.
दम टूटना to be exhausted.
दम न होना to have no guts.
दम निकलना to pass away.
दम लगाना to smoke.
दमड़ी भी न होना (पास में) to be penniless.
दर-दर की ठोकरें खाना to knock at one door after another.
दर्शन दुर्लभ होना to be seen rarely.
दाँत खट्टे करना to force the enemy into a tight corner.
दाँत तोड़ना to render powerless.
दाँतों तले उँगली दबाना to stand amazed.
दामन फैलाना to beg.
दाल न गलना to affect little.
दाल में काला होना to have something wrong.
दिन को तारे दिखाना to put in a very tight corner.
दिन को रात कहना to reverse the truth.

दिन दूना रात चौगुना बढ़ना to grow by leaps and bounds.

दिनों का फेरा run of good luck to be changed.

दिमाग़ आसमान पर होना to be very much conceited.

दिमाग़ की खिड़कियाँ खुली होना to have an open mind.

दिमाग़ लड़ाना to exercise one's brain.

दिल खट्टा होना to feel repulsed.

दिल छोटा करना to feel dejected.

दिल बाग़-बाग़ होना to be extremely delighted.

दिल में घर करना to be taken to heart.

दिल से निकाल देना to forget and forgive.

दुआ देना to wish well.

दुआ मांगना to pray for somebody's well-being.

दुकान उठाना a business to be closed for good.

दुकान जमाना to firmly establish a business.

दुनिया की हवा लगना to acquire worldly wiles.

दुनिया से कूच कर जाना to pass away.

दुम दबाकर भागना to turn tails.

दुःख का पहाड़ टूटना to be in terrible distress.

दूसरों का मुँह ताकना to look to others for help.

दृश्य देखते बनना a sight worth seeing.

दृष्टि फेरना to withdraw one's favour.

दृष्टि रखना to keep uner observation.

देह में आग लगना to get enraged.

दो की चार सुनाना to pay in the same coin along with interest.

दो रोटी कमाना to earn one's livelihood.

दोहरी चाल चलना to play a double game.

धक से रह जाना to be stunned.

धक्के खाना to be tossed about.

धाक जमना to command overwhelming influence.

धूप में बाल सफ़ेद होना to age without experience.

धूल चटाना to knock down.

धूल फाँकना to wander without a job.

धूल में लट्ठ मारना to make a random effort.

धोखा देना to play false.

धौंस जमाना to bluster.

ध्यान में न लाना to ignore.

ध्यान में उतरना to forget.

नकेल डालना to tame.
नज़र करना to offer.
नज़र दौड़ाना to look around.
नज़र बचाना to try to evade.
नज़रों से गिरना to be in bad books of.
नथने फुलाना to be in rage.
नशा उतरना vanity to be knocked off.
नस-नस पहचानना to know through and through.
नसीब सीधा होना to be in luck.
नाक काटना to defame.
नाक बचाना to safeguard one's honour.
नाक में दम करना to harass.
नाक रखना to save one's honour.
नाच नचाना to harass.
नानी मर जाना to feel lost.
नाम आसमान पर होना to be very famous.
नाम कमाना to acquire renown.
नाम डुबाना to lose one's reputation.
निगाहें चार होना to exchange glances.
निशाना बनाना to aim at.
निशाना बाँधना to take an aim.
नींद-भर सोना to have one's fill of sleep.
नींद हराम करना to disturb one's sleep.
नुकसान पहुँचना to suffer a loss.
नुकसान भरना to make good the loss.
नौ दो ग्यारह होना to turn tails.

पत्ता न हिलना everything around to be still.
पत्थर पिघलना a stony heart to be moved.
पर काट देना to render ineffective.
पलड़ा भारी होना to have a stronger case.
पसीने-पसीने होना to perspire profusely.
पहाड़ से टक्कर लेना to cross swords with a giant.
पाँव फूँक-फूँककर रखना to advance every step with care.

पाँव फैलाकर सोना to enjoy a carefree sleep.

पानी उतारना to disgrace.

पानी-पानी होना to be overwhelmed with shame.

पाप कटना to get rid of.

पास तक न फटकना to keep away absolutely.

पासा पलटना the tide to be turned.

पीछे पड़ना to harass continuously.

पीठ दिखाना to flee from the battle field.

पेट काटना to save money by imposing self-restraint.

पेट की आग बुझाना to fill the stomach.

पेट गिरना to commit abortion.

पेट पालना to earn one's living somehow.

पेश आना to treat.

पैर जमना to consolidate one's position.

पैर भारी होना to be in the family way.

प्राण हथेली पर लिए फिरना to face all sorts of risk.

प्राणों से हाथ धोना to lose life.

फंदे में पड़ना to be caught in a trick.

फूट-फूटकर रोना to weep bitterly.

फेर में पड़ना, निन्यानबे के to be unseemly crazy to amass wealth.

बखिया उघेड़ना to expose thoroughly.

बगलें झाँकना to be rendered witless.

बगलें बजाना to be exceptionally happy.

बदन में आग लगना to fret and fume.

बला मोल लेना to own up a trouble.

बहती गंगा में हाथ धोना to make hay while the Sun shines.

बाछें खिलना to be very happy.

बात न पूछना to care nothing for.

बात बनाना to talk much.

बातों में आना to be taken in.

बाल धूप में पकाना to age without experience.

बाल-बाल बचना to have a hair-breadth escape.

बेड़ा पार होना to achieve the end.
बोरिया समेटना to leave.

भाग जागना to have a run of good luck.
भाग फूटना to have a run of ill-luck.
भौं सिकोड़ना to frown.

मनसा वाचा कर्मणा through the mind, speech and deed.
मसें भीगना to be on the threshold of youth.
माँग उजड़ना to be widowed.
मिट्टी पलीद होना to be in a miserable plight.
मिट्टी में मिलाना to be ruined.
मिट्ठू बनना, अपने मुँह to indulge in self-praise.
मुँह काला करना to be disgraced.
मुँह खोलना to speak out.
मुँह देखते रह जाना to be taken aback.
मुँह फेरना to abstain (from).
मुँह बनाना to look displeased.
मुँह में ज़बान न रखना to be tongue tied.
मुट्ठी गरम करना to bribe.
मूँछ नीची होना to be disgraced.
मूँछ पर ताव देना to care for nothing in the world.
मूसलचंद, दाल भात में a wrong man in a wrong place.

यकीन आना to feel assured.
यकीन दिलाना to assure.
येन-केन-प्रकारेण by hook or by crook.

रंग उतरना to fade.
रंग चढ़ना to be in high spirits.
रंग जमना to be held in esteem.
रंग फीका पड़ना to fade out.
रंग में भंग करना to mar a happy occasion.
रग-रग से वाकिफ़ होना to know through and through.

रगों में खून दौड़ना to be excited.
रफूचक्कर होना to make good one's escape.
राई का पहाड़ बनाना to make a mountain 'of a mole.
राशि मिलना agreeably inclined to each other by temperament.
रोयें खड़े होना to be thrilled.

लंबी-चौड़ी हाँकना to talk tall.
लंबी तानकर सोना to enjoy a carefree sleep.
लकीर पीटना to follow the tradition.
लगाना-बुझाना to back-bite.
लहू पीना to trouble constantly.
लहू सफ़ेद हो जाना to become inhumane.
लाड़ लड़ाना fondle.
लेना एक न देना दो for no purpose at all.
लेने के देने पड़ना to lose while expecting to profit.

वक्त-बेवक्त at all times.
वचन पालना to implement one's promise.
वचन भंग करना to break a promise.
वास्ता देना to invoke the name of.
वास्ता पड़ना to be concerned with.
विपत्ति मोल लेना to own up avoidable calamity.
वीरगति को प्राप्त होना to achieve a heroic end.

शंख फूँकना to make a declaration of war.
शक्ल न दिखाना not to turn up.
शक्ल बनाना to wear a strange look.
शान मारना to boast.
शान में बट्टा लगना a fair name to be tarnished.
शामत आना to be in the grip of misfortune.
शेर होना to be encouraged too far.

सब्ज़-बाग दिखलाना to arouse high hopes in vain.
सर करना to conquer.

साँप सूँघ जाना to be rendered still.

साथ देना to keep company with.

साथ निबाहना to continue.

साथ लेकर डूबना to involve someone in a sure tragedy.

साफ़ छूटना to go scot free.

सामने आना to confront.

साये की तरह साथ-साथ रहना to shadow somebody.

सिट्टी-पिट्टी गुम हो जाना to be nervous.

सिर उठाना to rebel.

सिर ऊँचा करना to be proud.

सिर खाना to go on bothering.

सिर चकराना to feel giddy.

सिर चढ़ना to take too much liberty.

सिर थोपना to impose (upon).

सिर न उठाने देना to give no opportunity to rise against.

सिर पर आसमान उठाना to create a havoc.

सिर पर चढ़ाना to pamper a bit too much.

सिर पर पाँव रखकर भागना to show a clean pair of heels.

सिर पर सवार रहना to keep bullying.

सिर पैर न होना to make no sense.

सिर फिरना to be out of senses.

सिर लेना to own up.

सुख लूटना to enjoy.

सुहाग उजड़ना to be widowed.

सेहरा बँधना to get the credit for.

स्वाहा करना to ruin.

हँसकर बात उड़ाना to laugh away.

हँसी उड़ाना to make fun of.

हक पर लड़ना to fight for one's right.

हक मारना to usurp one's due.

हड्डी-पसली एक करना to thrash thoroughly.

हरा होना to be gay.

हराम कर देना to make (things) impossible.

हलका पड़ना to prove lesser.

हवा के घोड़े पर सवार होना to be in a great hurry.

हवा खाना to go for a walk.

हवा बँधना a reputation to be earned.

हवा से बातें करना to be moving at a terrible speed.

हवा हो जाना to disappear.

हस्ती होना to be existent.

हाँ में हाँ मिलाना to keep on flattering.

(किसी पर) हाथ उठाना to beat.

हाथ उतरना the arm-bone to be dislocated.

हाथ ऊँचा रहना to have an upper hand.

हाथ कट जाना to be helpless.

हाथ खाली न होना to be busy.

हाथ खींचना to withdraw support.

हाथ खुलना to be a spendthrift.

(किसी काम में) हाथ डालना to undertake a work.

हाथ तंग होना to be tight.

हाथ धो बैठना to lose.

हाथ-पाँव चलना to capable to work

हाथ-पाँव बचाना to keep oneself secure.

हाथ फैलाना to beg.

हाथ बँटाना to co-operate.

हाथ बिकाना to be a slave to.

हाथ मँजना to acquire a fineness (in doing a work).

हाथ में हाथ देना to give away in marriage.

हाथ से जाना to lose.

हाथ होना to have a hand in.

हाथ पड़ना a curse to come true.

हिसाब देना to render accounts.

हिसाब साफ करना to clear off the account.

हेकड़ी जताना to show arrogance.

होश सँभालना to come of age.

वर्गीकृत सामान्य शब्दावली

अन्न तथा भोज्य पदार्थ

अचार - pickle
अरारूट - arrowroot
आटा - meal
कढ़ी - curry
कहवा - coffee
कुल्फ़ी - ice-cream
गेहूँ - wheat
घी - clarified butter
चटनी - sauce
चना - gram
चपाती - cake
चावल - rice
चाय - tea
चीनी - sugar
जलपान - breakfast
जई का आटा - oatmeal
जौ - barley
तरकारी - vegetable
तिल - sesame
तेल - oil

दलिया - mash
दही - curd
दाल - pulse
दिन का भोजन - lunch
दूध - milk
धान - paddy
पनीर - cheese
पावरोटी - loaf
बरफ़ - ice
बाजरा - millet
बिस्कुट - biscuit
भुट्टा - maize
भोज - feast
मकई - maize
मक्खन - butter
मट्ठा - whey, butter milk
मलाई - cream
मांस गाय का - beef
मांस बकरे का - mutton
मांस सुअर का - pork
मिठाई - sweetmeat
मिश्री - sugar-candy

मुरब्बा - jam
मूँग - kidney-bean
मैदा - flour (fine)
मेथी - fenugreek
रात का भोजन - supper, dinner
रेंड़ी - castor-seed
रोटी - bread
शक्कर - loaf-sugar
शर्बत - syrup
शराब - wine
शहद - honey
सरसों - mustard

औजार

आरी - saw
करघा - loom
कुतुबनुमा - compass
कुदाली - shovel
कुल्हाड़ी - axe
कैंची - scissors
कोल्हू (तेली) - oil mill
कोल्हू (ईख पेरने का) - sugar mill
गुनिया - trying-angle
गोलची - gauge
चोसा - rasp
छुरा - razor
छेनी - cold chisel
ढिबरी - nut
तराजू - balance
परकाल - divider
पिचकारी - syringe
पेंच - bolt
पेंचकस - screw-driver
फावड़ा - spade
फर्मा (मोची का) - last
बरमा - auger

बरमी - drill
बंसी - fishing-angle
रंदा (छोटा) - trying-plane
रंदा (बड़ा) - jack-plane
रेती - file
रंभा - lever
लंगर - anchor
सबरी - jemmy
सिल्ली - hone
साहुल - plumbline
हथकला - spanner
हथौड़ी - hammer
हल - plough
हल का फाल - ploughshare
हाथ बाँक - hand-vice

खनिज पदार्थ

अभ्रक - mica
काँसा - bell-metal
कोयला (पत्थर का) - coal
खड़िया - chalk
खान - mine
गंधक - sulphur
गेरू - ochre
चकमक पत्थर - flint
चाँदी - silver
जस्ता - zinc
ताँबा - copper
तूतिया - blue vitriol
पक्का लोहा (इस्पात) - steel
पारा - mercury
पीतल - brass
राँगा - tin
शिलाजीत - bitumen
सुरमा - antimony
संखिया - arsenic

सज्जीखार - natron
सिंगरिफ - cinnabar
सीसा - lead
सफ़ेदा - white lead
सिंदूर - vermilion
संगमरमर - marble
लोहा - iron

गृहस्थी की सामग्री

अलमारी - almirah
कनस्टर - canister
कंघी - comb
कुरसी - chair
ओखली - mortar
गगरा - jar
चकला - pastry-board
चटाई - mat
चमचा - spoon
चलनी - sieve
चादर - bed-sheet
चाभी (ताली) - key
चारपाई - bed
चिमटा - tongs
चिमनी - chimney
चूल्हा - stove
छड़ी - stick
छाता - umbrella
टेबुल - table
टोकरी - basket
डिब्बा - box
ढकना - lid
तंदूर - oven
तकिया - pillow
तराजू - balance
तार - wire
ताला - lock

निजोरी - safe
थाली - plate
दर्पण - mirror
दियासलाई - match
पलंग - bedstead
पीकदानी - spittoon
बक्स - box
बढ़नी (झाड़ू) - mroomstick
बत्ती - wick
बर्तन - pot
बालटी - bucket
बेलन - pastry-roller
बेंच - bench
बोतल - bottle
मथानी - churn
मोमबत्ती - candle
रकाबी - dish
रस्सा - rope
रस्सी - string
लोटा - a small round metal pot
शीशी - phial
संदूक - box
सल्लाई - match
साबुन - soap
सिंगारदान - casket
सुराही - pitcher, jug
सूई - needle

कीड़े, मकोड़े इत्यादि

अजगर - boa
कछुवा - turtle
केंचुवा - earthworm
केकड़ा - crab
खटमल - bug
गिरगिट - chameleon
घोंघा - snail

छिपकली - lizard
ज़हर - poison
चींटी - ant
जुगनू - firefly
जूँ - louse
जोंक - leech
झींगुर - cricket
टिड्डी - locust
तितली - batterfly
बिच्छू - scorpion
मछली - fish
दीमक - white ant
मधुमक्खी (नर) - drone
मधुमक्खी (मादा) - bee
मेढक - frog
मेढक का बच्चा - tadpole
फन - hood
मकड़ा - spider
मकड़े का जाला - web
मक्खी - fly
मगर - crocodile
मच्छर - mosquito
बर्रें - wasp
रेशम का कीड़ा - silkworm
साँप - snake
शंख - conch
सीप - oyster

पक्षी

अबाबील - Swallow
अंडा - egg
उल्लू - owl
कठफोड़वा - wood-pecker
कबूतर - pigeon
काला (डोम) कौवा - raven

कोयल - cuckoo
कौवा - crow
गरुड़ - eagle
गिद्ध - vulture
गौरैया - sparrow
घोंसला - nest
चमगादड़ - bat
चील - kite
चोंच - beak
डैना - wing
तीतर - partridge
नीलकंठ - magpie
पर - feather
पिंजड़ा - cage
पंख - plume
पंडुकी - dove
बतख़ - drake
बतख़ी का बच्चा - duckling
बतख़ी - duck
बुलबुल - nightingale
बया - weaverbird
बटेर - quail
बाज़ - falcon
मुर्ग़ा - cock
मुर्ग़ी - hen
मुसैचा - eagle
मुर्ग़ - fowl
मुर्ग़ी का बच्चा - chicken
मोर - peacock
मोरनी - peahen
लवा - lark
शुतुर्मुर्ग - ostrich
सारस - crane
सुग्गा - parrot
हिरामन तोता - macaw
हंस - swan

पशु

ऊँट - (camel)	बारहसिंगी - hind
कुत्ता - dog	भालू - bear
कुतिया - bitch	भेड़ - sheep
खच्चर - mule	भैंसा - buffalo
खरगोश - rabbit	माँद - den
खरहा - hare	मेढ़ा - ram
गदहा - ass	मेमना - lamb
गाय - cow	मूसा - rat
गिलहरी - squirrel	मृग - stag
गैंड़ा - rhinoceros	लोमड़ी - fox
घोड़ा - horse	लकड़बग्घा - hyena
घोड़ी - mare	लंगूर - ape
चीता - panther	व्याघ्र - tiger
चूहा - mouse	शिकारी कुत्ता - hound
छछूंदर - mole	साँड़ - bull
जंगली सुअर - boar	सियार - jackal
झबरा कुत्ता - spaniel	सिंह - lion
टट्टू - pony	सींग - horn
तेंदुआ - leopard	सुअर - hog pig
नेवला - mongoose	सुअरी - swine
दुम - tail	हरिन - deer
पशु - beast	हाथी - elephant
पंजा - claw	
पिल्ला - puppy	**फल-फूल और वनस्पतियाँ**
बकरा - he-goat	
बकरी - she-goat	अखरोट - chestnut
बकरी का बच्चा - kid	अनन्नास - pine-apple
बछड़ा - calf	अनार - pomegranate
बछिया - she-calf	आम - mango
बछेड़ा - colt	आलू - potato
बिल्ली - cat	अंगूर - grape
बिल्ली का बच्चा - kitten	अंजीर - fig
बंदर - monkey	इमली - tamarind
बैल - ox	ककड़ी - cucumber
बारहसिंगा - stag	कटहल - Jack-fruit
	कमल - lotus
	कमलिनी - lily

कद्दू - pumpkin
काजू - cashewnut
कुकुरमुत्ता - mushroom
केला - plantain
खजूर - date
खरबूजा - musk melon
खीरा - gourd
खुबानी - apricot
गन्ना - sugar cane
गाजर - carrot
गुलमेहँदी - balsam
गुलबहार - daisy
गुलाब - rose
गेंदा - marigold
घास - grass
चंपा - magnolia
चकोतरा - citron
चमेली - jasmine
चिड़चिड़ा - snake-gourd
चुकंदर - beet
जामुन - blackberry
जैतून - olive
तमाखू - tobacco
तरबूज़ - watermelon
दाख - currant
नारियल - coconut
नारंगी - orange
नाशपाती - pear
नीबू - lemon
पपीता - papaya
पान - betel
पालक - spinach
पिस्ता - pistachio
पुदीना - mint
पोस्ता - poppy
पौधा - plant
प्याज़ - onion

फूलगोभी - cauliflower
बादाम - almond
बनफ़शा - violet
बंदगोभी - cabbage
बबूल - acacia
बेर - plum
बेंत - cane
बैंगन - brinjal
भिंडी - lady finger
मिरचा - chilli
मुनक्का - raisin
मूंगफली - ground nut
मूली - radish
मेहँदी - myrtle
रुई - cotton
लता - creeper
लहसुन - garlic
शरीफा - custard apple
शहतूत - mulberry
शकरकंद - sweet-potato
साबूदाना - sago
सुपारी - betel-nut
सेब - apple
सेम - bean

भवन तथा इनके सामान

अटारी - attic
अनाथालय - orphanage
अँगीठी - fireplace
आँगन - courtyard
ईंट - brick
कमरा - room
क़िला - fort
खपरैल - tile
खलिहान - granary
खिड़की - window

खूँटी - peg
खंड - storey
गिरजाघर - church
गुंबज - cupola
चबूतरा - platform
चूना - lime
चौखट - door-frame
छड़ - bar
छत - roof
छप्पर - shed
जाली (पत्थर की) - lattice
ज़ंज़ीर - chain
झरोखा - peep-hole
झोपड़ी - cottage
ड्योढ़ी - ante-chamber
तहख़ाना - cell
दरवाज़ा - door
दफ़्तर - office
देहलीज़ - corridor
धुवाँकश - chimney
नाबदान - drain
नींव - foundation
पत्थर - stone
परनाला - gargoyle
पलस्तर - plaster
पाठशाला - school
पागलख़ाना - lunatic asylum
पुस्तकालय - library
पेशाबख़ाना - urinal
फ़र्श - floor
बरसाती - portico
बरामदा - verandah
बोरसी - fireplace
बँगला - bungalow
मंदिर - temple
मसजिद - mosque
महल - palace

मीनार - steeple
मेहराब - arch
रसोईघर - kitchen
शहतीर - rafter
सराय - inn
स्नानगृह - bathroom
सिरमिट - cement
सीढ़ी - stair

मसाले और औषधियाँ

अजवाइन का सत्त - thymol
अदरक - ginger
अफ़ीम - opium
इलायची - cardamom
कपूर - camphor
कस्तूरी - musk
काली मिर्च - black-pepper
केसर - saffron
ख़मीर - yeast
कत्था - catechu
चंदन - sandal
जायफल - nutmeg
जावित्री - mace
तुलसी - basil
तेजपात - cassia
दालचीनी - cinnamon
फिटकिरी - alum
नमक - salt
मजीठ - madder
माज़ूफल - gall-nut
मिर्च - pepper
रीठा - soap-nut
लवंग - cloves
शोरा - saltpetre
सज्जीख़ार - alkali
सुपारी - betel-nut

सिरका - vinegar
संखिया - arsenic
सोंठ - dry ginger
सौंफ़ - aniseed
साबूदाना - sago
हल्दी - turmeric
हींग - asafoetida

युद्ध सामग्री

अणुबम - atom bomb
आक्रमण (चढ़ाई) - aggression
आक्रमण (धावा) - attack, offensive
कवच - armour
कारतूस - cartridge
खाई - trench
गोली-बारूद इत्यादि - ammunition
गोली - bullet
घरेलू युद्ध - civil war
घुड़सवार सेना - cavalry
घेरा - seige
जल सेना - navy
जंगी जहाज़ - battleship
तोप - cannon
तोप का गोला - cannon-ball
धमाके से फटने वाला बम - explosive bomb
नाकाबंदी - blockade
पनडुब्बी - submarine
परमाणु युद्ध - atomic warfare
पेंदी तोड़ गोला फेंकने वाली नौका - torpedo-boat
पैदल सेना, स्थल सेना - land force
प्रस्थान (कूच) - expedition
बम - bomb
बम वर्षा - bombardment
बमवर्षक विमान - bomber

बारूद - gunpowder
बारूदख़ाना - magazine
भोजन सामग्री - provisions
मनोबल - morale
युद्ध - battle, war
युद्ध के शस्त्र - armaments
युद्ध कौशल - strategy
युद्ध विराम - cease-fire
युद्ध बंदी - prisoners of war
रंगरूट की भर्ती - recruitment
रक्षा - defence
रक्षा कोष - defence fund
लड़ाकू वायुयान - fighter plane
विद्रोह - mutiny, rebellion
विमान भेदी तोप - anti-aircraft gun
विध्वंसक पोत - destroyer
संधि - treaty
सेना - army, troops
सेनागति - operation
सेनापति - commander general, commander-in-chief
शत्रु - enemy
शीत युद्ध - cold war

रत्न और आभूषण

अँगूठी - ring
कंगन - bracelet
कड़ा - bangle
कड़ी - link
कफ़ का बटन - stud
कर्ण फूल - ear-ring
काँटा (बाल का) - hairpin
काँटा (साड़ी का) - brooch
कील नाक की - nose-pin
चिमटी - clip
चूड़ी - bangle

जवाहिरात - gems
तमगा - medal
नथुनी - nose-ring
नीलम - sapphire
पन्ना - emerald
पेटी - belt
पैजनी - anklet
पुखराज - topaz
पोलकी - opal
फीरोज़ा - turquoise
बाजू - armlet
बिल्लौर - pebble
मानिक - ruby
माला - garland
मुकुट - tiara
मूँगा - coral
मोती - pearl
लटकन - locket
लोलक - pendant
हार - necklace
हीरा - diamond
हँसुली - neckband

वस्त्रादिक

अँगरखा - tunic
अँगिया - bodice
अँगोछा - napkin
अस्तर - lining
आस्तीन - sleeve
ऊन - wool
कंबल - blanket
कपड़ा - clothes
कमरबन्द - belt
कमीज - shirt
किनारा - border
किमख़ाब - brocade

कोट - coat
गद्दा - cushion
गुलूबंद - muffler
घूँघट - veil
चादर - sheet
छींट - chintz
जाली - gauze
जाँघिया - half-pant
ज़ीन - drill
जेब - pocket
टोपी - cap
तागा - thread
तौलिया - towel
दस्ताना - gloves
दुपट्टा - scarf
दुशाला - shawl
पतलून - pantaloon
पायजामा - trousers
फतुही - waistcoat
फ़ीता - tape
बटन - button
मख़मल - velvet
मलमल - linen
मोज़ा - stockings
रफू - darning
रुई - cotton
रूमाल - hand-kerchief
रेशम - silk
लबादा - cloak, gown
लहँगा - petticoat
साटन - satin
साफ़ा - turban
सूत - yarn

वृक्ष, पौधे, अंग

अंकुर - germ
अमरूद - guava
आम - mango
इमली - tamarind
कली - bud
काठ - wood
काँटा - thorn
गुठली - stone
गोंद - gum
चीड़ - pine
छाल - bark
छिलका - skin
जटा (नारियल की) - coir
जड़ - root
जीरा - stamen
टहनी - branch
डाल - branch
धड़ - stem
नस - fibre
पत्ती - leaf
फूल - flower
बरगद - banyan
बबूल - acacia
बीज - seed
बाँस - bamboo
रस - juice
रेशा - pulp
शाखा - branch
सरो - cypress
सागवान - teak

व्यवसाय

अख़बारवाला - news-agent
अध्यापक - professor
अहीर - milkman
इंजीनियर - engineer
कसाई - butcher
कारीगर - artisan
किसान - farmer
कुली - coolie
ख़ज़ांची - treasurer
खुदरा फ़रोश - retailer
गंधी - perfumer
गाड़ीवान - coachman
ग्रंथकार - author
जर्राह - surgeon
जहाज़ी - sailor
जादूगर - magician
जाँचने वाला - inspector
जिल्दसाज़ - book-binder
जुलाहा - weaver
जूता बनाने वाला - shoe maker
जौहरी - jeweller
टाइप बैठाने वाला - compositor
ठठेरा - brasier
डाकिया - postman
डॉक्टर - doctor
तेली - oil-man
दर्ज़ी - tailor
दलाल - broker
दवा विक्रेता - druggist
दाई - midwife
दाँत चिकित्सक - dentist
दूकानदार - shopkeeper
धाय - nurse
धोबिन - washerwoman
धोबी - washerman
नानबाई - baker
परीक्षक - examiner
पहरेदार - watchman
प्रकाशक - publisher

प्रबंधकर्ता - manager
फेरीवाला - hawker
फ़ोटो उतारनेवाला - photographer
बढ़ई - carpenter
बज़ाज़ - draper
बारिस्टर - barrister
भिक्षुक - beggar
भंडारी - butler
मछुवा - fisherman
मरम्मत करने वाला - repairer
मल्लाह - boatman
मालिक - proprietor
माली - gardener
मुनीम - agent
मुद्रक - printer
मुंशी - clerk
मेहतर - sweeper
मोची - cobbler
मोदी - grocer
रसोइयादार - cook
रोकड़िया - cashier
रंगसाज़ - painter
रंगरेज़ - dyer
लादनेवाला - carrier
लेखक - writer
लोहार - blacksmith
वकील - pleader
वैद्य - physician
शिक्षक - teacher
सोनार - goldsmith
सौदागर - merchant
संगतराश - sculptor
संपादक - editor
हज्जाम - barber
हलवाई - confectioner

शरीर के अंग

अँगुली (पैर की) - toe
अँगुली (हाथ की) - finger
अँगूठा (हाथ का) - thumb
आँख - eye
आँत - intestine
ओठ - lip
एड़ी - heel
कंधा - shoulder
कनपटी - temple
कमर - waist
कलाई - wrist
कान - ear
कोहनी - elbow
खोपड़ी - skull
गर्दन - neck
गर्भ - womb
गर्भाशय - uterus
गला - throat
गाल - cheek
गुदा - anus
घुटना - knee
चमड़ी - skin
चूचुक - nipple
चूतड़ - buttock
चेहरा - face
छाती (पुरुष की) - chest
छाती (स्त्री की) - breast
जाँघ - thigh
जिगर - liver
जीभ - tongue
जोड़ - joint
ठुड्डी - chin
तलवा - sole
तालु - palate
बाढ़ - jaw

दाढ़ी - beard
दाँत - tooth
दिमाग - brain
धमनी - artery
नख - nail
नथुना - nostril
नस - vein
नाक - nose
नाभि - navel
पलक - eyelid
पसली - rib
पीठ - back
पेट - stomach
पेडू - abdomen
पुतली (आँख की) - eyeball
पेशी (पुट्ठा) - muscle
पैर - foot
फेफड़ा - lung
बगल - arm-pit
बरौनी - eyelash
बाल - hair
बाँह - arm
भौंह - eyebrow
मसूड़ा - gum
मुट्ठी - fist
मुख - mouth
मूँछ - moustach
मूत्राशय - kidney
योनि - vagina
रक्त - blood
रीढ़ - backbone
रोमकूप - pore
ललाट - forehead
शिश्न - penis
हड्डी - bone
हथेली - palm (of hand)
हृदय - heart

शरीर के विकार तथा रोग

अंधा - blind
अल्पदृष्टि - short-sight
अम्लपित्त - acidity
अतिसार - diarrhoea
आतशक - syphilis
आँत उतरना - hernia
आँसू - tears
उबासी - yawn
कद - stature
कफ - phlegm
कय करना - vomit
कास - bronchitis
काना - one-eyed
कुबड़ा - hunch-backed
कोढ़ - leprosy
कोष्ठबद्धता - constipation
कृमि - worms
खाँसी - cough
खून की कमी - anaemia
गठिया - rheumatism
गर्भपात - abortion
गरमी - syphilis
गला बैठना hoarseness
गाँठ - tumour
गिलटी - tumour
गूँगा - dumb
गंजा - bald
घाव - wound
चक्कर - giddiness
चर्बी बढ़ना - obesity
चोट - hurt
छींक - sneeze
जुकाम - coryza
जूड़ी - ague
जंभाई - yawn

ज्वर - fever
ठंड - chill
डकार - belch
थूक - spittle
दमा - asthma
दर्द - pain
दर्द सिर - headache
दस्त - stool
वाद - ringworm
दुबला - lean
दूरदृष्टि - long-sight
नस चटकना - sprain
नींद - sleep
नींद न आना - insomnia
पथरी - stone
पसीना - sweat
पागल - mad
पागलपन - insanity
पित्त - bile
पीब - pus
पेचिश - dysentery
प्रदर - leucorrhoea
फुंसी - pimple
फोड़ा - boil
बलगम - phlegm
बवासीर - piles
बहुमूत्र - diabetes
बुखार - fever
बौना - dwarf
भगंदर - fistula
भूख - hunger
मस्सा - mole
मिरगी - epilepsy
मूत्र - urine
मोतियाबिंद - cataract
मोहासा - acne
लकवा - paralysis

लार - saliva
विष्ठा - stool
रोग - disease
लँगड़ा - lame
लू लगना - sunstroke
शीतला - small-pox
श्वेत कुष्ठ - leucoderma
साँस - breath
सूजन - swelling
सूज़ाक - gonorrhoea
संग्रहणी - sprue
स्वर - voice
हिचकी - hiccough
हैज़ा - cholera
क्षय - tuberculosis

– संगीत के वाद

चंग - harp
झाँझ - cymbal
डफ़ - tambourine
डुगडुगी - drum
ढोलक - tomtom
तुरही - bugle
नगाड़ा - drum
पियानो - piano
बाँसुरी - flute
बेला - violin
मसक बाजा - bagpipe
शहनाई - clarion
सितार - guitar
सीटी - whistle
हारमोनियम - harmonium

सम्बन्धी

अम्मा - mamma
उपपत्नी - co-wife
चाचा - uncle
चाची - aunt
जेठानी/देवरानी - sister-in-law
दत्तक पुत्र - adopted son
दत्तक कन्या - adopted daughter
दादा - grand father
दादी - grand mother
दामाद - son-in-law
नाना - grand father
नानी - grand mother
पति - husband
पत्नी - wife
पतोहू - daughter-in-law
परीक्षक - examiner
परीक्षार्थी - examinee
पिता - father
पुत्र - son
पुत्री - daughter
बहिन - sister
भतीजा - nephew
भतीजी - niece
भाई - brother
भांजा - nephew
भांजी - niece
माता - mother
मामा - maternal uncle
मामी - maternal aunt
मौसी - mother's sister
ससुर - father-in-law
सास - mother-in-law
संबंधी - relative
सौतेली कन्या - step-daughter
सौतेला पुत्र - step-son

सौतेला पिता - step-father
सौतेली बहन - step-sister
सौतेला भाई - step-brother
सौतेली माता - step-mother

लिखने-पढ़ने तथा दफ्तर के सामान

अख़बार - newspaper
अलमारी - almirah
आधी रसीद - counterfoil
आराम कुर्सी - easy chair
आलपीन - pin
आलपीन गद्दी - pin cushion
कलम - pen
कलमतराश - pen-knife
कागज़ - paper
कार्ड - card
काली स्याही - black ink
कोश - dictionary
खाता - register
गड़्डी - file
गोंद - gum
चिट्ठी का कागज़ - letter paper
चिमटी - clip
चौकी - bench
जेबी पोथी - pocket books
टिकट (स्टम्प) - postage stamp
टेबल - table
तार - wire
तिपाई - stool
दावात - inkpot
नकल करने का कागज़ - carbon paper
नकल करने की स्याही - copying ink
नकल करने की पेंसिल - copying pencil

नक्शा - map
निब - nib
निमंत्रणपत्र - invitation card
नीली स्याही - blue ink
परकाल - divider
पुकारने की घंटी - call-bell
पेंसिल - pencil
फ़ाइल - file
फ़ीता - tape
बंधना - fastener
भेंट करने का कार्ड - visiting card
मोहर - seal
रबड़ - eraser
रबड़ की मोहर - rubber stamp

रद्दी की टोकरी - waste paper-basket
रूलर - ruler
रोशनाई - ink
लपेटने का काग़ज़ - packing paper
लाल रोशनाई - red ink
लिखने की पट्टी - writing pad
लिफ़ाफ़ा - envelope
लेखा बही - ledger
सरेस - glue
सादा काग़ज़ - blank paper
सोखता - blotting paper
सैंड़सी, छेदने की - punch
होल्डर - holder

संख्याएं
NUMERALS

1	एक	One	I
2	दो	Two	II
3	तीन	Three	III
4	चार	Four	IV
5	पाँच	Five	V
6	छ:	Six	VI
7	सात	Seven	VII
8	आठ	Eight	VIII
9	नौ	Nine	IX
10	दस	Ten	X
11	ग्यारह	Eleven	XI
12	बारह	Twelve	XII
13	तेरह	Thirteen	XIII
14	चौदह	Fourteen	XIV
15	पंद्रह	Fifteen	XV

16	सोलह	Sixteen	XVI
17	सत्रह	Seventeen	XVII
18	अठारह	Eighteen	XVIII
19	उन्नीस	Nineteen	XIX
20	बीस	Twenty	XX
21	इक्कीस	Twenty one	XXI
22	बाईस	Twenty two	XXII
23	तेईस	Twenty three	XXIII
24	चौबीस	Twenty four	XXIV
25	पच्चीस	Twenty five	XXV
26	छब्बीस	Twenty six	XXVI
27	सत्ताईस	Twenty seven	XXVII
28	अठाईस	Twenty eight	XXVIII
29	उनतीस	Twenty nine	XXIX
30	तीस	Thirty	XXX
31	इकत्तीस	Thirty one	XXXI
32	बत्तीस	Thirty two	XXXII
33	तैंतीस	Thirty three	XXXIII
34	चौंतीस	Thirty four	XXXIV
35	पैंतीस	Thirty five	XXXV
36	छत्तीस	Thirty six	XXXVI
37	सैंतीस	Thirty seven	XXXVII
38	अड़तीस	Thirty eight	XXXVIII
39	उनतालीस	Thirty nine	XXXIX
40	चालीस	Forty	XL
41	इकतालीस	Forty one	XLI
42	बयालीस	Forty two	XLII
43	तैंतालीस	Forty three	XLIII
44	चौवालीस	Forty four	XIV
45	पैंतालीस	Forty five	XLV
46	छियालीस	Forty six	XLVI
47	सैंतालीस	Forty seven	XLVII
48	अड़तालीस	Forty eight	XLVIII
49	उनचास	Forty nine	XLIX

50	पचास	Fifty	L
51	इक्यावन	Fifty one	LI
52	बावन	Fifty two	LII
53	तिरपन	Fifty three	LIII
54	चौवन	Fifty four	LIV
55	पचपन	Fifty five	LV
56	छप्पन	Fifty six	LVI
57	सत्तावन	Fifty seven	LVII
58	अट्ठावन	Fifty eight	LVIII
59	उनसठ	Fifty nine	LIX
60	साठ	Sixty	LX
61	इकसठ	Sixty one	LXI
62	बासठ	Sixty two	LXII
63	तिरेसठ	Sixty three	LXIII
64	चौंसठ	Sixty four	LXIV
65	पैंसठ	Sixty five	LXV
66	छियासठ	Sixty six	LXVI
67	सरसठ	Sixty seven	LXVII
68	अरसठ	Sixty eight	LXVIII
69	उनहत्तर	Sixty nine	LXIX
70	सत्तर	Seventy	LXX
71	इकहत्तर	Seventy one	LXXI
72	बहत्तर	Seventy two	LXXII
73	तिहत्तर	Seventy three	LXXIII
74	चौहत्तर	Seventy four	LXXIV
75	पचहत्तर	Seventy five	LXXV
76	छिहत्तर	Seventy six	LXXVI
77	सतहत्तर	Seventy seven	LXXVII
78	अठहत्तर	Seventy eight	LXXVIII
79	उन्यासी	Seventy nine	LXXIX
80	अस्सी	Eighty	LXXX
81	इक्यासी	Eighty one	LXXXI
82	बयासी	Eighty two	LXXXII
83	तिरासी	Eighty three	LXXXIII

84	चौरासी	Eighty four	LXXXIV
85	पच्चासी	Eighty five	LXXXV
86	छियासी	Eighty six	LXXXVI
87	सत्तासी	Eighty seven	LXXXVII
88	अट्ठासी	Eighty eight	LXXXVIII
89	नवासी	Eighty nine	LXXXIX
90	नब्बे	Ninety	XC
91	इक्यानबे	Ninety one	XCI
92	बानबे	Ninety two	XCII
93	तिरानबे	Ninety three	XCIII
94	चौरानबे	Ninety four	XCIV
95	पंचानबे	Ninety five	XCV
96	छियानबे	Ninety six	XCVI
97	सतानबे	Ninety seven	XCVII
98	अट्ठानबे	Ninety eight	XCVIII
99	निन्यानबे	Ninety nine	XCIX
100	सौ	Hundred	C

अंशवाचक गिनती

1/2 आधा—Half (हॉफ़)

3/4 तीन चौथाई—Three fourth (थ्री फ़ोर्थ)

2/3 दो तिहाई—Two third (टू थर्ड)

1/4 एक चौथाई—One fourth (वन फ़ोर्थ)

1/5 पाँचवाँ भाग—One fifth (वन फ़िफ़्थ)

1/6 छठा भाग—One sixth (वन सिक्स्थ)

1/7 सातवाँ भाग—One seventh (वन सेवेंथ)

1/8 आठवाँ भाग—One eighth (वन एट्थ)

1/9 नौवाँ भाग—One ninth (वन नाइंथ)

1/10 दसवाँ भाग—One tenth (वन टेंथ)

क्रमवाचक गिनती

पहला — First (फ़र्स्ट)

दूसरा — Second (सेकंड)

तीसरा — Third (थर्ड)

चौथा — Fourth (फ़ोर्थ)

पाँचवाँ — Fifth (फ़िफ़्थ)	आठवाँ — Eighth (एट्थ)
छठा — Sixth (सिक्स्थ)	नौवाँ — Ninth (नाइंथ)
सातवाँ — Seventh (सेवन्थ)	दसवाँ — Tenth (टेंथ)

गुणवाचक गिनती

एक गुना — Single (सिंगल)	छह गुना — Six fold (सिक्स फोल्ड)
दुगना — Double (डबल)	सात गुना — Seven fold (सेवन फ़ोल्ड)
तिगुना — Three fold (थ्री फ़ोल्ड)	आठ गुना — Eight fold (एट फ़ोल्ड)
चौगुना — Four fold (फ़ोर फ़ोल्ड)	नौ गुना — Nine fold (नाइन फ़ोल्ड)
पाँच गुना — Five fold (फ़ाइव फ़ोल्ड)	दस गुना — Ten fold (टेन फ़ोल्ड)

More Dictionaries from Hippocrene Books:

ENGLISH-ALBANIAN DICTIONARY
0081　　ISBN 0-87052-480-1　　$12.50 cloth

ENGLISH-ARABIC CONVERSATIONAL DICTIONARY
Richard Jaschke
0093　　ISBN 0-87052-494-1　　$8.95 paper

CAMBODIAN-ENGLISH/ENGLISH-CAMBODIAN STANDARD DICTIONARY
0143　　ISBN 0-87052-818-1　　$14.95 paper

CZECH-ENGLISH/ENGLISH-CZECH CONCISE DICTIONARY
Nina Trnka
0276　　ISBN 0-87052-586-7　　$6.95 paper

DANISH-ENGLISH/ENGLISH-DANISH PRACTICAL DICTIONARY
0198　　ISBN 0-87052-823-8　　$9.95 paper

DUTCH-ENGLISH/ENGLISH-DUTCH CONCISE DICTIONARY:
With a Brief Introduction to Dutch Grammar
0606　　ISBN 0-87052-910-2　　$7.95 paper

FINNISH-ENGLISH/ENGLISH-FINNISH CONCISE DICTIONARY
0142　　ISBN 0-87052-813-0　　$8.95 paper

FRENCH-ENGLISH/ENGLISH-FRENCH PRACTICAL DICTIONARY
Rosalind Williams

0199	ISBN 0-88254-815-8	$6.95 paper
2065	ISBN 0-88254-928-6	$12.95 cloth

GERMAN-ENGLISH/ENGLISH-GERMAN PRACTICAL DICTIONARY
Stephen Jones

0200	ISBN 0-88254-813-1	$6.95 paper
2063	ISBN 0-88254-902-2	$12.95 cloth

CONCISE, PHONETIC ENGLISH-HEBREW/HEBREW-ENGLISH CONVERSATIONAL DICTIONARY (Romanized)
David C. Gross

0257	ISBN 0-87052-625-1	$7.95 paper

HINDI-ENGLISH PRACTICAL DICTIONARY
R.C. Tiwari, R.S. Sharma and Krishna Vikal

0186	ISBN 0-87052-824-6	$11.95 paper

HUNGARIAN-ENGLISH/ENGLISH-HUNGARIAN DICTIONARY
Magay Tamas, et al.

2039	ISBN 0-88254-986-3	$7.95 cloth

HUNGARIAN-ENGLISH/ENGLISH-HUNGARIAN CONCISE DICTIONARY:
With Complete Phonetics

0254	ISBN 0-87052-891-2	$6.95 paper

ICELANDIC-ENGLISH/ENGLISH-ICELANDIC CONCISE DICTIONARY
Arnold Taylor

0147	ISBN 0-87052-801-7	$7.95 paper

INDONESIAN-ENGLISH/ENGLISH-INDONESIAN PRACTICAL DICTIONARY
Helen and Rossall Johnson

0127	ISBN 0-87052-810-6	$8.95 paper

ITALIAN-ENGLISH/ENGLISH-ITALIAN PRACTICAL DICTIONARY
Peter Ross

0201	ISBN 0-88254-816-6	$6.95 paper
2066	ISBN 0-88254-929-4	$12.95 cloth

NORWEGIAN-ENGLISH/ENGLISH-NORWEGIAN DICTIONARY
E.D. Gabrielsen

0202	ISBN 0-88254-584-1	$7.95 paper

PILIPINO-ENGLISH/ENGLISH-PILIPINO CONCISE DICTIONARY
Sam and Angela Bickford

2040	ISBN 0-87052-491-7	$6.95 paper

POLISH-ENGLISH/ENGLISH-POLISH STANDARD DICTIONARY (Revised)
Iwo Cyprian Pogonowski

0207	ISBN 0-87052-882-3	$12.95 paper
0665	ISBN 0-87052-908-0	$22.50 cloth

**POLISH-ENGLISH/ENGLISH-POLISH
PRACTICAL DICTIONARY**
Iwo Cyprian Pogonowski
2041   ISBN 0-87052-064-4 $8.95 paper

**PORTUGUESE-ENGLISH/ENGLISH-
PORTUGUESE PRACTICAL DICTIONARY**
Antonio Houaiss and I. Cardin
0477   ISBN 0-87052-374-0 $9.95 paper

**RUSSIAN-ENGLISH/ENGLISH-RUSSIAN
PRACTICAL DICTIONARY:
With Complete Phonetics**
O.P. Benyuch and G.V. Chernov
0164   ISBN 0-87052-336-8 $10.95 paper

**RUSSIAN-ENGLISH/ENGLISH-RUSSIAN
DICTIONARY**
W. Harrison and Svetlana Le Fleming
2344   ISBN 0-87052-751-7 $9.95 paper

**SERBO-CROATIAN-ENGLISH/ENGLISH-
SERBO-CROATIAN POCKET DICTIONARY**
0136   ISBN 0-87052-806-8 $11.95 cloth

**SPANISH-ENGLISH/ENGLISH-SPANISH
PRACTICAL DICTIONARY**
Arthur Butterfield
0211   ISBN 0-88254-814-X $6.95 paper
2064   ISBN 0-88254-905-7 $12.95 cloth

SWEDISH-ENGLISH/ENGLISH-SWEDISH STANDARD DICTIONARY
Vincent and Kerstin Petti

0755	ISBN 0-87052-870-X	$11.95 paper
0761	ISBN 0-87052-871-8	$19.95 cloth

TURKISH-ENGLISH/ENGLISH-TURKISH CONCISE DICTIONARY

0569	ISBN 0-87052-241-8	$5.95 paper

TURKISH-ENGLISH/ENGLISH-TURKISH POCKET DICTIONARY

0148	ISBN 0-87052-812-2	$14.95 paper